Lessy broke away and stared into Ripley's eyes. They were smoky and half-closed with such an expression of ardor that she giggled.

"Mr. Ripley," she said. "You look at me like I was a peach cobbler myself. And I'm practically an old married lady."

He leaned forward once more. When she drew back, he winked broadly. "You aren't married yet, Miss Lessy. Ain't no sin in taking a last long look at freedom. I *am* from the haying crew, and they do say to make hay while the sun shines."

She was laughing at his teasing when over his shoulder she caught sight of a large, work-hardened blond man gazing at them in horror.

"Vassar!" . . .

—from "Making Hay" by Pamela Morsi

*   *   *

Turn to the back for a sneak preview of Pamela Morsi's next novel, Wild Oats!

Regency Collections from Jove

SUMMER MAGIC
SUMMERTIME SPLENDOR

Summer Magic

by
Pamela Morsi
Jean
Anne Caldwell
Ann Carberry
Karen Lockwood

J

JOVE BOOKS, NEW YORK

SUMMER MAGIC

A Jove Book / published by arrangement with
the authors

PRINTING HISTORY
Jove edition / July 1993

All rights reserved.
Copyright © 1993 by The Berkley Publishing Group.
"Making Hay" copyright © 1993 by Pamela Morsi.
"Summer Dreams" copyright © 1993 by Jean Anne Caldwell.
"Hog Heaven" copyright © 1993 by Maureen Child.
"White Heather" copyright © 1993 by Karen Finnigan.
This book may not be reproduced in whole
or in part, by mimeograph or any other means,
without permission. For information address:
The Berkley Publishing Group,
200 Madison Avenue,
New York, New York 10016.

ISBN: 0-515-11116-3

Jove Books are published by The Berkley Publishing Group,
200 Madison Avenue, New York, New York 10016.
The name "JOVE" and the "J" logo
are trademarks belonging to Jove Publications, Inc.

PRINTED IN THE UNITED STATES OF AMERICA

10 9 8 7 6 5 4 3 2 1

Contents

About the Authors

PAMELA MORSI ("Making Hay") is one of romance's fastest rising stars. Winner of the 1992 Rita for Best Historical Romance, Pamela is the author of *Garters* and the soon-to-be released *Wild Oats*. A former medical librarian, she lives with her husband and daughter in South Carolina.

JEAN ANNE CALDWELL ("Summer Dreams") is the author of the second book in the "Brides of the West" series entitled *Swept Away*. Jean Anne's first book was called "a joyous, fun-loving, and romantic romp" by *Romantic Times*.

ANN CARBERRY ("Hog Heaven") is the author of *Frontier Bride, Nevada Heat,* and the soon-to-be-released *Shotgun Bride*. She lives in Southern California with her husband, two teenagers, and a dumb-as-dirt dog.

KAREN LOCKWOOD ("White Heather") is the author of the Homespun historical romance *Harvest Song* and the soon-to-be-released *Winter Song*. She's married and the mother of three sons. Home is Idaho Falls, Idaho, where the long, cold winters give her plenty of time to dream of summer.

MAKING HAY

Pamela Morsi

Chapter One

"Then it's settled. You two will marry as soon as the hay is in." Widow Nora Green smiled across the table at the serious faces of her daughter, Lessy, and her soon to be son-in-law, Vassar Muldrow. "I'm just so tickled I could purely swoon," she added. "And I know, Vass, that your mother and daddy will be just as delighted."

The big, blond young man gave a slight nod of agreement and stole a careful, respectful glance toward his future bride. "They couldn't be more delighted than me, ma'am."

Four years earlier, when Nora's husband, Tom, had died, Vassar Muldrow, the youngest son of a distant cousin from Arkadelphia, had come to help out on the Green farm. It had been a good thing for all concerned, and from the first day the widow had held secret hopes of a match. Hopes that had now materialized.

"You can't be calling me ma'am anymore." Nora Green was beaming. "It just ain't family sounding. You just call me Mammy, like Lessy does." She nodded firmly. "You call me Mammy Green."

Vassar's smile was broad and friendly. He was a quiet and serious young man; the widow saw his smiles rarely, but considered them worth the wait. The wide slant of his mouth and the seemingly small brilliant white teeth made his rather plain farmboy face glow with good looks. "I'd be honored, Mammy Green."

"What kind of wedding are you wanting?" She looked fondly at her only child.

Her daughter, just turned twenty, sat demurely across

the table from Vassar. Her pale brown hair was parted
very straight down the middle, each side tightly braided
and rolled into two carefully secured swirls at the back
of each ear. Excitement glittered in her eyes, but she held
tightly on the reins of her enthusiasm.

"I don't think we need a big to-do," she told her mother
quietly. "I think if we just get the preacher to marry us on
the church steps after service, then we could come back
here for the wedding supper."

Remembering her own elaborate ceremony, Nora Green
frowned slightly. "That ain't much of a wedding, honey.
You sure you don't want something fancy and grand? I've
got a little money saved up, and a girl only gets married
oncet."

Lessy cast a glance at Vass that seemed almost hopeful.
His look was open and unassuming, but she shook her
head. "There's no need to pull a fuss," she said with a
lightness that didn't fool her mother for one minute. "You
save your money, Mammy, for something important. We'll
be just as married without some showy shindig. Vass and I
are quiet people."

If the widow's murmur of assent didn't quite ring true, it
was clear that Vassar's nod of approval was all that Lessy
noticed.

"I just want you to be happy," her mother said.

Both young people turned to look at her curiously, as if
it had never occurred to them that they wouldn't.

"Do you want more pie or coffee?" Lessy asked her
young man.

Vass shook his head and patted his belly with contentment. "I couldn't eat another bite."

Lessy rose to help with the dishes, but her mother waved
her away. "I'll wash up these things. You two are officially
engaged." She smiled warmly at Vass. "I think that means
you can go walking out with my daughter alone now."

Vassar's cheeks reddened, and he appeared more ill at
ease about the prospect than delighted. "Do you want to
walk out with me?" he asked Lessy.

She blushed also as she nodded her agreement. With

roses in her cheeks and sparkles in her eyes, her rather ordinary appearance blossomed to genuine comeliness. Vass looked away.

Helping her out of her chair, he offered his arm like a swain at a dance. Lessy took it, her expression blissful. As the widow watched them step out onto the front porch, she shook her head.

There was something about this engagement that wasn't exactly right.

A half moon was rising in the eastern sky and turning the hot summer evening silver gray in its light. The young couple strolled casually from the front porch of the farmhouse down the path that led past the corncrib, into the peach orchard, and toward the pond.

"It's a pretty night." Lessy took a deep breath. The warm summer scent of ripening fields and maturing fruit always pleased her, but tonight it could have been pouring rain, and she would have been happy. Her spirit soared within her.

Vass nodded as he surveyed the fleeting light critically. "The weather's been just about perfect this year. Corn and oats were good, the stock is near fat enough for market, and your peach trees are still producing when they were nearly to breaking limbs with fruit a full month ago."

Smiling, Lessy agreed. "It's been a very good year." She gave him a shy glance. "I just hope that's a good omen for a wedding."

Vassar kept the serious gaze of his pale blue eyes straight ahead. "We don't need any omens, Lessy. We've had four years of getting to know each other. This is not some dizzy craziness that will pass with the first rough row to hoe. There aren't many couples who are as sure of wanting a marriage as we are."

"Of course, you're right." Looking up at him, Lessy's heart was in her eyes. She felt as dizzy and crazy as the first day they'd met. Vass was big and blond and tanned ruddy from working in the Arkansas sunshine day after day. And his long, thickly muscled arm so close to her own was strong and warm, even through the thin covering of his near-threadbare cotton shirt.

Vass glanced down at her and gave her a small smile of encouragement before he looked away, assessing the grove around him and the fields farther on.

"The hay is about ready," he said. "I wrung out a handful today, and it broke near as clean as celery. I suspect to get the haying crew up here any day now."

"That soon," Lessy answered, delighted.

Vass nodded. "If the weather holds, we'll have it all in the barn in three weeks' time."

"So I guess we should plan on the wedding about the end of the month." It was a statement, but she looked up at Vassar as if it were a question.

"Sounds fine," he answered. "I'm glad we're just having a quick marry-up."

Lessy cleared her throat and nodded determinedly. "A big wedding does seem like a waste of money."

"More than that. It's sure a kind of foolishness for a couple such as us. It isn't like marriage is going to be a big change in our lives."

Lessy raised her eyes in surprise.

"I mean, of course it's a change," Vass hastily corrected himself. "But it's . . . well . . . you're not leaving home, and I'll not be working a new farm. Our lives will be pretty much what they've been for the last four years."

Lessy made no reply, but Vass noticed her biting her lip nervously and tried again to explain. "You'll go on doing what you do every day," he said. "And I'll go on doing what I do. Things will be just the same. Except, of course, that we'll be a . . . a . . . sharing a room." Vass rubbed his palms nervously against his trouser legs.

Her face flushing bright crimson, Lessy could only nod in reply. Vass took her speechlessness as concern.

"Now, please don't start to worry about that, Lessy," he said. "I promise it won't be as bad as you're thinking."

She looked up curiously, but when she met his eyes, she dropped her gaze again in embarrassment. Vassar gently patted her hand.

"I want children as much as any other man," he told her quietly. He swallowed and looked away from the woman beside him. Once again he felt a twinge of regret. She was sweet and innocent and deserved a better man than he. "I'll try not to bother you excessively."

"I know you won't," Lessy whispered, her face flaming with humiliation.

They hurried on, as if moving out of the fragrant peach orchard would move their thoughts into new directions as well. When they reached the edge of the pond, they could go no farther. Both of them stared out over the water, wistfully, as if wishing for the courage to look at each other. Lessy's grandfather had dammed up a small creek when he'd first arrived in this part of Arkansas. The pond was so well established now, only those who knew it was man-made could distinguish it from a natural water hole.

A spindly willow tree grew on the bank, and the couple stopped beneath it. Vassar leaned against the tree trunk as Lessy gazed out over the water listening to the croak of the frogs and the rattle of crickets.

He no longer held her arm.

"Have you thought what you want to do with your peach money this year?" Vassar asked.

She smiled, grateful that he'd introduced a safe subject for discussion. The peach orchard had been Grandma Green's pride and joy, and she'd willed it separately to Lessy. Since she was a little girl, every year that the peaches made money, Lessy spent it on whatever she pleased.

"Mammy and I thought we could send for some dress silk from the catalog. Mammy says a woman needs something new to get married in." In her mind she could picture herself in a beautiful gown, Vass standing beside her . . . perhaps looking at her proudly . . .

When he made no further comment, Lessy finally asked, "What do you think I should do?"

He shrugged. "I was thinking we might could raise some birds on this pond. A few ducks and geese wouldn't be much of a worry. And there ain't nothing like a big old fat goose in the roasting pan."

A vision of her dreamed-of silk gown fluttered into oblivion. "Then waterfowl it is. Mammy and I can make over one of the dresses that I already have."

"You really don't even need nothing new since you're marrying me," he said. "I think you look mighty pretty in your regular Sunday-go-to-meeting."

Her regret over the loss of a wedding dress was soothed by the compliment. Vass made so few. Lessy giggled and covered her face with her hands and then peeked out to look at Vassar. He was grinning and pulled himself to his feet. Moving to stand in front of her, he took her hands in his own.

It got very quiet between them as they both stared at their clasped hands. Vassar looked away and took a deep breath before turning back to her.

"With us betrothed now," he said, "I guess a kiss would be in order."

Lessy smoothed a wispy lock of hair that had escaped the tightly twisted braids and raised her chin bravely. "Yes, I suppose that would be all right."

With only a slight hesitance Vassar leaned closer. Gently, oh, so gently, he pressed his mouth against the soft, rosy cushion of her lips. Lessy inhaled the raw, sweet scent of him and felt the heat of his nearness. The soft touch of his lips was so brief, barely lingering, over almost as soon as it began.

Vassar stepped back, ran a nervous hand through his hair, and cleared his throat. "We'd best get back to the house. Your Mammy will be worried."

The Widow Green did not appear to be the least bit worried when Lessy returned home. Her mother was sorting through the wardrobe in their bedroom and humming pleasantly to herself.

"Mammy? What are you up to?"

With a gesture toward the sorted clothes strewn across the bed, she answered, "I just thought I'd get some of this packing done before the haying crew arrives and we get so busy."

"Packing?" Lessy plopped on the side of the bed, her expression puzzled. "Are you going somewhere?"

Nora Green looked up and shook her head, chuckling. "Did you think I'd expect you to move into the little room with Vass?"

Lessy hadn't thought about it at all.

"Of course you two should have the front bedroom," she said. "It was meant for a married couple."

Lessy glanced around uneasily at the room she had shared with her mother for the last four years. It suddenly seemed a strange and alien place. When she'd imagined sharing a room with Vassar, she'd always seen herself crossing the threshold of the little one added onto the back of the house where she'd spent her childhood. It had been Vassar's room since the day he had come to live with them. It was almost as if she couldn't remember a time when he hadn't been there.

"We wouldn't want to run you out of this room," she protested. "This is the room you shared with Daddy."

Widow Green reached out for her daughter's hand. "It was, indeed, the room I shared with my husband, and it will be the room you share with yours."

A mixture of delight and anxiety skittered inside Lessy, and she averted her eyes.

She had wanted to marry Vassar Muldrow since the first day that she had seen him, a few weeks after her father's death. She was sad and scared and confused. Although she had always been close with her mother, Daddy was so very special. He'd called her Gopher-Girl for her love of gardening, tree planting, and any other dirt-digging activities. And he'd given her confidence in herself.

"You can be anything you want to be, Gopher-Girl. Your life is like a batch of your mama's bread dough. You can shape it into a standard loaf, twist it into cur-licues, or you can tie it into sailor knots. It's all up to you."

Lessy had smiled at him skeptically. "I suppose I can

make my hair blond and my eyes blue and turn into Sugie Jo Mouwers if I want."

Her father had raised his eyebrows in surprise at the mention of the exuberant young daughter of one of the neighboring farmers. "I don't doubt that you could if you put your mind to it," he'd said. "But I hate to see you aiming so low."

"Aiming so low?"

Tom Green nodded thoughtfully. "Poor Sugie Jo ain't got nothing much in this world but *pretty*. You, Gopher-Girl, have the chance to be whatever your heart desires. You've just got to figure out what you want in this world."

And she had. She wanted Vassar Muldrow.

Not three weeks after they'd laid her beloved father in the ground, Cousin Jake and his sons had shown up to help harvest the cowpeas. She could remember, as if the image were burned into her brain, her first look at Vassar Muldrow. He was standing in the back of the wagon unloading their gear. His golden-blond hair seemed almost burnished in the sunlight, and his tall, broad-shouldered physique made him appear a giant of a man. Heartsore and lonely for the man who called her Gopher-Girl, Lessy needed the strength she'd seen in those young shoulders and was drawn to the pain in those murky green eyes that seemed to mirror her own.

"Nora, this is my youngest boy," Jake had said to her mother as he gestured to Vass. "He's the one I wrote you about. He ain't much one for talking, but he's a good hand and a hard worker."

Vass had glanced in their direction and given them an excessively polite nod of acknowledgment.

Lessy had felt a catch in her throat and a jolt in her heart. He doesn't *have* to talk, Lessy thought to herself. I'll be happy to do his talking for him.

Her sigh of sweet remembrance caught her mother's attention.

"Lessy-mine, you're not worried about sharing a bed with this man, are you?"

Her cheeks pinking only slightly, Lessy shook her head.

"No, Mammy," she said. "I've been around the farm long enough to know pretty much what happens. And Vass says it won't be as bad as I think."

Her mother's mouth dropped open in surprise before she threw her head back and laughed. "Lord-a-mighty, you and Vass are the strangest pair of cooing doves I ever laid eyes on. Not as bad as you think?" The Widow Green shook her head in disbelief.

"Is it that funny?" Lessy asked, unable to keep the hint of pique out of her voice.

Nora reached over and patted her hand affectionately. "No, honey, you know I wouldn't make fun of you or Vass. You are both the dearest to me on this earth. But I swear you two have the funniest ideas of courting that I've ever come across in all my born days."

Lessy raised her chin, still slightly defensive. Their courting had been unique. In fact, it had been like no courting at all. Vass never wooed her or sent her flowers or carried her to a barn dance or church supper. He was a shy man and didn't like social occasions. Although Lessy had once reveled in carefree fun and meeting with friends, she now only wanted to do what Vassar wanted to do. And what Vassar wanted to do was farm.

"It's normal for you to be a little scared of your marriage bed," Lessy's mother was telling her. "And it's right for Vass to try to reassure you. But, I'll swanny, he has a strange way of going about it."

Lessy didn't want to talk about Vass. "Did Daddy have to reassure you?"

Nora Green nodded. "He surely did. I was three years younger than you are and had been so sheltered I thought the difference in men and women was the clothes that they wore."

Lessy laughed and shook her head, refusing to believe her mother's claim.

"I was scared near to death," her mother told her. "But when your daddy realized why, he snuck me down behind that big old barn at Granny's place and kissed me till I was breathless. I was so het up, I told him I didn't want to wait even one more day. It was only your daddy's good sense that kept us from making our marriage bed in that damp grass."

"Oh, Mammy!" Lessy giggled. "I can't imagine you and Daddy sparking behind the barn."

"Well, it's the truth." Her eyes were soft with the memory. "But if you tell it at church, I'll deny every word." Nora Green pointed her finger at her daughter threateningly, and both dissolved in laughter. "If my memory serves me right," her mother continued when they'd regained composure, "these warm summer days can fire up a young man's blood and a young woman's, too. Many a young couple have met the preacher *coming back* from the well. More than one have lived to regret it. I never heard tell of a pair that were sorry they'd waited till the wedding day."

Lessy leaned forward and hugged her mother tightly. "Don't worry, Mammy," she said. "There is not even a question. Vass and I are going to wait."

Nora looked at her daughter for a long moment and then nodded in agreement. "I guess I should know that. Vassar is a mother's dream. He's polite, respectful, honorable, and upright. But when a man's in love, it'd be hard to fault him for stealing a kiss or two."

Lessy's smile held, but the pleasure behind it faded, and she lowered her eyes to the cotton petticoat that she held in her hands.

Chapter Two

The singing woke him. Every morning, as regularly as the sunrise or the cock's crow, Lessy Green sang as she stoked the fire in the stove and set coffee to boil. Today it was a cheery but subdued "On the Banks of the Ohio." Vassar was just grateful it wasn't "Ta-Ra-Ra-Boom-De-Ay"!

Without opening his eyes, he sluggishly rolled to a sitting position on the side of the bed. His feet touched the cold boards on the floor. I am awake, he told himself. He allowed his left eye to open to a squint. With a moan he closed it again, and only pure strength of will kept him from falling backward onto the bed.

Vassar hated mornings.

"It's the devil's own laziness in that boy!" one of his aunts had told his mother. "Never heard of a farmer who didn't love the first light of day."

Vass didn't know if he loved it. He tried very hard not to see it.

The gentle tapping on the door diverted his attention from his own weariness, and he blindly rose to his feet and felt his way across the room.

He pulled open the door wide enough only to reveal his face.

"Good morning, Vassar. It's a beautiful day outside. Breakfast should be ready in about twenty minutes."

The sweet shy voice held a revitalizing power, and Vassar obligingly opened his eyes fully for the first time. Lessy stood, fresh-scrubbed and pink, in his doorway. The neat braids on either side of her head were precise and perfect. The plain calico work dress she wore had been carefully pressed to best advantage, and the sun-bleached apron tied around her waist was as clean and neat as lye soap and a washboard could make it.

"Morning." His voice was deep and gravelly.

Vassar took the pitcher of warm water she offered, and with a nod that he hoped conveyed his thanks, he shut the door. Then he staggered to the washstand. He poured the water into the basin and set the pitcher aside before bracing himself with both hands and leaning toward the spotted shaving mirror. He grimaced at the wavy reflection he saw there. Farming would be a better line of work if it didn't start quite so early in the morning.

He closed his eyes once more and almost managed to fall asleep again standing up. His own swaying motion startled him awake, and he looked at his reflection in the mirror with distaste. "Lazy slugabed!" he accused. His tone held real anger and self-disgust. Like most men, Vass had weaknesses. But unlike most, Vass knew that his own failings, his own flaws, had and could cause infinite pain and unending regrets. His own weakness had ruined lives, innocent lives and guilty ones, also. Since coming to the Greens', he'd determined never to let his weakness show again. So, leaning forward, he scooped a double handful of the warm water and splashed it on his face. Like it or not, the days started early in Arkansas.

By the time he made it to the kitchen, at least he'd begun to look more like a hardworking farmer than a rounder after a wild Saturday night.

Lessy was alone, still sweetly singing. Without a word to her, Vassar reached for the pristine bucket that hung by the churn. Lessy glanced over at him, a warmth of pride lighting her face.

"Oh, I've already done the milking."

Vassar gave a grunt of acknowledgment before he hung the bucket back on its nail. He looked on top of the cupboard to see the elm splint gathering basket was missing.

"Eggs?" he asked.

"Mammy's gathering them now," Lessy answered.

He nodded with gratitude and regret. He was late again. What must Lessy think of the man she'd agreed to marry? Milking was surely his task. And although many women gathered their eggs, his father had always both milked and gathered while Mama cooked breakfast.

With a mild feeling of failure Vass seated himself at the table, his pride in shambles. Lessy was perfect. A perfect woman destined to be a perfect farm wife. He eyed her as she bustled about. Cheerful and steady, Lessy's hardworking life and happy disposition shamed him. Leaning his elbows on the table's edge, he put his head in his hands. He rubbed his eyes to try to dispel the lassitude that still lingered there, but he could easily have drifted off again had Lessy not set a mug of steaming hot coffee in front of him.

"Thanks," he muttered.

He took a sip as Lessy moved to put the biscuits beside him, singing again.

She had a pretty voice, and Vass was grateful for it. But how could anyone be so dang cheerful at daybreak! The screen door slammed as Nora Green returned.

"Best get that breakfast on the table, Lessy," she said before turning her attention to Vass. "I saw a dustcloud out to the west—bet it's the haying crew coming down the road."

Vass made to rise, but the widow stayed him. "You can't be putting in a day's work on an empty stomach."

Agreeably Vassar accepted the plate of bacon, biscuits, and grits Lessy set before him. "How many eggs do you want?" she asked.

"Give him a half dozen," Nora answered for him. "That's a big man you've got to fill up, Lessy, and a long day ahead of him."

Vass was wide awake when the haying crew led by Roscoe Doobervale pulled up into the yard. Roscoe had been doing business at the Greens' farm since before Lessy was born. He was a fellow of about Mammy Green's age and sported a bushy gray mustache that seemed constantly in need of trimming.

"Blessed day to you, Vassar," was the older man's greeting.

"Looks like a blessed day for hay cutting, if you're ready."

Roscoe nodded and gestured toward the men who were just beginning to jump down from the back of the hay wagon where their gear was stowed. Trailing behind the wagon, like stray dogs following a sausage truck, were the machines that made modern haying a quick and reasonable task for a half dozen men. Vass immediately found his steps leading him to the shiny mechanical wonders. Almost with reverence he gently caressed the cold, brightly painted metal of the rake bars.

"You know most of these boys," Roscoe said, interrupting Vass's communion with the farm implements.

Looking up hastily, dismayed at his own bad manners, Vass acknowledged the men in the crew who were familiar to him. "John, Angus, Claidon."

Handshakes were exchanged.

"That boy is Angus's," Roscoe said, pointing at a ruddy-complexioned young man in his teens. "His name's Tommy. And this here is Ripley. He's quite a hand with the machinery. He's got that newfangled haykicker of mine slipping through the fields like a knife through butter."

A man in his mid-twenties jumped from the back of the wagon. There was a sauntering laziness to his walk, but no shortage of implied power in his thick muscular arms and thighs. His coal-black hair hung in loose curls around his head, and bright blue eyes gazed out of a strong, handsome face. He gave a friendly nod to Vass, his smile was broad and his teeth straight and white, and one long, deep dimple curved down his left cheek. The new man was only a few inches shorter than Vassar and had to look up only slightly to meet his gaze. After wiping his hand casually on his trousers, he accepted the offered handshake. Vassar's huge bearlike paw was much bigger than Ripley's own, but his grip was of a man to his equal.

"Pleasure to meet you, Mr. Green. You got some fine good fields a-growing here."

"The name's Muldrow, Vassar Muldrow." He glanced around with pride. "I grew the fields, but they aren't mine. The Widow Green owns this place."

Ripley nodded with polite apology at his mistake and then raised a teasing eyebrow as he glanced around at the other men. "Widow, huh? I'm right partial to widows."

His words brought a guffaw of laughter from the rest of the crew. Vass felt vaguely unsettled.

"That Ripley's got him a gal on every farm we've been through this year," John Crenshaw explained. "I suspect half the gals in Arkansas are expecting him to come back at the end of the season and put a ring on their finger."

Claidon Biggs slapped Ripley on the back and said in a feigned whisper, "And half the menfolk'll be praying for the same thing when those gals' bellies start swelling up like watermelons."

Vassar felt awkward but grinned in camaraderie.

Old Roscoe shook his head with disapproval. "There's more truth to that than I want to think about."

"I swear I don't know how he does it," John said. "He just smiles that pretty smile and talks some pretty talk, and them gals are clinging to him like ivy on bramble vines."

Ripley shrugged with feigned innocence and chuckled good-naturedly.

Vass was grinning more easily now. "I hope you don't set your sights on Widow Green. She ain't much of a woman for foolishness. My daddy sent me here for her to straighten out my ways. You start talking pretty to her, and she's liable to wash your mouth out with soap."

Ripley nodded, his words open and friendly. "Thank you, Muldrow. I consider myself warned. And call me Rip—everybody does."

Vass slapped Rip on the back.

It took the better part of the morning to unload all the equipment. The crew would be camping out near the hay barn, where they could shelter in case of inclement weather.

Vass began hitching up the teams to the equipment and found Ripley at his side. He'd already noticed the man had a good mind for tools and implements as well as a quick wit. Rip had kept up a steady stream of conversation, which more than once brought a blush to Vass's cheek and a grin to his lips.

" . . . and so the Quaker stood back a moment and recovered himself, and then he reached over and patted that mean old milk cow on the flank and said, 'Nay, Bossy, I shall not strike thee. But on the morrow I'll sell thee to a Baptist, and he'll beat the hell out of thee!' "

Vass chuckled at the image and shook his head. But as he reached over to take the tie from Ripley, he saw the young man's gaze was looking past him.

"Well, well," the handsome young man drawled with a grin. "The widow might not be quite my style, but that one with her would be *worth* getting a mouth washing for."

Curiously Vass turned to see Mammy Green and Lessy setting up the dinner table in the yard beside the house.

"That young one will do me just fine," Rip was saying. "I ain't close enough to see if she's pretty, but she's got a handsome way about her. See how she moves. It's like her feet don't touch the ground at all."

Following Ripley's gaze, Vassar watched Lessy walking around the table. It *was* kind of an interesting walk. He'd never noticed it before.

"That's Lessy. Widow Green's daughter."

Rip's grin widened. "Her daughter? You've been holding out on me, Muldrow. Dirty Devils awaiting, I'll be slicking my hair back when I go a-sparking her."

Words sticking strangely in his throat, Vass finally managed to cough out a curt reply. "Miss Green is my intended."

Ripley turned his attention back to Vass. His eyebrows were raised in surprise before he grinned wryly and with a feigned look of disgust folded his arms belligerently across his chest. "Well, if that ain't a jackass pa-toot! Why didn't you say so in the first place? You let me get my hopes all up and then tell me the gal is claimed. You warning me off?"

Vassar scoffed and shook his head as he hooked the traces to the crupper. "There's no need for 'warning you off,' Ripley. Lessy is a quiet, hardworking woman without a thought in her head for flirting or vanity."

Rip raised a speculative eyebrow. "Two peas in a pod, hey?"

Vass shrugged. "More like two sheaves of grain," he said. "We've grown up together these last four years and have common goals for ourselves and the farm. We have a shared past and have expectation for a shared fate."

"A shared fate?" Ripley whistled with admiration. "Now, I've told a gal or two that we were *destiny*, but I sure never made it sound as doggone boring as you do."

Vass felt stung. "Maybe my Lessy *likes* boring."

Ripley shook his head. "The gal may like *you*, but they ain't *no* gals that like boring."

The platter of fried chicken was so heavy it took both Lessy and her mother to carry it. Feeding seven working men was a chore, and the two had started cooking the midday meal as soon as Vass had left from breakfast.

"Is that everything?" Lessy asked, surveying the heavily laden table.

"Good graces, I've forgot the bread!" Widow Green exclaimed. "Go call the hands to dinner and bring those loaves on your way back."

Lessy hurried to the back porch and clanged the triangle loudly with the wand that hung from it by a string. With only a hasty glance toward the men near the barn, she stepped into the kitchen to get the bread. Six perfectly brown crusty loaves, still warm from the oven, were already piled in a wicker basket. She grabbed it up, but before hurrying out, she hastily checked her reflection in the small looking glass imbedded into the inlay of her mother's china cabinet. Her hair was still in place, but she smoothed it nonetheless. Her brown eyes were big, too big she thought, and too close together to be truly attractive, but she didn't really mind. Her nose, however, was thin and straight and sharp. Without thinking, she tapped the end of it with her index finger, a habit she'd formed years ago when Sugie Joe had told her that it came to a point like a butcher knife.

Reassured, Lessy let her fingers drift to the underside of her lower left jaw. A bout with smallpox as a youngster had left three small craters there that never shrank even after being massaged with cream treatments or browned with sun. Vassar was too kind to have ever mentioned the marks.

With a determined huff, she fought back the wave of self-pity that had churned up inside her. In fact, Vass really never commented on her appearance. Vass was not a man to be lured with a pretty face or charmed by vain foolishness, she mused. There was no flour on her nose or grease splatters on the bib front of her apron. She was clean and neat. That was all a good woman was expected to be. Raising her chin with determined pride, she headed out to the table spread under the maple tree.

Vass had already seated himself at the head of the table when Lessy set the basket of bread in front of him. He looked up and smiled. Her heart lifted with the flash of his white teeth, and shyly she returned his grin with one of her own.

Clearing his throat, he placed his elbows on either side of his plate and clasped his hands together before laying his forehead against the knuckles. "God, our blessed Father," he began.

Lessy squeezed her eyes together tightly and sent up the silent prayer that she offered so frequently these days. *Thank you for sending me Vass. Help me to be the wife that he needs*.

When Vassar offered a deep baritone amen, Roscoe seconded it loudly, and the table of men eagerly reached for the bowls of food within their grasp.

Scrutinizing the contents of the table once more, Lessy nodded reassuringly to her mother seated at the end of the table before picking up a pitcher of ice water to fill the goblets on the table.

"Lessy, you remember Roscoe," her mother said, gesturing to the older man on Vassar's right. Lessy gave him a welcoming nod. "It's good to see you, Mr. Doobervale."

Widow Green introduced the rest of the crew to her daughter as Lessy filled their glasses and politely repeated their names. When Lessy made her way around the table to the young man at her left, he turned to her and offered his hand.

"Ripley, ma'am," he said. His eyes were bright blue and warm with laughter as he looked at her.

Rather awkwardly Lessy transferred the pitcher from her right to her left hand before offering hers. Glancing down, she saw her palm was damp from the coolness of the water she carried. Self-consciously she pulled it back and wiped it on her apron, then flustered with embarrassment, she offered her hand once more. The young man did not, as she expected, give her a hearty handshake, but merely grasped her long slim fingers in his own and gave them a most delicate squeeze.

"What a delight to meet you, Miss Green," he said, his eyes twinkling as they looked straight into hers.

"Nice to meet you, too, Mr. Ripley," Lessy replied. She was slightly taken aback by the warmth of his greeting and a little concerned that he still held her hand.

"Please, call me Rip," he said, dropping his voice ever so slightly. "You are Miss Lessy, I believe. May I be permitted to address you by your given name?"

His formal question seemed so out of character with his flirtatious tone that Lessy almost giggled. "That would be fine."

"Lessy." He repeated the name slowly, thoughtfully, rolling the *s*'s off his tongue in a caressing way. "It is a diminutive of Celesta, I presume."

"Why, yes."

Ripley cocked his head slightly to one side and let his eyes explore her head and shoulders. "Celesta. It means heavenly, you know."

She nodded slightly.

His tone softened with warmth. "And the name does suit you . . . Lessy."

A strange something skittered across her stomach at the unexpected compliment. She felt immediately ill at ease and fought the desire to drop the water pitcher at his feet and hide her unheavenly face from his gaze. Purposefully collecting herself, she leaned forward slightly to pour water into Ripley's goblet. She felt somehow safer with her hands at work until she cast a glance at the handsome young man only to catch him eyeing her bosom. With a nervous start she jerked back from the table, managing to spill a very cold dollop of water on Rip's trousers.

"Oh, I'm sorry!"

Ripley wiped at the water on his thigh and gave her a careless gesture of unconcern. "I suspect I needed a little cooling off."

His remark brought a snorty chuckle from the youngster across the table from him.

Lessy's eyes were immediately drawn to Vass. He sat silently at the head of the table watching the byplay, his green eyes looking at her in a way she found strange and unfamiliar. She felt suddenly as embarrassed and exposed as if wind had thrown her skirts over her head and her best drawers had been in the wash. Their eyes caught, and she flushed and looked away.

Glancing down at the man beside her, Rip's bright smile was open and friendly. The stranger seemed to offer a safe haven from new feelings that were distinctly uncomfortable.

As if in apology for some slight he'd caused, Ripley turned his attention to his plate, and Lessy moved on down the table to fill the glasses of John Crenshaw and Claidon Biggs, before taking her place to the left of Vassar.

"Muldrow tells me you are about to become his bride," Ripley said.

Blushing, she spared a hasty glance toward Vass. "Yes." Her voice was a shy whisper. "As soon as the hay is in."

Rip's smile broadened into a grin as he looked around the table. "Then I pity this crew," he said. "With a lovely bride like Miss Lessy awaiting, Muldrow will drive us like Missouri mules!"

The men around the table chuckled. Rip gave Vass a challenging grin. Staring back at him silently, Vass continued to chew his food.

"What about you, Mr. Ripley?" Lessy asked. "Have you got a wife or a sweetheart waiting for the end of the season?"

Tommy McFadden laughed loudly this time with the less than delicate enthusiasm of youth. "Rip's too smart to fall into some gal's trap!"

Lessy raised her eyebrows in surprise at the words; Ripley just gave a shrug.

"I just haven't found that right woman, Miss Lessy," he said. His smile widened and his expression softened. "Seems every time I meet a girl I could think about marrying"—he turned to glance down the table meaningfully at Vassar—"some other fellow's already claimed her."

Lessy's cheeks sparkled with bright warm color at his implied compliment. What a rogue he was! And what a gentleman. She smiled with shy pleasure at Ripley for a timid moment before grabbing up the basket before her and offering it across the table. "You didn't get any bread, Mr. Ripley. I baked this myself, and some say I've quite a knack for it."

Chapter Three

The sky was still an inky blue as Lessy made her way out to the barn to milk. Vass had said he would tend to the cow this morning, but she hated to wake him. And with seven men to feed in addition to her regular chores, she wanted to get an early start on the day. Mammy was helping, of course. But she was letting Lessy lead, giving her a chance to prove what a good farm wife she could be. Lessy welcomed the chance. She wanted Vass to be proud of her.

She let herself into the door of the barn, and the sweet, warm smells of clover and alfalfa assailed her. Like everything else on the farm, the barn was nearly as clean as a church. Vassar believed that cleanliness being next to Godliness meant animals and farm buildings as well as personal hygiene.

"Morning, Sissy," she said to the big buff-colored Guernsey that stood in the first stall. Lessy quickly gathered up some feed for the cow, and stepping past her in the stall, scattered it evenly in the trough. Sissy wasn't willing to wait as Lessy neatly spread her morning meal. She pushed her big, anxious head up under Lessy's arm, trying to push her out of the way.

"For shame, Sissy!" Lessy scolded her as she patted the cow sternly on the cheek. "A lady has got to learn some patience at the breakfast table."

Sissy's reply was a loud unconvinced moo.

"You going to sing with me this morning?" Lessy gave the cow one loving caress on the flank before she left her to her eating and gathered up her stool and pail. She

24

hummed a tune that was playing in her head, though she didn't know the words. It was a sweet, light tune, cheery and fresh, a tune Vass often hummed. She thought of it as Vassar's song. It made her feel close to him to hear the sweet sounds coming from her own lips.

Lessy heard the crackle of hay underfoot only a moment before a fine tenor voice joined in her song.

> "Millie's brother's gunning for me,
> And the fault is mine, they say.
> She lost her drawers at the Sunday School picnic,
> And I'll ne'er regret that day."

"What are you singing!" Lessy's eyes were wide with shock as she stared at Ripley leaning indolently against the stall post.

Rip's grin was wide, his eyes were bright, and his stance was teasing, hands in his pockets, arms folded across his chest. "You were the one humming the tune," he said. "I just joined in with the chorus."

"But those words, I—" Lessy sputtered, her face flaming with embarrassment.

"At least I only sang the chorus," he said. "Why, the verses of that naughty ditty would put kinks in your hair faster than a curling iron!"

Lessy's face was fiery red. "I didn't know the words," she protested.

Rip folded his hands in front of him and surveyed the blushing young woman before him. His lips twitched and his eyes danced, but his tone was gentle. "It's a drinking song, Miss Lessy. You hear it bellowed by a hoard of galoots at the top of their lungs when they're out on a round. It's called 'Plowing Millie.' "

It seemed impossible that Lessy's eyes could get any bigger, but they did. She nearly choked on her own words. "Oh, dear," she began. "Mr. Ripley, I never—well, I really didn't . . . I—"

Rip held up a hand to silence her. "I'm sorry I embarrassed you, Miss Lessy. I heard your sweet voice humming that wicked little tune, and I just had to join in. I shouldn't have let you know the words."

"Oh, no," Lessy assured him. "I am very grateful that you did. I hum that tune quite often, and I certainly . . . well, I wouldn't want anyone to . . . to, well . . . to get the wrong idea."

Rip hunkered down in the stall next to her and smiled with genuine admiration. "Miss Lessy, nobody would get the wrong idea about a woman like you," he said. "You are sweet and warm, and when you give your heart to a man, he'd never have cause to doubt."

Lessy smiled, her face flushed with pleasure. "Well, Mr. Ripley, that is certainly a glowing endorsement."

"Every word of it is true."

"You don't even know me."

"I know enough." His voice was a low gruff whisper. "Things about you just shine on through. I know that you are strictly the marrying kind."

Lessy turned her attention back to the cow. "Well, aren't most women?" she said. "And I am to be married shortly."

"Yes, that's what I hear. And I certainly envy Muldrow his good fortune."

Lessy turned to look at him. Surprised and puzzled at his words, she was not sure if they were not just flattery.

Before she could make a determination, Rip's fingers reached out to lightly trace the curve of her jaw and tenderly caressed the tiny white circles he found there.

"I know what these are," he said.

Lessy blushed and pushed his fingers away. "They're pockmarks."

"Pockmarks!" Rip sounded horrified. "No, ma'am," he said firmly. "I'm absolutely sure this is where the fairies kiss you in the dead of night."

She giggled. "No fairies are kissing me in the dead of night."

"No? Maybe it's Muldrow." He hesitated a moment and touched the tiny scars again before his voice dropped to a husky whisper. "Lucky Muldrow."

A tiny whimper of surprise and shock escaped Lessy's lips as a strange tingly feeling emanated from his hands to her flesh and throughout her body. Her pulse jumped and a covey of butterflies took flight in her stomach. Her hands stilled at their work. She did not so much as blink, feeling frozen in place.

Her eyes wide, Lessy stared at the handsome man beside her who was looking at her in a way no one had before. She could feel the depths of heat in his eyes, and ripples of anxious excitement quaked through her body.

Vassar! her mind whispered his name as a plea. The trembling inside her made her think only of Vassar.

The heavy humid silence between them held for one full minute.

Sissy made a noisy complaint and stamped her hind foot threateningly. Lessy jumped slightly, startled. The cow's interruption broke the spell, and she jerked away from the warm male hand that caressed her.

"Mr. Ripley, please."

He immediately withdrew and made apology. "Forgive me, Miss Lessy," he said. "Morning and mockingbirds always get the best of me. They get the best of any man, I suspect."

Lessy wondered.

His words were made with such a boyish sincerity and an impish grin that her discomfiture ceased immediately, and she found herself smiling and shaking her head at him. He was flirting with her. The idea of a handsome young man making pretty talk to a plain farm woman that was practically married filled her with delight.

"I've got no time for foolishness this morning," she said. "I've got a big breakfast to get on the table and a whole day's chores to do."

His grin widened. "Don't let me stop you, Miss Lessy. It's my ambition to one day marry myself a right-living farm gal and watch her a-working all day long."

Lessy threw him a look of mock exasperation as he chuckled and leaned indolently against the stall. Contentedly she continued her milking with his eyes upon her.

"So do you flirt with all the women you meet?" she asked him.

Clutching his hand to his chest dramatically, he assured her that it was not so. "Not all the women, certainly," he said. "Just most of them."

In response Lessy turned the teat she held in her hand in his direction and squirted the toe of his workboot with warm milk.

Rip raised his hand like a captured criminal. "Don't shoot, ma'am. I'm unarmed."

When the milk was just foaming along the top of the pail, Lessy pulled it out of Sissy's way and handed it to Rip.

"Don't spill it," she admonished him as if he were a youngster.

"I'll do my best, Miss Lessy," he assured her.

She hung the three-legged milking stool on the side of the stall before leading Sissy out the back of the barn. Lessy removed her halter and gave the milk cow a grateful slap on the rump.

"See you at sundown, Sissy."

With lazy grace Sissy leisurely strolled away from the barn without so much as a backward glance and began her morning inspection of the pasture.

Lessy watched her for a minute before turning back to Rip, who stood in the doorway, milk pail in hand.

"I can take that now," she told him as she came back into the barn.

"It would be my pleasure to carry it for you, Miss Lessy," Rip answered with a flourish of his hand indicating that she should lead the way to the farmhouse.

The two were laughing together as they stepped into the back door of the farmhouse. Vass was leaning against the cupboard, coffee cup in hand, but with his eyes closed. At the sound of their entrance, he stood up straight as an arrow and stared in surprise.

"Good morning, Vass," Lessy said sweetly. "You're up early."

"Morning, Muldrow," Ripley said. "Where do you want this milk, Miss Lessy?"

Lessy turned her attention back to him. "Let me get the cheesecloth, and you can strain it into the milk can."

Vass watched them work with a strange catch in his heart. "You're up early, Ripley," he said.

The young man smiled at him, his straight white teeth glimmering in the dim morning light of the kitchen. "I'm an early riser," he said. "I can hardly wait for the days to begin."

Vass took a large swig of coffee and winced as it burned his mouth. He had tried to be an early riser this morning. He'd forced himself out of bed at the first cock's crow. But apparently it hadn't been early enough. Ripley had already been slicked up milking and laughing with Lessy before he'd even got both eyes properly opened.

"Stop that or I'll hit you with a frying pan!" Vass heard Lessy warning. Turning toward them, he saw Rip with the last bit of milk in the pail threatening to douse Lessy.

"Turnabout is fair play," Ripley stated, his eyes bright with mischief. "You squirted milk on me—I pour it on you."

"Not if you want biscuits."

"Ah, biscuits." Rip's grin widened. "Quick bread made from your sweet hands, Miss Lessy, would taste to me like manna from heaven."

Lessy giggled with delight. Her pink cheeks and bright smile were very alluring.

Vass cleared his throat uncomfortably. A stab of hot jealousy seared his heart. She and Rip looked so happy together. Their talk was soft and flirty. Vass envied that talk.

But it could never be that way for him, he admonished himself. He respected Lessy too much. Vass would never risk the loss of control a flirtation might provoke. Other men could play with fire, but Vassar's own carnality had already burned too many.

The mower cut a wide swath toward the right of the wheels as it moved across the meadow. John Crenshaw sat high above the team, pulling a line as straight as an arrow. In front of him, Roscoe and Vass walked through the knee-high grass, searching the ground for hidden dangers to horse or cutting blade. Behind the mower Claidon Biggs, Angus McFadden, and his son stirred the worst of the cutting with rakes. The hay would have to be fluffed and separated to dry. The haykicker would do most of that, but still hand labor could spot a potential problem that might break a rake spine and set men and machinery back a day or more.

At a distance Ripley drove the haykicker. He stood on the crossbar, reins in hand, as he guided the shiny piece of farm equipment into the cutting. The haykicker scooped the hay from the ground with spikes and tossed it into a wooden cagelike bin. The bin, connected to the wheels, tumbled the grass over and over as it moved, getting both sunlight and breeze into it. Sometimes known as a tedder, the haykicker took the place of dozens of women and children who in days long past would have been asked to follow the mower or scythe and toss and shake the cut by hand. The newfangled modern machine was able to stir the grass and then evenly spread it against the ground to dry in neat windrows. Fresh-cut hay would not be safe stored in a barn. Damp grass took to rotting and became as combustible as kerosene on a fire grate.

From the shade of the front porch Lessy watched their progress as she shucked corn. Squinting, she could almost make out Vass in the distance. His familiar straw hat hid his face from view, but the breadth of his shoulders made him easily distinguishable from the others.

Grabbing up the next ear of corn, she clasped the husk at the blackened tip of the silks and ripped it down with one swift, smooth motion. Snapping off the stem, she pulled the rest of the husk with it and began stripping down the fine silks that clung so tenaciously to the ridge rows.

She wanted Vassar Muldrow. For four years now she had wanted him more than anything in her life, and she'd gone after him with everything she had.

Within days of his arrival on the farm, Lessy had known

that he was a serious-minded worker. He had no time
for frolic or foolishness. It was as if he held his fears
and feelings in fine leather harness with a sharp steel
bit to pull up when necessary. Lessy admired his control and emulated his example. But her heart cried that
there was more behind his stern facade. That the pain
behind his eyes was real and raw and that surely she could
soothe it.

But he would never let her close. He would never let
anyone close who threatened the restraint that bound him.
Lessy understood almost immediately that like catching
a chicken in the henhouse, to catch Vassar Muldrow she
must scratch as hard and crow as loud.

Lessy was, by nature, neither quiet nor thoughtful. She
loved life in a way that she couldn't quite tamp down.
A warm, open girl, she loved to laugh, to run, to sing
in the sweet air of morning and the purple shadows of
closing day. She had been a high-spirited child who ran
wild through the meadows and climbed every tree in the
orchard. But overnight she had become a quiet young
lady of decorum and responsibilities. A lady that Vassar
Muldrow might want to marry.

And the change had not gone unnoticed. Her mother's
brow was furrowed more than once over the metamorpho-
sis. The people at church assumed it was her father's death
that "calmed young Lessy down." But she thought that her
mother knew the truth. The truth that love had conquered
Lessy Green.

It had been an improvement, Lessy thought to herself. It
had been time for her to grow up and assume the dignity of
womanhood. She would have done so, sooner or later, had
Vassar not arrived. But since he had, there was no reason
why she couldn't take it on in a way that was calculated
to please him.

Watching young Vass, Lessy had come to know him. He
looked at Sugie Jo Mouwers. But he was more comfortable
talking to Maizie Watson, the preacher's wife. He played
dominoes and chinkerchecks, but he preferred to spend
his evenings reading the *Farm Bulletin*. He could sing

quite fair and was light on his feet at the local dances.
But he was happier walking the land and humming to
himself.

Lessy watched and had learned. She was now as easy
to talk to as the preacher's wife, totally content with an
evening of reading, and openly stated her preference for
farm activities over social outings.

In point of fact, Lessy did love the farming life and
had never dreamed of a different life. But though she'd
become everything Vass wanted, for four long years Vass
had fought the love that she offered.

Having plucked the last stringy thread of cornsilk from
the roasting ear, Lessy threw it into the basin and grabbed
another from the basket.

Now Lessy had won him at last. Their marriage was
only weeks away. And she and Vass were now perfectly
matched.

Grabbing the dark husk tips of corn, she ripped down
with her usual efficiency. She gave a startled little cry and
dropped the ear abruptly. A big, furry green and brown
corn borer lazily crawled along an eaten-out path of ker-
nels. She shuddered slightly before determinedly jerking
up the corn and flicking the hideous worm into the pile
of husks bound for the compost heap. She hated creepy,
crawly things, especially corn borers. It was amazing how
they could hide so completely in what appeared to be a
perfectly developed ear of corn.

Lessy snapped off the wormy piece and threw it in the
husk pile before she cleaned the silk out of the untouched
portion and continued her work.

Again she gazed across the fields to the hay meadow.
The haykicker made its noisy way behind the men and
mower, and Lessy's eyes were drawn to it. Her lips widened to a smile.

That Ripley was about the best-looking fellow she'd
ever seen in her life. And with his pretty face came a
silver tongue. That man could talk snakes into buying
shoes. Her memory strayed to the touch of his hand on her
cheek. She tutted to her self and shook her head. Clearly,

Mr. Ripley had a way about him that was likely fatal to the female sex.

Ripping open another ear of corn, this time more hesitantly, fearing more corn borers, she absently wished that Vass had some of those winning ways. Then she forcibly pushed the thought from her mind. If Vass was not the romantic type, then the romantic type was not what she wanted.

Chapter Four

It was full dark before Vass stepped in through the back door.

"You still at it?" he asked of Lessy, who was still noisily puttering about the kitchen.

She shook her head and smiled at him warmly. "I'm just getting a little ahead for tomorrow. Mammy's already gone to bed, and I was really waiting up for you."

Clearing his throat uncomfortably, Vass cast a nervous glance toward the bedroom Lessy shared with her mother. Being alone with her was surely asking for trouble.

"You want to go walking out?" The question was asked almost incredulously. Everybody on the farm had been working almost nonstop since daybreak, and the whole crew was bone tired. If Vass didn't go to sleep now, he wouldn't be able to rise until noon tomorrow.

"Oh no," Lessy assured him quickly. "I know you're tired, and . . . well, the barnyard and the orchard don't seem quite our own with the hay crew staying there."

Vass nodded in agreement.

"I'd just like to sit in the parlor a few minutes if you'd like to," Lessy said. "Perhaps we could just visit a little, tell each other about our day."

Tiredness aside, an unchaperoned evening in the parlor was something that Vass knew he should discourage. Still, they were betrothed, and a few moments of his time during a busy working day seemed such a simple request.

Vassar nodded. Lessy was more precious to him than anything he'd ever worked for in his life. She deserved heaven on earth, he was sure of that. Unfortunately, he had a lot less to offer. If she wanted a bit of companionship, it was certainly his duty as well as his pleasure to provide it.

Stimulating conversation, however, was not one of Vassar's strong points, and as the two settled themselves on opposite ends of Mammy Green's brocatele divan, he began his usual turn of phrase.

"Did you see that new haykicker out there? Is that some kind of machine or what? I'd be sitting pretty with a piece like that hitched behind my team."

"It's a very fancy machine," Lessy agreed.

"We got a lot done today."

"Oh?"

"Yep. If it keeps up this way, we may be done by the end of the week."

"That's wonderful."

As the subject concluded, a long pause ensued.

"How are the hens laying?" he asked finally.

"Only nine this morning," she answered. "But you know how much they hate this heat."

"Hmmph," Vass agreed. "What about Sissy—she don't look to go dry?"

Lessy shook her head. "Sissy's just fine. She seems to be in the prime of health. I think she spends the hot afternoons sitting down in that shady spot in the little creek."

"Umph," he agreed. "I saw the garden as I came in. It looks plenty big still. You've got enough tomatoes out there to feed the Arkansas Guard."

Lessy smiled warmly and tilted her head to give him a welcoming look. "I know how much you love tomatoes."

Vass smiled back, his face flushed with pleasure, and cleared his throat absently.

"The peach orchard looks—"

"Vass." Lessy interrupted him gently. In her mind's eye she saw the corn borer inside what looked to be a perfect roasting ear. "Let's talk about something else."

"Something else?"

"Something else besides the farm. That's all we ever talk about, it seems. We just talk about the farm. Why don't we talk about something else tonight."

"Well, sure, Lessy," he agreed. "We can talk about whatever you want."

The two sat smiling silently together for a long moment.

"Sure hope this weather holds," Vassar blurted out finally.

Lessy nodded. Silence.

"There's talk at church about a harvest revival," she said.

Vass nodded. Silence.

"I see your mother is fixing to switch rooms with me."

Silence. Lessy blushed furiously, and Vassar coughed, mentally kicking himself in the head.

The room became quiet once more. Vass scanned the ceiling boards as if topics for conversation might be written upon them.

"Roscoe told me that he and his wife took the train to Kansas City last year," he said finally.

"Oh, really?"

"Um-hum. He said they just drove the buggy up to DeQueen to catch the train, then sat back and watched two states go by from their window."

Lessy sighed. "That sounds wonderful."

"You like traveling?"

She giggled. "I wouldn't know," she told him. "I've never been anywhere."

Vass smiled. "Well, I don't care for it much. It's a lot of heat and bother, and I like sleeping in my own bed. But maybe we could go up to a stock show or something sometime. Just so you could say you've been somewhere."

"Oh, no, please," Lessy said. "I wouldn't want to go just for me. If you don't like traveling, then we'll just stay here."

His expression softening, Vass reached over to take her hand and squeezed it gently. "Sweet Lessy, I believe you are a sainted angel that God sent to me."

He ascribed the vivid blush that swept her cheeks to modesty. Lessy seemed disconcerted, giving him quick encouraging little smiles and then dropping her gaze to her hands.

Vass searched his brain for lighter topics. Perhaps they could discuss last Sunday's sermon. Unfortunately, he didn't remember a word of it. He grabbed upon and then discarded numerous subjects because they were farm-related. When he was almost ready to give up in defeat, Lessy spoke.

"You know, the funniest thing happened to me today," she began.

"What?" he asked.

Lessy shrugged, a little unsure of herself. "Well, it's really . . . I probably shouldn't even tell you this."

"Tell me," he insisted with a warm, open smile. "After a hard day's work a man needs a bit of humor come evening."

"Well, it was really quite embarrassing, actually," she said. "Sometimes our most embarrassing moments can really be very funny."

Vass chuckled with agreement, remembering some of his own. "I can't imagine what you could ever be embarrassed about," he said. "But I'm sitting with my ears perked, waiting to hear."

Lessy smiled a little shyly before giving a big sigh of resignation. "You know that tune you hum all the time?"

"Tune?"

"You know, the tune you hum while you're working."

"I hum?" He looked at her quizzically. "I didn't realize it."

"Yes, you are always humming this tune. I swear, every time I get near you or we're working together, you start humming this tune. I've come to think of it as sort of a part of you."

Vass was still smiling but shrugged in disbelief. "I can't imagine what it is."

"It goes—" Lessy hummed a few bars. Her rendition was a little off key, and Vass listened intently before he shook his head without recognition.

"Well, it's called—" She hesitated and then swallowed a giggling blush. "It's called 'Plowing Millie.' And I was humming it in the barn, not knowing what it was about. And that Mr. Ripley came in and started singing it. I declare, I must have turned every shade of red in the sunset."

Her words had run together rather quickly, but as she spoke, Vassar's eyes widened in shock and his jaw dropped open far enough to drive a team through.

In memory he saw himself, his older brothers, and their friends sitting behind the corncrib back at his daddy's farm. They were drinking root beer and pretending it was the real thing. Between swapping stories and speculation about women's anatomy, they sang the raunchy beer tunes of hardened rounders.

> Sweet Millie whined
> Now please be kind.
> I almost am a virgin.
> Except for Joe and Cousin Moe
> And the baseball team at Spurgeon.

"Ripley sang that song to you!" The words came roaring out of Vassar's mouth with such fury that Lessy jumped.

"He sang the chorus, Vassar, only the chorus," Lessy insisted quickly. "He said that the verses weren't proper for me to hear."

"Nothing about that song is proper for *you* to hear."

Vass had risen angrily to his feet, and his hands were clenched in suppressed rage.

"It was my fault," Lessy insisted. "I was the one that was humming the song after all."

Vass turned to look at her, his eyes wild. "It was not *your* fault," he told her, keeping his voice deliberately controlled. "You would never think of doing anything shady or wicked."

Vassar was perfectly clear about whose fault it was. It was his own. What evil demon in his soul had him humming whoring ballads in the presence of a lady! *Be sure your sins will find you out* was more of a promise than a threat. Every day, every day, he tried to be worthy of Lessy, to be worthy of the woman of his dreams. But still he couldn't manage to live up to the man she believed him to be. He couldn't live up to the man that she deserved. His past sin might be forgiven, but the wickedness that still haunted his thoughts and his nights was not so easily vanquished.

"I need to take a walk," he announced as he moved toward the door.

Lessy hurried after him. "You're not going to do anything to Mr. Ripley?"

Vass looked back, surprised. "No, no, of course not." She was such a darling. Concerned for him, concerned for Ripley, never a thought to the terrible misdeed he had done, exposing her to the lowness of his own weakness. Vass reached over and patted her shoulder comfortingly. "I just need to be alone a while."

Pulling his hat from his head, Vass reached up to wipe the sweat from his brow. The teams had stopped moving, and the men had moved to the shady side of the horses as Lessy made her way through the group with cool water fresh from the well.

Beside him, Roscoe Doobervale spit a wad of tobacco into the new-mown field. "Don't like the looks of those clouds to the west," he said. "That's more than a chance shower, I'd stake my best boots on it."

Vass glanced in the direction he'd indicated and nodded his head. "I suspect we'd best get what we can into the barn and let the rest meet the rain."

He didn't hear the old man's reply as his attention was

drawn to the end of the wagon. Lessy and Ripley stood together, talking and laughing as if it were the easiest thing in the world. Rip was looking down into her eyes, his smile wide and his expression flirty. Lessy was looking back at him with only the palest flush of modesty on her face. What she told him made Ripley laugh, a deep hearty baritone, and she joined in with a tinkly giggle.

Watching them, there was little doubt in Vassar's mind that they had found something other than farming to talk about.

"Hey, Miss Lessy," Biggs called out. "Did you bring all that water for Ripley, or can the rest of us have some?"

Momentarily startled, Lessy looked at the water bucket in her hand as if she'd forgotten its existence. Then she gave Rip a feigned look of censure and shook her finger at him threateningly. "That's why you're trying to sweet-talk me! You want to keep this water within easy reach."

Ripley hung his head and placed his arms before her, wrists crossed like a guilty criminal asking to be led away. Lessy shook her head as she moved away, offering water to the rest of the men.

Vass valiantly attempted to focus his attention on what Doobervale was saying, but his eyes kept drifting to Lessy, whose cheeks were pink.

True to his word, he hadn't spoken to Ripley about the song. It was not Rip's fault, he'd concluded. It was surely his own. In the long night as he'd walked the peach orchard, he'd mentally cataloged his long list of sins.

He had wanted Lessy even before he'd ever seen her.

"It's no shame to have desire, son," his father had told him that long-ago summer. "But there is a place for it, and that place is the marriage bed."

Vass had hung his head in shame before his father. Shame had become his most familiar emotion. Shame was how he felt, and shame was what he'd brought, on his family and others.

"It just happened," he'd confessed to his father. "I don't know how it happened, it just did."

What had happened was Mrs. Mabel Brightmore. The wife of an aged and somewhat stodgy husband who was the local Granger representative. Mr. Brightmore was out of town quite frequently on business, and he'd hired Vass, then only seventeen, to take care of the heavy chores.

Those heavy chores had turned out to be more burdensome than he'd ever imagined. That long, blissful summer of his seventeenth year had been a sensual feast for a young man nearly starved. Mabel was enraptured with the broad young shoulders and the blushing innocence of the neighbor's boy.

"You don't know how lucky you are," she'd told him more than once as they lay in the lazy afterglow of an afternoon's illicit pleasures. "Why, your brothers and all your friends would just be green jealous if they knew that you and me were having such a good time."

He had felt lucky. He was hot and eager, randy and lucky. After a taste of the forbidden, he hadn't been willing to go back to being just another farmboy. It no longer mattered if Mr. Brightmore was due home any minute; they loitered in his bed illicitly. And if he were in the field, they could linger in the hayloft. And while the quiet, honest man spoke to his neighbors of farming concerns, Mabel and Vassar whispered coarse and wicked words in the seclusion of the Brightmore buggy or the broad daylight of Shady Creek bridge.

And Vass had thought himself the luckiest man on earth. Then his luck ran out.

"Harlot! Jezebel!" Vass could still hear Mr. Brightmore screaming through his tears. He'd surprised the two of them behind the men's privy at the Granger Hall. Nearly every man, woman, and child in Arkadelphia had been there. They'd heard Brightmore's words, they'd stared at Mabel's disheveled clothes, and they'd witnessed Vassar's shame.

It was only his father and Reverend Watson who had kept old Brightmore from killing Vassar where he stood. There had been times when Vass had wished he had. Mabel left the county in disgrace. His parents could hardly hold their heads up in town. They decided to send him away.

"Hard work and your cousin Nora's moral values will keep you on the straight and narrow," his father had prophesied. "The only young woman within miles is little Lessy. And she is the kind you marry, not the kind you lust after."

But lust after her he had. She'd smiled her sweet innocent smile, and he'd gone as hot and hard as if Miss Mabel had run a long fingernail up his thigh.

Lessy was the kind of woman a man married, his father had said so. Even Vass could see the truth of that. Marriage was the perfect idea, he'd thought at first.

"That Lessy sure looks like Grandma Rooker," his father said to him that first day.

Vass had studied her face. He remembered his great-grandmother only vaguely and could see nothing of the withered visage he remembered in the young, smooth cheeks before him. Still, Pa had said that it was so. And he found it disconcerting to imagine desire and lust with a ringer for Grandma Rooker.

So every time he looked at her, he thought of Grandma Rooker so he could keep his thoughts pure. And he'd managed to mend his ways.

Within a year he knew that to have a saint like Lessy for a wife would be more than any man could ask of heaven. But his dreams were still filled with sinful thoughts . . .

Lessy was standing in front of him now, offering a dipper of cool water and looking at him curiously.

"What on earth are you thinking about, Vassar?" she asked. "I'll swan, you look to have your mind half across the globe."

He took the dipper and drank it down. "Looks like it's going to rain," he said with a gesture toward the western sky.

Lessy turned to look in that direction, raising a hand to her brow to shade the afternoon sun from her eyes.

"How far away is it?" she asked.

Vass had allowed his eyes to drop to the curve of her

bosom and then mentally cursed himself for his weakness. He brought his gaze to her face to find her looking at him.

"What?" he asked with a nervous cough.

"The rain. How far away is the rain?"

"Oh! Late this evening or tonight, I suppose," he said. "I hope it clears up by morning. I'd hate to lose more than a day."

Suddenly Ripley was there, his arm slung casually around Lessy's waist, his voice loud and teasing. "You hear that, honey," he said. "Your bridegroom is so anxious to tie the knot, he's wishing the rain away. Never heard tell of a farmer doing that in all my days."

"Plenty do it in a flood," Doobervale piped in.

Rip gave a little moue of agreement and nodded his head. "A flood, you are right about that. And what we've got here is a flood of love."

The crew chuckled at his words, clearly enjoying the joke on the young couple.

Lessy laughed also as she elbowed Ripley playfully. "You are the biggest sack of foolishness God ever put into the body of a man."

Rip grinned at her. "And what does a sweet little farm girl like you know about men's bodies?"

Lessy's hand flew to her mouth in shock. Vass felt his whole body going tense, and his jaw set dangerously.

"Whoops," Rip said quietly as he caught sight of Vassar's expression. With exaggerated motions he withdrew his arm from Lessy's waist and stepped back with his hands up in a gesture of surrender. "Just teasing, Mr. Muldrow, sir. What's a wedding without a little good-natured teasing?"

The humorous murmurs from the other men seemed to be in agreement, so Vass let his anger go.

Although not completely. A part of him continued to simmer that Ripley had made suggestive remarks to Lessy.

And that she hadn't fainted away in shock and horror.

Chapter Five

The rain had arrived just after darkness fell, but it had not dissipated with the dawn. Dismal gray clouds hung overhead, and a slow steady shower rained down on the farm.

Lessy slogged through her chores with less enthusiasm than usual. Vass had been avoiding her since their talk in the parlor, and she feared that he thought the worst of her. She knew Vass to be a very moral, very upright gentleman. He must be horrified by her commonness.

Sugie Jo had once complained bitterly about how men—all men, young and old, rich or poor, farmer or tradesman—turned into twelve-handed boars in rut when they found themselves alone with a woman. Lessy was sure that Sugie Jo exaggerated, as was her nature, but even Mammy said a fellow was likely to try to steal a kiss.

Vassar, however, had never so much as made an improper suggestion.

And she was beginning to suspect why.

Vass, her Vass, had hummed a naughty ditty as he worked beside her. It seemed that Vassar perhaps wasn't the stalwart young man she thought him to be. Perhaps it wasn't his high moral nature that kept him at a distance from her. Perhaps it was something lacking in herself. When he was alone with her, he thought about farming. If he were to be alone with Sugie Jo, would his thoughts be different?

"All work and no play makes the bride look tired on her wedding day!"

Lessy started at the unexpected voice and turned in the

direction of the caller. She spied Ripley seated underneath the tarp that the men had raised over their little camp. A light glowed from a lantern beside him, highlighting his face.

With a wave of his arm he called her over.

She walked closer, within easy speaking distance but still far from the tarp. "I can't come in there," she protested.

Rip gave her a look of long-suffering patience. "Now, Miss Lessy," he said with light sarcasm. "It is broad daylight, and anybody within a half mile of the farmhouse can see us plainly. Come on inside and get out of the rain. I've got something to show you."

Lessy hesitated a minute more and then shrugged. Rip was absolutely right. The tarp may be where the men slept, but on a day like this it was hardly a private assignation. She stepped beneath the cover of the tent and pulled the sodden rain bonnet from her hair.

"Where are the rest of the men?" she asked.

Rip shrugged. "In the barn, I suppose, cleaning harness."

Lessy nodded. It seemed a likely occupation on such a day. "Why aren't you helping?"

"I will if they ask me," he said. "But if they don't notice that I'm not there, I'm not about to point it out."

"You'd rather sit out here and do nothing?" Her expression was incredulous.

"I'm doing something."

"What are you doing?"

"Drawing."

"Drawing? Pictures? Oh, let me see!" There was enthusiasm in her voice as she hurriedly seated herself beside him.

Rip seemed amused at her excitement and a little apologetically handed her the paper he was working on. Lessy stared at it curiously. The pen and ink drawing was all circles and perfectly straight lines. She couldn't quite make out what it was supposed to be. Biting her lip nervously and glancing at him under lowered lids, she turned the picture upside down, hoping the image would reveal itself. It did not.

"It's lovely," she said politely.

Rip laughed out loud and leaned over to squeeze her shoulders. "Lovely? Well, ma'am, you must really have farming in your blood to see a side-loading packer binder and think it lovely."

"A side-loading packer binder?"

Her expression was so dumbstruck, Rip squeezed her shoulders again. "Yes, Miss Lovely Lessy. This is my latest design. I've been working on it all summer. Hope by fall to sell it to one of the farm implement companies, McCormick or Ralston maybe."

"You design farm implements?"

Rip nodded. "Indeed I do." He pulled a tablet wrapped in sealskin from his grip. "I've designed machines that will do everything on a farm but kiss the babies."

"Let me see."

He did, showing her page after page of neat, intricate mechanical drawings.

"If what you really do is design farm equipment, why are you working on a hay crew?"

Rip shrugged. "I *design* equipment," he said. "You only make money if you *sell* your designs."

"But you said McCormick or Ralston—"

Rip shook his head. "I'm dreaming," he admitted. "They have more engineers and draftsmen in those companies than ticks on a blue hound. They aren't very likely to buy something from outside when they can get it from their own people for free."

"But you keep trying."

"Can't stop," he said. "Once you start a thing, it kind of gets in your blood and you can't get away from it. It doesn't seem to matter what the truth is or if it's the right thing to do. Once you've invested a goodly amount of time on something, it seems you just can't quit it. It's funny really."

Lessy didn't think it was a bit funny. That was exactly

what she had done with Vass. She'd decided that she wanted to marry him, and she'd pursued him obstinately. Now she was only weeks away from the wedding, and she was wondering if their perfect matchup was full of corn borers.

"If I had a lick of sense," Rip was saying, "I'd quit this nonsense and find me a real job."

"No, not that," Lessy told him. "If you had a lick of sense you'd go into business for yourself."

Rip laughed humorlessly. "Me and whose bank?"

"You don't need a bank, you just need some farmers with a little money to invest. And there is no better place to find those than right here. We've had three good harvests in a row. Folks here about are looking for a good place to put what's stuffed in the mattress."

"Nobody around here even knows me."

"They don't have to know you, just your designs. I'm no engineer, but some of the farmers around here know a lot about equipment. If it's really good, they'll be able to tell."

Ripley shrugged, not quite dismissing her idea.

"I can see it now," she said. "Rip Ripley Farm Machinery." She hesitated. "No, that will never do. What is your given name?"

"My given name?"

"Your given name. John Ripley, Will Ripley, Chester Ripley?"

He shook his head. "Just Ripley, ma'am. My name is such an embarrassment, *I* don't even remember it anymore."

Lessy nodded. "All right. Then Ripley and Sons—that sounds very official, don't you think? The kind of long-term solid company a farmer can trust."

"I have no sons."

She waved away his concern. "Believe me, when you own your own manufacturing company, some woman will marry you up real fast."

"They might try."

Lessy laughed. "Oh, a confirmed bachelor. I suppose

you know that women love a challenge."

His expression was careless and his shrug teasing.

"Seriously, though," she said, "I believe that we should all try to find a way to achieve our heart's desire. It is such a waste of our gifts if we don't."

Ripley's expression became solemn. "I'm going to do it someday. I just have to wait for the right time, settle down, and get started."

"I could ask Vassar to have a look at your drawings, if you like," she said. "I'm sure he has money to invest."

Her sincerity and determination showed clearly on her face, and the sight brought a warm tenderness to Ripley's smile. He brought a hand to her cheek and smoothed away a damp tendril of hair that clung there.

"You are really a fine kind of woman, Lessy. You are surely what God had in mind when he used the word *helpmate*."

Lessy's eyes widened, and she shook her head in disagreement. "No, I'm not really like that," she confessed. "I pretend to be that way, but I'm really just foolish and selfish."

Rip's expression turned quizzical. "What a strange thing to say."

Lessy blushed. "It's true," she said quietly. Suddenly she wanted somebody to know the truth. "I'm really not as hardworking and temperate as I seem."

"You're not?" Ripley clearly did not believe her, but was intrigued by the possibility.

"I . . . well, I started acting that way for Vass."

Raising an eyebrow, he looked at her curiously. "Vass wants you to act hardworking and temperate?"

"Oh, no. I mean yes." She was both confused and embarrassed at her own revelation. "Well, he doesn't know that it's an act. He thinks I really *am* the person I've been pretending to be."

Rip leaned closer, resting his hand on his chin. "And why have you been pretending to be some other person, Miss Lessy?"

"I'm not exactly pretending to be another person. I'm

just . . . well, I'm trying to be the woman that Vass would want to marry." She lowered her head shamefully. "I can't believe I've told this to you. It's really terrible, isn't it?"

She looked up to find Rip grinning ear to ear. "Yes, Lessy, it is very terrible, a sin of major proportions to allow your intended to think the best of you. But, truth to tell, I've never met a woman—or a man, either—that was exactly what he seemed to be before the wedding."

"Well," Lessy admitted, "maybe most folks are on their best behavior before the wedding, but I'm just an out-and-out liar. Vass doesn't know that I have a temper or that I daydream during Sunday School or that I only like gardening because it gives me an excuse to dig around in the dirt like a gopher."

Rip laughed with delight. "I doubt he'll care. When a man's in love, he can forgive a lot in a woman."

"What if he's not in love?" Lessy's words were only a whisper.

Rip took her chin in his hand and raised her eyes to his. "None of that nonsense," he said. "Vassar Muldrow is so much in love, he looks like a mule hit between the eyes with a poleax."

She was doubtful, but she didn't want to confess the rest. "But he's in love with someone I've pretended to be."

Rip shook his head. "He's in love with you, Lessy Green. Believe me, when that man is kissing your sweet lips, the last thing he's thinking about is what occupies your mind during Sunday School."

That was the problem, Lessy thought with despair. He didn't seem to want to kiss her.

The rain finally stopped late in the day, and the sun came out with blistering ferocity. Steam rose from the ground in eerie little patches, and the men were as wet from sweat as if they were still working in the rain.

Because dinner was early and the day had been a slow one, it was expected that Vass and Lessy would walk out after supper. Both knew that it would appear strange if they did not. But both would have forgone the experience if they'd been offered the chance.

Vass rose from the table and offered Lessy his arm in a most gentlemanly fashion. This action drew a tableful of catcalls, and the two embarrassed young people could not get away from the group quickly enough. They walked in silence as far as the peach orchard, when the strain became too much for Lessy.

"I'm sorry about the song," she said. She didn't look at him, and unable to gauge his reaction, she blundered on. "It was the kind of distressing moment that a woman should have just forced herself to immediately forget. I should never have passed on the incident like a careless piece of gossip."

"It was all my fault, Lessy, and I do beg your forgiveness. But please let us not talk about it anymore."

Lessy nodded agreeably as she mentally berated herself for once again bringing the subject up. Talking so openly and easily with Rip had loosened her guard. She had to remind herself how Vass preferred women who were more upstanding.

Conversation waned as Vass was loath to bring up the farm for discussion and Lessy was second-guessing every thought that came to mind.

"Did you know that Mr. Ripley does mechanical drawing?" she asked finally.

Vass looked at her curiously. In memory he could see the two of them with their heads together giggling like children. It was an incongruous image, but one that had him stinging with jealousy. "No, I was not aware of that," he said.

"Well, I saw some of his drawings today, and I really think that you should have a look at them."

"Really?"

With the natural confusion of the nonmechanically minded, Lessy explained the side-loading packer binder, the double row corn planter, and the other implements that she had seen. Vass listened with some interest as he watched the enthusiastic expression on Lessy's face. Was she enthusiastic about the machines or about the man?

"He's really quite talented, and I thought you might look at his work and give him your opinion."

Vass nodded. "Well, certainly I would. Roscoe said that he was very handy with the equipment, but I never would have guessed he had ideas for machines of his own."

Lessy smiled. "He says the implement companies are not interested in inventions from outsiders. But I think he could go into business for himself if his ideas were sound and he had some farmer investors to back him."

"It's certainly possible," Vass said, slightly surprised by her enthusiasm. He'd never doubted that Lessy had a keen mind; she always agreed with him. But she'd never come up with ideas of her own.

"You like Ripley, don't you?" His question was somewhat abrupt.

Lessy was momentarily taken aback. "Well, yes, of course I like him. He's a very entertaining man. He tells such funny stories, I swan, he has me laughing all the time."

Vass wondered if he himself ever made her laugh. At that moment he couldn't remember a single time.

"The fellows tell me he's very popular with women," Vass said tentatively.

Lessy giggled. "I'm sure that he is. My lands, if the things he says to me are any example, he must be breaking hearts all across Arkansas."

Because she said it with good humor, Vass didn't tell her that her little joke was very likely true.

"I didn't see Rip in the barn today. Where did you talk to him?"

Lessy couldn't meet Vassar's eyes. "Under the tarp," she said a little too hurriedly. "We were just sitting under the tarp to be out of the rain."

Having been beneath that tarp on several occasions, a mental image flashed through Vassar's brain of an eight by ten foot space that was a long row of bedrolls—men's bedrolls. The color drained from his face.

"We were just getting out of the rain," Lessy said again when she saw him pale.

His thoughts whirling in confusion, Vass imagined that he saw Lessy, his Lessy, laying back on a tattered bedroll that smelled of men. Her eyes were not trusting and innocent, but earthy and eager. And he saw himself kneeling down before her. In his mind he clutched the hem of her calico work dress and raised it to her waist with indecent haste.

He quickly tried to think of Grandma Rooker. But this time the old trick didn't work.

"Nothing happened!" Lessy's nervous insistence finally brought Vass back to reality.

"Of course not, Lessy," he assured her, although he gripped her hand a bit tightly. "With a woman like you, I know that nothing untoward would happen."

Lessy hesitated a moment before responding with a tentative thank-you.

They continued their walk silently in the direction of the pond. Vass kept his eyes straight ahead, trying not to think of Lessy in sinful ways. Although it was hard since she was right beside him, smelling of soap and starch.

Lessy's mind was also in turmoil. Did he trust her so completely because he believed her to be so virtuous or because he saw her as so undesirable?

In the growing darkness near the pond, neither saw the puddled evidence of the day's rain until Lessy slipped in the mud. Her boot slid out from beneath her, and she was headed for an indecorous splat on the soggy ground.

"Oh!"

Her cry was hardly out of her mouth before Vassar was there. He more than caught her—he wrapped his arms around her and whisked her out of the mud, lifting her against his chest.

For Lessy the moment was almost heart-stopping. The startled surprise of a near splash in a mud puddle was immediately followed by this evidence of masculine strength as the man after her own heart held her closely against his.

Vass stepped back and held her only a moment longer than necessary. The welcome weight of the woman in his arms nearly stunned him brain-numb. He wanted to bury his face in the cool softness of her throat, taste her lips, and explore her with his tongue. He wanted to send his hands a-roving the sensuous hills and valleys of the woman in his arms. He did none of these.

"I'm sorry, Lessy, I led you right into the mud," he said as he stood her upright on what seemed to Lessy to be very shaky solid firmament.

Her feet touched the ground, and he dropped his arms from her. But Lessy did not move away.

"Vass?" Her voice was only a whisper.

He looked at her face only inches from his own and swallowed nervously.

"Vass?" she whispered again.

"Lessy." Her name came out a gravelly plea.

"Kiss me."

"Lessy."

"Kiss me."

He swallowed. His heart was pounding like an infantry drum during full frontal attack. The scent and warmth of her skin still clung to his shirtfront. His hands trembled with desire. Kiss her? Oh, yes, he would kiss her. He would kiss her and hold her and pull her to the ground, right here in the mud, and make her his, truly his, as he had always wanted.

Painfully he set his jaw against his inclination and forced himself to step back.

His retreat stabbed Lessy like a wound, and tears stung her eyes.

"Don't you want to kiss me?"

"Of course I do," he insisted. His voice was still a little shaky, and he wiped his sweating palms against his trousers before he placed his hands gently on her shoulders. Leaning down he brushed her lips as lightly as he had before. It was the way Lessy might have kissed her mother. Even Lessy's inexperience in such matters could not hide from her that his was not a lover's kiss.

"We'd best go back to the house," he said.

Lessy nodded, her heart in her throat. With a kiss like that she was sure a man might easily be thinking about what occupied her thoughts during Sunday School.

Chapter Six

"Yoohoo! Yoohoo!"

Lessy was pouring the last cup of breakfast coffee around the table when the rattle of a rig on the drive captured her attention only an instant before she heard the call.

"Yoohoo! Lessy!"

Rip looked up from a conversation with Angus, his glance furrowing to incredulity.

"Who is that?"

Lessy waved her arm broadly in greeting.

Dressed in a bright pink gingham that was cut much too form-fitting for farm work, Sugie Jo Mouwers bounced excitedly on the wagon seat, her blond curls fluttering in the breeze as she waved a dainty pink handkerchief.

Beside the pretty young woman, Joseph Mouwers sat stern and stoic as was his nature, making it difficult for all to imagine how such a straight and narrow worker ant, solemnly doing his duty, could have ever fathered such a frivolous butterfly as Sugie Jo.

"Morning, Mr. Mouwers." Vass offered the greeting as the wagon pulled up before the house. "Morning, Miss Sugie Jo."

"Is it true? Is it finally true?" Sugie Jo's questions were high-pitched with excitement and aimed at both Vass and Lessy. Not waiting for an answer, she scrambled down from the wagon with only minimal assistance from Vass to wrap her arms eagerly around Lessy. "Tell me! I couldn't wait another day to hear it for myself. Are you and Vass really getting married?"

Lessy blushed and gave Vass a shy glance before nodding affirmatively.

"Yeeeek!" Sugie Jo began jumping up and down, her arms around Lessy, taking her along. "I'm so excited! It finally happened! I knew it would. I just knew it."

Joseph Mouwers managed to ignore his daughter's girlish glee as if he were both deaf and blind. "Figured after that storm you all wouldn't be in the fields today," he said to Vass with a nod to Roscoe coming up beside him. "Suspect you'll be checking harness and sharpening implements today."

Vassar nodded.

"With all these men drawing wages," Mouwers said with a disapproving gesture at the men still seated at the breakfast table, "I thought you might as well work on mine, too." He indicated the plow blade he carried in his wagon and the disk harrow that trailed behind. "If you are bringing your crew to my place next, I don't want you getting used to loafing away your time."

Doobervale bristled.

Joseph Mouwers had a way of bringing out the devil in the best of Christians. Vass was used to stepping in to smooth things over.

With familiarity that made for unconcern, Sugie Jo pulled Lessy away from the men. "I want to hear everything!" she declared dramatically. "Don't even keep the most private of details from me!"

Lessy smiled and shook her head at her exuberant friend. "Sugie Jo, there really isn't that much to tell."

"I don't believe a word of it! I want the whole truth. Was the moon full? Did he go down on one knee? Did you say yes right away or leave him dangling a week or two?"

Lessy giggled at the ridiculousness of the idea. From the corner of her eye she spotted Rip and immediately motioned for him to come over.

"I want you to meet this really sweet fellow that's come with the haying crew," Lessy said as Rip walked toward them. "I know you two are just going to like each other immediately."

Sugie Jo looked up, but her expression darkened. By the time Rip stood at their side, his face was a mask of disapproval and his mouth was drawn into one thin line.

"Sugie Jo, this is Rip Ripley. He works on Mr. Doobervale's crew, and he designs the most impressive-looking farm machines you ever saw." Lessy turned back to Rip. "This is Sugie Jo Mouwers. She and her family are our closest neighbors, and we've been friends since we fit in the same laundry basket."

Lessy's smile was wide with pleasure at the introduction but faltered slightly at the curt nods of acknowledgment her friends exchanged.

"Miss Mouwers."

"Mr. Ripley."

Rip's smile was reserved for Lessy as he took his leave, professing an urgent desire to help the other men. Surprised, Lessy turned to her friend in question.

"Do you two know each other?"

Sugie Jo shook her head. "No, I don't know him. But I know his type."

"His type?"

The pretty blonde nodded, her curls bouncing affirmatively. "He's one of those sweet-talking heartbreakers," she said. "As pretty as a baby skunk and a whole lot more dangerous. You'd best stay away from that one, Lessy. He's nothing but trouble."

Lessy's mouth dropped open in surprise. "He seems like a perfectly nice young man to me."

Sugie Jo nodded sagely. "I'm sure that Eve thought the serpent to be just a friendly lizard, too."

Later as the two picked beans in the garden, Lessy told about her engagement.

"So it's really not going to be that big of a change," she said with an air of feigned maturity. "We'll just go on living the lives we've always lived."

Sugie Jo didn't giggle at that—she laughed out loud. "Lessy Green, I swear you've got no more sense of things than a rabbit." She stopped to pull off the bright pink bonnet and shake her curls in the barest of morning breezes. "Here you are just weeks away from doing the *big naughty* with the fellow you've been pining after for four years. And you talk as if it's of no more importance than switching Sunday School classes."

Lessy raised her chin defiantly. "I think all the stories we've heard about this man-woman thing are just made up. I think it's not really so much."

"Well, you're wrong," Sugie Jo insisted. "The *big naughty* is even bigger than we ever thought."

Lessy was skeptical. "It's just nature, like growing up or having a baby. All those things they say about getting weak-kneed and falling off the edge of the world, that's just talk."

"It's not just talk," her friend insisted.

"How would you know? I'm the one that's betrothed."

Sugie Jo raised an eyebrow loftily. "I guess you've forgot that *I* was engaged to Homer Deathridge all last winter."

Staring at her friend for a long moment, the import of Sugie Jo's words finally soaked in and Lessy squealed in scandal-shocked delight as she leapt across a half dozen rows of snap beans to grasp her friend around the waist.

"You did the big naughty with Homer Deathridge?" Lessy's whisper was half awe—half horror.

"Not the whole thing," Sugie Jo assured her with a nervous glance around to assure herself there was no one within earshot.

"How much?"

Sugie Jo hesitated. "I let him touch me."

"On your bosom?"

"Oh, for heaven's sake," Sugie Jo complained, shaking her pretty blond curls with disbelief. "You can't even get engaged without letting them touch you there! No, silly goose, I let him really touch me, touch me down there."

Her eyes widening with shock, Lessy gave an involuntary glance toward Sugie Jo's skirts.

"Down there?"

"Through my clothes, of course."

"Of course!"

A hushed, uncomfortable silence fell between them. Lessy swallowed nervously.

"So how did it feel?" she asked finally.

Again Sugie Jo hesitated, as if wavering about her admission. "*Wonderful.*" The word exploded from her, and Sugie Jo blushed furiously before covering her mouth with her hand and emitting an earsplitting screech.

The two young women clasped hands and began jumping up and down in giggling glee.

"You just wait," Sugie Jo promised. "When Vassar lays his hands on you, you are going to think you've died and gone to glory."

Lessy hugged her tightly, trying to hold in the thrill and anxiety and fear that curled up inside her.

"If it was so wonderful," she asked finally, "why did you break off with Homer?"

Sugie Jo shrugged. "Oh, I'm not silly enough to think that Homer's the only fellow who could make me feel that way. And I think Daddy liked him better than I did. That, in itself, is enough to worry a gal into breaking it off."

It was near noontime before Joseph Mouwers had his blades all honed to his liking. He flatly refused an invitation to luncheon, stating tactlessly that the Widow Green's cooking never set well on his stomach.

"I hope I see you again before the wedding," Sugie Jo told Lessy as they parted. " 'Cause I'm sure I won't see much of you afterward. I bet that Vassar keeps you within hugging reach from then on."

Lessy smiled with delight at the prospect, but reality couldn't quite be ignored. As she watched the Mouwerses driving away, Sugie Jo bouncing up and down on the seat, her father staring straight at the horses in front of him as if he were completely alone, Lessy couldn't help but worry. Would Vassar ever want to touch her? And if he did, would she really think that she'd died and gone to glory? Or was that special feeling only for pretty girls like Sugie Jo?

"Come help me pick peaches." Lessy's words were more in the nature of a command than a request, and Rip immediately discarded the gearing box design he was working on to follow her.

The sun was shining brightly this afternoon, making it hot and muggy, but all were hopeful that by tomorrow the fields would be dry enough for haying.

Lessy had been uncharacteristically quiet both at breakfast and the noon meal. Even now her thoughts appeared to be elsewhere as she made her way to the orchard, an empty bushel basket hanging from her left hand.

Ripley had to hurry to catch up with her, and when he took the basket, her smile of thanks seemed more sad than grateful.

"Not many peaches left," he said conversationally as they walked through the neat rows of tall, well-tended trees.

"It's late in the year," she agreed. "But I never let a peach go to waste." She spied a bright yellow fruit with a rusty red blush on its cheek and reached up on her tiptoes to pull it down. "It really takes more time to pick what's left than when the trees are full, because you have to move the ladder with you constantly."

Taking her words as a suggestion, Rip retrieved the folding ladder that leaned against a nearby tree trunk and began following Lessy with it in hand. They stopped at first one tree and then the next as she climbed up the ladder to reach the higher limbs that held a few stray ripe peaches.

Her thoughtful expression caused worry lines to form on her brow.

"This is a mighty fine orchard, Miss Lessy," Rip told her, trying to lighten her mood.

Lessy smiled gently, her voice a soft whisper. "My grandmother planted it. When I was young, I thought of it as my own secret hideaway where everything that I ever wanted would always come true." Suddenly recalling herself, she cast off the hint of dreaminess in her expression. "Vass said pecans would have been better."

Rip's expression was puzzled as he raised an eyebrow in disagreement. "I like peaches."

"Me, too," Lessy agreed as she climbed up the ladder. "There is nothing better than fresh peach cobbler. But Vass is right, pecans would have been more practical."

Rip held the ladder steady as she reached a high and heavy branch. Lessy could feel the heat of his gaze upon her. The strangeness of the feeling caused her to speak more rapidly than she would have.

"Pecans are easier to grow," she said. "And they keep much better than peaches, even when they are in preserves. And when there's a need to cull the trees, the wood of the pecan is valuable in itself. Peachwood is good for nothing."

"I don't know about that," Rip said with a smile. "My mama used to make some mighty fine switches from the tree in our yard."

Lessy giggled at his comical expression of remembered pain as she gently placed another bright, blushing peach in the basket. "With pecans you're free of the time spent handpicking. You can simply shake the nuts down from the trees without a worry about breaking or bruising them." Lessy nodded determinedly. "Pecans are definitely a more practical orchard tree."

Rip brought a handful of sweet-smelling ripe peaches and laid most of them carefully in the basket. One, the darkest, ripest, most perfect, he held out to her like the temptation in the Garden of Eden. "Practical should not be a woman's first concern," he said. "And what's most fine to have in this world is not always the easiest to get. Lots of the best things in life are clearly not practical." He waved the peach slowly under her nose. The sultry, sweet scent assailed her. "Music and dancing and laughing aren't what you'd call practical, but life wouldn't be nearly so happy without them."

"Well, certainly we wouldn't want to give up our humanity for practicality," she said, grabbing the peach from him, unable to resist taking a large greedy bite. It was sweet and juicy, and Lessy's tongue darted out to capture the juice that threatened to drip down her chin. "But pecans over peaches seems a very small compromise to make."

Rip came to stand in front of her, holding the ladder between them. "It's the little compromises like that, Miss Lessy, that will take all the sweetness out of a life."

Lessy let his words pass, hastily dropping her gaze and moving along to the next tree. But as they continued their way through the cooling shade of peach boughs, her mind dwelled upon them.

Stopping, she took another bite from the peach he'd given her, tasting the sweet, sticky smoothness that could never be supplanted by the finest-tasting pecans. "Ripley," she asked, as if she could no longer keep her silence, "how important is it to a man that his wife be pretty?"

The young man was a bit startled by the question. She was unwilling to look at him directly, which gave him opportunity to observe her discomfiture. "You thinking of your friend, Miss Mouwers?"

"Oh, no," Lessy insisted. "I was just asking. But you didn't like Sugie Jo."

"I liked her fine," he said. "What's not to like? She's a fine looker for sure."

Lessy was puzzled. "You didn't act like you liked her."

"Just being careful," he replied. "She's one fine looker who is a-looking to get married. So I don't want her looking in *my* direction."

"But she's very pretty."

Rip nodded in agreement.

"So how important is it to a man that his woman be pretty?"

Ripley turned to look at her. "For most men it's very important," he said at first and then hesitated as if thinking. "Well, I guess it's pretty important." Stopping completely, he shook his head, and with a light chuckle as he bent over to catch her downcast eyes he told her finally, "Maybe it ain't a bit important at all."

Lessy folded her arms across her chest stubbornly in disapproval. "Which is it?" she asked. "Very important, pretty important, or not important at all?"

Rip looked at the young woman with some curiosity and a good deal of cockiness as he leaned indolently against a tree trunk. "Miss Lessy," he said, "it's all three."

She raised an eyebrow.

"To find a woman, a man's got to notice her. If he passes by her in church without ever speaking, it ain't likely they'll ever be together. But if she's a fine looker, say like your friend, Miss Mouwers," he said, "then it's not likely he'll pass by without seeing her."

Lessy nodded. "So it's very important that she be pretty."

Rip shook his head. "Now, most of us fellows meet a gal through family or friends, and usually you get to know her a bit before you'd ever think of walking out with her. If she's pleasant and sweet, you're interested whether she's eye-popping or no. But still, when a man's got that gal on his arm, he wants her to be looking good. He wants the other fellows to be green with envy. That makes a fellow feel pretty cocky. But a man won't bother to sashay around with a woman he don't cotton to."

"So it's pretty important," Lessy said.

Rip reached out a hand and raised Lessy's chin. He looked into her eyes. She was no beauty, but there was strength and substance to her that held a lure all its own. His smile was warm and bright. "When it comes to walking out, yes. But you said *wife*, Miss Lessy. In a wife it ain't important at all."

Lessy's eyes widened with surprise.

"Us country boys may act the fool," Ripley told her. "But most of us are smart enough to know that a pretty child at sixteen may not be worth her weight in beans as a helpmate at forty-five. It's what's inside a woman that makes you choose her for a wife. Her heart, her soul, her dreams . . . that makes a man want to live a lifetime with her. If the feeling and yearnings all fit, it don't matter if the gal is belle of the county or fit to wear a cowbell."

His words scoured a rough tenderness in Lessy's heart, and she blinked back a burning in her eyes that she feared might be tears.

"But what if the man doesn't really know who she is inside? And what if he thinks the woman to be a good helpmate but can't bring himself to sweeten toward her? Could a man marry a woman that he has no . . . no yearning for?"

The tears were welling, unwanted, in the corners of her eyes, and she tried to drop her gaze from Rip's expression that had been teasing and sweet but had now turned tender and concerned.

With a hint of anger in her motion, she cast the half-eaten peach in her hand into the distant grass. "I'm just being foolish—" she began, trying to turn away.

Rip did not let her. He slipped his arm around her waist and pulled her close to him. "Are you being foolish, Miss Lessy? Or is it that big farmer of yours who's a fool?"

Standing in his arms, Lessy looked up at the dark, handsome face above her, and she knew he was going to kiss her. He did not hold her tightly, and his hesitation was clearly to give her time to retreat. She did not.

His mouth touched hers with skill and confidence. He traced the line of her lips with his tongue, causing Lessy to startle.

Ripley grinned at her innocent surprise. "The sweetest peach in Arkansas," he whispered against her as he opened her mouth to get another taste.

"Dadburnit!" Roscoe swore. "This wagon jack ain't worth throwing into the scrap heap."

The men around him were nodding their heads in agreement, but Vass only chuckled. "Now, you can't go blaming this poor hardworking little jack for not being able to do something that I told you would need a rope and pulley."

Doobervale threw up his hands in defeat. "Lord love you, Muldrow, I'm just grateful you ain't a betting man, or I'd a lost money on this one."

The empty hay wagon was bogged down in the mud on the low side of the barn. Young McFadden, in the ignorance of youth, had left it there when he'd driven it out of the field. Doobervale had insisted that a wagon jack would be enough to rescue it. He might have been right if they'd begun working at it early in the morning, as they'd planned. But after hours of tool sharpening, both their own and Mouwers's, the muddy ground had hardened, holding the wagon wheels to it like molasses turned into hard candy.

"Get me that rope and tackle that I left on the floor of the harness room." Vass directed the order to young Tommy, whose cheeks were still alternately pale and flushed with the humiliation of his mistake. "We can throw it over the ridge pole of the barn and get all the leverage we need." Vass looked up to the timber that extended out from the peak of the barn roof, wondering if there would be enough rope.

"With a whole crew of men this shouldn't be too much of a chore." Glancing around, a furrow came into his brow. "Where's Ripley?"

Doobervale shrugged with unconcern. "That one is the very best to have when a man's working with equipment. But he's got a real aversion to putting his back into a job."

The men around him chuckled.

"Ripley," Claidon Biggs declared, "don't never lift nothing heavier than a petticoat if he can help it."

These words gained guffaws all around, and young McFadden, hoping to get himself back in with the boys, added his own little joke. "I know that's got to be true," the boy claimed. "Here we are sweating over a stuck wagon, and I spied him walking out into the shade of the peach trees with Miss Lessy."

The laughter the boy had hoped for fell a little flat as Vass gave him a sharp look. Without further comment Vassar hoisted the rope over the ridge pole and set up the pulley. He worked with certainty and efficiency born of habit, but his thoughts were elsewhere.

Lessy and Ripley alone in the peach orchard? It just didn't seem proper somehow. Lessy was so innocent and trusting. A man like Ripley might take advantage of her sweet nature. In his memory he could hear the two of them laughing together in the kitchen. And she was so enthusiastic about his drawings. They had been alone together under that camp tarp. Could that no-account rounder be whispering pretty words to his Lessy? Vass could hardly keep his feet in the spot. As soon as he assured himself that the knotting was secure, he handed the end ropes to Doobervale.

"I need to get a drink of water," he announced lamely. Walking away, Vass didn't dare to look back on the bewildered expressions of the men he'd left.

Making no pretense of even going near the house, he headed straight to the peach orchard. The thoughts in his mind spun in wild imagining, but he wouldn't focus on them. Lessy was in the orchard with Ripley, and he was merely going to join them. He was only going for a friendly chat. He was only going to ask Ripley to come help with the wagon.

Lessy broke away from the kiss and stared into Ripley's eyes. They were smoky and half-closed with such an expression of ardor that she giggled.

His mouth dropped open with surprise.

"Mr. Ripley," she said. "You look at me like I was a peach cobbler myself. And I'm practically an old married lady."

His surprise melting into delight, he leaned forward once more and teased her lips with his tongue. When she drew back, he winked broadly. "You aren't married yet, Miss Lessy. Ain't no sin in taking a last long look at freedom. I *am* from the haying crew, and they do say to make hay while the sun shines."

She laughed at his teasing and had actually raised her lips for more of his special brand of haymaking when over his shoulder she caught sight of a large, work-hardened blond man gazing at them in horror.

"Vassar!"

Ripley jumped away from her as if shot from a gun.

His face pale and pained, Vassar Muldrow paced slow, heavy steps toward them.

Lessy had never thought of Vass as a man of violence, but the expression on his face, normally so calm and controlled, was frightening in its intensity.

"Don't hit him, Vass!" Lessy said, bravely stepping in front of the handsome dark-haired man. "It's my fault, not his. I let him kiss me. I wanted him to."

Her words had the same effect on Vass as being kicked in the stomach by an ornery mule. He paled and sweat broke across his brow.

Ripley easily stepped around Lessy, his hands held high in a gesture of surrender. "You want to punch me, Muldrow?" he said. "Well, take your shot. But it was nothing more than a stolen kiss, and it was headed nowhere."

Vassar's face was now florid, and his breathing came in frightening puffs of anger, but his eyes, as he looked at the couple before him, were full of pain. He swallowed hard.

"Doobervale needs a hand at the barn," he said to Ripley, his tone brooking no question.

The young man glanced toward Lessy. "Are you going to be all right?" he asked her. "Are you safe with him?"

Before Lessy could nod her assurance, Vassar exploded. "What kind of man do you take me for? She's been safe with me for years before she ever knew you existed!"

Lessy nodded to the young man to go. Vass stood, fists clenched until Rip had walked away. Then, with a sigh that seemed to wilt the steel in his backbone, Vassar took a step closer, leaning against the ladder as if he could no longer stand on his own power.

Hearing the pained gasp of his breath, Lessy watched him squeeze his eyes together as if to hold back the tide that threatened to pour from them. Her own eyes were now swimming with tears that she tried to wipe on her apron.

"I'm so sorry Vassar," she managed to choke out. "I have lied to you, so many lies, I'm not the woman that you think I am. I am lazy and frivolous, and I let a man kiss me just because I wanted him to. I've deceived you into believing that I am better than I am, but I never meant harm. Can you ever forgive me?"

It was as if Vassar had not heard her words. "Don't worry, Lessy," he said. "I should have seen this coming. I did see it—I just didn't want to believe it true. I'll see that he marries you up good and proper. I'm wise to his ways and reputation, and I won't have him leaving any broken hearts on this farm."

"What?"

"A fine woman like you is not to be dallied with and left behind. I'll see that he stands up to his responsibilities if it takes a shotgun to do it."

She gawked at him, swiping at her eyes distractedly. "Responsibilities?"

"He's not the kind of man I would have wanted for you, Lessy. But there ain't a man living that's half good enough to husband you. I guess he has no more faults than me."

"Vassar, what are you saying?"

"I won't stand in your way, Lessy. I know that you love him, and I care too much for you to hold you back."

Then he left.

"Oh, Mammy! What am I going to do?"

Lessy's tears dampened the cotton quilt that covered her bed, darkening the bright yellow and blue patterns of Sunbonnet Sue.

Rip had come to the porch right after dinner. She hadn't seen Vassar in the background, but she knew he was there as Ripley, with genuine apology in his voice, gave a gentle and impassioned plea for her to honor him in matrimony. Speechless, Lessy had fled from the sight and had been lying across her bed crying her heart out ever since.

Her mother seemed less concerned than entertained. "Lord-a-mercy, I've never seen that Vassar in such a lather as at the supper table. If looks were bullets, that Ripley boy would have more holes in him than a sieve."

Nora Green, clad in her nightgown, stood before the mirror at the washbowl and combed the tangles out of her long gray hair as she listened to her daughter's pitiful sniveling.

"I can't marry Ripley, Mammy," Lessy declared adamantly. "He's funny and sweet, but I just don't love him."

"Well, of course you don't," her mother agreed easily. "You love Vassar and you have ever since you laid eyes on him."

Her mother's words started Lessy wailing again. "But Vass doesn't want me, not now. Maybe he never has. He never saw the real me, just the perfect angel I pretended to be." The words were a pitiful whine that ended with Lessy face-buried in the quilt. "I tried to tell him in the orchard, to confess at last about how I'd tried to trick him, but he wouldn't listen."

In fury and frustration Lessy pounded the feather tick beneath her. "I can't believe I was so foolish! It was as if I'd taken leave of my senses completely." She moaned piteously.

Raising her tear-stained face to her mother, she admitted her culpability. "I just wanted to know if I was pretty enough," she said, shamefaced. "I wanted to know if I could attract a man on my own. If maybe I could have attracted Vass for *me*. Oh, Mammy, I want him to want me for . . . well, not for my hard work and my high morals, to want me for . . . oh, for sweet things and sinful things."

Nora Green lay the brush on the chiffonier and moved to the bed, where she knelt and began rubbing her daughter's back in the strong circular motion that had comforted her daughter when she was still a baby. "Lessy, Lessy," she told her coaxingly. "There is nothing sinful about wanting your man to desire you. And nothing unnatural about wanting a little bit of romance. The man you marry must see more in you than a strong back and a willing hand."

"But that is exactly what he does see. It's all that I've let him see."

Shaking her head, Mammy didn't agree. "If he'd known you for only a few months of this *perfect pretense* you've been putting on, then I'd worry. But no one can keep up a lie for four years! The truth about who you are comes shining through you every day, in the way you move and the songs you sing. Believe me, even if his eyes don't see you as you really are, his heart does."

Lessy looked at her mother, wanting desperately to believe her. "But I've ruined everything, Mammy," she said. "I've kissed Ripley, and now Vass wants me to marry him."

"Pooh!" Nora waved away the complication. "That load of manure smells to high heaven. Vassar Muldrow wants you for himself. He thinks *you* want that Ripley fellow. And the only way he's going to know any different is if you swallow your pride and tell him yourself."

Lessy's breath caught in a shuddering sigh.

"But the kiss, Mammy?"

"What about the kiss?"

Lessy's cheeks were flushed with shame. "I liked it, Mammy," she said. "I liked it a lot."

Nora rested her chin in her palm thoughtfully. "Did you want it to go on forever?"

"Forever? No."

"Did you feel like you were home at last?"

"Home? We were in the peach orchard."

"Did your heart tell you that you couldn't live without that man?"

Lessy blushed and shook her head. "No, Mammy. My heart kept wishing it was Vassar who kissed like that."

Nora grinned, her expression now completely unconcerned as she shrugged. "That Ripley is the kind of fellow that's been with lots of women, Lessy. A man may learn a few tricks about kissing women that way. Now, maybe your Vass ain't as wise in loving ways. But it ain't an unpleasant study, and I'm thinking you two could learn together."

Lessy swallowed hopefully. "Do you think so, Mammy? Do you think Vass could learn to kiss me like that?"

Her mother chuckled. "I suspect he'd be willing to die trying."

For the first time in hours, Lessy smiled. Maybe things were not as hopeless as they had seemed.

"Of course he'll learn to kiss me like that when we're wed," Lessy assured herself happily. "Why, he's so fine and upstanding, I don't suppose that Vass has ever kissed a woman before in his life."

Out of the corner of her eye Lessy caught a strange expression on her mother's face. "What is it, Mammy?"

Nora began readying herself for bed as if she hadn't heard Lessy's question.

"Mammy?" Lessy's tone was insistent.

Hesitating, as if weighing her words, Nora Green finally shook her head. "I think that he has."

"You think that he's kissed women before?"

"Yes." Her answer was firm and simple, but there was something in her mother's tone of voice that prompted questions in Lessy's mind.

"What is it, Mammy? Is there something you should tell me?"

Sighing heavily before she answered, Lessy's mother seemed clearly unhappy about the revelation she was about to make. "I understand from Jake that the main reason he wanted Vass to come out here and work for us was to separate him from a woman."

Lessy's eyes widened with surprise, and a lump of anxiety settled in the back of her throat. "He was in love with another woman?"

"I don't know if he loved her. He was . . . ah, seeing her."

Jealousy warred with confusion in Lessy's mind. "Why didn't he marry her? Did Cousin Jake not approve of the match?"

Lessy's mother cleared her throat nervously and looked her daughter straight in the eye. Nora hoped she was ready for the truth. "I don't believe it was possible to approve or disapprove, Lessy. The woman was already married."

Staring at her mother in stunned silence for several seconds, a tiny puff of disbelief emerged from Lessy's mouth before she rolled over on her back to contemplate the ceiling.

"Vassar Muldrow and a married woman." She whispered the words incredulously. Her Vass, the purest of souls, the finest of men, the noblest of the breed, carousing with another man's wife. It was a shock. She didn't know him any better than he knew her.

Her mother blew out the lamp before coming to bed. With a gesture of her hand she urged Lessy to her own side of the bed and crawled in to tuck them both in for the night. "He was young, Lessy, and it was a long time in the past. These things happen sometimes in life," she told her daughter in a sympathetic whisper. "It's best neither to judge nor ruminate. Just put the past behind you and go on. Like that kiss you shared with young Ripley, it was a mistake better outlived and forgotten."

"We don't know each other at all," Lessy whispered, her gaze still focused on the dark ceiling above her.

Chapter Seven

Vass saw her bringing the water bucket when she was still half a hayfield away. He'd tried to avoid her for the last three days, and he'd managed to do a pretty good job of it. The woman he'd hoped to marry just a week ago had become a polite stranger, and he supposed it was all for the best.

He began moving away from the group. He didn't want to be close when she dipped water for Ripley. He didn't want to see them laughing, their heads together like happy children. He wanted her to be happy. But wanting her to be happy and watching her be that way with another man were not the same thing.

The bright gold of newly cut hay touched the deep summer blue of the sky behind her. Lessy was like a painted picture on a feed calendar. In his heart she had never looked more beautiful. And she did walk as if she floated off the ground, Vass thought to himself. And then hated that it was Ripley who had pointed it out to him.

He turned away from the sight of her and began hand-raking a long swath of alfalfa. There was a tiredness in his movements. He hadn't slept well for days. He'd always wondered what the early mornings were really like, and now he knew for sure. Frequently he was still awake when they arrived.

The hay was nearly all in the barn. By this time tomorrow the crew would be gone. Would Ripley be staying here with them? Or would he be taking Lessy with him until the season was done? He hoped it was the latter. Within a month he could get things in order and head back to Arkadelphia. He didn't think he could stand to live even a day at this farm with Lessy as a bride to another man.

Strangely his thoughts flew to Mabel Brightmore. Not to sweet memories of illicit indiscretion or wild stories of misspent youth, but to the pain he'd caused her poor old husband. For the first time he thought past his own sin to the pain Brightmore must have felt knowing another man claimed his woman's love. Now he, too, felt that pain.

"I brought you some water."

Vass started at the voice behind him and turned to see Lessy, her hair tucked in a bright blue bonnet smiling up at him in her so-familiar fashion.

He glanced over at the other men.

"Oh, I left them a bucket," Lessy said, guessing his thoughts. "But I brought this jar for you."

"Thank you," Vass said quietly. "But you needn't have gone to the trouble."

"I wouldn't have if I'd thought you'd stay near the men to get a drink, but you've been avoiding me so much, I

was afraid you might be fainting in the field from thirst."
Her complaint was warm with teasing.

Vass smiled, slightly embarrassed, then took a long
drink from the blue quart jar that Lessy handed him.

"It's good," he said, as if the comment were a compliment to her cooking.

With a sigh, Lessy nodded her thanks.

The two looked at each other for long moments, each
wishing for something important to say. They had always
talked. The farm, the future, the day-to-day workings of
life, had come easily to their tongues. But they had never
talked about anything important. They had never talked
about the feelings they held inside. Now, in his heart,
Vass knew that any words were too little and too late.
He had never deserved her. He would never be worthy
of her, but he did still want her. Vass now wished he'd
thrown caution to the wind.

But she'd turned to another man. The fact jolted him
back into his sad reality, and he took another swig from
the jar just to occupy himself.

"I'm not marrying Ripley," Lessy announced calmly,
although her hands were shaking.

Vassar's heart stopped for an instant, and his eyes widened in surprise. Then they narrowed in anger. "Is that
no-account trying to worm his way out?"

Lessy sighed and shook her head. "No, he still wants to
wed." She laughed lightly. "I don't know what you said to
the man, Vass, but you've sure put the fear of God in him.
He seems almost desperate to marry me." She took a deep
breath before looking him straight in the eyes. "But I'm
not having him, not now, not ever."

His expression lightened slightly, but concern was still
evident in his features. "I know how you must worry," he
said. "But I'm sure that he cares for you. How could he
not? And he's not so bad a fellow, and those rounder ways,
well, for certain, Lessy, he's the kind of man to give them
up when he's wed."

"I'm not worried about his rounder ways," Lessy said.
"I just don't love him."

She was so matter-of-fact that Vass was momentarily taken aback.

"Of course you do," he insisted.

"No, I don't, Vass. I simply don't. Why would you think so?"

"I saw you in the peach orchard, Lessy," he said quietly. "I know you. And you're not the kind of woman to . . . well,"

Lessy's cheeks were bright red with embarrassment, but she bravely bit her lip before she spoke. "That's what you don't understand about me, Vass. I am exactly that kind of woman. I am exactly the kind of woman to do all kinds of silly foolishness. I'm just a regular, ordinary woman with as many faults as any of my gender."

"What?"

"I tried to tell you that day, Vass. I am not the sweet, hardworking young farm woman who thinks everything you think and wants everything that you want. That's just what I've pretended to be."

"You are perfect," Vass told her.

"No, Vass. Truth is, I'm far from perfect. Before you came I was as averse to chores as any other farm girl. I could hardly wait for Sundays to see my friends, and I spent my free time with them laughing and gossiping and getting into foolishness. I don't want to spend my peach money on waterfowl for the pond. I want the fanciest silk wedding dress this county has ever seen. And I want to be kissed and sparked and spooned along the edges before I'm safely wed. And if the man I love isn't willing, I am certainly weak enough that another man will do."

Vass saw the tears that had formed in her eyes, and he knew he should reach to comfort her, but he was frozen in place.

"I love you and I have since the first day you drove up in the yard. And I tried to be perfect for you, Vassar, because I believed that you were perfect. I assured myself that you could never want me as myself, so I made myself become someone else. Someone as perfect as I believed that you were. Daddy used to tell me that my life was like bread

dough. I could shape it and form it into anything I ever
wanted. And he was right about that, Vass. I just didn't
understand that I would still be bread even if I fashioned
myself as a heart of gold. I can't be perfect for you,
Vassar."

He lifted his hands, denying her words. "Lessy, I'm not
perfect myself."

"I know that, Vass," she said. "You like to sleep late,
and you're a little single-minded at times, and you work
too hard. I was so busy loving you that I blinded myself
to your faults and your weaknesses as I wanted to blind
you to my own. But I cannot blind myself to the fact that
you don't seem to want me, Vass. You don't want me as
a man wants a woman."

He swallowed hard. Her confession was frightening in
its erroneousness, its honesty, and its potential. Maybe it
was not over. Could there still be a chance for him to have
the woman that he loved?

"I have more faults, Lessy, than those you've mentioned," he said evenly. "I have a . . . well . . . a weakness
for women that I've tried not to show you."

Lessy looked up into his eyes, still trusting. "Mammy
told me about your 'woman trouble' in Arkadelphia," she
said. "It's truly none of my business, but I wished that
I'd known it sooner. Then maybe I would have realized
that it wasn't my own, very human nature that kept you
at a distance, but your own lack of desire for me."

Vassar's face was rigid.

"You wanted a good little farm wife that would do
everything right but wouldn't press on your heart, wouldn't
demand your love in return. Do you still carry a torch for
that married woman in your past?"

He shook his head. "No! Lessy, of course I don't."

Lessy nodded only slightly. "Well, I am glad about that,
I suppose." She swallowed bravely. "I've already said that
I love you, and I can tell you now that I always will. I just
wish that you had a weakness for me the way you had a
weakness for her. That's what I came out here to tell you
after all." Her chin was raised with challenge, and her

stance was willful with her arms folded stubbornly across
her chest.

"I may never wed. I may live my whole life as an
unloved, dried-up old maid. But I'd rather do that than
have a man that I'd have to pretend with. Or a man that
would have to pretend to wanting me."

Eyes narrowing in anger, Lessy jerked the mason jar out
of his hand. Fury stiffened her spine as she turned to go.
Vass stared after her with stunned disbelief. Who was this
wild fiery woman who was living in sweet little Lessy's
body? Who was spitting fire at him from soft-spoken little
Lessy's mouth? Who was stomping angrily away across
the hayfield, the soft floating walk of Lessy now an alluring
sultry sway of hips that enticed him with every step?

"Lessy!"

His call stopped her dead still, but she didn't turn around.
Vassar began to run. Standing stiffly in the field, she didn't
once look back as he called her name over and over as he
raced toward her. Reaching her side, he grabbed her arm
and pulled her toward him. His heart pounded in his chest
as he drew her to face him.

"Lessy." He spoke only a little above a whisper.

"Vassar," she answered, her voice as quiet as his own.

A thousand thoughts jumbled in his mind. A thousand
excuses and a thousand explanations jockeyed for first
confession from his tongue. But the words that came out
were from the heart, not the head.

"I love you, Lessy. I love you. I haven't given more
than a thought to Mabel Brightmore since the day I came
to this farm. I want you, Lessy. How can you ever doubt it?
I can't get up in the morning because I spend all night long
dreaming that I hold you in my arms." His eyes burned
with a feverish glow. "Make that dream come true for me,
Lessy," he whispered. "Take me, boring, slugabed, and all,
and I will spend the rest of my life learning to love you
for who you really are."

He leaned forward and wrapped his arms about her
waist. "I love you, Lessy," he said. "I love you whoever
you are."

Pulling her close, Vass lowered his mouth to hers. It was a kiss of fire, a kiss of desperation, a kiss of passion. Lessy's own arms circled his neck and pulled him even closer as she answered the question in his touch. His lips were greedy, eager, starving at her mouth, and he could not pull her near enough to ease the ache that gnawed at him.

Lessy, too, felt her flesh jittering like lightning in the clouds of a summer storm. She couldn't keep her hands still as they wandered the wide breadth of his shoulders and caressed the soft blond hair at the nape of his neck.

One of Vassar's big sun-browned hands slipped low on her back and pressed her more tightly against him. He rubbed himself against her in a rough and lusty manner, and her own eager response and moan of shocked delight urged him on.

Vass broke the kiss from her mouth to trail his lips along her throat. Greedily his tongue flickered against the tiny marks on the underside of her jaw that had long lured him. He pressed her bosom tightly to his chest, feeling her soft tempting roundness and the hard, eager nipples. Struggling valiantly he managed to get exploring fingers between his heated flesh and her own.

Lessy threw her head back in delight and bit down painfully on her lip, trying to control the waves of pleasure that were coursing through her.

Vassar's other hand slid down her backside, clutching her bottom and squeezing her gently before venturing down the back of her thigh.

Pressing his face against her bosom, he heard and felt the rapid pounding of her heart. She wanted him as he wanted her. And he was loath to wait another minute.

He dropped to his knees in front of her and lay his cheek gently against the soft curve of her belly. Here she would receive his love, and here she would carry his children. He pressed his lips to the warm soft cotton of her skirt for one long struggling moment of thrilling enticement before he raised his eyes to hers.

He fought for breath and the right words to say as he took her hands in his own. Bringing her knuckles to his lips, he kissed them ardently, submissively, like a slave to a queen.

"Do you believe now that I want you, Lessy? Can you doubt it?"

He ran his hands eagerly along her thighs, and her eyes widened in shock and wicked delight.

"Marry me, Lessy," he pleaded. "Marry me and allow me to learn everything there is to know about the woman that I love. Marry me and find out the truth about the man who has dreamed of being your husband since the day that we met."

Lessy dropped to her knees beside him in the grass and whispered yes as again they embraced. Unashamedly they kissed and caressed each other in the blind passion of new love. Lessy trembled at his touch, and Vass struggled with control as the flame of their love set the kindling of desire to blaze.

Vass would have laid with her, there in the fresh-mown hay of the summer afternoon, and she would have let him. There was no shame or sin in what they felt. Vows unspoken had already been said with the heart.

But the hoots and hollers of a rowdy haying crew penetrated their blissful heaven, causing them to jerk away from each other in disbelief and embarrassment.

"The men!" Lessy squealed shamefaced as she hastily pulled together her bodice that inexplicably had come undone.

Vass hurriedly moved in front of her to shield her from the eyes of the yammering yahoos waving and shouting from near the hay wagon.

"I forgot that they were there," Lessy admitted and then foolishly began to giggle.

Vass caught her mood and chuckled, also, before shaking his head with self-derision. "I swear, Lessy. I forgot that there was anyone else in the whole world."

Epilogue

The train shuddered to a stop at the new clapboard station. The porter put down a block of steps, and two young children scampered down from the train followed by Lessy and Vassar Muldrow.

"Lena June!" Lessy called out to the little girl. "Mind your brother while your daddy and I get the bags."

The porter handed down two well-worn grip sacks and received both a tip and a thank you from Vass.

Lessy looked around the clean, modern new station in a town that hadn't even existed when the two had taken their first trip, their honeymoon trip, nearly eight years ago.

Theirs had been the fanciest wedding that the county had ever seen. Vassar had worn a brand-new suit that was swell enough to get buried in. His dad and brothers had made the trip from Arkadelphia to stand up with him. And both his mother and Mammy Green had worn new store-bought dresses from Kansas City.

Lessy's fine white gown had been silk and lace, which she had fancifully embroidered with tiny ducks and geese around the bodice and hem.

They had delayed the wedding several weeks to come up with all the finery, including satin ribbons on the church pews and dripless candles of pure white from the Montgomery Ward catalog.

"We are only going to marry once," Vass had said. "We want the public symbol of it to be as special as our private happiness."

Poor Reverend Watson had become a little anxious for

the day to arrive. The young couple had become so calf-eyed and openly affectionate, they had become a near scandal and a clear embarrassment to the community. Lessy giggled even now at the memory of the hang-dog expression that had been on Vass's face those last few nights when they'd had to part at bedtime.

Finally, when they'd stepped out of the church, laughing and delighted to be Mr. and Mrs. Vassar Muldrow, he'd lifted Lessy clear off the ground and twirled her around like a whirligig until they were both laughing and dizzy and the congregation thought them half crazy. With almost discourteous haste, they'd made their getaway in the brightly festooned buggy as if they could hardly wait for the privacy of their honeymoon Pullman car to Kansas City.

"What are you thinking about, Lessy?" Vassar asked as he managed to grasp both bags in one hand and chivalrously took her arm. "You've got a faraway look on that face I know so well."

She grinned suggestively. "It's so nice to be able to ride the train all the way home," she said. "My least favorite part of our yearly vacations was always that long buggy ride home from DeQueen."

"That buggy ride was downright romantic until we had two wild Indians that we have to practically tie to the buggy."

Lessy smiled wryly and nodded agreement.

"Tommy, Lena June, don't go running off," he called sternly after the children, who seemed much in danger of doing exactly that.

As the couple made their way off the platform, to the newly bricked street that was the pride of the brand-new town, the children followed in their fashion. With a blast of whistle and a smoky puff of steam, the train headed on down the track to Texarkana.

"Look, Daddy!" the little boy squealed, pointing a chubby finger at a new, brightly colored billboard next to the station.

The two adults surveyed the signboard as Lessy read

it aloud. " 'Welcome to Peach Grove, Arkansas. Population 1,895. Home of Ripley-Muldrow Agricultural Works. Arkansas Machines for American Farmers.' "

"That's our name!" young Tom exclaimed with a delighted giggle.

Vass gave a wry grin and a long-suffering sigh. "That Rip can never seem to remember the 'silent' in 'silent partner.' "

Lessy waved away his objection. "It's a good name. You *are* the one who helped him get started."

Vass shook his head. "We've received plenty of compensation for that over the years. It was only a little investment that paid off. It was Rip's business, his designs, and his hard work that made the company one of the finest in the country and gave this little community a bit of commerce and enterprise aside from farming."

Lessy couldn't argue that.

"He should have called it Ripley and Sons," Vass said firmly.

Lessy giggled at his affronted puffiness. "That would have been a good name for it, considering all the sons that he has. It seems like poor Sugie Jo is in the family way nearly all the time."

Vass grinned. "And such big boys they are, too." His eyes were wide with feigned innocence. "Why, that oldest of theirs, nearly nine and a half pounds the day he was born! And a full three months early at that."

"Vassar!" Lessy hissed through her teeth. "The children."

Her discomfiture only brought a deep chuckle and a broader smile to his face. "Now, Lessy honey, don't be acting all proper and saintly on me now. If there is one thing I've learned about the woman that I've married, it's that she is plainly just as fraught with human frailties as I am."

As the children moved on up ahead of them, Vassar began to hum a familiar tune, and taking up the challenge, Lessy joined in, quietly singing the bawdy words that her husband had taught her and that she now knew by heart.

"She was curved and plump
And broad of rump
And her drawers were pink and frilly.
As years may pass, I'll oft recall
That day spent plowing Millie."

SUMMER DREAMS

Jean Anne Caldwell

Prologue

Smoke from a cigar curled around the tall man's chiseled features, partially hiding the ragged scar that did nothing to mar his tanned face. Only the cool depths of his blue eyes belied the casualness with which he made his way through the crowd at Tattersalls. A few of the patrons nodded their greeting as he passed by, but most kept their distance from the "Elusive Earl." It was a rare occasion indeed that he made an appearance.

With the authority of one who knows his position, Richard Michaels, third Earl of Gloxbury, took his place at the head of the crowd. Only those he counted as friend ventured to take the liberty of standing next to him. Richard preferred it that way.

He had come to bid on Lord Wesley's colt. Not that he wanted the colt, but it was his way of ensuring that his good friend and neighbor got the fair price he needed to pay off his most pressing debts. What with Lady Wesley's longtime illness and three years of bad management of his estates, the viscount's pockets were embarrassingly slim. Richard would have given the money to him outright, but he knew the old man's pride would have kept him from accepting.

With the bidding about to begin, Richard let his gaze wander about the room. The corner of his mouth lifted in a self-satisfied smile when he spotted Julian Bromly, the Viscount Humbly, across the way. He could put aside his worry of keeping the bidding brisk on the animal. Richard knew he had merely to show an interest in the colt and Julian would overbid.

Although Richard carried the mark of Julian's rage, Julian held the grudge. Ironic. Even after all these years, Bromly bitterly refused to admit that Richard was the best judge of horseflesh.

The auctioneer cleared his throat and declared the bidding was to start at five hundred pounds. Richard started to raise his glove when Bromly called out his bid. Surprised, Richard lifted a dark brow.

"I have five hundred pounds, gentlemen," the auctioneer sang to the crowd. "Who will up the offer?"

Richard waited to see if there were any other bidders before he signaled the auctioneer. "Fifteen hundred pounds," he countered, knowing that while the untried colt wasn't worth much more than twelve hundred, his offer would undoubtedly goad Julian into increasing his offer. Even if it didn't, Lord Wesley would be more than pleased with the bid as it stood.

"Two thousand pounds!" Julian almost shouted.

The anger in Julian's voice told Richard what he wanted to know. Not only did Julian want the colt, but he had hoped to walk away with it for a small portion of its worth.

Richard had heard that since his father's death, Julian had taken to spending his newly acquired inheritance with wild abandonment. At two thousand pounds, Lord Wesley was getting a fair price, but it would be interesting to see how plump Julian's purse had become.

Richard waited until he had Julian's eye, then raised his glove one more time. "If Lord Humbly is willing to pay two thousand pounds, I can only believe the colt has to be worth at least thirty-five hundred," Richard stated. "And that is my bid."

A murmur rumbled through the crowd. Everyone knew of the hatred between the two rivals and all eyes turned to Lord Humbly.

Even from this distance Richard could see Julian struggling with the decision of whether he should go any higher in order to redeem his pride. Having decided to help him with his decision, Richard arched a dark brow and smiled broadly.

Julian's face reddened at the challenge. "Seven thousand pounds!"

A hush fell over the crowd.

Richard turned to the man standing down the way from him. "What say you, Lord Wesley? Is seven thousand pounds a fair price?"

The viscount, who had been watching the proceedings in a euphoric state of shock, had to be nudged by the gentleman standing beside him before he was able to reply.

"Y-yes, Richard, s-seven thousand pounds seems most fair."

"Fine. Then I shall conclude my bidding," Richard stated. "The colt is yours, Bromly."

With that, he turned and started back through the stunned crowd. He hadn't gone far when he felt a hand fall roughly on his shoulder. The others backed away when he turned. He wasn't surprised to discover Julian had stopped him.

All the old hate boiled deep within him. "Unhand me, Bromly," Richard said through clenched teeth. "I am no longer eleven years old. If you took a bottle to me today, you would be feeling its edge, not me."

Julian dropped his hand. "You deliberately bid me up on that animal, Michaels."

"I came intending to bid on the colt. You cannot blame me for your insane need to best me."

Julian didn't say anything for a moment, then he laughed grimly. "You came out of your precious seclusion for the colt, yet let me take him from you?"

Impatiently, Richard smiled down at him. "I'll leave you to think about that," he said before turning to leave.

"Were we short of funds today, my lord?" Julian taunted.

Richard pivoted about. Those near backed away to see anger whiten the scar against Lord Gloxbury's tanned face. Hatred hung in the air between the two men.

"If I had thought the colt comparable to any in my stables, your paltry bid of seven thousand pounds would not have stopped me."

Julian gave an insolent grin. "And you own the fastest

horses in all of England, is that it?" he taunted. He leaned toward Richard. "Are you willing to put a little wager on that?"

Richard let his eyes trail from Julian's puffed face, down past the front of the mustard-colored embroidered waistcoat to the padded legs of the puce pantaloons he wore. Perhaps it was time he met this tasteless mannequin's challenge.

"I will do one better than that, Julian. I will be returning to Kingsley Manor for the summer. Each year the village hosts a race at their Summer Festival. I will pay ten thousands pounds to anyone who can beat my horse."

"A local race?" Julian scoffed. "What competition can there be in that?"

"The number of entries will have to be limited, of course. But then I shall see that it's open to all horses across England. An impartial party will decide who the lucky entrants will be."

"I will see to that," Alistair Mayberry stated, stepping forward.

"Agreed, then. And you, Julian?"

"Agreed! But I would like to put another proposal to you. I propose that if your horse loses, you forfeit him to me."

Richard's dark brows dipped in a frown. "And what are you risking, Julian?" he asked, then raised his hand to forestall Lord Humbly's answer. "Keep in mind, there is not a horse in your stables worthy of my time nor my groom's to come collect him."

"Then name the stakes."

"Being spared the disastrous efforts of your tailor would be more than enough for me."

Julian itched to strike his glove across the earl's cheek, but only a fool would test Richard's skills. "You may merely look the other way if my fashionable wardrobe calls attention to your lack of one."

Richard grinned at Julian's weak insult. "I would prefer your exile for the next five years," he said. "India should suit me fine. Now, good day, gentlemen."

Chapter One

"Marry you!" Dorina shouted once she could get her breath again. "Never!"

She could tell by the redness of his face that her words had momentarily angered Lord Humbly, but that suited her just fine. He was a vulgar man. His vulgarity was one of many reasons she always tried to avoid his company, but her mother had made a point of leaving them to themselves today.

Normally she tried not to let him see how his unpleasantness affected her, but there was no point in trying to finesse her reaction to his announcement now. Almost choking to death on her glass of lemonade pretty much told the gentleman seated across the small wicker table that it had come as quite a surprise.

Although he was sixteen years her senior and ran with an unsavory crowd, Dorina had known Julian Bromly for the entire eighteen years of her sheltered life at Willowtree Manor. Julian was a cruel and pompous ass at the best of times. As a husband, he would be intolerable.

She knew that her best hope in eluding him would be to act as vulgarly as possible. Surely he was hoping a wife would be a credit to him. "Your attic must be in desperate need of repairs," she added, almost surprising herself with her nerve. "Otherwise, why would you think I would consider marrying an overdressed popinjay such as you?"

His cruel gray eyes darkened. "Because I am now the fourth Viscount Humbly . . . and a very wealthy man," he added with an affected nasal twang.

She leaned toward him and lowered her voice. "And why would I care who you are?"

Appearing to scrutinize her through his new jeweled quizzing glass, Julian gave her an indulgent smile. "My dear Miss Stevens, someone who is as unfashionable as you should take it upon herself to care, or before long you'll find yourself sitting on a shelf. After all, I doubt your parents will bestir themselves to take a hand in helping you find a more eligible party. Since I have decided it is time to take a wife, I think it most generous of me to consider you for the honor. After all, there aren't many men who would be so willing to rescue you from this godforsaken place."

"So terribly self-sacrificing of you, Julian," Dorina said, her words icy enough to pluck out of the air and cool her glass of lemonade. She knew that her unfashionably dark curls and tanned face made her an unlikely candidate as a Diamond. It was so like Julian to point that out.

It was only out of her respect for Julian's dead father, she told herself, that she didn't fetch her target pistol and shoot the irritating gnat. That and the fact that killing Julian wasn't worth hanging for.

"You needn't thank me," Julian said smugly as he came around the table to assist her from her chair. "Your parents have already expressed their gratitude."

Dorina ignored his hand and stood. "You have already spoken with my parents?" she asked, stretching to her full height.

With the tip of his finger Julian flipped open his enameled snuffbox and pinched a small portion of the special blend. After a few delicate snorts, he returned it to his pocket. "It is customary to ask the father's permission before approaching your intended."

"A shame you wasted your time, Julian. I am not your intended, nor do I ever plan to be."

Unconcerned he reached out and tweaked her cheek. "It's already been decided, my little one. Our engagement is to be announced at the ball following the Summer Festival." Before Dorina could put forth an argument, Julian pulled her boldly into his arms and covered her mouth with his.

The kiss was wet, hard, and demanding. Disgusted, Dorina tried to pull from his arms, but her struggles only seemed to inflame him. Finally she stood stiff in his arms. As she suspected, his ardor quickly cooled at her meek compliance.

He grasped her chin between his fingers, then looked down into her dark green eyes. He knew the anger he saw smoldering there should displease him, but this was not the time to challenge Dorina's unladylike independence. Once married to him, she would soon discover who was the lord and master of her body . . . and her soul.

"I can see you are in need of some practice, my dear, but that is as it should be." He smiled wryly as he straightened the front of his lavender waistcoat. "But then, the tiresome duty always falls to the husband, doesn't it."

Dorina could not fathom how a gentleman as nice as the old Lord Humbly could have sired such a toad.

Even knowing that he would make her pay, she could not resist challenging him one last time. With a sly grin pasted on her face, Dorina batted her eyelashes provocatively and said, "If the task is so distasteful to you, my lord, I'm sure I can get one of the stableboys to relieve you of the duty."

She watched the telltale redness of his anger rise like a storm from the recesses of his intricately tied cravat, flooding past the high stiffened points of his collar to wash over his outraged countenance.

"Dorina," he said in a deep, even voice, "I do not find your words the least humorous. You are mine and make no mistake about it. So you'd do best not to threaten me again. I don't take kindly to casual intimidation, my dear. I may take it into my head to exercise my marital privileges before the wedding night and give you a little taste of what being mine means."

It took all Dorina's efforts to keep from lifting her hand to the side of his arrogant face. With an anger surprisingly in check, she answered him. "And you would do best to withdraw your offer, my lord, before you leave for London.

Only then will you be free to present it to someone who is willing to bow humbly at the altar of your most *generous sacrifice*."

Before he could reply to her insult, Dorina swept from the room. There'd be hell to pay for this before the day was out, but she didn't care. She wouldn't marry the man and that was that.

"How dare you throw Lord Humbly's offer back in his face like some ungrateful child," Dorina's mother ranted not for the first time in the past hour. "He has been most helpful, offering to help your father with a few pressing matters."

"Money, Mama?"

"You needn't sound so snippy, Dorina. We merely find ourselves short of . . . well . . . funds to cover a few tiresome obligations. Lord Humbly understands perfectly, and I will not have you treating him in this disrespectful manner. Have I made myself clear?"

A terrible suspicion began to take form in Dorina's mind. Had her parents been borrowing from the viscount, meaning to eliminate their debts by marrying her off to Julian? If so, she hadn't a chance against their schemes. The social whirl meant everything to them. Hadn't they spent most of their time in London, leaving her to wile away the last eighteen years at Willowtree without a second thought?

"I understand everything perfectly, Mama," she finally said.

Amelia Stevens carefully adjusted a stray blond curl. "I knew once you grew accustomed to the idea, you would see the value in this union. You aren't getting any younger, Dorina, and Julian is such a sweet boy and—"

"Mama, thirty-four is hardly a boy, and sweet! Julian was never sweet. He is a monster and shall always be one."

"Now, Dorina, Julian has matured over the years. Surely you are not going to hold any childish pranks against him forever, are you?"

"Childish pranks, Mother? He was twenty-one when he drowned all Suki's kittens to punish me for saying I didn't like his waistcoat. And what about the time when he got so drunk he took that broken bottle to the Earl of Gloxbury's son, scarring him for life."

"A childhood fight between two mere boys. No more," she said, dismissing the accusation. "Those things happen. It could just as easily have been Julian who walked away with the scar."

"How can you say that? Julian was eighteen years old and the earl, only eleven. It wasn't a childhood fight between two young boys. It was the criminal act of a drunken bully who let the superior horseman's skills of an eleven-year-old inflame him with an uncontrollable bout of jealousy. Julian did it out of spite, Mother. Pure and simple."

"How would you know so much about it? You couldn't have been much more than a babe at the time."

"Ask any one of the servants who were here at the time. They all remember. What I don't understand is why Julian was never punished."

"That's not for you to worry your head about. Things were settled between their fathers, and that is how it should be."

Dorina had heard the rumors often enough. Most everyone was willing to speculate on what exactly had been the arrangements of a settlement for ruining the life of a young man. It was said that afterward the earl could no longer stand the sight of Julian and had taken his family to live at another of his estates. Now, other than a few close friends, the young "Elusive Earl" of Gloxbury kept to himself. To this day the matter remained a mystery.

"Would you hand me my lace shawl, dear?" Amelia asked, bringing Dorina out of her daydreaming. "I mustn't be late to the Bedfords' tea. Lady Winifred dropped me a note saying the Earl of Gloxbury is due at Kingsley Manor, and she must fill me in on the latest gossip."

Dorina had always harbored a fantasy of the earl returning to Gloxbury and demanding a long overdue justice from Julian. Well, if he had returned, maybe the rest of her dream might very well come true, also. If the Elusive Earl *was* at Kingsley Manor, she hoped she would have the opportunity of meeting him.

A smile slipped across Dorina's lips. It would be interesting to learn if Julian had timed his hasty retreat to London to the earl's return. From everything she'd heard, sixteen years had not served to mellow the rivalry between the two.

Dorina retrieved the cream lace shawl from the clothespress. "Will the earl be staying long, Mama?"

"Yes, and it's all Julian's fault. Why he lets that man repeatedly make a fool of him is beyond me."

"The earl made a fool of Julian?" Dorina asked, intrigued. If that were true she would have given her entire quarterly allowance, if she had one, to have been there to see his downfall.

Amelia ignored her daughter's question. "If he wasn't forever trying to best the man, the earl would have stayed where he belongs. Now with all this nonsense of a horse race, no one can talk of anything but the ten-thousand-pound purse. Your father and I agree it would be better to postpone the announcement of your engagement until the ball at the Summer Festival. That way our news will not be overshadowed by this ridiculous wager."

"There's to be a race?" Dorina gasped. "One for ten thousand pounds?"

At the suspicious note of excitement in her daughter's voice, Amelia turned her attention from the mirror. "Don't get any foolish ideas in that head of yours. I know you think yourself an excellent horsewoman, Dorina, but young ladies do not ride in races."

"But ten thousand pounds, Mama." If she could only manage to win the race, she would not have to worry about her parents forcing her to marry Julian. She and her governess could take a small cottage on their own, and she would never return.

"It does not matter—Lord Mayberry is the one to pick the horses that are to run, and he would never allow a woman to enter her horse. And I would never allow you to humiliate Julian in this manner."

"I will not be Julian's bride, so it doesn't signify."

Amelia stood and snatched the shawl from Dorina. "Make no mistake, my little naive minx. You have no say in the matter. Your father and I have already given our consent to the marriage, and before I am through with you, you will be glad to give yours."

She left Dorina standing with her mouth dropped open and her heart beating wildly. Never had her parent spoken to her in this manner. Up until now they had left her on her own to run all of Willowtree. Never interfering, never questioning what she did.

Now it looked as if she would be forced to marry Julian. Unless . . .

No, it would never work. Shut away here in the country as she was, how was she to find another suitor richer than Julian? No one had that kind of wealth. No one . . . no one but the earl, that is.

The thought seemed to ignite a fire deep within her that no amount of logic could smother. It was said the earl would never marry because there was not a maiden in all of England who could look upon his countenance long enough to wed him.

Well, they'd been friends once, and Dorina remembered him as kind. Dorina would wed him, scar and all. Perhaps since Lord Humbly had scarred him, surely the earl would understand her plight.

Everyone knew that earls must marry someday. After all, it was their duty to produce an heir. Well, if he agreed to her plan, not only would he get the wife he needed, but he would also be getting a small token of revenge on Julian.

Yes, she'd be paying a visit to the earl one of these fine mornings. A casual meeting on her morning ride would do most nicely. In the meantime, she needed to learn more of the race.

Chapter Two

"Hell's bells!" Dorina Stevens swore under her breath as she glared up at the tall dark stranger through the ruins of her once stylish coiffure. If the man's reckless actions hadn't landed her backside in this muddy patch of bog, she might have admired his glossy black hair and piercing blue eyes. After all, the intriguing devil-may-care looks he sported were quite a change from the other young men of her acquaintance.

To be truly fair, she would have to admit the gentleman was of a more mature age than most of those she knew; but, aside from the scar that ran down one side of his tanned face, age had treated him well. Much more so than Julian. Even so, she could swear she saw a suspicious twinge of amusement tugging at the solemn line of his full lips.

"Go ahead and have your fun," she demanded. "I hope you know you've ruined everything."

Having dismounted, Richard Michaels reached down to assist the fetching young miss to her feet. "Other than muddying your attractive riding habit, what other crimes are you attempting to lay at my feet?"

"You've ruined my chance of catching a glimpse of the Elusive Earl."

Richard stiffened at the nickname the more frivolous of the *ton* had bestowed upon him merely because he elected to keep his distance from the matchmaking efforts of the mothers who were willing to sacrifice their daughters to him—all for the sake of his wealth and title.

He was well aware of the young lady's scrutiny and

knew she hadn't overlooked the bold scar that had blighted
his countenance—and his heart—since the tender age of
eleven. Odd she hadn't recognized the vulgar badge of his
identity as that of belonging to the earl.

"If I have truly ruined your chances, then you should
be thanking me, not berating me," he announced.

Dorina removed her crushed bonnet. "Thanking you!
Whatever for? My horse has ran off, and I am covered
with mud—all thanks to you."

Her green eyes sparked with fire, and Richard found
himself smiling. "Ah, but then I saved you from having to
view the horror of the earl's terrible affliction." He paused
and studied her a moment. "I've been told it can be quite
daunting."

Dorina forgot her anger for a moment. Here was someone who actually knew of the earl. "Is the sight so awful?"
she asked breathlessly.

Her innocence almost made him feel handsome. "Some
ladies have been known to faint at the very sight of
him."

"How dreadful."

Richard held his breath at the words. Without thinking,
he traced the ragged edge of his scar. "You can hardly
blame them," he said, the old bitterness lending a sharpness
to his words.

"I most certainly can," Dorina answered without hesitation. She had not missed the involuntary path of his
strong, slim fingers, and her heart almost broke at her
faux pas. The stranger was obviously comparing his own
scarred face with that of the earl. "It was not his fault
that he carries the scars of that awful Julian's drunk-
en rage," Dorina almost shouted in her rush to redeem
herself. "And anyone who has no more sensitivity than
to call attention to his affliction by fainting deserves the
same fate."

Richard reached out and touched her cheek. "What a
fierce little kitten you are."

Dorina could almost feel her heart soar at the husky
emotion in his deep voice but knew she mustn't let the lure

of a handsome face detract her from her goal. While there was something about the stranger that fascinated her, the Earl of Gloxbury was her objective. Only a wealth greater than the one Lord Humbly had inherited would sway her parents now.

Even to her inexperienced eye, Dorina could see that the stranger in his worn tweeds would never fit that bill. He was probably one of the hopefuls come to check out the site of the big race. She could not say that she blamed him. The lure of ten thousand pounds to prove that you had the fastest horse in all of England was a lot to pass up.

Dorina ran a critical eye over the stranger's mount. The horse was magnificent. There was no denying that, but Dorina knew, if given the chance, her Moondancer could beat him.

"Did you come hoping to gain a position in the big race?" she asked.

A smile touched his lips. "You might say that."

"The countryside has been crawling with those who think they might win. It has been a long time since our small village has seen such activity. The local merchants are all singing the earl's praises for the trade the size of the winner's purse has brought to our little town."

"And already counting the coins they will bring in at the Summer Festival no doubt," he said half to himself.

Using her handkerchief, Dorina wiped at a glob of mud which had adhered itself to the white cuff of her riding habit. "You can hardly berate them for that," she said. "Since the old earl left and then the viscount and his son followed not long after, there has not been much business to sustain them these past years."

"With all the drunken brawls the viscount's son was known to host, I would imagine it brought in a lot of revenues to the area."

Dorina was surprised at the stranger's bluntness. "I take it you do not care for Lord Humbly."

"I care nothing for bullies—or spoiled little boys who never seem to grow up."

"I must agree," Dorina said as she gazed up into the

stranger's handsome face. "The old viscount spoiled Julian terribly. I do believe there is nothing Lord Humbly is not capable of doing if he takes the notion. But enough about that . . . that toad. What do you know about the earl?"

The stranger's blue eyes darkened. He stared over her shoulder as if lost in thought. "I doubt anyone truly knows him. Least of all me."

Dorina grasped the folds of her skirt and shook the wet leaves that clung to her hem. "Even so, he is most generous to have put up such a fine purse for the race this year. This will be the greatest horse race Gloxbury has ever known." Having finished, she straightened, then pursed her lips together in a pout. "I only wish I were a man so I could run my horse."

Smiling, Richard plucked another leaf off the sleeve of her jacket. "Your horse is fast, is he?"

His action took her quite by surprise for a short moment. Then the annoying fact that because she was a woman and therefore unable to ride in the race set her anger to boiling anew, putting all thought of any impropriety from mind.

"Moondancer is the fastest horse in all of England," she stated. "Everyone hereabouts knows that."

Her fierceness brought a smile to his face. "You forget, as a relative stranger to Gloxbury, there is no way I would be privy to such information. Besides which, none of it matters. Even if you were able to ride your horse, mine would win."

Dorina was not used to having her opinion challenged, especially where a horse was concerned. She squared her shoulders and glared up at him. "Such a shame your education in horseflesh is so lacking," she said with a huff. "And just when I was beginning to form a liking for you. Now I must know who you are. I refuse to think poorly of anyone without at least knowing his name."

Richard scowled. "Which name would you like? I have been called many things."

"None of them to your liking, I would say."

Richard bowed slightly. "How very perceptive of you."

"Then what am I to call you when I dredge up these unflattering thoughts of you?"

Intrigued by the fact that his disfigurement had not been the thing to turn this beautiful young lady from him, Richard hated to tell her that he was the Elusive Earl she sought to catch a glimpse of. But Richard had learned long ago that there was no way he could hide from his legacy.

"I am Richard Michaels," he finally said, then waited for the awful truth to wash her features in embarrassment.

"Michaels? Why do I think I should know that name? Is your family from around here?"

"We lived here once, but that was a long time ago," he answered.

"That's probably why it seems so familiar," Dorina said. She had always prided herself in her judgment of others, and Richard Michaels seemed a likable fellow.

She leaned her head to one side and studied him a moment. "The name Richard does not seem to fit you somehow," she said, dismissing the nagging thought that there was more to it than that.

Richard smiled at her bluntness. "And what name would you give me?"

"I think I would call you William," she answered. "Like William the Conqueror. But do not take it as a slight," she hastened to add at his silence. "Richard is a very nice name, but it seems rather timid. William sounds so strong—and noble. A name much more befitting a strong noble face such as yours."

Richard had a difficult time maintaining his surprise, not only at her cavalier treatment of his flaw, but also because William was the name of his father—a man Richard had once resembled and Julian's father had always despised. It was a mutual dislike. The old viscount had courted Richard's mother, but she had married the earl. Richard sometimes wondered if the viscount had encouraged the bad feelings between Julian and himself as a means of exacting some sort of sadistic revenge on Richard's father.

"I much prefer Richard," he said with a devilish grin. "Like Richard Lion-Heart."

"Oh, my, that is a noble name," she breathed.

He laughed in spite of himself. "You would refer to me as strong and noble, despite my misinformed insistence that my mount is faster than yours?"

Dorina looked up at him. "If you knew me, Mr. Michaels, you would know I am nothing if not fair. I've always believed a person's views can be changed, but they must learn to live with what else they become."

"I am pleased to know that I am not past all hope of redemption. But now I feel it only fair that you give me your name as well."

Dorina chewed on her lip a moment. She didn't want anyone to learn that she ventured so far from home without her groom, yet at the same time she felt she could trust this stranger. "Dorina. Dorina Stevens."

"Maurice Stevens's daughter?" he asked. "You live at Willowtree?"

"Hell's bells!" she declared, the words slipping out before she could stop them. Despite the cool morning air, she could feel her face growing red. It wasn't bad enough that he knew her parents and was bound to tell them of her folly, but she had to compound her crimes by uttering aloud the first words that came to mind.

"You must swear you'll not tell anyone you saw me," she whispered.

"Or of your choice of words?"

"I apologize for my cursing. Too much time spent with my horse in our stables. My parents have threatened to send all the grooms away if I don't stop. But at least I am trying to curb my tongue."

"Apology accepted," he said, attempting to keep his lip from quivering in amusement. "You're a long way from home, Miss Stevens."

"You talk as if I were some young miss just out of the schoolroom. I am almost nineteen and know the country-side like—"

Her face suddenly went pale as she stared at him.

"What's wrong?" he asked, ready to catch her should she faint.

"Michaels! Now I remember. You're him. You're the . . ."

"The Elusive Earl? Yes, I'm afraid so."

"But you said . . . I mean, your scar . . ."

"Quite hideous, isn't it?"

"No! I mean not at all. In fact, it lends your face an air of—intrigue—and dark mysteries—and—and hidden passions." She knew she was babbling but she couldn't stop.

"You need not try to romanticize it. It was not gotten in the glory of war. No one called upon me to fight Napoleon." He took her hand and laid it against his cheek. "Your precious Lord Humbly did this because he couldn't abide the looks of me. Ironic, isn't it? Afterward he could bear the sight of me even less, yet he seeks me out and harasses me at every opportunity."

Finished, he reached down, spanned her tiny waist with his hands, and swung her up onto his horse.

"What are you doing, Lord Gloxbury?" she squealed.

He swung up behind her. "I would think that would be obvious, Miss Stevens. I'm taking you home." After a few trying moments of attempting to locate the other stirrup hidden beneath the generous folds of her riding habit, Richard gave up and urged the horse forward.

Dorina settled herself against his broad chest and tried not to think about the strange flutter that had arisen in her breast. "I'm grateful for the ride, my lord, but I must insist you let me down. My parents—"

"Would never forgive me if I left their daughter to make her way home from here."

"You must trust me when I say it will cause more of a stir if I show up with you than if I am a trifle late. Besides which, when Moondancer shows up at the stables without me, my groom will come looking for me."

"And will he know that you traveled so far afield today?"

Dorina cast him a glance ensured to leave him in little doubt as to her opinion of his question. "That is a risk I am willing to take, Lord Gloxbury. To accept your assistance now might further complicate, let alone compromise, a carefully planned strategy."

He returned her glance with a wicked grin. "If you have set out to intrigue me, Miss Stevens, you have done a most thorough job of it. Dare I ask what this plan might be?"

"Most certainly not!"

He had not missed the redness of her face, nor had he forgotten that she had come this far to catch a glimpse of him. "We shall see," he said, then touched his heel to his mount's side. The horse immediately responded, and Dorina was forced to nestle comfortably into his arms. "Yes, we shall see."

Dorina tried not to dwell on the note of confidence in his words. If she was fortunate, her parents would be still to bed and would not notice her return. If not, she would more than likely be forced to endure a lecture on how a lady hoping to marry such a fine prospect as Julian Bromly should conduct herself.

They rode on in silence until they reached the drive leading up to her front door. Richard brought his horse to a stop at the iron gateway.

"Now let's hear your plan," he stated.

"What?"

"This carefully planned strategy you spoke of. Let's hear it."

"It can be of little interest to you, my lord, so if you will be so kind as to lower me to the ground, I will be ever so grateful."

He didn't move his arm. "Not until you tell me," he answered.

Lord Gloxbury was beginning to annoy Dorina, and she told him so. But the devilish grin on his lips had a way of distracting her, and she almost missed his taunt of delivering her to the front parlor and depositing her in her father's lap.

"You would do that to get your own way?"

"Most certainly," he assured her. "Now tell me. Why did you wish to catch a glimpse of me? Because, if you were thinking to seduce me in order to race your horse against mine, you needn't waste your time. Lord Mayberry will be picking the horses that will run."

"Why, you arrogant . . ." Dorina raised her hand to slap him, then thought better of it. Lord Gloxbury looked the type to slap back. "If you must know, I had no plans to seduce you. My goals are much higher than a horse race. My plan, Lord Gloxbury, is to marry you."

Chapter Three

Dorina lay back against her bedchamber door, holding her breath at the memory of what she had blurted out. Her announcement had worked better than she could have ever imagined. She had shocked him to such an extent that she was able to slip down off his mount without him trying to stop her. It wasn't as if she'd lost anything by confessing her plan to him. Now that she'd met him, she had to admit it would never have worked. Despite everything she had heard about his scarred face, Richard Michaels could have anyone he wanted as a wife.

With the Summer Festival only a month away, she had no time to waste chasing after such an unrealistic dream. She'd just have to look elsewhere for a suitable husband.

A knock at her door sent her scurrying across the room.

Dorina's young maid, Tess, didn't wait for an answer but burst into the room. "The Reverend Harold Layton . . . be in . . . the front parlor, miss," she managed to get out between her rasping gasps of breath.

"Finally," Dorina whispered to herself. "He certainly took long enough."

"Pardon, miss?"

"Tell him I will be down shortly."

"But he seemed . . . most anxious to speak with your parents, not you, miss. I know they won't be up for hours yet, but you asked me to warn you if anyone asked after them. What do you want me to tell him?"

"Don't get yourself all in a dither," Dorina warned. "He's here to see me. He asked after my parents as a courtesy only. Besides, if you recall, Lord Humbly was the one I was referring to, not the vicar."

Tess dropped her gaze to the apron she had twisted into knots. "I'm sorry to have gotten it wrong again, miss."

Dorina smiled. Despite Tess's inability to grasp even the most rudimentary of rules governing the conduct of a proper lady's maid, Dorina preferred her over her mother's more experienced one.

"That's fine, Tess. I would rather you warn me of everyone than miss warning me of Lord Humbly. Now go belowstairs and tell Harold to wait."

"Yes, miss," Tess said over her shoulder as she left the room.

"And offer him refreshments," Dorina added.

She and Harold had been close all their lives, and she knew if anyone could help her out of her dilemma, it would be him. After all, being four years older, he had gotten her out of any number of scrapes when they were growing up. It was only the years since he had become vicar that he had begun to question the wisdom of their escapades and Dorina had been forced to become a lady for lack of a conspiratorial companion. With a loveless marriage to Julian as the stakes, surely he would not balk at helping her now.

The young vicar was finishing off his third apple tart when Dorina completed her story.

Harold sat his napkin aside. "You could marry me," he said with a resigned sigh.

She knew his lack of enthusiasm should vex her, but she didn't think it was the time to point it out. "You are a dear to say so, but I value your friendship too much to tie you down to such an unsuitable match." She reached down and snatched a crumb from his plate. "Besides, your morals are too high to run away with me and your income too low to secure my parents' consent."

Dorina stood and took another turn around the room. "No, Harold, we must put our heads together and decide who among our acquaintances would be most willing to set aside the lack of a dowry for an amiable wife."

Harold cocked a blond brow. "Amiable?" He didn't bother waiting for her protests but continued his scolding. "You'd better come up with another incentive, Dorina. Everyone hereabouts is well aware of your managing ways."

"What a gentleman you have become of late," she said sarcastically.

"Don't get your feathers ruffled with me, Dorina. Remember I was the one you dragged along on your schemes when we were growing up."

Dorina flopped down on the cushion beside him. "And you were such fun before you chose to become a vicar. I swear ever since then, you have become right down stodgy."

"It's your fault I decided to turn away from our hoyden ways, and you know it."

Dorina picked up one of the petit point pillows tucked into the corner of the sofa. "I can't believe you still blame me for all this."

"After that last escapade of yours I felt I owed my soul to God for sparing us the humiliation of being caught. If the Earl of Gloxbury was ever to find out that I turned your mare in with one of his stallions, there would be hell to pay."

"You talk as if I planned that poor Rosebud would form an unhealthy attachment for the earl's horse. It wasn't my fault, I tell you. It was the fault of that groom for riding the earl's stallion past her pasture each morning, enticing her with the savage grace of that big brute. Personally, I did not see what she saw in him."

"That did not justify what you had me do."

"Would you rather Rosebud had pined away until she was nothing but skin and bones?"

"Heavens, no!" he thundered. "She looked bad enough by the time we realized what was ailing the tart."

"Harold! You, a vicar, calling my poor Rosebud a tart?"

Harold could feel the heat creeping up from his collar. The last five years hadn't changed much. Dorina had a way of making him lose control of the conversation when she was plotting one of her schemes.

"Well, that's what she was," he said in his defense. "And her capricious yearnings could have landed us in front of the magistrate's bench. Gentlemen are most particular about their horseflesh, and well you know it."

"You needn't sound so critical, as if I had deliberately set out to cheat the man. I would have paid if I could have spared the funds. Moreover, it was to be Rosebud's last colt. Can you blame her for wanting to voice her opinion as to who the father was to be? Besides it wasn't as if we took something that was irreplaceable. Why, I'm sure the earl's stallion has since sired any number of—"

"Dorina! We will not discuss this any further. What you talked me into doing was wrong, and if I did not know how much store you set by Moondancer, I would insist you turn the colt over to the earl as compensation for your sins."

"Harold Layton, I'm surprised at you. You would separate a colt from its mother? All these years and I never believed you could be so cruel. You are as heartless as Julian."

Refusing to be intimidated, Harold stubbornly crossed his arms and glared at her. "Moondancer is four years old, Dorina. Rosebud hasn't given him so much as a passing look in over two. So don't cast me in the role of a cruel villain."

"Well, then, you must at least help me secure a husband by the Summer Festival to redeem yourself. For if I am forced to marry Julian, I shall never forgive you."

"If it was anyone other than Lord Humbly, I would say I could live with that, but I agree, we must prevent this wedding." He leaned back in his chair and closed his eyes in thought. "What you need is someone who is so smitten with you that he has failed to notice your overbearing ways."

Dorina snatched up the petit point pillow that was resting in her lap and swatted the vicar over the head.

Harold jumped to his feet. "What the . . . Why did you hit me?"

"Because you have this annoying habit of reminding me of what I've become. After all this time of my parents leaving me and the servants to manage basically on our own, I doubt you'll change me."

Harold glared down at her. "You are fortunate that I am of a forgiving nature or I would walk out of here and leave you to your marriage."

"You wouldn't," Dorina wailed.

"You're right. I wouldn't wish my worse enemy to be married to him."

"Then help me think of someone."

Harold started to sit, then thought better of it. "Give me a moment."

With long strides he walked the length of the room and back, then came to a stop in front of her. "Lord Compton has yet to take a wife. Although he's definitely not one to stir a woman's heart, he *is* likable enough."

Dorina shook her head. "Unfortunately, his intolerance of our country air gives him a perpetual red nose and a pair of watery blue eyes that even a pocket of linen handkerchiefs has a difficult time keeping pace with."

"A woman looking to spend the rest of her days at the mercy of Julian Bromly best be keeping all her options open."

"I said I was desperate, Harold, not dead. Now, who else is there?"

"None that I can think of."

"Then we must look among those we don't know."

Harold did not like that glint he saw in her green eyes. "And how would you suggest I do that? Run an advertisement in the London *Gazette* or the *Post*?"

Dorina's lips curved in a smile at the notion. Thank goodness the race was already bringing visitors to the area. Julian was right. Being tucked away as she was at Willowtree, there hadn't been much opportunity of meeting many young men. But perhaps spreading a bit of gossip that she owned the fastest horse in all the county, then hinting that Moondancer might be for sale, might lure a few young men her way.

Chapter Four

Richard Michaels tossed the reins of his horse to the stableboy and mounted the front steps of Kingsley Manor. No matter how hard he tried to put the young lady's declaration from his mind, he found himself returning to it over and over again.

But marry him? Who had put that bee in her pretty little bonnet? He was well aware that the ugliness of his scar had prompted any number of thoughtless pranks over the last sixteen years, and he couldn't help but think this was but another one.

Rarely would an instigator make himself known. None wished to test Richard's skills of dueling pistols across a field of honor. No, they much preferred to put some unsuspecting dolt up to it. He had to admit Dorina did not look to be a fool, but marriage to him? A handsome woman like her did not need to go begging to a stranger.

Unless . . .

Richard's lips turned down in a bitter frown. It was his wealth. It was the only thing that made any sense out of her declaration. Dorina was looking to snag her line into a rich husband.

*   *   *

A good night's sleep and a warm breakfast did not lay to rest the earl's nagging suspicions that Dorina Stevens was hiding something. The woman had ridden all the way to his estate just to catch a glimpse of him—to ascertain for herself if his affliction was so devastating as to grant him ineligible to wed.

For a half crown, he would turn the tables and show her what it felt like to be an item of someone's morbid curiosity. No, on second thought, a half crown wouldn't be necessary. He'd do it for nothing.

Pushing away from the breakfast table, Richard ordered his mount to be brought around.

Although a cold chill crept up the back of her neck and her heart felt as if it were lodged in her throat, Dorina kept Moondancer down to a sedate trot. For over a week now, whenever she set out for her morning ride, she'd had the feeling she was being watched. With all the strangers in the area, all hoping to claim the earl's fine purse, it wouldn't do for them to see Moondancer's speed. That privilege would be reserved for the gentlemen interested in her proposition.

She had wanted all inquiries to be referred to her, but Harold had insisted that he be the one to decide who would be included in her offer. Once he found a likely candidate, he would discreetly approach him with the proposition. No one was to know who owned Moondancer until he had agreed to the terms. Was it possible someone had already learned of her horse?

Dorina let her gaze travel casually over the edge of the forest that bordered Willowtree. She thought she caught a glimpse of movement, but she couldn't be sure. As jumpy as she had become, it could be nothing more than her imagination.

She had purposely picked the early morning to avoid being seen. Perhaps even that was becoming too risky now. With a sigh she turned back toward home.

Dorina pulled her horse up short at the sight of a lone horse and rider on the hill. Two dark silhouettes cast against the rising sun, they conjured up all manner of frightening fantasies. The least of which was the possibility that someone meant to have Moondancer, with or without her.

She quickly searched the edge of the meadow for the path that cut through the woods. She grimaced to realize it lay halfway between her and the stranger.

Without a moment's hesitation she reached back and slapped Moondancer's rump. He responded immediately, and Dorina was forced to lean forward and hang on. Her stylish bonnet with her favorite feather was the first to be lost in the wind. The careful arrangement of her black curls was the next to go, but Dorina refused to check Moondancer's speed. If the stranger was able to keep to his pace, he would catch up with her at the path.

"Faster, Dancer," she urged. "Faster. We shall not let this interloper get his hands on you, boy."

Richard marveled at the sight before him. The woman was actually getting more speed out of the big gray stallion. Hawk would have to stretch himself to catch them now. Never had he thought to come across a horse that would challenge his own mount. Much less one ridden by a slip of a woman.

Richard reined in at the path. He turned to greet her when she flew by him, a vision of blue riding habit and black curls. Without hesitation he took off after her. Her mount obviously was familiar with the paths that crisscrossed through the trees, for Richard soon lost sight of the pair.

When he realized she had the advantage, he turned Hawk back and returned to the meadow. He'd had a chance to see part of the estate during his week of following her, and he had an inkling of where the path came out. If he was wrong, he still knew where she lived.

Dorina pulled up on the reins when she realized that Moondancer had lost the horse and rider. Riding alone was becoming too dangerous. As much as she hated to, she was going to have to roust out one of the stableboys to accompany her on her morning rides. At least until the race was over. It was something she rarely did anymore. It always proved a waste of time. For when she let Moondancer have his head, none of the stableboys were ever able to keep up with them anyway.

She caught a glimpse of movement out of the corner of her eye when she broke from the trees. Pulling up on the reins, she turned to catch a better look.

The earl. It had been the earl all the time. She brought Moondancer to a halt.

"That's quite a mount you have there," he said, tipping his beaver felt. "He almost beat Hawk."

Dorina ignored his polite smile. "Why are you following me?" she demanded.

"I wished to catch a glimpse of you," he answered coolly, then added, "In much the same manner you did of me."

Dorina could feel her face grow warm, but she was never one for backing down. "Unless you are doing it for the same reasons as I, I suggest you go about your business and leave me to mine."

Richard took in the wild disarray of curls and the arrogant set of her shoulders and decided he wouldn't let her off so easily. He urged his horse to circle the young stallion.

"Deep chest," he said. "Good, strong muscles not too close-coupled." He let his gaze travel down her stiff back and past her small waist. "Definitely not goose-rumped, either," he added.

Dorina turned, trying to catch his eye. "I thank you for your approval, my lord, but I must insist that you be on your way."

Richard leaned forward and laid his crossed arms on the neck of his mount. "Now dismount."

"What?"

"I said dismount." He reached for her reins. "However am I to see if you are coon-footed unless you dismount and stand for my inspection."

Dorina clasped her whip firmly. "Lord Gloxbury! I am not a horse, and I'll thank you to stop this here and now."

His blue eyes darkened. "Nor am I some spectacle set out for *your* observation and amusement."

Dorina bit back the words that came readily to mind. If she were honest with herself, she would admit she deserved his anger. She had indeed treated him abominably.

"You are correct. I do owe you an apology, but I had not thought to disturb you with my curiosity. It was not done to embarrass you or in any way cause you discomfort. I had heard that your . . . your face was . . ."

"A sight worthy of the circus?" he finished for her.

"Oh, my no," she said. "I mean yes. I had heard it was so, but now I can see that the rumors were wrong. You have a most handsome face, my lord. A handsomeness that is only enhanced by your scar."

"And you thought to marry such a face?"

Dorina had never backed down from a bad situation before but somehow sensed she should make an effort to do so now. To stay and mince words with the earl was only making an embarrassing situation worse.

"I said it to shock you, nothing more. And the plan succeeded, for you let me down."

Richard studied her a moment. Even from this distance he could smell the jasmine perfume she wore. He wanted to believe her, but he had grown more and more cynical over the years.

"It won't work a second time," he warned. He was pleased to see he'd surprised her. "Oh, yes, I can see it in your face. You mean to say something totally outrageous in hopes of shocking me again."

She ventured a glance at him. "Would you have me believe my saying I meant to marry you shocked you?"

Richard had a difficult time keeping his lips from answering with a smile. "I have to admit, your declaration was original. It took me quite by surprise."

Dorina tossed him a wicked grin. "I've found the truth often does that to a man."

Before he could question her further, she nudged her mount around his and was down the short lane to her stables. Richard allowed his gaze to follow her.

"You've not seen the last of me!" he shouted after her.

Dorina's heart was beating wildly at her boldness by the time she reached the stables. She couldn't recall when she'd enjoyed a confrontation more. For all Lord Gloxbury's gruff manners, there had been a decided twinkle in his eyes when he scolded her. She suspected he might have found himself equally entertained.

If Lord Gloxbury stayed at Kingsley Manor much longer, he was certain to hear of the rumor that there was a horse to beat his right here in Gloxbury. After seeing Moondancer run, it wouldn't take much to guess to whom the horse belonged.

Despite her fears, a smile tipped the corners of her mouth. She wondered how long it would be before he paid a visit to confirm his suspicions. The thought crossed her mind that Lord Gloxbury might be willing to take her up on the offer of marriage if it would mean keeping Moondancer out of the race, but then daydreams were always more pleasant to dwell on than the cold realities of her dilemma.

Julian had made it a habit to break his fast at the club of late. It was the only way he was given a moment's peace anymore. Having opened yet another note, he looked up from his morning correspondence and cursed.

"Everyone and his dog is boasting that they have the fastest horse in all of England," he informed Lord Mayberry across the breakfast table.

Lord Mayberry continued to spread the thick strawberry jam on his muffin. Other than Bromly's whining, he couldn't recall when he'd had so much fun.

"With so many to choose from, Bromly, we are bound to find one which can match paces with Michaels's stables."

"That's the problem. There are so many responses, even if we lived to be a hundred, we would never be able to sort them all out."

Lord Mayberry set down his muffin and studied Bromly carefully. He had never much cared for the man, but then he knew even less about Lord Gloxbury. Furthermore, he didn't much care who won the blasted race. His only stake in the matter was the excitement his contribution had generated among his cronies. Nothing doing but Bromly was forcing him to dip his oar in the water again.

"First thing we have to do is have a look at the horses. Seeing how they perform should eliminate more than three quarters of them."

Julian picked up the pile of letters and tossed them across the table to Lord Mayberry. "And how would you think we should go about accomplishing that? There has to be more than twenty queries there, and that's just this morning's post. I have thirty-seven more like them at my lodgings."

Lord Mayberry shoved the letters back to Lord Humbly. "You surprise me, Bromly. If you spent half the time thinking this thing through that you spend on selecting your wardrobe, you'd have found any number of suitable nags days ago."

Julian twisted his mouth in disgust. "Ones that can beat Michaels's horses?"

Lord Mayberry ignored the barb. "The first thing we do is ignore these letters," he said. "Then post a notice in the London *Gazette*. State that we will be viewing the horses at your estate from two to four each afternoon. If we tire of it, we can always have your trainer take over for us. In fact, it might not be a bad idea to have him overseeing the entire thing. I should be there, of course, seeing as I'm to have the final say as to which horses are to run in the race."

It was the one stipulation that set Julian's blood to boiling. His pride still smarted from Richard's stunt at Tattersalls, and he would have liked to have had the means of Richard's downfall exclusively in his hands, but he knew he'd have to settle for the rules Mayberry was willing to bend. It had taken Julian the better part of two weeks of boot licking, but he'd finally got the old boy to let him sit in on the selections.

There had to be a horse somewhere that could beat Richard's. He smiled. Given the terrain picked for the race, there were always ways for riders to see that their competition didn't finish. The only problem with his plan was that the other horses would have to keep up with Richard's in order for it to work. He'd need some damn good sprinters for that. If Dorina still had that big stallion of hers, he knew just the horse.

Chapter Five

Dorina found Lord Gloxbury sitting beside the stream the next morning, the lines from his two fishing poles trailing in the sun-dappled water. She had slackened her hold on the reins, and Moondancer made his way under the trees to the water's edge.

"Good morning, Miss Stevens," the earl said without turning. "Would you care to join me? The fish are so hungry this morning they're even nibbling at my poor fare."

Dorina looked over the top of her borrowed spectacles and eyed the undisturbed lines with skepticism. "Perhaps you should remind them they must wiggle the line to let you know the degree of their appetite."

Richard opened the leather pouch on the ground beside him. "Don't let their indifference bother you. I grew so tired of pulling them in while I waited for you to come by that I left the bait off the line," he said before turning to grin up at her. "I hoped . . ."

He stared at her a moment before realizing it was the wire-framed spectacles that were different. "Where in the devil did you get those?"

"From my governess," Dorina answered, pushing the smudged glass orbs back in place. "What do you think? Do I look dreadful enough?"

"You wish to look dreadful?" he asked as he climbed to his feet. Without asking her permission, he took the reins from her and lead Moondancer to one of the trees lining the bank of the stream.

"Oh, yes," she answered. "The gentleman my parents wish me to marry—only he isn't much of a gentleman—is due to visit today. He's quite particular about one's looks, and I was hoping the spectacles would put him off."

Having secured her mount, Richard lifted his hands to help her down. She didn't turn away from him but slid easily into his arms. It was as if he didn't have the ugly scar marring his face.

"Won't your parents question your need for the spectacles?" he asked, hoping to keep her attention diverted from noticing his affliction.

"I had thought of that, also, but then, my parents have not spent much time at Willowtree, so it should not be too difficult to convince them that I have been wearing them for quite some time."

Richard searched her face as he took her hand and led her over to the stream. He could detect no bitterness, just a sense of resignation.

"Am I to assume, then, that you are left at the mercy of the servants most of the time?"

Dorina laughed at his seriousness. "To their mercy sounds as if one were helpless. I'm afraid I'm not as docile as all that. With no parents about to temper my ways, I've turned out quite the opposite. In the long run my independence has proved to be quite a handful for the staff. Why, I have even had the hiring and firing of my own governesses since I was fourteen."

After seating her on the blanket, Richard handed her one of the poles and took his place next to her, deliberately sitting with the scarred side of his face to her. It was his perverse way of challenging her to accept him or leave him alone.

"Are you saying your parents run off to London and leave you here to manage the household?" He shook his dark head. "I know it isn't considered fashionable to drag your children around to all the social functions, but I've never heard of one abandoning one's offspring to fend for themselves at such a tender age."

Dorina pulled in her line and dangled the naked hook in his face. "I guess it has something to do with growing old. You forget the simplest things."

"Are you referring to your parents or me?"

"Both," she answered without hesitation.

He couldn't take offense to a comment accompanied with such a radiant smile. "You had better be more pleasant to me, or I shall make you bait your own hook," he teased.

"Then I will attempt not to take my frustrations out on you. It's just so terribly disheartening to have one's parents take notice of one at the very time when you want their attention the least."

He handed her the baited line. "From that I am to presume that after all these years of neglect, your parents have recalled their responsibilities and are now taking over?"

"You make it sound so heartless. It's not that I think my parents don't love me in their own way. It's merely after rarely seeing me, they still thought of me as this little girl all dressed in ruffled dresses covered with ribbons and lace." She paused to throw her line into the stream. "I do believe learning that I was soon to be nineteen took them quite by surprise."

Richard tossed his line in beside hers. "It didn't take them long to recover from their shock if they have managed to secure you a husband in such a short time."

"I think they have wanted me to marry Julian for y—"

"Julian Bromly?" he asked sharply.

How had she forgotten? The scar. Of course, the earl would be shocked to hear of the engagement. Dorina reached out to touch his arm. "It's not as if I want to marry Lord Humbly, you understand. I think him the most dreadful of men."

"Then you must tell your parents you will not marry him."

Dorina caught her lower lip between her teeth. "I've tried," she finally admitted. "They're not much for listening at the moment. Lord Humbly has promised to pay some pressing obligation or another, and that's all that matters to them."

Richard's mouth went dry. It was the IOUs he held that had prompted this wedding. It didn't surprise him that Julian would use Stevens's debt to his advantage.

"Well, tell them again," he demanded, surprised to hear the frustration in his voice. It was not his fault that her father thought to avoid his gambling debts in this manner. It was none of his business, he told himself. Even so, he knew if he hadn't been clasping his pole so tightly, he'd have taken her by the shoulders and shook her and made her do as he asked.

It took all his concentration to school his features, but it wouldn't do for him to let her see his hatred. Only calm reason would convince her now. "Take it from me, Miss Stevens, Julian is not a fit husband for you—or anyone."

When she didn't reply, Richard ventured a quick glance. What he saw tore at his conscience. Gone was the bright sunshine that seemed to follow her around—only to be replaced by a little-girl-lost sort of gray cloud.

If she had been a spring day, he would have said the fog had rolled in. But she wasn't. She was more like the wild roses that grew along the lane—you were annoyed at the spot they picked to make an appearance, but their uninhibited beauty touched your soul into forgetting their bold intrusion.

As if she felt his gaze on her, Dorina turned to him. "If you were to allow me to run in your race, Moondancer would win the ten thousand pounds. Then no one could force me to marry him."

"What would you do with it? Run away?"

Dorina glared at him. "There is a small cottage in the village that Har—the vicar says I could get for a little of nothing."

Richard was pleased to see the fire back in her eyes. "Even if I could get your horse in the race, which I can't, I already hear that there is a mystery horse in the area that will win."

Dorina quickly turned her attention back to her fishing pole. "Have you seen this horse yet?" she asked casually.

Richard had not missed the blush that crept up her cheeks. So that was the game. Although he had questioned the vicar thoroughly last evening, he had learned nothing of the owner. All Layton would say was that certain conditions went with the ownership of the horse—conditions that had nothing to do with price. He'd be willing to wager a neat purse that they were in this together.

"No, I have not seen the animal," he said, hoping her pride in Moondancer would give her away. "But then, the locals are bound to have some favorite. I've found it to be so any number of times. It gives them something to talk about over their ale."

"This horse is the fastest in all of England," she snapped. "And that's what the race is about, isn't it?"

"Are you saying this horse can even beat yours?"

Too late, Dorina realized her mistake. The words did not set easily on her tongue, but she knew she had to say them or the earl would soon guess her secret.

Deliberately she had let the tip of her pole drop in the water, then made a great show of lifting it out. She twisted the wet line through her fingers like one of the stableboys had shown her. "I think I'm getting a nibble," she said.

"I asked if the horse can beat yours," he repeated.

The distraction hadn't worked. She grasped her pole in frustration. He wasn't going to let up until he satisfied his curiosity. He didn't mind at all that it put her in an awkward position. If she said no and word got out, then all Harold's efforts to help her catch a husband would be for naught. Yet she hated to admit to this man that she had lied all along and that there was another that could beat Moondancer.

The fish that pulled on her line took her by surprise, and Dorina jumped to her feet. In her haste she lost her balance and tumbled into the stream. The next thing she knew, Lord Gloxbury was lifting her out of the cold water.

"What will you try next to avoid answering my question?" he asked, inhaling the scent of her perfume.

My, but his smugness was beginning to annoy her. "The horse can win over mine," she finally mumbled, her teeth chattering.

"Interesting," he said, giving her wet costume a thorough examination before he covered her with the blanket. "Perhaps I should return to the vicar and try to purchase him."

It would serve him right to find out that she came with the deal he wanted to strike, Dorina decided. Perhaps there was justice in this world after all. She met his grin with one of her own. "I think that would be wise of you, Lord Gloxbury. I've seen this horse run. Unless you wish to lose the race, I'd do everything possible to add him to my stables."

"Sounds a lot like a dream," he said, letting her slip down the front of him. "And not all dreams are pleasant, Dory. Some become nightmares."

"Not summer dreams," she breathed.

There, let him think on that for a while.

"Marriage!" Richard shouted up at the man who brought him the news. "You're saying the owner of the horse refuses to part with the animal unless the buyer is willing to wed her?"

Richard's man of business was not one to rehash his presentation. Always one to memorize his findings word for word, it dismayed the old man to have to verify the interpretations of his information by others. He did what was asked, then reported his unbiased findings. "So it would seem, m'lord," he reluctantly replied.

"But that's ludicrous, Perkins."

"It's not for me to say, m'lord, but it did seem to presume a might too much."

"Well, I will not keep you from your duties any longer. You may go."

"Thank you, m'lord," he said as he nodded his white head and left.

Richard sat in thought in the dark study long after the old man had closed the door. Richard had known by the wickedness of her grin that Miss Stevens had some nefarious scheme brewing, but he had to admit this took him quite by surprise. It was a temptation to tell the vicar he'd accept the terms. It would certainly teach the little vixen a lesson.

He knew she didn't want to marry Lord Humbly, but her plot to get out of it was almost as dangerous. Did she really think she'd land an honorable husband this way?

He was ready to inform the vicar his thoughts on the asinine plan when it came to him that the vicar had never said the bride was to be Dorina. In fact he had been most adamant that the identity of the bride was to remain a secret until the exchange of vows. He had been so certain when he'd asked to talk with the vicar that the mystery horse was Moondancer, he had not even entertained the idea that it would belong to anyone but Dorina. But what if the horse did belong to someone else—a dried-up prune of a spinster who thought to use this opportunity to snag a husband? It would certainly explain Dorina's parting challenge.

What was it Dorina had said to him while her mouth was wreathed in that wicked grin? *"Unless you wish to lose the race, I'd do everything possible to add him to my stables."*

But marriage? She had once said she'd come to propose to him. Had it truly been merely a ruse to get him to let her go? Or had it contained a grain of truth? If not for that grin, he would have said it had. But that grin had dared more than merely that he accept the terms a mystery lady had set forth.

It was obvious that she was saying the horse could beat any of his. The rest of it was too ludicrous to even contemplate. No one would agree to marry someone just to ensure getting their hands on a horse, even if it did turn out to be the fastest in all of England.

What Miss Stevens didn't know was that she had over-played her cards when dealing with him. Her grin told him she knew about the terms and that only a desperate man would agree to such an arrangement. Even so, it wouldn't hurt to try to discover the identity of the lady—and her horse—and as far as he could see, there was only one way to do that. He'd have to convince Perkins that it was time the old man took a wife.

*   *   *

In her excitement Dorina grabbed the vicar and gave him a generous hug. "We have an offer?" she shrieked in his unprotected ear.

Harold pried her arms from around his neck. "Dorina, will you please contain your enthusiasm for a minute? You don't even know who it is yet. Now, if you will sit down, we'll go over the details."

Dorina did as he asked, but she was sure she didn't have to ask who had accepted her offer. She was sure it had to be Lord Gloxbury. After all, she had practically dared him to talk to Harold. She looked up at the vicar. It was difficult to maintain a calm demeanor when she was to make such a fortunate alliance.

Trying to keep the smile from her lips, Dorina calmly rearranged the folds of her skirt. "I'm ready now," she said once she was sure her features were carefully schooled.

"The gentleman who has made the offer is a Mr. Silas Perkins. He's a little old, but from what I can ascertain, he has a steady income. I have made arrangements to . . ."

The light had gone from Dorina's eyes. If he didn't know her better, he was sure the news had shocked her. "Dorina, is there something wrong?"

She smiled to hide her disappointment. It was only an offer like many others she was likely to receive. Obviously Richard had been too busy to speak with the vicar yet.

"Please continue, Harold," she said in a most gracious voice. "What else do you know about this Mr. Perkins?"

"As I was saying, being Lord Gloxbury's man of business, Mr. Per—"

"Lord Gloxbury's man of business! He sent his man of business?"

Harold hurriedly scanned his notes. "It says nothing about anyone sending him, Dorina. According to the offer he signed, he is prepared to marry you provided he gets to see the horse run."

She reached across the desk and grabbed the papers from his fingers. The offer was pretty straightforward. It added no more conditions than she would have expected, but she couldn't shake the feeling that Richard was behind this. Could an earl have that much influence over his staff? As soon as the question formed in her mind, she knew she had her answer. Money had a way of opening all doors, and from all she'd heard, Lord Gloxbury was known for having more than his share.

She'd be willing to wager Mr. Perkins would next insist that Lord Gloxbury be present when she raced Moondancer. She had to admit Richard's plan was extremely clever. Not only would he not be committing himself to marriage, but if she were to marry his man of business, he would have the opportunity of acquiring Moondancer for his own stables.

She looked up at Harold. "Once I'm married, Moondancer then belongs to my husband, doesn't he?"

Harold nodded.

"Well, we must put our heads together on this. There has to be a way to prevent that from happening, and once we've found it, tell Mr. Perkins we accept his offer."

Let Lord Gloxbury see his chance to get Moondancer slide through his fingers. She would have her husband and her horse.

Chapter Six

"She accepted your offer, did she?" Richard tried to sound casual despite the knot that had formed around his chest. Well, how was he to feel? he asked himself. He had all but offered the man a lifetime of happiness if only he would pursue the intriguing proposal put forth by the vicar.

Perkins, who had now grown accustomed to the idea of marrying the beautiful Miss Stevens, smiled broadly. "I'm to meet with the young lady this evening."

"Wonderful, Perkins." Richard rubbed his hands together. "Then tonight we shall know the true identity of our mystery lady."

Perkins's smile fell like a rock in water. "But . . . but . . ."

"Yes, Perkins?"

"You assured me the lady was Miss Stevens, my lord." He ran his finger under his starched collar, cleared his throat, then continued, "While I would be most pleased to tie the knot with her, I don't know that I'd be willing to give up my freedom for anyone else."

"Freedom? What freedom? You spend all your waking hours now pouring over my account books." Richard wasn't about to let the bait squirm off his hook this close to catching his fish. "Ten thousand pounds, Perkins. Think on it. That should be more than sufficient cause for you to pursue this arrangement."

He could see from Perkins's face that the money was not what had captured the man's interest. The lady was the issue. Richard should have never pointed Dorina out and painted that vivid picture of the lady's charms. Somewhere along the way Perkins had developed a few romantic notions of his own about the young miss.

"What if I tossed in that cottage near Brighton I inherited a few years back for you and your new bride? Would you be willing to at least meet with this young lady?"

Perkins maintained his solemn frown. "I'll not be promising to marry her?"

"No, all you have to do is meet her. I'll even come with you. If our mystery lady isn't Miss Stevens, then you may back out of the arrangement."

Perkins relaxed. "That seems fair enough."

"Good. Now that we have that settled, when are you to see the horse?"

"The horse?"

"Miss Stevens's dowry was to be the horse which could beat mine at the Summer Festival," Richard reminded him. "You do recall the reasons for this marriage, don't you?"

"Yes, not only am I to get the beautiful Miss Stevens as a bride, but you will pay me the ten thousand pounds the horse would have won in the race."

Richard's gray eyes narrowed at the light that seemed to radiate from Perkins's thin face at the thought of his new bride. His shy little business manager appeared to have shed his previous aversion to the marriage. Richard was hard-pressed to know if he was pleased or miffed at the change. He'd do best to stick to the business at hand.

"And I am to get the horse," he added.

"You get the horse," Perkins repeated, as if in a daze.

Richard could have sworn the man was in danger of lifting his feet off the floor and floating across the room. "Then if that's all, Perkins, I will meet you here this time tomorrow evening to accompany you to the vicarage."

The little man turned and walked to the door. "And I get the cottage near Brighton for me and Miss Stevens."

Damn! The man had lost his crackers. That was the only possible explanation for this sudden case of puppy love. It would have pleased Richard better if the man had looked on his upcoming nuptials as a duty to his family to marry rather than his entrance to heaven.

He had merely thought to find Miss Stevens a husband. A decent man to be sure. One so shy he would but worship her from afar. Certainly not one who thought to cut his own teeth on her innocence.

Dorina sat in the darkened corner of the vicar's study, a heavily veiled black bonnet and shawl concealing her true identity from the two gentlemen entering the room. With a smile on her face she studied their reactions to her grim costume. There was no hiding Mr. Perkins's dismay, nor Lord Gloxbury's surprise, which he quickly replaced with something suspiciously resembling amusement.

"Gentlemen," Harold said in his official manner of introduction. "I would like you to meet the young woman who owns the horse in question."

Richard stepped past his man of business to take the woman's hand. If he hadn't already known it was Miss Stevens, the jasmine perfume would have given her away.

"Such a pleasure to meet someone who recognizes the value of a fast horse and is willing to share his grace and speed with the others of us who admire such animals."

Dorina didn't answer but merely nodded her head, acknowledging her agreement with his assessment of her.

"Miss, ah-h-h . . ." he prompted. She didn't respond to his inquiry, but he could have sworn he could feel the barely suppressed laughter through her gloved fingertips.

What game was this vixen playing now? Didn't she realize he knew who she was the moment he walked into the room? Anyone but Miss Stevens would have shrunk from the sight of his scar.

"You may call me Louise for now," she said, adding a pronounced lilt to her words in an effort to disguise her voice. When he didn't answer, she cocked her head to one side and peered up at him through the dark lace. "I'm surprised that someone as handsome as you, my lord, has escaped the feminine wiles of some pretty miss until now," she said, deliberately mistaking him for the intended bridegroom. "But then, none offered you the fastest horse in all of England to sweeten the offer, did they?"

Harold quickly grabbed Mr. Perkins by the arm. "Lord Gloxbury merely came to meet you, Dor—Louise. On behalf of his man of business," Harold said, pushing the shy man forward. "This is Mr. Perkins. He is the one wishing to marry you."

Dorina slid her hand out of Lord Gloxbury's, then patted the seat beside her. "Come sit here, Mr. Perkins. I wish to discuss horses with you."

The little man tossed Lord Gloxbury a glance that bespoke his panic. "I can't say as how I know much about horses."

"Then you merely wish to marry me for the ten thousand pounds my horse will win for you," she prompted. "That's fair enough."

It all sounded so cold and heartless, and Perkins, who found himself growing quite fond of Miss Stevens, rushed to redeem himself. "My dear Miss Stevens, given the opportunity, I would have married you with or without your horse."

Miss Stevens! Dorina snatched the veil and hat from her face. "How very gracious," she said through clenched teeth. "Miss Stevens, is it? And how did you come to discover my name, Mr. Perkins?"

Although the object of his affections was not looking at him, Silas couldn't hold back the flood of embarrassment at his *faux pas*. "Lord Gloxbury, he . . . well, he told me of your predicament and how if you didn't find a husband soon, you would be forced to marry Lord Humbly. And seeing as how I will have to marry someday—family duty and all that—I agreed to approach you on the subject."

Dorina continued to stare at Richard, but the cold mask of his gaze never wavered. A chill skittered up her spine. It was easy to see why men feared him. Well, he'd not scare her with his frown.

"Tell me something, Mr. Perkins," she asked. "Lord Gloxbury will have to marry someday himself, won't he? I mean family duty and all that."

Silas knew from the sarcasm in her voice he was making a mess of things. Nothing he said to Miss Stevens seemed to come out right. But then, it was very disconcerting to have her staring at Lord Gloxbury that way when she meant her questions for him.

"Lord Gloxbury has no plans of marrying, Miss Stevens. The terrible scar and all," he added in a whisper.

Dorina let her gaze drift back to the little man. "Scar?" she asked. "What does his scar have to do with him not marrying?"

Richard's voice filled the room. "I'll answer that, if you don't mind, Miss Stevens."

When she returned her attention to the earl, the look on his face sapped her response from the tip of her tongue. His eyes were the gray-blue of a winter storm. Never had she seen such anger. Bitterness like the hot melting wax of a burning candle seemed to drip down the length of his hard-muscled body. She trembled as he crossed the room to stand before her.

"I'll have no one's pity, Miss Stevens, nor a wife who shrinks from my touch," he said, running the back of his hand along her cheek. His sad smile mocked the tremors that coursed through her body at his nearness.

"Nor will I have one who lies awake at night dreading the sound of my footsteps should I choose to visit her bed," he added in a hoarse whisper before he strode from the room.

Dorina stood staring at the door long after he left, her heart crying out after him: I would welcome your footsteps, my lord.

The resounding rhythm of Moondancer's hooves pounding down the beaten path broke the early morning silence but failed to drown out Dorina's troubled thoughts. Even though she had no wish for anyone to see her dressed in her father's old riding breeches, Dorina no longer cared who was witness to the stallion's speed. Nothing seemed to matter now. It had been a week since she had seen the earl, and her heart still ached at the memory of his words.

Up until now all she had thought about were her own problems. Not once had she considered that others might have had to live with something far worse than she was to face.

Dorina crouched low over Moondancer's neck and gave him his head. The sudden rush of wind tugged brutally at her unbound hair and brought tears to her eyes as she felt the stallion respond to the rare taste of freedom.

A wonderful combination of power and grace, Moondancer was born to run. With powerful strides he covered the length of the meadow, then turned. Faster and faster they rode until the bushes at the edge of the path became a green velvet ribbon trailing beside them.

All too soon they arrived back at the stables. Dorina reluctantly brought her horse down to a sedate walk. Despite the distance he had carried her, Moondancer remained eager to go again. It was a shame to have such a horse and not have the chance to prove his worth at the Summer Festival.

Since Mr. Perkins, there had been few inquires about the horse. None of them satisfied Harold's standards. As the day of the race grew closer, it looked as if Mr. Perkins would be her choice. She had liked what she had seen of the quiet reserved man but knew in her heart Mr. Perkins would come to regret his decision. Her tendency to take charge couldn't help but smother any attempt he made to put himself forward. She had even tried telling him so, but he had argued that his position as Lord Gloxbury's man of business took up most of his days and that he had no intention of interfering with the running of the small estate Lord Gloxbury intended to settle on him on the occasion of their marriage.

She should have been grateful that Lord Gloxbury was encouraging Mr. Perkins to marry her, but somehow the knowledge only brought a tightening to her chest. But the earl didn't want her pity, she reminded herself as she slipped from Moondancer's back. Returning to Kingsley Manor after all these years had to have dredged up enough unpleasant memories.

"Do you always dress like a stableboy for your morning rides?"

Dorina acknowledged neither Julian's terse words nor his presence but led Moondancer into the stable, forcing Lord Humbly to follow. She handed the reins to a groom.

"My good man," Julian bellowed. "If you would but use the small brain your Maker gave you, you would see Miss Stevens does not need your assistance. But I do. Now tie that horse to the stall and come help me off this brute."

Dorina swirled around. "Moondancer needs to be cooled out. And you, my lord, need to leave."

Julian rode his mount up beside her. With slow deliberation he ran the tip of his riding crop down the side of her slim neck. "Lord, you're beautiful when you're angry."

She snatched the whip from his hand. "And you are disgusting at all times." She broke the whip over her knee, then walked away.

"That's quite some horse you have there, Dorina," he said in an overly loud voice. "I hadn't realized how fast he was . . . until this morning." Julian was pleased to have her stop. Even her stiff back as she turned to him awakened a small measure of lust in him.

Now that he had her undivided attention, Julian lowered his eyes, feigning disinterest. With a deceptive casualness, he pulled his leather riding gloves snug. "I think I shall talk with your parents about adding him to my stables."

"You will be wasting your time, Julian. Moondancer belongs to me."

He eased his mount to the door. "A mere technicality, love!" he shouted over his shoulder. "As your husband, he will soon be mine anyway. I can't see that your parents will object to receiving a generous sum for him beforehand."

From all she had witnessed lately, she feared what he said was true. If her parents hadn't listened to her pleas about not marrying Julian, they would certainly not listen concerning a horse.

Chapter Seven

"You can always sell the horse before he talks with your parents," Lord Gloxbury suggested as he stepped from the shadows at the back of the stables.

Dorina had had about all she could take for one morning. "It is not bad enough that Julian was following me. You had to follow me, also?"

"Only in case you were in need of my services," he said with a nod. "I was out for my morning ride when I caught a glimpse of your uninvited escort."

Why this man always managed to invoke both her gratitude and her anger at the same time was puzzling, but she wasn't about to dwell on it now. "Then you saw Moondancer go through his paces?" she demanded.

Richard spread his arms and smiled. "With such an impressive display of speed, you didn't really expect me to look the other way, did you?"

"It doesn't matter even though he's in the final leg of training. I will tell you the same thing I told Julian. Moondancer is not for sale. He goes to the man who will agree to marry me."

"Lord Humbly offered to marry you," he pointed out as he walked to the edge of the stall where Moondancer was being rubbed down by one of the grooms. "At least, with me the horse would be safe."

Richard circled the stall. "I owned a horse years ago that was a lot like Moondancer," he said. "Challenger had the same speed. And the same grace of form when he ran. A real champion."

Dorina could feel her knees growing weak at the astute comparison. It was plain to see that Lord Gloxbury was checking Moondancer for flaws. She knew he'd find none. Other than his color, gray, Moondancer was a pattern copy of his father—Challenger. Dorina held her breath waiting for him to ask who the sire was.

Dare she hope that he would not ask, but instead would want Moondancer enough to agree to her conditions? With Lord Gloxbury as her intended, she need not hide the engagement.

Having finished his inspection, Richard turned to face her. "I'd like to purchase Moondancer."

Her disappointment lasted but a moment. How dare he play with her this way? He knew why she could not sell.

"So that's it," she said bitterly. "You thought to get the horse but not me."

Richard searched her face. There was no mistaking the anger that tinged her cheeks a becoming shade of pink. He had upset her. With her shoulders thrown back, her hair a tousled mass of black curls, and eyes a deep sea green, she resembled a warrior. He could picture her standing on England's shores fighting Napoleon at the side of her lover.

She should always wear her hair down, he thought. Such a prize should not go to Julian, but how could he make her understand it couldn't be him? It would not be easy

soothing her ruffled pride. Life with him would be one
of seclusion most of the time. He had his investments, his
estates, and his horses. That was his life—one no woman
should be forced to accept and one he could not change.

The green in her eyes darkened noticeably. She was
demanding an answer from him.

"It is not that I don't want you, Dorina. For the thought
has crossed my mind many a time late at night that my
bed but needs you to warm its sheets and drive away the
loneliness. It is that I choose not to take a wife."

She had not realized she was holding her breath until his
answer forced it from her. How dare he say he wanted her
in one breath, then say he will not have her in the next?

"Then you shall not have Moondancer, my lord. I will
marry your Mr. Perkins, and it will be his bed I warm. Then
I will find some way to get Moondancer in your precious
race. Have no doubts, my lord, Moondancer shall beat any
horse you might have in your stables. And I shall take great
pleasure in my husband collecting the ten thousand pounds
from you."

A need he had not felt in years spilled over in his veins as
he watched her walk away. She was beautiful—much like
a spirited mare—and he couldn't help but notice how the
outline of the riding breeches swayed in all the right places,
bringing an embarrassing snugness to his own. He'd pay
ten thousand pounds to own her, the hell with her horse.

Harold set aside his correspondence and faced his guest
across the large oak desk. "I've lain awake for four nights
now, Dorina, and I've decided I can't let you go through
with this."

Dorina may have changed her clothes and tidied her hair,
but the anger that had prompted her decision to marry Mr.
Perkins was still as strong as when she'd shouted her
intentions to Lord Gloxbury.

"You promised, Harold," she said bitterly.

He stood firm. "You haven't seen Mr. Perkins since that
night, have you?"

"Well, no. But what does that have to do with it?" Before

he could answer, Dorina gasped. "He hasn't changed his mind, has he?"

"No, and I doubt that he would." Harold paused. "I think the man fancies himself in love with you now, and I'll not have him hurt."

Dorina sank back against the cushion of her chair. She had not anticipated this. Surely she had expected to be a good wife, but emotions and love—this was something she was not prepared to deal with. Not now. Not with the shame of Lord Gloxbury's rejection so fresh in her heart.

She stood to leave. Harold was right. She couldn't marry Mr. Perkins. But what was she to do about Moondancer? If Harold was to be of any help, she'd have to tell him of her disastrous morning.

Harold listened while she told him of Julian's threat to buy Moondancer and Lord Gloxbury's suggestion that she sell the horse to him instead.

"It would certainly make sense to do as the earl says. If you could verify a sale of the horse before Julian buys him from your father, then he would be safe."

Dorina paced the room several times before answering. "I'll not sell Moondancer to Lord Gloxbury."

"Whyever not? If you would but recall, he has first claim to the horse anyway," Harold pointed out calmly, hoping his frustration with her stubbornness would not show.

The manner in which Dorina carefully avoided facing him told him there was more to it than not wanting to part with the horse. "At times, Dorina, I believe you cause half your problems by refusing to accept the simplest solutions."

She suddenly stopped her pacing of the study and whirled around.

Heaven help him, she'd come up with another scheme.

"Why can't *you* buy Moondancer?"

"Me!" he bellowed. "Wherever am I to find the money it would take to buy a horse like Moondancer?"

"That's just it. I can sell him to you for anything I like."

"Then what are you going to use to entice a young man to run away with you?"

Dorina took her seat again. "If I sell him to you and you can manage to get him in the race, Moondancer will do the rest and we'll be ten thousand pounds richer. With that much money, I need not marry at all. It will surely pay my father's debts with enough left over for my own home."

She looked so happy Harold hated to be the one to point out that, at her age, her parents could still try to force her to marry Lord Humbly, but she had to be told. Her calm acceptance of his reminder was more upsetting than the ranting and raving he had expected.

"Not if I leave England," she finally said, rising from her chair.

Harold didn't like the suggestion any more than he liked the suspicious light in her eyes. There was no end to her schemes, and he was sure he'd like this one even less than the last.

"A friend of mine told me of a ship leaving for America not ten days after the race. Her sister was to be traveling on it. Once I have the money in hand, I will leave."

"A young woman cannot travel that far without a companion."

"But a woman disguised in widow's weeds could," she said with a smug smile on her face as she swept from the room.

With her plan decided, Dorina was determined not to let anything deter her. As soon as she reached home, she sent one of the stableboys back to the vicarage with Moondancer, a signed bill of sale, and a note pointing out that he not waste any time getting Lord Mayberry to choose the horse for the race.

Next she turned to her neglected stack of correspondence and began writing her notes of acceptance to several invitations. With the Summer Festival less than three weeks away, the entire countryside had taken to entertaining the unexpected London guests who had come for the race. Her friend Lucy Melbrook's tea later in the afternoon would mark the first of many engagements she would place on her social calendar. It would be her way of saying good-bye to all her friends.

Having finished her notes, she handed them to the footman for delivery. He in turn handed them to the butler, but not before taking the liberty of scanning the folded missives and passing on the information gleaned to Lord Gloxbury's liveried footman who waited down the lane.

Lucy Melbrook's staid butler, Carlton, opened the double oak doors to the parlor, then stepped aside for the earl to pass. Once the notable had paused at the threshold, Carlton threw back his shoulders and in the sober tone of his profession announced the arrival of Richard Michaels, Earl of Gloxbury.

Dorina choked on her sip of tea as Lord Gloxbury stepped across the room to his hostess. Her *faux pas* was nothing compared to the gasps of the other five ladies perched on various chairs around Lucy Melbrook's parlor.

It was the first time Dorina had seen Lord Gloxbury in anything but tweeds, and the effect was devastating to her fragile peace of mind. She found herself taking a deep steadying breath.

The snowy white linen of his intricately tied cravat stood out in bold contrast to the otherwise somber blackness of his attire, calling attention to the silken waves of his thick black hair. Even the coldness of his blue eyes could not detract from the savage handsomeness of his tanned face.

Every eye in the room appeared to follow Lord Gloxbury's pantherlike grace. It was no wonder, Dorina thought, for her own heart appeared to have lodged in her throat with her tea.

Two chairs down she could hear Lucy stumbling over her words of welcome. It was obvious her friend was also smitten with Lord Gloxbury's overpowering maleness.

Suddenly Dorina no longer wanted to share Richard with her friends. Lord Gloxbury was hers. The thought caught Dorina completely off guard. When had this happened? It was disconcerting to realize the cruel knife of jealousy could stab so swiftly at someone's heart without prior warning.

Like a lion protecting her only cub, Dorina let her gaze travel around the room. By the time she reached Lucy, her concern was not for who might be trying to capture Lord Gloxbury's attention, but whether Richard had noticed the rudeness of those who stared and whispered behind their hands.

One glance at the taut muscles playing along the hard line of his stubborn jaw told her he had missed nothing. His blue eyes met hers, and she knew why he'd come. It was his way of showing her that this was what a young lady should expect if he were to marry her. It was easy to see that he only meant to come, make his point, and then leave. He always had to be so bloody right.

Well, she'd not let anyone off that easily. Both Lord Gloxbury and her friends needed a lesson in manners.

She patted the cushion beside her. "Fetch yourself a cup of tea, Lord Gloxbury, then join me here. I, for one, am dying of curiosity about this grand race of yours, and I'm certain there are others who would like to know a few of the details."

"Oh, my, yes," Lucy said, pleased that someone had helped remind her of her duties as hostess. "Even my dear George has been hoping to secure a position in the race."

Dorina carefully avoided Lord Gloxbury's frown as he sat down beside her. She gave her tea a brisk stir. "I hope he has more luck than I. Why, I have written Lord Mayberry no less than three times about my Moondancer, and he has yet to answer."

"You didn't, Dorina!" Lucy gasped. "Whatever will your parents say when they hear that you have tried to enter your horse?"

"It does not matter. I sold Moondancer to the vicar today." There, it was out. Lord Gloxbury no longer had a reason for pursuing her.

"I can't say I'm sorry," Lucy said with a sigh. "That horse frightened me beyond belief."

"Yes, a wise decision," Richard said, then lowered his voice and mumbled, "Sort of like eating your cake and having it, too."

Dorina grabbed up her spoon and danced it across her cup of tea again. "I believe Harold plans on leaving for London first thing in the morning. Seems Lord Mayberry and Harold's parents have known each other for years."

Richard sat down his cup and stood. "I wish to thank you for inviting me to tea, Lady Melbrook," he said with a gracious bow before turning to take his leave of Miss Stevens.

"I shall stop by the vicarage on my way home," he told her. "If the reverend is planning on racing Moondancer, he might be in need of a recommendation from me. Good day, Miss Stevens."

Dorina paced the length of Harold's study and back. "He wouldn't intervene for me, yet the moment you have the horse, he hands you a recommendation."

Harold was used to Dorina's temper and knew it was best to merely sit and wait for her anger to cool.

"You should have seen the smile he gave me when he said it," she ranted at him. "I wanted to rip it off his face, toss it to the floor, and stomp on it."

"Why are you so upset?" he asked her calmly. "You even said he accused you of still owning Moondancer, despite the sale. Doesn't it sound as if he did this for you, also?"

Dorina sank down in one of the leather chairs, all the fight gone out of her. "He merely means to ease his guilty conscience for not marrying me."

"Damn, Dorina! You didn't ask him to, did you?"

"Vicars shouldn't curse," she pointed out.

"Neither should they remain silent and not confess their past crimes—such as who really owns Moondancer. Now tell me you didn't ask Lord Gloxbury to marry you."

Dorina dropped her gaze. "I suppose I may have brought it up," she mumbled.

"May have brought it up?" he urged.

Dorina glared at him. "You needn't look so self-righteous, Harold. The noble earl turned me down," she added bitterly. "He informed me he does not plan on taking a wife."

Ah-hah! thought Harold. So that was it. After all these years of breaking hearts, Dorina had finally managed to lose her own. And if he wasn't mistaken, the earl had a few of Cupid's arrows sticking from his, also.

Chapter Eight

Dorina pulled the mother-of-pearl-handled hairbrush through the tangles of her hair and winced at the pain. It was her own fault, she told herself. Harold had found a groom willing to ride Moondancer, but she couldn't seem to let go of the duty. The horse had been too much a part of her for too long. With her parents always in London, Rosebud, then Moondancer, had been everything to Dorina. It was a tie hard to break.

Besides, it gave her something to think about other than Lord Gloxbury. Over the last week he seemed to have accepted an invitation to every function that Dorina had. The entire neighborhood was abuzz with the news of his attendances, and it wasn't long before the success of one's party was being measured on whether the Elusive Earl had made an appearance or not.

Dorina would have been pleased to point out to Lord Gloxbury how his scheme to prove the extent of his ineligibility as a husband had appeared to have backfired if his continued presence hadn't added to the distress of her already wounded heart. Even learning that Harold had secured a position in the race had not lifted her spirits. She decided that love was hell—and God was dealing out a double portion of it just for her.

Having brushed her curls into some semblance of order, Dorina rang for her maid. She would wear her new pink gown today. The one with the silver ribbons. Lucy was having a luncheon down by the lake today, and Lord Gloxbury was invited. She had lain awake most of the night planning how she would sit all prim and proper in

Lucy's new white fan chair. The high back would provide the perfect backdrop for her new gown. She had fantasized for days about how beautiful he would think her. Lord Gloxbury may insist that he did not want her for his wife, but she was darn well going to show him what his stubbornness was costing him.

Dorina pulled the bell cord again. Where was that maid of hers? If she didn't come soon, Dorina would be late, and how was she to get the white fan chair if she was late?

She was almost at the point of dressing herself when her maid hurried into the room. "Lord Humbly's here, miss," she said breathlessly. "He's waiting downstairs."

"Did you tell him I was on my way out?"

"Yes, miss, but he says he knows it and is waiting to take you up in his carriage."

Dorina held her arms up so Tess could slip the gown over her head. "He can wait forever," she said from inside the folds. "I can't be late for this party. I have to get that chair."

Tess frowned. "Miss Lucy's giving away a chair, miss?"

"Never mind, Tess. Help me with this sash. I want it tied just so."

Tess frowned at the provocative manner in which Dorina had crisscrossed the silver ribbons on the bodice of her gown, boldly outlining her generous breasts. It wasn't that her mistress didn't usually take pains with her toilette, but it was unlike her to call attention to herself in this way. Something was definitely in the wind.

Following Dorina's instructions, Tess pulled the ribbons tight, crossed them again in back, then brought each one forward. With a snort of disapproval, she handed them back to Dorina.

Dorina ignored her censure and tied the ends into a generous bow under one breast. While the effect was sure to get the attention of every male present, she only cared about one. Lord Gloxbury. If it captured his attention, the censure of the other ladies present did not matter.

After a final look in the mirror to see that all was as brazen as she hoped, Dorina grabbed up her reticule and gloves from the bed and hurried out the door. With Lucy's house twenty minutes away, she hurried down the stairs.

"My, my. What have we here?"

Julian's voice stopped her dead. She had forgotten all about him—and the spectacles.

"Oh, hell!" she mumbled as she turned and ran back up the stairs. Why did Julian have to pick now to come calling? She had a chair to get to.

And now he had heard her cursing. Whatever was happening to her lately? Ever since her parents had called her to account for it, the words seemed to be sprinkled throughout her conversations like pepper on one's eggs.

Her patience sorely tried, Dorina grabbed up the spectacles from among her combs and brushes, propped them up on her nose, then left her room again. Her progress down the stairs was much slower the second time. Every other step or so, she was forced to stop and lift the wire frames to see the steps.

"What do you want, Julian?" she almost shouted by the time she reached the last one.

He stared at the thick spectacles and cringed. If he didn't know what she looked like without them, he would be tempted to cry off. Once they were married, he'd make sure the things got lost.

"I came after my horse," he finally said. "He's not in the stable. Where have you put him?"

"I've put him nowhere, Julian. You'll have to ask the man who owns him now."

"I own him!" he bellowed. "And I demand that you tell me where he is."

Dorina ignored his shouting and glanced at the hall clock over the top of her spectacles. Drats! The chair was sure to be gone now. She tapped her foot impatiently.

"Do you have a bill of sale, Julian?"

He smiled smugly. He had expected her to ask and carried it in his coat pocket. "Here," he said, whipping it out.

Dorina lifted the glasses to have a look. "I'd be going back to London and asking Father for your money back if

I were you. This paper says he sold you Moondancer on the twenty-fourth. And I happen to know we didn't own him on the twenty-fourth."

"What do you mean?"

She tossed the paper back to him, then settled the spectacles back on her nose. "I sold Moondancer to the vicar on the twenty-third. Now, good day, Julian. I have to hurry. I have an engagement with a chair."

Dorina found herself besieged with offers to be escorted down to the lake, where Lucy's servants had set up tables laden with such delicacies as to tempt the most jaded of appetites. While on any other occasion she would not have minded, Dorina had another objective in mind. Ruthlessly she selected Matthew Huxley, Lord Carford, a young man from London, then sent the others on their way.

"Damn!" she silently cursed when she reached the lake. Lady Margaret had her chair.

It took Lord Carford a moment to come down from his euphoric cloud to realize that the beautiful young lady on his arm had said something and he had failed to respond. After standing outside the garden doors for the last twenty minutes in hopes of being her escort, he had been unforgivably inattentive. In humble apology he bent his head close to hers.

"Pardon?" he asked politely, hoping she would be of a mind to repeat it.

"What does she need that chair for?" Dorina demanded.

Lord Huxley followed her gaze. He could see nothing amiss with Lady Margaret's occupancy of the chair in question, but then sometimes there was no understanding the whims of women.

"To sit on?" he asked innocently.

Dorina shot him a withering glance. "She doesn't need that chair. She has already brought Thomas up to scratch."

She tightened her hold on his arm and nudged him forward. "Please ask her to move."

His heart sank to the heels of his new Hession boots. Ever since arriving in Gloxbury a week ago, he had been attempting to capture the lovely Miss Stevens's attention. Now he had it and was on the brink of losing it, for he had no idea of how he was to go about doing as she asked. Honesty required that he tell her so.

Dorina was not to be put off so easily. "You need merely to say you need it for one of those elderly ladies standing over there."

Embarrassment warmed his collar. "But . . ." he started to protest, then let it drop.

"Never mind," Dorina snapped when she saw Lord Gloxbury step through the garden doors and proceed along the path to the lake. If she was going to do something, it would have to be quickly.

"Merely follow me, and whatever I say, you need only agree."

Before he could say yea or nay, she stooped down and dipped her finger into one of the flowerbeds bordering the lake, then was off. Matthew had to hurry to catch up.

"Good afternoon, Lady Margaret," Dorina said so sweetly that Matthew wondered if his hearing was in need of attention.

"Miss Stevens."

"I'm reluctant to bring this to your attention, but I feel you would never forgive me if I let you continue without pointing out that you have a most unbecoming smudge on your cheek."

"I do?" Lady Margaret all but screeched as she reached up to cover the spot.

"Oh, no, not there," Dorina said sweetly. "Here." With that she placed a large mark on Lady Margaret's porcelain cheek. Having finished, she glanced at her glove in dismay.

"Oh, my!" she exclaimed. "Why, I have managed to soil my glove, too."

Fearing to attract undue attention, Lady Margaret leaned forward in the chair. "Did you get it all?" she asked in a whisper.

Dorina tossed a glance over her shoulder at Lord Huxley. "What do you think, Lord Huxley?"

The man didn't say anything. He just stood there staring down at the smudge on Lady Margaret's cheek.

"It's most noticeable, isn't it?" Dorina asked sweetly as she stepped on the toe of his boot.

Lord Huxley came out of his shock and swallowed the lump that had suddenly risen in his throat. "Yes-s," he somehow managed to answer.

Dorina wanted to swat him for his lack of enthusiasm. She could see Lord Gloxbury making his way through the guests. If she didn't get the chair soon, she might as well forget it.

She placed her hand on Lord Huxley's arm. "Don't you think you should escort Lady Margaret back to the house so she can use the powder room?"

"Oh, yes. Yes." He extended his arm to the young lady. "Please allow me to escort you?"

Dorina restrained herself from diving into the chair when Lady Margaret stood. She waited until they had gone a few steps up the path. "That's it," she said to herself, then sank into the chair only moments before Lord Gloxbury walked up to her. Drats, he didn't even give her enough time to arrange her skirts and strike just the right pose.

"Good afternoon, Miss Stevens," he said.

His husky voice sent chills up Dorina's arms. Not trusting her own voice under such conditions, she merely nodded her acknowledgment, then settled herself back in the chair.

"You're looking exceptionally beautiful this afternoon," he added.

Dorina caught herself before uttering "it's the chair." Demurely she lowered her eyes. "It must be—"

"The glasses!" he exclaimed. "You aren't wearing those atrocious glasses."

Dorina glared up at him. Damn! How was she to get him to think romantic thoughts when he made her forget what clever thing it was she was going to say.

"Lord Humbly is not expected," she said in her coldest manner.

"Ah, yes, our nemesis," he said with equal sarcasm. "No need to look the aging spinster if Lord Humbly is absent."

Richard's attention was drawn to the new arrivals. "You're certain he's not coming?"

Dorina did not like the look in Lord Gloxbury's eyes. "Why?" she asked, a knot forming in her chest at the suspicion she already knew the answer.

"He's making his way around the luncheon tables now."

"Hellfire and damnation!" she cursed to herself.

Richard raised a dark brow. "Hellfire and damnation? I thought you were giving up cursing."

Dorina wasn't in the mood for niceties. She had come to make one last attempt to get Lord Gloxbury to reconsider marrying her, and Julian's presence was going to ruin everything.

"Well, you needn't look at me like that, Lord Gloxbury. If they can preach it in the church services, I can say it to myself. Besides which, if your parents were forcing you to marry that cruel . . . inhuman . . ."

"Bastard?" he offered softly in her ear as Lord Humbly stepped up to them.

"Exactly!" Dorina answered with a conspiratorial grin at the murderous frown on Julian's red face.

"You left before I could ask if you wanted to accompany me in my new carriage, my dear," Julian stated coldly.

Even though Richard had promised himself he would not get involved in this matter, Lord Humbly's tone was too much like the one he had used when Richard had had to deal with him. Odd how he resented Julian's high-handed treatment all the more when it was directed toward Dorina.

"Why would Miss Stevens wish to ride with you when I had already asked her to accompany me?" He knelt on the grass beside Dorina and gazed lovingly up into her eyes. "Dory appreciates a good team of horses, don't you, love?"

Dorina couldn't have answered if her life depended on it. All she could do was return his gaze as she felt herself sink deeper and deeper into the clear blue depths of his beautiful eyes.

Julian had never been accused of being blind. Neither had any of his friends, he thought, fuming to notice that others had stopped their conversations to observe his byplay with Lord Gloxbury. He had heard of Gloxbury's growing popularity, but he had hoped the rumors were false.

"She also appreciates the touch of a handsome man," he returned smugly, wishing the barb were sharp enough to slice through Lord Gloxbury's other cheek.

The gasp of those listening was unmistakable. They were horrified at Julian's rudeness. Dorina could see Richard's self-control slip a notch. While her own hatred for Julian knew no bounds, she'd not let Richard be drawn into her fight. And there was only one way to turn Julian's hatred from Richard. She must direct it back to herself.

Dorina reached out and took Richard's cold fingers. She squeezed them until he returned his attention to her. "You're so right, Julian," she cooed, keeping her eyes on Richard. "I do appreciate the touch of a handsome man."

Julian minced angrily in front of her. "Very well, you may flirt now, Dorina, but after our engagement is announced tomorrow night at the ball, I shall have more say over those you choose to bestow your glances on."

Richard squeezed her hand in warning. "After Moondancer wins the race tomorrow, Dorina shall be a woman of independent means, Julian. She will no longer need her life to be guided by the financial purse strings of her parents."

Julian was momentarily taken back by the news. "But she sold Moondancer."

"To the vicar," Dorina added. "To be given over after the race."

His hatred was like a white fire waiting to consume her if she stepped too close.

"Your parents will never allow you to refuse me," Julian said smugly before turning back to Richard. "Just remember, if she wins, I win. And the ten thousand pounds will make a nice dowry to collect on my wedding day."

Chapter Nine

Dorina stood quietly the next morning while Tess slipped the white gown trimmed with small embroidered roses over her black curls. Her mind kept returning to Julian's odd comment. How would Julian win if Moondancer did?

Would her horse winning the race today truly cost Richard more than just the ten thousand pounds? She had tried questioning Lord Gloxbury further after Julian had walked away, but he had merely laughed and said not to worry. Julian was more than likely referring to the fact that Richard's pride was on the finish line also.

While Lord Gloxbury's explanation seemed logical, Dorina couldn't shake the feeling that there was more to it than he was telling her. Was she perhaps making more of it than she should? After all, Julian was always one to go out of his way to try to prick someone's pride.

"How about these for your hair, miss?" Tess asked for the second time.

Dorina glanced at her maid's reflection in the cheval glass. In her hands Tess held up two clasps for Dorina's hair. The tiny cluster of ruby and glass beads hung in varied lengths from the miniature bouquets of tiny summer rosebuds, cleverly disguising the small vial of water needed to keep the flowers fresh on such a warm day.

"How lovely, Tess! Wherever did you get them?"

"Lord Gloxbury sent them over with this note."

Dorina grabbed the missive and ripped open the seal. "Oh," she said in disappointment. "He's merely wishing me luck in the race today."

"Sit down now, miss, so I can put these in proper," Tess said as she held out the chair. Dorina plopped down. "And don't look so sad," she added with a big smile on her face. "I happen to know your parents received a note from the earl, too."

Dorina spun around in her chair. "What did it say, Tess?"

"I'll tell you if you promise to sit still. Lord Humbly's coach should be here any minute, and you don't want to be late. That man's liable to take off the footman's head if his horses have to stand."

"What was in the letter, Tess?" she almost shouted.

Tess glanced at the door, then leaned close to whisper, "He's invited your parents and you to sit in his box for the races."

Dorina thought her heart would burst. Surely that meant he had changed his mind about asking for her hand.

"Hurry, Tess. We mustn't make Julian wait."

"You cannot make me sit with that awful man!" Amelia Stevens screeched at her husband.

Maurice Stevens sighed as if the weight of the world were on his shoulders. Her constant nagging always had a disastrous effect on his ability to tie his cravat.

"How many times must I say it? Until Julian pays the IOUs Lord Gloxbury holds, you would do best to humor him. You must admit, he has been most patient with me. Not once has he brought up the outstanding notes."

Amelia dropped down on the edge of the bed. "Oh, why hasn't Julian just paid off the man so we won't be haunted by his polite presence?"

Maurice's hand slipped and the tie ends of his starched neckcloth fell from around his neck—a rumpled heap. Another one ruined.

"Probably because our daughter stubbornly refuses to acknowledge this engagement. If you could but—"

"You'll not lay this at my feet," Amelia snapped. "I warned you not to gamble with the man. From everything I've heard, he has the devil's own luck." Amelia's gaze dropped to her gloves for a moment before she met her husband's eye.

"You don't suppose the man cheats, do you?"

Amelia had never seen her husband's face turn that particular shade of red before. Why, he had even crushed the new neckcloth he had just picked up. "That's it, isn't it? The man cheats at cards."

Maurice grabbed her arms and shook her. "Don't you dare say that to a soul. Not only would Lord Gloxbury never cheat at cards, he would put a bullet through anyone who suggested he did."

"Oh," was all Amelia could get past the frantic beating of her heart. How had she ever forgotten about Lord Gloxbury's skill with his pistols?

Bright colored silk covered the various boxes that lined the starting point of the race. Dorina did not know how Lord Gloxbury managed to arrange it, but when the horses were brought out for the race, her family was seated in the earl's box. A footman served them refreshments and apologized for Lord Gloxbury's absence. The earl was giving last-minute instructions to his groom.

Amelia leaned across Dorina to talk to her husband. "If I knew the earl was not going to be here, I would have invited Julian to join us."

Dorina ignored her mother's pointed rebuke and watched the grooms lead the horses and riders down the path and back. Everyone was careful to avoid the white line of powder across the field where the horses were to begin the race.

"Isn't that Moondancer, Dorina?" Amelia asked, pointing her parasol at the big gray stallion.

"Yes, Mama."

"It was a shame you sold him. He looks as if he might have a chance of winning this race."

Dory raised her eyes heavenward and bit back the curse that came to mind. "You forget, Mama, if I had not sold him, he would still not be mine. Remember you meant to sell him to Julian."

"So I did," she said. "So I did. And Julian was most upset to lose him, I might point out. You would have done well to consider that if Julian were to race Moondancer and win, the ten thousand would have been yours, too."

Dorina did not like the way her father stared at her but didn't say a word. It was as if something had just now occurred to him. Perhaps it was her guilty conscience that made her wonder if he knew why she had sold the horse to Harold. She was grateful for Lord Gloxbury's arrival. It served to distract her father from whatever train his thoughts had taken.

"I hope Samuel made you comfortable," he said as he took a seat between Dorina and her father.

"Oh, quite," Maurice said, but Amelia kept her lips stubbornly pursed and said nothing.

A trumpet blew and all eyes turned to the lineup of horses. Dorina held her breath as the flag was held aloft. This was it. If Moondancer won, she would be off to America. Away from Julian's threats—and Richard's arms.

The flag dropped. A deafening roar rose from the crowd as the horses plunged across the starting line. Down the meadow they went, neck and neck. Everyone rose to their feet. Standing on the tip of her toes, Dorina saw three horses take the lead. Moondancer was not among them.

Disappointment washed over her. She felt someone touch her hand and turned to find the earl's head next to hers.

"Do not worry, Dory, at that pace they will quickly tire themselves out. Our grooms will hold their mounts back. It is always best to conserve their speed until it is needed at the finish."

His breath on her cheek kindled a fire deep inside her that had nothing to do with the warm day. What would it be like to wake up next to him in the mornings—to be held in his arms at night? Her heart picked up a beat at the unladylike thoughts that had taken wing.

What would she do once she left England? In all of America there would be no one for her. After falling under the earl's spell, Dorina found that all men had paled in his presence. If only this invitation to view the race could mean more—if only it could mean that he wanted her as much as she wanted him.

A roar from the crowd brought Dorina back to reality. "They're coming in together," echoed and reechoed through the crowd.

"It looks as if you might lose, Michaels," Julian said as he sauntered up to the earl's box.

"The race isn't over yet, Bromly."

Dorina glanced from one adversary to the other. Hate seemed to hang thick in the air like a heavy fog, choking the life out of everyone.

"It's the vicar's horse!" someone shouted. "The vicar's horse be the fastest in all England."

"Did you see that, Dory?" Harold asked, running up to grab her hand and pull her out of the door to the box. "Moondancer won by a nose!"

Dorina looked back over her shoulder. The earl and Julian seemed to be in deep discussion about something that appeared to please Julian to no end. She tried to catch Richard's eye, but whatever Julian was saying to him had put that cold shuttered look back on the earl's face. Dorina knew it had cost Lord Gloxbury ten thousand pounds, but she had hoped he would stand beside her and share in her happiness.

Harold tugged at her arm. "Let's go collect our prize, Dory."

"But the earl," she said as he led her away. "I don't think he's pleased."

Harold's eyes followed hers. "I don't know why he'd be upset. If it hadn't been for his putting in a word with Lord Mayberry, Moondancer would not have been running in the race."

"He knew Moondancer might beat his horse, didn't he?"

"That's the way I see it. Jolly good sportsman, isn't he?"

Dorina stopped. "But it cost him ten thousand pounds."

"Cost him more than that was what I heard."

"What do you mean?"

"I heard the earl stood to lose Hawk to Julian if a horse beat his."

Dorina couldn't let that happen, even if it meant she would have to marry Julian. His horses were all that mattered to Richard. She broke away and ran back to her chair.

"I didn't win!" she shouted. "I didn't win!"

Amelia glanced around her in embarrassment at the commotion her daughter was making.

"Whatever are you shouting about, child?" Amelia said. "Of course you didn't win. You sold Moondancer to the vicar."

"No, I didn't sell Moondancer," she said, keeping her eyes on the earl. "Moondancer was never mine to sell. I bred Rosebud to Challenger without the earl's permission."

From the screech and the thud, Dorina knew her mother had collapsed in a faint. Her father would have to deal with her now. She couldn't let Julian take Hawk from Richard.

"Moondancer legally belongs to Lord Gloxbury," she stated.

Julian raised his voice in protest. "This cannot be! You put Dorina up to this, Michaels."

"You would call Dorina a liar?"

The deadly look in Lord Gloxbury's eyes kept Julian from answering.

Richard tipped Dorina's chin until she was forced to meet his gaze. He looked deep into her eyes. She was giving up everything for him.

"I suggest you go home, Julian," he said, keeping his eyes on Dorina. "Then pack your things before my men do it for you. Five years is a long time to be without your favorite boots."

Julian's face burned red. "But you can't do this," Julian warned. "You lost!"

Richard didn't argue but raised his hand to summon his men. "Please show Lord Humbly home. I wouldn't want him to miss his ship to India."

When Julian was out of sight, Richard returned his attention to Dorina. "I wondered when you were going to tell me."

"You knew all the time?"

"Not at first. I'd almost forgotten the report of my groom seeing two children leading a gray mare down the road late one night. After all, five years is a long time. That and the unmistakable lines that marked the colt as having been Challenger's son."

Dorina stepped closer. "I'm sorry I deceived you," she said, staring deep into his eyes. She knew she was going to lose him, and it nearly broke her heart.

"I don't plan on claiming my rights to the colt, Dory. You and Harold proved to be better breeders than my man. None of Challenger's other colts come close to the speed I saw in Moondancer today. The ten thousand pounds is yours."

Her joy was short-lived when he turned and walked away. She had lost him.

She didn't argue when Harold took her arm and helped her into the carriage that was to take them home. Her mother sat in the opposite seat and glared at her. Dorina started to say she was sorry for all the embarrassment she had caused them but decided it would do no good. Her mother was not of a forgiving nature.

Harold signaled the coachman, then climbed in beside her. She thought her heart would break as something seemed to die inside her.

They had just reached the edge of the grounds when the coach rolled to a stop and the door opened. Richard stood outside.

"Don't forget to post the banns this Sunday, Harold," he said with a broad grin.

"You have asked her parents?"

Dorina felt a knife tear at her heart. Lord Gloxbury was getting married after all—but not to her.

"I think they'll agree. Want do you think, Dory?"

"Me?" she asked. How was she to know what he said? She could hear almost nothing past the terrible ripping of her heart.

"Our marriage."

"Now, see here," Amelia squealed. "We will say who our daughter is to marry."

For the first time in his life Maurice decided he would have his say. "Shut up, Amelia, and let him talk."

Richard tossed the scraps of paper in Mr. Stevens's lap. "Your notes, sir. The way I see it, if you could sell your daughter to Lord Humbly, you could sell her to me for the same sum. At least with me your daughter will be loved and cherished, for I plan to fulfill all her summer dreams."

A tear slipped down Dorina's cheek. "Damn! It's about time."

Richard shook his head. "Hold up on the banns, Harold. My housekeeper will have to supervise the making of a large batch of soap for this young lady's mouth before I'll tie the knot."

HOG HEAVEN

Ann Carberry

Chapter One

Confusion, California 1878

"Loralie! You're not listening to me!"

Loralie Davis looked up from the bread dough she was kneading. She used the back of her right hand to push her falling blond hair out of her eyes and left a long streak of flour along her lightly tanned cheek.

The tall, broad-shouldered man wore a familiar frustrated expression. His hat brim was gripped in both hands, his curly brown hair flopped over his forehead, and his brown eyes were locked on her. Only the frown on his lips marred an otherwise *very* handsome face.

"Of course I'm listening, Gabe." She smiled and he sucked in his breath. "Don't I always?"

He mumbled something she couldn't quite catch and then went on with his lecture. Loralie smiled to herself and went back to kneading the dough. He meant well, she knew, but Gabe just didn't understand that money and success were simply not important to her. With Gabe's deep voice echoing in the background, Loralie raised her gaze and glanced quickly around her little kitchen.

The paint was chipping, and some of the garishly flowered wallpaper was bubbling and peeling off the walls—and still she loved it. The battered sink and creaky pump handle, the scarred counter, and even the table she was working on now, with the initials of long-grown children carved into the top. Sunshine spilled through the shiny windows, and a hot summer breeze lifted the starched white curtains over the tiny potted flowers on the windowsill.

She didn't need a big, fancy house like Gabe's. All she needed was this little farm. This one little corner of the world where she could decide how things would be done.

Gabe groaned. "Loralie, you're doing it again."

She shook herself and smiled sheepishly at her neighbor. "I *am* sorry, Gabe."

His full lips twisted, and his black brows rose over sharp brown eyes.

"I *am*. Really." With a flick of her wrists she opened a clean dish towel and laid it atop the dough. "Would you like some lemonade? I have to let this rise again anyway before I bake it. . . ."

Gabe sighed. Just once he wished that misty, dreamy-eyed expression she wore so often meant that she was thinking of him. But he knew better. "All right, Loralie. Lemonade."

She grinned and ushered him out through the front parlor and onto the wide porch. "You sit here in the shade, and I'll be back in a shake."

The screen door slammed behind her. Gabe shook his head, disgusted. What was wrong with him, anyhow? He owned the biggest ranch in this part of the country. His face wouldn't win any prizes, but it wouldn't exactly stop a train, either! Plenty of money, fine home, didn't drink, and he only cussed when he was really pushed. He slapped his hat against his thigh. Why the *hell* ain't she interested?

He muttered a curse under his breath and crossed the porch gingerly. He didn't much care for the loud creaks and groans the wood was making. Hell, the place was falling apart around her lovely ears, and she didn't even notice! If she wasn't careful . . . if she didn't take *some* of his advice, this ol' place was going to hurt her! That thought had been giving him nightmares for months.

Carefully he sat down on one of the tiny chairs clustered around an even smaller table. Propping his booted feet up on the porch rail, he stared across the road at his own place.

Just a few hundred yards separated the Curran ranch from the Davis farm, but it might as well have been miles. Even from here Gabe could make out the well-made, man-size furniture set out on the veranda that wound completely around his two-story home. The pale blue house with sparkling white trim fairly glittered in the hot afternoon sun. Two giant elm trees in front and a matching pair in back tossed splotches of shade over the structure, and he knew that inside, the house would be deliciously cool.

Gabe shifted uncomfortably and wiped his dark blue bandanna over the back of his neck. Not like Loralie's place. He was willing to swear that the damn cabin caught every bit of summer sun and hugged it to itself greedily. And the way the house was situated, it didn't get the strong cross breezes his did when the windows were thrown open.

Why the hell was she so blasted determined to hold on to the place? Lord knows, he told himself, he'd done everything he could to try to make it easier on her, but she refused to listen! Every time he tried to talk to her about paying off her bank note, she simply brushed his concerns aside and said that she would take care of everything. If he knew what was good for him, he'd just back off and let the bank foreclose.

But if the bank took away her farm, Loralie would have to leave. And he couldn't stand that.

He squinted up at the cloudless summer sky. Hell, if they didn't get some rain pretty soon, he told himself, it might not only be Loralie losing her place.

The screen door swung open with a complaining screech, and Gabe shot to his feet.

"Oh, please, Gabe. Sit down." She quickly crossed the few feet separating them and seated herself on the chair opposite him. "It's much too hot to be jumping up and down."

He let his gaze wander over her lazily. Long tendrils of her soft, golden-blond hair fell from the knot on top of her head and lay alongside her heart-shaped face. Her wide green eyes were set beneath delicately arched brows and her full pink lips were curved in a smile. The collar of her pale peach shirt was unbuttoned and the fabric folded back, displaying an enticing deep vee of golden brown flesh. Only one more button stood guard over her high, firm breasts, and Gabe had to force himself to look away.

She handed him the tall glass and watched as he tipped it up and drained the lemonade in a rush. The long line of his throat drew her eyes down to the open collar of his sweat-stained blue work shirt. Warmth that had nothing to do with the heat of the day filled her. Try as she might, Loralie couldn't ignore the feelings Gabe Curran stirred in her. But she wasn't about to give in to them.

Ever since she'd come to the farm, Gabe had proved himself a good friend. And a terrible distraction. Having him so close all of the time was beginning to wear on Loralie's nerves. Especially when he looked at her like she was a prize turkey at Thanksgiving.

She took a long gulp of her lemonade and tore her gaze away from Gabe's strong suntanned profile. Instead, she looked out over her very own yard. Hard to believe it had only been six months since Aunt Agatha had died and left the place to her. She shook her head. It seemed to her as though she'd been on her little farm forever.

Sadly, Aunt Agatha would never know just how much her legacy had meant to Loralie. It had come at a time when she'd needed it desperately. Agatha had made it possible for Loralie to leave San Francisco and live her own life. Make her own decisions. Here in the little town of Confusion, California, there were no Patrick Terwilligers to tell her what to do. And that was exactly the way she wanted it.

Her fingers tightened around her glass, and she made a deliberate effort to push all thoughts of the past from her mind. She wouldn't let even the *thought* of Patrick ruin this day for her.

"What are you thinking?"

Loralie's gaze shifted back to Gabe and found him staring at her in a way that sent a tremor of longing shooting through her body. For just a moment she allowed herself to bask in his obvious admiration. Not for the first time Loralie wished that things could have been different between them.

Quickly she straightened up. No point in wishing. She wasn't about to let a man rule her life again, and if Gabe Curran was unwilling to remain strictly a friend, so be it.

"I wasn't thinking anything in particular, I'm afraid," she

said and pretended not to notice his sigh of disappointment. "But I *am* worried about my garden. . . ." She stood up and walked past him to the edge of the porch. Leaning on the rail, she looked out at her vegetable patch. She'd planted the seeds only a couple of months before, and now she was beginning to harvest a few of the more eager plants.

"Why?" Gabe's voice came from directly beside her. He had the most disconcerting habit of sneaking up on a person.

She moved away a bit. "Why what?"

He took a deep breath and expelled it in a rush. "Why are you worried about it?" He waved one hand at the seemingly flourishing patch of earth. "Looks fine to me."

"Right now, yes." She chewed at her lip. "But we need rain."

"Huh!" Gabe snorted, turned around, and leaned his behind against the porch rail. "That's what I've been trying to tell you, Loralie! At least, partly. Don't you *ever* listen?"

She smiled and shrugged. Loralie wasn't about to tell him that the *last* time she'd listened to a man, she'd lost every cent she had in the world, as well as any faith she might have had in men.

Gabe sighed. "A well. I told you not a half hour ago that you should let my men dig you a well. Then you wouldn't have to worry about carting water out to your plants or whether it rains or not."

"Oh," Loralie said softly, "I don't think that will be necessary, Gabe. It's sure to rain soon." She looked out over her property. "Besides, I'd like to leave the land as it is. I like it just fine. And it's good for me, carrying water out to the garden."

"And you don't want a fence around it, either, I suppose?"

She laughed. "Of course not. That would be such a bother."

"Maybe, but it would keep the animals out." Gabe stretched his long legs out in front of him and crossed his booted feet at the ankles.

"Why would I want to do that?" She looked at him and smiled. "Animals have to eat, too. There's plenty for all of us."

Gabe slammed his fist down against the side of the rail. "Dammit, Loralie, don't you understand? You've *got* to take care of this place, or it won't be able to take care of you!"

"I know but—"

He threw his hands wide and shouted, "No *buts*! You either fix this place up, or you're going to lose it! Either it'll fall down by itself, or the bank will come and take it!"

The creaking wood suddenly snapped with a noise like a pistol shot. Loralie jumped back, startled, and watched helplessly as Gabe, eyes wide with surprise, fell through the broken porch railing to the dirt four feet below.

Chapter Two

Loralie peered over the edge of the porch, fingertips pressed against her lips in the hopes of stifling the bubble of laughter choking her.

Gabe lay sprawled just at the edge of her vegetable patch. As she watched, he raised himself up on both hands and looked at her. His legs still spread-eagle, his hat on the ground beside him, he cocked his head and nodded grimly.

"There. See? This is what I was talkin' about." He sat up straight, lifted his arms, and shrugged. "This could have happened to you. You could have been hurt."

"Are *you* hurt, Gabe?" she whispered unsteadily.

"No, I ain't hurt!" He pounded on the ground with one clenched fist. "But you could have been!"

She shook her head. "But it's such a *little* drop, Gabe. . . ."

He muttered something she didn't catch and chose to ignore.

"I promise. I'll have Virgil fix that railing right away."

Gabe snorted and looked around wildly at the vegetables as if asking them to listen to the crazy woman on the porch. "Virgil? *Fix* something? You mean you're gonna ask that hired hand of yours to *work*?"

Loralie's spine stiffened. Defensively she said, "Now, don't start on Virgil again, Gabe Curran. You know as well as I do that the heat is hard on him."

"Hah!" He shook one long finger at her. "He's been usin' that excuse since I was a boy! He don't like the heat, can't work in the cold, windy days make him sneeze, and a calm day gives him the 'itchies.' "

Loralie bit her bottom lip, desperately trying to curb her smile. He'd just given a wonderful description of Virgil Huntsacker. But still, it was none of Gabe Curran's business who Loralie hired to work her farm. If she wanted to make an old man comfortable, give him a home, that was her business.

"Virgil will fix the railing," she said.

"Yeah, well. I'd purely like to see *that*." Gabe reached for his hat and came up on one knee. "That is the *laziest* man I ever saw!"

"You should have a bit more compassion for Virgil. He's an old man."

"*Old*? Hell, he's more than old! He must've been ninety when I was a boy! But it doesn't make one spot of difference. How do you think he got to be that old, anyway?" Gabe knelt on one knee and nodded at her abruptly. "I'll *tell* you how! By gettin' every soul he ever met to take care of him. Don't think that man ever did a day's work in his life." Gabe pushed himself to his feet, started to speak again, but stopped suddenly, his eyes wide.

A low, rumbling, snorting sound accompanied by heavy, irregular breathing came from behind him. Just as he turned to see what he should have been expecting, Gabe heard Loralie shout, "No, Alfonse! No!"

It was too late. Six hundred pounds of pale, angry hog rushed at Gabe. Snorting and wheezing, Alfonse charged the man's legs and narrowly missed. He lumbered into a turn and charged again, but the man leapt onto the porch just ahead of the big animal's snout.

"Are you all right?" Loralie asked, her hands still locked on Gabe's forearms.

"Yeah." Gabe looked away from the huge hog pawing the ground in frustration. He stared down into Loralie's concerned gaze and smiled. She was finally in his arms. All it had taken was him nearly getting killed by a crazy walking side of bacon.

When he jumped for the porch, she'd just naturally grabbed at him to pull him to safety. And she hadn't moved away. The warmth of her hands seeped through his shirtsleeves, shot up his arms, and spread through him like a wildfire. His hands at her narrow waist, he felt Loralie's rapid breathing and knew she shared the feelings swamping him. Her face only inches from his, Gabe couldn't contain himself any longer. He bent down slowly and brushed her lips with his own.

He heard her quick intake of breath and felt her tense up beneath his hands. Then she stepped away. Gabe's arms dropped to his sides as he watched a shutter drop over her features.

"Ah . . ." Loralie turned from him and walked to the front steps. "I'll take Alfonse to the back so you can get home."

"Loralie, I don't need you to protect me from that damn hog."

She smiled, nodded, and continued on.

"Loralie, I want to talk to you," he said quietly.

She stopped, hesitated for a moment, then started walking again. As she crossed the ground below him, she glanced up. "I think it's best if you just go home now, Gabe." Loralie walked right up to the snorting animal, laid her hand on his head, and said, "Come, Alfonse. Mr. Curran is leaving now, and I think it's time for your bath."

Stunned, Gabe watched as the tall, willowy woman

walked to the back of the cabin followed by the huge, complacent hog. He stood alone for a long moment and wished with all his heart he had that kiss to do over again. If he had, it wouldn't be a gentle touch. It would be a long, deep caress that would shake her to her toes and convince her they belonged together.

He pulled a lungful of air into his body and shot it out again. Jamming his hat onto his head, he stomped across the porch, down the steps, and stalked off toward his house.

It grated on a man to know that the woman he loved doted more on a hog than she did on him.

Loralie leaned against the back of the cabin and ignored Alfonse's snuffling at her feet. She crossed her arms over her chest and willed her heartbeat to slow down, her breathing to steady. Unfolding her arms again, she glanced down at her hands and wasn't surprised to find them trembling. Just that one brief kiss had sent her emotions reeling and the blood rushing through her veins.

Alfonse nudged her leg with his snout and leaned his massive body against hers affectionately.

Loralie smiled, reached down, and scratched behind the hog's ears. His snorting got louder, more contented. She shook her head slowly as she realized that Alfonse had more sense than she did. At least *he* had tried to run Gabe off the property.

Loralie let her head fall back against the rough wood wall. Staring blankly into the fiery summer sky, she whispered, "Oh, Alfonse, what am I going to do?"

"Don't you track that dirt all over my clean floor!"

Gabe stopped dead and slowly backed up through the front door onto the wide whitewashed porch.

Tessie followed him step for step, swinging a well-used broom over the dry clumps of dirt he'd carried in on his boots.

"Gabe Curran, how many times I got to tell you to keep them durn boots off my floors?" The short, round older woman with graying red hair pointed at him with the broom handle. "You know as well as me that Mondays is floor-scrubbin' days."

"Yes, ma'am, Tessie, I know."

"How the hell'd you get so dirty, anyway?"

He scowled at her.

"That hog again?"

"Partly."

Tessie shook her head slowly. "Can't figure why that dumb animal hates you so."

"I don't know and I don't care."

Her brow wrinkled up, Tessie pursed her lips in thought. "You know, almost as soon as the critter was born, he started lookin' on you with a black eye."

Gabe sighed heavily. "I remember." That damn hog had always been trouble. Giving him to Loralie was supposed to have been a blessing to him as well as her. It would provide her with meat for months and allow Gabe to walk down the road without lookin' over his shoulder.

But, he taunted himself, she'd ruined his plan by making a damn pet out of the ornery animal. *Alfonse*, for godsake. And if that wasn't bad enough, his own prize brood sow was forever trotting across the road to go visit the durn pig. He'd even heard that Loralie had named the sow Henrietta.

He sighed, then looked up when Tessie started in again.

"Can't be just the hog botherin' you. It's been quite awhile since the last time you dirtied up my floors."

Gabe hopped on first one foot, then the other as he pulled his filthy boots off. "I know, Tess. But I was so dang mad, I just forgot."

"Hmmph!" She set the business end of the broom on the porch and leaned on the handle. "Loralie, is it? Why don't you just marry that girl and be done with it?"

Gabe dropped his boots, and the heels thudded on the wooden floor. Hands on narrow hips, he smirked at his housekeeper/self-appointed mother hen. "Now, there's a *fine* idea. Don't know why I didn't come up with it myself!"

"Me, neither."

His hands fell to his sides, and he shook his head helplessly. "Tessie, she won't hardly stand close to me! Most times, she acts like I ain't even there! Now, just how the hell am I supposed to marry her if she can't see me for dust?"

Tessie's generous outspoken mouth twisted into a frown. "Beats me how any of you men ever get married. What do you mean, she don't *see* you?" She took a step closer and jabbed his chest with her forefinger. "What is it you figure she's up and watchin' at six o'clock in the morning, *every* morning, when you ride out? Your horse?" She shook her head. "Not likely."

Gabe's eyebrows shot straight up. "She does?"

"Yeah, she does." The broom handle in the crook of her arm, Tessie straightened the hang of her perfectly starched white apron. "Though the Good Lord alone knows why. . . ."

"Tessie . . ."

"No, sir." Her blue eyes narrowed. "If you can't see that woman needs you, then your eyes is a sight worse'n mine." She inhaled deeply and blew the air out with a nod in Loralie's direction. "Why, that ol' place of Aggie's is about to come down to a pile of kindlin'. Don't know what's holdin' it up as it is!"

"That's what *I* told her!" Gabe turned and stared at the cabin across the road. "But she says she'll have Virgil fix it."

Tessie snorted. "Then you'd best get her outa there quick. If she's dependin' on *Virgil*, she's gonna need you more than ever!"

Gabe sighed, turned away, and plopped down onto the nearest chair. He should have known better than to start Tessie in on Virgil. But he was so upset, he hadn't been thinking. Now he'd have to listen to her for hours. He closed his eyes and let his head drop back on his neck. Tessie's irate voice rang out in the otherwise still afternoon.

"Virgil Huntsacker! Why, that lazy, no-good, two-timin' son of a three-legged mule! He ain't been nothin' but trouble for the last forty years! Tell *me* about Virgil, will ya? Well, boy. Just you let me tell *you* a thing or two . . ."

Gabe sighed and frowned. If Virgil hadn't jilted Tessie at the altar forty years ago, they'd probably all be a lot happier.

Chapter Three

The next morning Loralie watched Gabe until he passed from sight around the bend in the road. He sat a horse so well, it was as if he became part of the animal. For a moment she let herself remember the nattily dressed men in San Francisco, taking their hired horses out for a canter in the park. Not one of them had the grace, the look of tightly leashed power that Gabe Curran possessed. Loralie sighed and let the ivory lace curtain drop back into place.

Every morning it was the same thing. Up before the dawn, make a pot of coffee, then stand in the shadows of the front windows and watch Gabe ride off to start his day. She couldn't even remember how the little ritual had started. She only knew that she couldn't stop. Didn't want to stop. There was something about the early morning hush, the untouched day that called to her. And as for staring at Gabe, well, she couldn't seem to help herself.

If only he weren't such a *nice* man. If he were as pompous and patronizing as Patrick Terwilliger had been, Loralie would have no trouble at all ignoring his very presence. But instead, he was beginning to wear her defenses down with his little kindnesses. Taking her into town in one of his carriages so she wouldn't have to walk, bringing her loaves of bread fresh from Tessie's oven. He'd even hung a new door on the back of the cabin for her.

She smiled and remembered how he'd sent one of his men to plow up a patch of land for her vegetable garden right after she'd moved in. Of course, she reminded herself, he'd also tried to tell her what to plant, how often to water, when to harvest and where to sell it to get a good price.

Shaking her head, Loralie turned for her bedroom, pulling at the tie of her robe as she went.

Loralie snorted indelicately. Actually, if Gabe were forty years older, fifty pounds heavier, and bald, he'd be the perfect *image* of Patrick Terwilliger. She gritted her teeth at the memory. Patrick was a friend of her late father's. And just like her father, he had professed to know what was best for her. It was his duty, he'd said, to watch out for her. He'd taken every cent of her inheritance, invested it . . . and promptly lost it.

If not for Aunt Agatha leaving her the tiny cabin, Loralie, with no other choices open to her, would have been forced to *live* with the Terwilligers.

She shook her head, determined to keep the past *in* the past. Loralie straightened her shoulders and lifted her chin defiantly. She'd had quite enough of bossy men trying to tell her how to live. Attractive or not—tempting or not—she would not allow Gabe that kind of control over her.

Because when all was said and done, despite his best intentions, Gabe Curran was a man—and men wanted control.

She slipped her robe off and grabbed up a skirt and blouse. As she got dressed, Loralie told herself that she would just have to try harder to ignore her wishful thinking and to remember what was most important to her.

Independence.

Tessie was right, Gabe crowed. This time he'd paid attention and had seen Loralie for himself, peering out her front window as he rode past.

The black stallion he rode pranced nervously in the road, anxious to be off and running. Gabe reached down and patted the animal's neck. Grinning, he turned in the saddle and stared back the way he'd just come. Maybe he *wasn't* beating his head against a stone wall after all. If she was watching for him, she *must* be at least a *little* interested. His horse snorted and shook his great head restlessly.

"All right, boy, we're goin'." Gabe lifted the reins, kneed his horse, and trotted on toward town. He'd get his business finished, then head back home. There'd be plenty of time to do a little courtin'.

"I surely do feel bad about this, Miss Loralie." Virgil groaned and eased himself down onto the rocking chair. "It don't seem right, you fixin' that rail and all. . . ."

"Never you mind, Virgil." Loralie lifted the hem of her long black skirt up to her waistband and secured it there with two clothespins.

Virgil gasped, blushed furiously, and looked away.

Loralie ignored him. She felt cooler already. And she was still decently covered. The long white ruffled petticoat she wore dusted over the tops of her bare feet, and she curled her toes self-consciously as she looked down at them. Of course, she *should* be wearing shoes, but it was so hot already . . . and at least on her own property it was all right. Wasn't it?

She shook her head and reached for the hammer. It was pointless worrying about what was or wasn't proper. After all, that was one of the main reasons she loved her little farm. There was no one to spout rules at her. Glancing up at the older man on the porch, she smiled to see he was pointedly looking in the opposite direction.

"It's all right, Virgil," she coaxed. "My limbs are covered."

He didn't turn. One gnarled, sun-browned hand rubbed across his gray-stubbled jawline, and he said, "Not by much, they ain't. What would folks think?"

"If they have any sense, they'll think I'm a clever woman finding a way to work in the sun and still stay cool."

He snorted.

She sighed. "Does it matter what folks think, Virgil? We're alone here. No one else will know."

Virgil's narrow shoulders shrugged. "Don't reckon there's any way I can stop you . . . is there?"

"No." Loralie grinned at the man's back. "Now, will you tell me what it is I'm supposed to be doing here?"

"You got to hammer that rail back into them posts."

Her lips quirked slightly. She'd figured *that* much out for herself. "Where are the nails?"

"Yonder." He crooked a thumb over his shoulder, indicating the corner of the porch.

Loralie leaned over, opened the brown paper sack, and pulled out a handful of nails. After sticking them in her mouth, she hooked her hammer under the waistband of her skirt and picked up the fallen rail. As she tried to find a way to balance the rail, hold a nail, and swing the hammer without an extra hand or two, she heard Virgil's rocker start creaking. Her eyebrows shot up. Maybe Gabe was right about Virgil Huntsacker after all. His back was fine this morning until he'd gone to look over the porch. Then he'd somehow managed to kink himself up while lifting the railing.

She sighed and shook her head. It didn't matter anyway. She still had to fix the porch. And she wanted it done before Gabe saw *her* fixing it. No sense in feeding the man's fire.

After wiggling halfway under the rail, she balanced it carefully on one shoulder, pulled a nail from between her lips, and positioned it just right. Then she dragged the hammer free and began to tap on the nail head.

"It's gonta take you all day if you hammer at it like that."

Loralie shot a glare at the back of Virgil's head. If he wasn't going to do it, then she wished he'd keep his comments to himself.

Slowly, carefully, Loralie tapped the nail into place. She told herself it didn't much matter if it went in a little crooked. As long as it went in. Her shoulder was aching as she began the second nail. In fact, as the minutes crawled by, her whole body began to cramp up. With her right leg stretched out for balance and her left curled under her, Loralie felt her muscles bunch. The sun beat down on her back, and under her sheer, short-sleeved white shirt, perspiration rolled down her flesh, adding to her discomfort.

Virgil rocked contentedly on, and as Loralie struggled with the rail, she found herself resenting every comfortable creak of his chair.

Finally one side was finished. Now, if she could just stretch for a moment or two before doing the other side . . .

"You all done, are you?"

Through clenched teeth Loralie said, "Just about." Then she groaned softly as she stretched her arms and legs. One glance at the hot sun high in the summer sky told her she'd been working quite awhile longer than she'd thought. She pushed her flyaway blond hair up out of her eyes, then tugged at the collar of her damp, clinging shirt. For one brief, tempting moment, she considered slipping out of her blouse and working in her chemise.

She shot a quick look at Virgil. No. He still couldn't bring himself to look at her, dressed as she was. If she was to peel down to her shimmy, the man would probably have a stroke.

Loralie sighed heavily and rolled her head around on her neck. Men really did have the best of things in the world, she acknowledged. Not only were they their own masters (and their wives'), but they could work out in the open, half-clothed, and no one thought a thing about it.

Lord, it was hot! She ran the back of her hand over her forehead and wished she had the time to sit down in the shade with a cool glass of lemonade. In fact, visions of the icehouse in town began to swim in front of her eyes, and it was all she could do to force herself to stay put.

Virgil's rocker creaked again, but this time it was an odd tearing sort of creak. Loralie looked up and her heart sank. It wasn't the rocker at all. It was the railing. As she watched, the wood pulled free from the porch post, its crooked nails groaning in outrage.

Before she could do a thing to stop it, the railing dropped to the porch with a clatter, then tumbled off to the ground.

"Don't think you had them nails set proper," Virgil intoned, without bothering to turn around.

Loralie took a long, deep breath, slammed her balled fists on her hips, and stomped one foot furiously. Immediately she gasped and dropped to the dirt. Tears filled her eyes as she reached for her right foot and pulled it into her lap. Unwillingly, she forced herself to look at the sole of her injured foot. One of the shiny new nails she'd bought at the general store was imbedded in the center of her arch.

"Ooooh," she whispered and bit at her bottom lip.

"Somethin' wrong?" Virgil had at last quit rocking.

"I stepped on a nail." Loralie hated the whining tone in her voice, but she couldn't seem to stop it.

"Well, hell." Virgil's rocker started in again. "Pull it out, girl, there's work to be done."

She glared at him but knew he was right. She should just pull it out. Tears of pain welled up in her eyes as the foot began to throb. For heaven's sake. She was acting like a child. Loralie squared her shoulders determinedly, breathed deeply, and didn't lose her courage until she looked at the nail again. She moaned and closed her eyes, knowing she had to get the darn thing out and that it was going to hurt!

"Are you all right?"

Gabe. She looked up. He was heading toward her, his gaze concerned. Loralie had never been so glad to see anyone in her life.

Chapter Four

"It's a good thing you come along, Gabe," Virgil said, risking a glance over his left shoulder. " 'Pears she's done hurt herself, and with my back bein' out like it is, well . . ."

Gabe shot the older man a disgusted look, then dropped to squat beside Loralie. Her brilliant green eyes shone with unshed tears, and he watched her bite into her bottom lip to still its trembling. He gave her a half-smile, then lowered his gaze to the foot she cradled in her lap.

Teeth clenched in sympathy, Gabe studied the nail solemnly. It had gone in deep. The sole of her foot was dusty, but he could see the pale flesh around the nail already starting to bruise. Unconsciously his eyes began to travel the length of her bared leg. The sun beat down on her milky white skin, and it was all he could do to remind himself that she was in pain. To help the situation a little, he reached over, grabbed the edge of her petticoat, and pulled it down over her calf. He didn't think he could stand that kind of distraction much longer.

"Is it . . . deep?" Loralie whispered.

He turned to look at her and was almost undone by the worry and pain in her eyes. Somehow he managed to keep himself from wincing when he lied and said, "Not too deep, no." Gabe knew it wouldn't do any good to tell her the truth. It was going to hurt like the very devil when he pulled that nail out—but why should she know that ahead of time?

"Don't much matter how deep it is, y'know . . ." Virgil interrupted. His rocker moved rhythmically, the creaks and groans accompanying his deep voice. "Why, I knew a fella one time stuck himself like you done, Miss Loralie."

She sniffed.

"Shut up, Virgil," Gabe snapped. But the old man ignored him.

"Yessir," Virgil continued, "he got that ol' nail out awright, but the durn foot rotted somethin' awful! Finally the doc had to cut it clean off."

Loralie gasped.

Gabe clenched his jaw, reached down, and yanked hard on the nail. It came out so quickly, she didn't have time to realize what he'd done.

"Now that I think on it," Virgil mused, "fella wasn't never the same after that. But we always knew when he was a-comin' our way on account of that slide, stomp walk of his!"

Gabe said, "It's out." But Loralie was listening in apparent fascination to Virgil.

"Oh, Lord," Loralie whimpered. "Gabe, is that true? Will that happen? Will they cut my foot off, do you think?" Her fingertips flew to cover her mouth. "Oh, I couldn't stand it! Slide, stomp!"

Gabe patted her hand ineffectually. "Loralie, it's out. Nothing's gonna happen to your foot." He turned a vicious glare on Virgil Huntsacker's back. "Virgil, why don't you get off that damn rocker and walk over to my house. Tell Tessie what happened and that we'll be there directly."

The rocking stopped. Virgil started to push himself out of the rocker and then dropped back to the seat with an absurdly exaggerated groan. "Oh, land, my pore ol' back. I'd admire to help you out, Gabe. I surely would. But these ol' bones just won't let me."

"Lazy, good-for-nothing, addle-brained . . ." Gabe's whispered diatribe faded off as he met Loralie's troubled gaze. The old fool'd only made things worse. Ignoring Virgil, Gabe grabbed Loralie's injured foot and squeezed it until a few drops of blood appeared.

"That hurts!" she said and tried to pull away.

"I know it does, but it's got to be done. Want to get out any dirt or such. . . ." He plopped down on the dirt and pulled her into his lap. Gabe yanked the bandanna from his neck and grabbed for her foot again, but she jerked it out of his reach.

"What're you doing now?"

He scowled at her, lunged across her body, and took hold of her foot. While she squirmed anxiously, he gently wrapped the blue square of linen around her foot. "I'm not going to hurt you, Loralie," he muttered. When he'd finished his task, he raised his gaze to hers. Then slowly his eyes moved over her features. His left arm snaked around her waist and pulled her even closer.

Before she had time to realize what he intended, Gabe's mouth lowered to hers. And this time he gave her the kiss he'd been dreaming about for months.

Slowly at first his lips moved over hers. Teasing, touching, exploring the feel and taste of her. Then, when he felt her respond, he urged her mouth open and dipped his tongue into the warmth of her. She gasped slightly, and he felt her arms slide up his shoulders to encircle his neck. His heart pounding, Gabe heard the rush of his own blood in his ears and lost himself in the incredible feel of her.

When her tongue timidly began to stroke his, Gabe knew that he was closer than he'd ever been to losing complete control of himself. Somewhere in the back of his mind a small rational voice whispered that he was moving too fast. But he ignored it and continued kissing her.

"What's goin' on back there?" Virgil called.

Loralie jerked back away from Gabe. Her fingertips covering her lips, she stared at him, wide-eyed.

"Nothin's goin' on, Virgil. I just took the nail out is all." Gabe's eyes never left Loralie's face, and he wished heartily he knew what was going on in her head.

Loralie finally looked away from him. She rubbed one hand over her mouth as if wiping away his kiss and her own reaction to it and tried to push herself to her feet.

But Gabe was too fast for her. In one smooth motion he rose, bent down, and scooped her up in his arms.

"What are you doing?" she asked.

"I'm keeping you from walking on that damn foot and getting dirt in that hole."

"Oh." She crossed her arms over her chest and said, "Fine. If you'll just carry me to the porch . . ."

"Nope."

"What?"

"I said, nope." He started walking. Not toward the front of the cabin but toward the road. Toward *his* house.

"What are you doing?" She uncrossed her arms and tried to push out of his grasp.

"Don't waste your time, Loralie." He glanced down at her and tightened his hold. "You'll get down when I want you to get down."

"There is no reason for this. If you will simply take me home, I can see to myself."

"Sure you can. And the minute I leave, you'll be up and running around . . . prob'ly go right back outside and try to finish that damn rail."

"I didn't break my leg, Gabe. I'm perfectly able to walk."

"Not if you don't have sense enough to wear shoes."

"I was hot."

"Yeah, well, now you're hot *and* hurt."

She shifted again, and he stopped dead.

"Y'know, unless you want to get dropped on your behind, you best hold still."

Loralie quit moving. Then she looked at him out of the corner of her eye. "Why did you kiss me like that?"

Gabe started walking again. He kept his gaze fixed on his house and answered softly, "To keep your mind off that damn nail."

"Oh."

He glanced down at her and added, "*And* because I've wanted to do that since the first time I laid eyes on you."

Loralie looked up, met his gaze briefly, then hurriedly turned away. "Oh."

Gabe used one hand to turn the doorknob and throw the heavy oak door wide. He didn't seem to notice when it slammed into the wall.

His bootsteps rang out on the polished wood floor as he crossed the wide hall. Loralie paid no attention to where he was going. She was much too busy admiring his fine home.

Vases filled with fresh flowers were everywhere, and the mixed perfume scented the cool rush of air moving through the length of the house. The walls were painted a delicate cream, and the dark wood trim gleamed from frequent polishing. She glanced up the wide curved staircase leading to the second floor and wished she had the time to explore the house at her leisure. In the six months they'd been neighbors, it was the first time she'd been inside Gabe's house. Not counting the kitchen, of course. She'd stopped by there once to ask Tessie how to make bread.

Loralie fought down a smile as she remembered the woman's horrified gasp of surprise that a full-grown woman wouldn't know how to bake bread! Explaining that she'd much rather *sketch* a loaf of bread than make it didn't help Loralie's case much, either.

When Gabe pushed open another door, though, all of

Loralie's mental ramblings ceased. Instead, she stared around her in awe and wonder. Books. Thousands and thousands of books. Her head turned slowly as she let her gaze move lovingly over the floor-to-ceiling bookcases that ringed the huge room.

Gabe didn't notice her facinated stare. He marched across the muted pastel area rug and set her gently down in an overstuffed floral armchair. Then he reached behind him, grabbed a footstool, and slid it under her injured foot.

"You sit still." He looked down at her, his features stern. "I'm going to get Tessie. I'll be right back."

Loralie nodded slowly, her eyes still moving over the varicolored spines of the books lining the walls. When he left the room, she leaned over and looked behind her. Still more books. Most were stacked neatly on the shelves, and some lay on the corner of a huge desk in the back of the room. Still others littered the seats of chairs, and some were even piled haphazardly in a corner.

Shaking her head, Loralie straightened, leaned back in the chair, and smiled. How she would love a room like this. To her right was an immense stone fireplace, with shining brass andirons and a stack of logs already laid. Heavy forest green drapes hung at each of the four windows, now closed against the afternoon sun, making the room cool and dark. A sudden soft breeze sent the drapes fluttering and allowed flashes of sunlight to dance across the bookshelves. On the pale varnished mantel over the fireplace stood small framed daguerreotypes of smiling people she didn't recognize.

But it was the books that held Loralie in thrall. Slowly she pushed herself up out of the chair. Balancing on one foot, she hopped to the nearest bookcase.

Chapter Five

Gabe's long-legged stride carried him to the huge square kitchen in moments. "Tessie?" He glanced around the empty room, then hurried across to the back door and flung it open. "Tessie?" His gaze swept the well-tended backyard and the path to the corrals and barn. No one.

He pulled back inside and shut the door. Well, where the hell is she? Disgusted, he walked to the nearest cupboard, reached inside, and pulled out a chipped blue tin basin. He slapped it down on the scrubbed pine counter and turned for the sink. He grapped up a towel off the freshly washed stack, held it under the pump for a moment, then wrung it out. He set the wet towel down beside the basin and walked to the pantry and flung the doors open.

The double doors wide, Gabe sighed his frustration. A small rectangular room, the pantry shelves stretched from the ceiling to the floor, and each shelf held hundreds of items. From pickling jars to calico fabric, from sacks of flour and sugar to extra saddle blankets. It was going to take him forever to find what he was looking for without Tessie's help.

Muttering under his breath, Gabe began to rifle through the supplies.

"Been tryin' to get that woman to the house for months—always said no—so danged independent—" He held up a small canister and squinted at the label. "My tobacco." He frowned thoughtfully. "And Tessie said it was all gone!" Gabe set the jar down by the door and went on with his search—and with his mumbling. "Don't know what it is about that woman—so bound and determined to keep her

distance, you'd think I had the smallpox or somethin'—"
His fingers closed around the neck of a half-empty whiskey
bottle. He drew it out, stared at it for a moment, then gave
the empty kitchen a quirk of his lips. Carefully he put
the bottle back where he found it. "None of my business if Tessie has a nip now and again. . . ." Down on
his knees now he rooted through the bottom shelf. Pushing
and shoving at the jars, bags, and bottles, something shiny
caught his eye. When he brought it out into the light, he
smiled briefly. Jenny's belt buckle. Solid silver with a
longhorn steer etched into it. Gabe had ordered it months
ago for his youngest sister's birthday.

His eyes widened as he stared down at the silver steer.
Jenny. And Anna. Oh, Lordy, and James. Gabe's fingers
curled around the cold buckle. In his concentration on
Loralie, he'd completely forgotten his sisters and brother
would be comin' home soon. They always came back for
the summer. Gabe dragged a deep breath into his lungs,
then shoved the belt buckle back into its hiding place and
continued rummaging through the pantry.

Time was running out. Not only was the bank getting
ready to foreclose on Loralie's place, soon his *own* home
would be crawling with people. He was going to have
to hurry up his courtin' some before his family arrived.
If Loralie thought *he* was bossy—his brother and sisters
would make her run for the hills!

He crawled over to the last shelf, his knees smarting on
the wood floor. Finally Gabe found what he'd been searching for. He grabbed up the bottle, carried it into the kitchen,
then splashed a goodly amount of the strong-smelling liquid
into the basin. Moving carefully, he headed back toward the
library, snatching another towel off the kitchen counter as
he went. He made one more stop. In case of emergencies
Tessie kept several rolls of bandages in the linen closet off
the dining room. He grabbed one, slammed the closet door,
and kept going.

Maybe, he told himself, now that he finally had Loralie
in the house, he should just try to think of a way to make her
stay. Gabe rounded the corner, and as he stepped through

the library doorway, he told himself, with Tessie in the house, too, Loralie couldn't say that it wouldn't be proper.

His gaze went directly to the overstuffed chair where he'd left her. She was gone.

"Blast it!" he said aloud to no one. "Where'd you go now?"

"Over here."

He spun around and watched in disbelief as Loralie, her injured foot held up behind her, hopped along the length of the far bookcases. "What are you doin'?"

She threw him a quick glance over her shoulder, then looked back at the books. "Oh, Gabe," she said, sighing delightedly, "this is a *wonderful* room!" She wobbled slightly and grabbed the edge of the nearest table for balance.

Gabe moved quickly. He set the pan and towels on the floor in front of the overstuffed chair, then hurried over to Loralie's side.

She snatched at the hand he offered gratefully and leaned her weight against him. "You never told me you had all these books!"

Gabe watched her, a smile on his face. He ran his thumb over her knuckles as she held on to him for support. Her green eyes shining, her features aglow like a child at Christmas, Loralie reached out with her free hand to run her index finger over the leather-bound books.

"Burns, Shakespeare, Dickens," she mumbled. "Oh, Emerson! My favorite." Loralie flashed him a brilliant smile.

"Mine, too," Gabe agreed quietly.

Loralie looked at him thoughtfully, as if bewildered by his admission.

"What's wrong?" Gabe chuckled. "Think the books were just for show?"

A half smile tugged at her lips. "No, it's only that I never expected *you* to care for poetry."

"You'd be surprised at the different things I care for."

The warmth of their joined hands seemed to blaze up suddenly, and Loralie jerked free of his grasp.

Gabe's fingers rubbed together as if unsure what to do without hers to hold on to. After a long uncomfortable silence he said, "Let's take care of that foot."

"What?" She glanced down. "Oh. It's fine now, Gabe. Doesn't even hurt too much anymore." Loralie hopped back a pace, keeping one hand on the table.

Gabe took a step closer. "It may not hurt much, but it ain't fine, either. We're gonna clean it out now, Loralie." He bent quickly and lifted her up into his arms. Looking down into her face, he added, "Whether you like it or not."

She blew out a disgusted sigh, crossed her arms over her chest, and resigned herself to the inevitable. She'd already learned that it was impossible to push herself out of his strong arms.

He carried her back to the big chair and plopped her down onto it. Seating himself on the footstool before her, he edged it back a bit and slid the liquid-filled pan in between them on the floor. Then he picked up her injured foot, propped it on his right leg, and began to unwrap the makeshift bandanna bandage.

Loralie sniffed and looked around. "What *is* that smell?"

"Hmmm?" His fingers smoothed over the puncture mark on her skin, careful not to press too hard on the already purpling flesh.

"That smell." She tugged at her foot, but Gabe held it firmly.

"Oh. That." Without another word Gabe, holding on to her ankle, set her foot down into the pan.

She screamed, jumped up, then sat down again, hard. Kicking at him with her free foot, Loralie tried to make Gabe let go. She even landed a couple of good kicks to his shoulder and arms, but he didn't budge. Tears streamed down her face as she tried desperately to twist away from the liquid fire imprisoning her foot.

"Just stop it!" he ordered. "It'll all be over in a minute."

"What . . . is . . . that?" she gasped out between gulping cries.

"Kerosene."

She jumped up again, but Gabe pushed her gently back onto the chair.

"Kerosene? *Why?*"

"Ah . . ." He stalled for a moment. "Someone once told me that it's good for makin' sure no infection sets in." Gabe looked up at her, an apology in his deep brown eyes. "I'm sorry, Loralie. I know it must burn like hellfire—but better this than gettin' sick and . . ."

She gulped noisily. "Gettin' my durn foot chopped off?"

He'd wanted to slug Virgil for shootin' his mouth off earlier. But maybe it was for the best. Her listenin' to that story would maybe convince her that he was right. "Yeah."

Loralie's teeth bit down on her bottom lip, and Gabe knew she was making every effort to stop crying. And he appreciated it. Lord, he hoped he'd never have to see her cry again. Her tears tore him up inside something awful.

Finally Gabe pulled her foot from the kerosene. Bringing it up to his lap, he carefully used the wet towel he'd brought to wash away the last of the kerosene. His hands moved tenderly over her bruised flesh, and after a long moment he risked a glance at Loralie. She'd stopped crying, though a few tears remained on her golden sun-touched cheeks. Her green eyes shimmering, she watched his hands smooth over her foot as if waiting for pain to begin again.

"It's all right now, Loralie. I'm finished."

She pulled one deep, shuddering breath into her lungs and forced a halfhearted smile. "I'm sorry I kicked you, Gabe."

He shrugged.

"But you should have warned me."

He shook his head. "Then you'd have just worried about it before time. Woulda made things worse is all."

She pulled at her foot, but he held it fast. His fingers smoothed over her arch and slid up to her ankle. Slowly Gabe's thumb drew warm circles on her skin, and he felt her body relax under his touch. He looked up at her face and found her eyes closed and a half smile curving her lips.

He smiled and slid one hand to her calf.

Loralie shifted deeper into the cushioned chair, and Gabe felt her other foot slide up his leg to his lap. He grinned and watched her almost purr her contentment.

Feather soft, the tips of his fingers moved over her leg and back down to her injured foot. She took a deep, shaky breath and stretched her other leg out until the arch of her good foot rested against his aching groin. He rolled his eyes and gritted his teeth as his fingers continued with their gentle explorations.

With every slight movement of her foot against his already throbbing body, though, Gabe felt his own control dissolving.

"Gabriel Curran!" Tessie shouted from the hall. "What do you think you're doin' tearin' up my kitchen that way?"

Chapter Six

Loralie jerked upright and yanked her feet off his lap.

Gabe groaned when she kicked his crotch accidentally, then he snatched her injured foot back and held it on his lap. He glowered at Tessie as she marched through the open doorway.

"What're you thinkin', boy? Rootin' through my pantry like . . ." Her tirade faded when she finally noticed Loralie. "Well, land's sake. What happened here?"

"It's nothing," Loralie said and shifted uneasily.

"What have you been up to?" Tessie frowned at Gabe, her foot tapping impatiently on the shiny wood floor.

"Gabe didn't do anything," Loralie said quickly. "I stepped on a nail and—"

"You poor thing." Tessie was all concern. Then her nose

wrinkled up and she sniffed. "Is that *kerosene* I smell?" She looked around the room anxiously. "Gabe, what did you spill it on?"

"I didn't spill any. It's in the basin here." He picked it up with one hand and held it out toward his housekeeper.

Her eyes wide, Tessie gasped, "You didn't stick her foot in this, did you?"

"Yes, he did. And it was quite painful."

"I should guess so." Tessie crossed the room and snatched the basin away from Gabe. "And I know just who give you this idea, too." She paused for a deep breath and went on. "Oh, don't you give me that frown, mister. These dang newfangled ideas. Some bacon grease woulda done just fine. And it wouldn't have hurt her any, either."

"Bacon grease?"

"Yes, bacon grease." Tessie shook one finger at him. "Don't come at me like that. You had plenty of it rubbed on your hurts when you was a boy . . . and it ain't done you no harm, has it?"

Loralie tugged at her foot again, but Gabe hadn't released his hold a bit.

"I don't know about harm," he yelled at the short, round woman, "but it *would* explain why that damn hog never could stand to be around me. I probably still stink of it!"

"Hmmph!" Tessie held out one hand to Loralie. "You come on with me, I'll finish you up, hon."

"*I'll* finish the bandaging." He met Tessie's stony gaze with one of his own. "Why don't you go upstairs and fix up Anna's room? Loralie'll be staying with us for a couple of days."

"What?" Loralie looked from one to the other of them, her head shaking firmly. "No, I'll be going home."

"Much as I hate to give him any credit a'tall," Tessie said with a brief nod at Gabe, "I got to go along with him on this one. You can't take care of yourself hoppin' around on one foot!"

"With a bandage I'll be just fine, thank you all the same."

"And how are you gonna walk?" Gabe spoke up and

Loralie looked at him.

"I'll limp."

"And get dirt in that hole in your foot?"

"I'll wear shoes."

"Not for a few days you won't."

"Gabe, I can't stay here."

"Why not?"

"I have animals to tend to for one thing."

"Virgil will do it."

She cocked her head and stared at him silently.

"All right," Gabe acknowledged. "*I'll* do it."

"And what about my garden?"

"You ain't leavin' the country, Loralie. It's just a couple of days!"

"It wouldn't be proper."

"Don't you worry none about that," Tessie said with a meaningful glance at Gabe. "I'll see to it you ain't bothered any."

Indecision was written plainly on Loralie's features. But suddenly Gabe had an idea. One he was fairly certain would convince her to stay.

"You can use the library any time you want to. . . ." Gabe's voice was soft, inviting. He watched as the thought took hold in her mind. She bit at her lip, obviously torn as to what to do. But when her gaze began to move longingly around the room again, Gabe was sure he'd won.

"All right," she said slowly, "but just for a couple of days."

Gabe grinned.

Tessie nodded and left to make Loralie's room ready.

"But you have to feed Alfonse for me."

Gabe sighed and looked up at her smiling eyes. For the chance of having Loralie actually living in his house, he was willing to put up with just about anything.

Even the hog from hell.

Gabe yelled something and waved his arms around wildly. Loralie laughed and told herself she was glad she couldn't hear him. She stared down at the yard from her second-story bedroom window and chuckled again as Gabe started to walk toward her house. The sow he'd tried to chase off was just a few steps behind him, trotting along happily.

"Good for you, Henrietta," Loralie whispered with a grin. "Don't let him boss you around."

Gabe turned suddenly, saw the huge sow lumbering after him, and threw his hands up in defeat. When he and the hog marched off toward her place, Loralie turned away from the window at last.

She gripped the arms of the big whitewashed rocking chair she sat in and studied her injured foot. Wrapped tightly in bandages and propped up on a pillow-covered footstool, it looked much worse than it was. She should have insisted on going home. It wasn't as though she was helpless. She could walk, or rather, hop. As if to prove it to herself, Loralie pushed up from the chair and lowered her foot to the floor.

Breathing deeply, she took a determined step and winced at the sharp, throbbing pain shooting up her leg. Hopping unsteadily, she made her way to the big four-poster bed against the wall. Once there, she eased herself down onto the thick feather mattress covered by a sky-blue flowered quilt, then leaned back against a bank of fluffy pillows in freshly starched cases.

She let her gaze move over the room Tessie'd prepared for her. An oak dresser and washstand stood along one wall. Two rocking chairs with a small table between them holding a lamp for reading were just opposite. White lace curtains hung at the windows and danced lightly in the afternoon breeze. Just beside the bed on the right was a door. Loralie had already tried to open it. It was locked. Which only served to feed her curiosity. Maybe she'd ask Gabe about it later. Or Tessie.

Yawning, she settled herself back against the pillows and closed her eyes. But sleep eluded her. Instead, she saw Gabe's deep, soft brown eyes apologizing for hurting her. She felt again the touch of his fingers as they moved over her leg. If Tessie hadn't come in just then, Loralie wasn't certain *what* might have happened. All she knew was, she'd

never known anything like that before. The warmth from
his hands had enveloped her in a soft, cozy haze where
the only thing that mattered was the tingling sensation his
fingers brought to her skin.

And his gentleness. He'd held her and tended to her as
if she were made of fine porcelain. It had seemed right,
somehow, for him to hold her and care for her. Loralie'd
forgotten how good it felt to be fussed over. To know that
you were important to someone.

A curl of warmth spread through her body. She kept her
eyes closed and remembered the kiss they'd shared only a
couple of hours before. If she concentrated, Loralie could
almost taste Gabe's mouth again. Feel his warm breath on
her face. The spiral of desire strengthened and her heart
raced in response.

Deliberately she opened her eyes, sending her memories
skittering off into the late afternoon sunshine slanting into
her room. Her breathing ragged, she fought to stop the fire
building in her blood.

Slowly Loralie turned onto her right side, curling her
knees up close to her chest. Her left hand smoothed over
the quilt top and came to rest on the pillow beside her. Absently
she stared at the shining brass doorknob on the locked door
as if expecting it to turn. Loralie licked her suddenly dry
lips. She had a feeling about where that door led.

And if she was right, she was in trouble.

Gabe opened the door as quietly as he could. She hadn't
answered his gentle knock and supper would be ready soon.
He wouldn't bother her, he told himself. He just wanted to
peek in at her, make sure she was all right. Creeping across
the polished floor, Gabe went to her bedside. Curled up on
her side, she lay with one hand under her cheek, the other,
palm up, on the pillow beside her. He was sorely tempted
to lean down and kiss her, but he didn't. In fact, he wouldn't
even wake her for supper. She'd looked so exhausted lately,
he was sure she could use the extra sleep.

She worked so hard on that little place of hers. Gabe's
teeth ground together in frustration. It was too much for

any one person to do alone. And Lord knew, Virgil was
no help. Why, when Gabe went to feed the animals, he'd
found Virgil still rocking complacently on the front porch.

Alfonse had been so glad to see Gabe, the hog hadn't
even bothered to raise a fuss. Although, Gabe told himself, the real reason might be that Henrietta had come
calling, too. Even that damn hog realized that he'd rather
have Henrietta than be alone. Why couldn't Loralie figure
that out?

She sighed in her sleep, and Gabe shook his head. She
shouldn't have to work so hard. She shouldn't have to do
everything for herself. Couldn't she see that he only wanted
to love her? To *share* her life, not take it over?

Somehow, he *had* to convince her.

Carefully he lifted the extra blanket from the end of the
bed and spread it over her. She sighed again and shifted
position in her sleep. Lying half on her back, the vee
collar of Loralie's shirt hung open revealing the swell of
her breasts. For a long moment Gabe watched her, his
breathing strangled, looking his fill of treasures he'd longed
for for months.

Before he could stop himself, he reached down and gently drew one finger down the curve of her breast. She
moaned, and his index finger smoothed over her flesh, then
dipped into the warmth of her cleavage before moving to
caress her breast once more. His breath caught when he saw
her nipple harden and strain against the sheer fabric of her
blouse. Gabe swallowed heavily and risked giving the erect
bud the slightest touch of his thumb and forefinger.

Loralie shivered, murmured something and turned toward
him unconsciously.

He groaned and straightened up. Slowly he turned, took a
few steps, and closed her bedroom door. Deliberately then,
he walked back to the bedside. But this time he pulled open
a drawer on the night table. He snatched up the brass key
that lay inside and used it to open the locked door that
Loralie had wondered about earlier.

With the connecting door to his room standing open,
Gabe looked down at the woman he loved. He wanted

her more than anything else in the world. But he wanted her awake. And as hungry for him as he was for her.

He left the door open in case she needed something in the night.

Gabe couldn't sleep. He blew out a rush of air, grabbed a feather pillow, and stuffed it behind his head. Staring at the ceiling, he tried desperately to get his mind off the woman sleeping in the next room.

It was no use, though. During supper and all through the long evening that followed, all he'd been able to think of was Loralie. And now, in the middle of the night, with Tessie snoring downstairs, he was still wide awake—and dreaming. Images kept forming in his tired mind. Images of him and Loralie together. Talking, laughing, kissing . . . He cursed softly and pushed himself off the bed.

He snatched his Levi's off a chair, pulled them on, then crossed the dark room to the nearest window. He yanked on the drape cord, and moonlight spilled into his room. With his hands braced on either side of the big window, Gabe stared blankly down at the darkness.

He heard a soft cry at almost the same time the thud came from the next room. Quickly he raced to the connecting door and found Loralie, sitting on the floor, wide awake and hopping mad.

Chapter Seven

"Are you all right?" Gabe squatted down beside her. Loralie's blond hair was messed from sleeping and fell loose and soft around her shoulders. She cradled her injured foot in her lap and looked at him.

"Yes," she ground out, clearly more frustrated than in pain.

"What happened?"

She glanced at him ruefully. "I, uh, needed to use the uh . . ."

Understanding dawned and Gabe fought down a smile. "Let me help you," he offered quietly.

Loralie opened her mouth to refuse, then sighed heavily. "I suppose I don't have much choice."

He bit the inside of his cheek to keep from smiling, and quickly, before she could change her mind, he scooped her off the floor and into his arms. Gabe stepped through the open connecting doorway, crossed his room, and opened the door into the hall.

From over his shoulder Loralie's gaze flitted over Gabe's room. Pale moonlight danced over the huge bed, and she shivered involuntarily.

"Cold?" he whispered.

"No," Loralie answered. Then added silently, just in trouble.

With Gabe waiting in the hall, Loralie finished her ablutions quickly, then gave herself a quick look in the oval mirror hanging on the cream-colored wall. Her hands moved over her hair, trying to smooth it into submission, but it was no use. She stared sternly into the reflection of her own eyes and mumbled worriedly, "Careful now, miss. That connecting door leads to more than you're ready for . . ."

A soft tap on the door and she heard Gabe say, "Did you call me? Are you all right?"

Still looking in the mirror, she shook her head. No, she wasn't all right. Not at all. Even the sound of his voice sent a tremor up her spine, and Loralie knew without a doubt that this would be the *longest* night of her life.

She opened the door and said, "Everything's fine."

He smiled at her, and the tremor in her body spread until she could barely stand. When Gabe picked her up and held her closely against him, her fingers locked behind his head. The warmth of his naked shoulders flooded her and she found herself studying the line of his jaw and throat. How his curly brown hair fell against the back of his neck. How the broad, tanned expanse of his chest was smooth except for a few dark, curly hairs between his flat nipples. Loralie let herself enjoy the strength of his arms and the gentle hold he kept on her.

Her gaze lifted to his face, and she felt a sudden desire to touch the lock of hair that fell across his forehead. To run her fingers over his features, to touch the full, warm lips that had kissed her so thoroughly.

Gabe glanced down at her and came to a dead stop. "If you keep lookin' at me like that, Loralie," he whispered harshly, "I'm liable to forget my high-minded notions and—"

"And what?" She met his gaze squarely and felt warmed by the fire in his dark eyes.

His arms tightened around her, and she could see that his jaw was clenched. He pulled a deep breath into his lungs and took another step or two down the hall before he stopped again. "Loralie."

"Yes, Gabe." She watched the muscles in his jaw twitch.

"You know how I feel about you. . . ."

"I think so," she whispered and ran one finger along his tight jawline.

He groaned and looked down at her. "Then let me say it, so you'll know for sure."

Loralie knew what was coming. She knew, too, she should stop him from saying it. If she didn't, everything between them would change. There would be no chance for a friendship. All of the feelings she'd tried so hard to hide over the last few months would be out in the open. Oh, she'd told herself that she didn't love him . . . that she only *cared* for him as you would a dear friend . . . but it was more than that. So much more that it scared her to think about it.

How had this happened? She'd never intended to fall in love. Rather, she'd been determined *not* to. And still somehow, Gabe Curran had crept into her heart almost unawares.

But even knowing that she loved him, Loralie wasn't sure she could *marry* him. Handing over control of her own life to a man . . . even Gabe, was too frightening.

If she said yes to him now, all she would be willing to promise him would be this one night.

But would that be so wrong? Wasn't she allowed *something*? Couldn't she let herself know what it was like to be loved by a man? She looked up into his eyes again and knew that she wouldn't stop him. If only for that night, she would let herself love and be loved.

"I love you, Loralie." He bent his head and kissed her softly, briefly. "Always have. Since the first day I saw you. And right now I want you so much, it's hard to breathe." As if to prove his point, he pulled a strangled breath into his lungs.

"But," he went on, and Loralie was held captive by the gentleness in his eyes, "I also love you enough to take you right back to your own room. Now." He licked his lips, and Loralie followed his tongue with her eyes. "You just say so, darlin', and I'll lock that door between us and give you the key."

Her heart thudded painfully in her breast. How could she say no to such a man? His gentleness. His kindness. Since the day they'd met, he'd done nothing but try to help. And now he offered her the gift of his love without demanding a thing in return. Could she have been wrong about Gabe Curran? All these months, could she have been misunderstanding his motives?

Slowly, hesitantly, her left hand reached up and cupped his beard-stubbled cheek. She felt his breath catch when her thumb moved over his flesh in a soft caress. But still he waited, holding himself in check. It was up to her, Loralie knew, and suddenly she realized that at that moment nothing was more important to her than being in Gabe Curran's arms.

"Don't lock the door, Gabe." Her voice was low, husky with her need for him. She guided his head down to hers, and when their lips met, she sighed and opened her mouth to him.

Gabe groaned softly and his arms tightened around her. For a long breathless minute his tongue caressed hers, and

Loralie gave herself up to him. She arched her body against his and ran her palm lightly over his chest. The hard, warm strength of him sent splinters of delight shooting through her, and when his hand cupped her behind, she wiggled in his grasp, wanting more of his touch.

He lifted his head almost reluctantly, his teeth tugging gently at her bottom lip. Loralie tried to pull his mouth back to hers, but he only smiled, held her close, and hurried down the hall to his bedroom. Once inside, he nudged the door shut with one foot and, his gaze locked with hers, carried Loralie to the giant four-poster bathed in moonlight.

With one hand he reached down, grabbed the quilt and sheet, and tossed them to the foot of the bed. Tenderly then, he set Loralie down in the center of the mattress and pressed her back against the pillows.

He lay down beside her and propped himself up on one elbow. Slowly, tantalizingly, Gabe drew his index finger down the length of her throat. With a hypnotic, feather touch, he explored the nape of her neck, the pulsing hollow at the base of her throat, and then moved on to the warm valley between her breasts.

Loralie shifted position and closed her eyes, allowing herself to be wooed by the gentleness of his touch. She hardly noticed when he unbuttoned the nightgown Tessie'd fetched for her from home, then began to tug at the ribbons. With the release of each ribbon Gabe bent and kissed the warm, pale flesh he'd exposed. By the time her breasts lay bare under his gaze, Loralie's body quivered with the need for his lips against her skin.

His tongue smoothed over one breast, flicking teasing, warm darts at her too-sensitive flesh. She opened her eyes and watched his mouth close over her erect nipple. Loralie gasped and ran her fingers through his hair, pushing against the back of his head, hoping to keep his mouth on her body as long as she could. The edges of his teeth played with the small pink bud, and then his lips closed around her and he began to suckle her. The pulling, drawing sensation was more than she could bear. Twisting and writhing, Loralie felt a damp, warm heat flood her and an unfamiliar ache begin at the apex of her thighs.

Gabe seemed to understand. His hands moved to the waistband of her skirt, and in seconds it was off and falling to the floor. He pulled away from her then, and she cried out softly for his return.

"I'm not leavin' you, darlin'," he murmured. "Not now. Not ever."

She lay still, and when he spread her legs wide and knelt between them, she only hoped he would end the aching that seemed to grow stronger with his every touch.

Gabe leaned over her, his mouth and tongue moved over her skin. Loralie licked at her lips and struggled for air. Her body jerked when his tongue and teeth moved over her belly and down her left thigh. Her head tossing from side to side on the feather pillows, Loralie bent her legs and tried to arch closer to him. To his mouth. To his tongue. To the heat only he knew how to quench.

She heard him chuckle softly, and then she felt him leave the bed. Her eyes closed, she heard the whisper of cloth and knew he was removing his jeans. Before she could urge him to hurry though, he was back, his hands running up and down the length of her legs, his lips following the path his fingers created.

And then suddenly his fingers moved to the core of her and she jumped, startled at the intimate touch and surprised at the force of her pleasure.

"Gabe, what—"

"Hush, Loralie," he whispered. He leaned over her and kissed her mouth tenderly while at the same time his fingers sent shooting stars up through her body.

Loralie opened her eyes and looked up into his. Her hands reached for him, and she rubbed her palms across his chest, her fingernails scraping gently over his hardened nipples. She smiled to see him jump as she had earlier and pulled him close so that she might suckle him. When her lips closed over his nipple, Loralie heard him groan in response.

Then his fingers slipped inside her body, and she knew nothing except the sweet sensation of his hand moving in and out of her warmth. His thumb moved gently over the hard bud of her sex, and Loralie thought she would die from the pleasure he brought.

"Ah, Loralie," he whispered in her ear, "I must be inside you. I have to feel your warmth. I need to be a part of you. . . ."

"Yes, Gabe," she answered, though he'd already moved to kneel between her thighs. She raised her head to look at him. He cupped her behind in his hands and lifted her hips slightly. When he pushed his body into hers, Loralie saw his eyes close in delight and then she forgot everything but the incredible feeling of being joined with him.

Locked together, they moved as one, each of them striving for the release that waited just out of reach. He leaned over her and their mouths clung together, sharing their very breath.

Loralie moved her hips, instinctively inviting him deeper inside. Then Gabe's hand slipped down between their bodies and he stroked the core of her. Her pleasure seemed to feed his, and together their bodies shook with the jolting, shuddering spasms of delight they'd both waited for for so long.

Chapter Eight

She snuggled in closer to him, and Gabe tightened the circle of his arms. Her breath on his chest, he felt the pounding of her heart and knew his own matched it. Releasing her momentarily, he tugged at the sheet and quilt covering them, pulling it higher over her naked shoulder. Then he ran his hand softly over Loralie's back and the arm she'd wrapped around his middle.

His eyes wide, astonished, Gabe stared up at the beam ceiling. Never had he imagined that lovemaking could be like that. So much more than a joining of bodies, he felt as though their souls had touched, and he knew nothing would ever be the same for him again. He knew, too, that he could never let Loralie go. It would kill him.

"Gabe?" she whispered and smoothed her palm over his chest.

He caught her hand in his to still it. The slightest touch from her burned across his flesh like a branding iron.

"What?" Gabe smoothed her hair back from her forehead.

Loralie leaned her head back to look at him. "I didn't mean for this to happen, Gabe."

"I know, darlin'." He kissed her brow gently.

"I tried so hard to keep my distance. . . ."

He chuckled softly. "You surely did."

"But"—her finger touched the base of his throat—"I couldn't."

Gabe lifted her finger to his mouth and nibbled at it.

Loralie shuddered slightly and closed her eyes. "I didn't *mean* for this to happen," she said again.

"Neither did I," he said quietly.

She smiled ruefully and looked at him. "Didn't you? You even had a connecting door into my room."

He frowned down at her in mock outrage. "*That* is not why you were put in that room, Loralie."

"No?" She pulled her finger from his lips and ran it lightly over his dark whiskered cheek. "Why then? And why do you *have* a connecting door to a guest bedroom?"

Gabe chuckled. "You got a real suspicious mind, Loralie. You know that?"

Her eyebrows shot up. "Don't you have an answer for me?"

"Yes, missy. I do." He flipped Loralie onto her back and leaned over her. She smiled up at him and drew her fingers across his nipples. Gabe gasped and dropped soft kisses across her brow, down her nose, and finally her mouth. "We put you in that room because Tessie sleeps downstairs." Another kiss. "And if you needed somethin' in the night, she wouldn't be able to hear you." Another kiss, this one a little deeper. "And as for that connectin' door . . ." His tongue stroked the outline of her lips. "This room used to be my folks' room." Gabe's right hand moved down over the sleek line of her waist and along the curve of her hip. "They had that door put in when my sister Anna was little."

"Sister?" she whispered and moved against his hand.

"Uh-huh." His hand moved down over her thigh and up across her abdomen. "She had bad dreams sometimes. Woke up cryin'." Gabe moved to kiss her neck, his teeth and tongue drawing a harsh sigh from Loralie. "When the folks died, I moved into this room. For Anna's sake." His mouth continued to trace warm patterns on her skin.

"Mmmm . . ." She sighed, cocking her head slightly to give him access. "Didn't know you had a sister."

"*Two* sisters and a brother," he corrected, then moved to lick her hardened nipple. Loralie's body jerked in response, and he lifted his head to meet her smiling gaze. "I love 'em all dearly . . . but do we *have* to talk about 'em *now*?"

She shook her head and reached for him. As her arms closed around him, Loralie's legs opened to welcome Gabe again.

"Well, come *on*, if you're comin', Henrietta," Gabe called. He glanced over his shoulder and smiled as his prize brood sow trotted up to him. Then his gaze shifted, and he found himself staring at the house as though he could see through the walls and into the library, where he'd left Loralie only moments before.

She'd looked like a queen, propped up on the big cushioned setee. Pillows under her foot, stacks of books within easy reach, and a pitcher of lemonade with a plateful of Tessie's cookies on the table beside her. It had taken every ounce of strength he possessed just to leave the room.

Deliberately Gabe breathed deeply, turned back toward her farm, and started walking. He had to feed Alfonse again. But he was feeling so good, even the thought of dealing with that durn hog didn't bother him. He started whistling softly, and Henrietta's hooves tapped perfect rhythm.

"Well, hey there, Gabe!"

Gabe's whistle stopped abruptly. "Virgil," he said and nodded at the man. Gabe looked around quickly. The porch railing still lay where it had fallen the day before. He wasn't surprised.

Virgil stepped over the rail and walked slowly to Gabe's side. "How's Miss Loralie doin' today?"

"Better. Foot's still swollen some. . . ."

"Yep." Virgil shook his gray head. "Swellin' comes first, then the *real* trouble sets in."

Gabe frowned at him. How the old coot had avoided somebody shootin' him long ago was a mystery. "Her foot's fine, Virgil."

"Yeah, at first . . . it would be."

"Oh, for . . ." Gabe started walking toward the back of the house. "What have you been doin' since yesterday, Virgil?" He glanced at the garden. "I see it ain't been the weedin'."

Virgil moaned. "I was aimin' to. But this ache come on me, down low in my back. Felt just like that time I got a Injun arrow in me. Throb? Whooee!"

Gabe rolled his eyes and kept walking, Henrietta right behind him. As they rounded the corner of the little house, the sow shot out into the lead and hurried over to her true love, Alfonse. They exchanged greetings in a series of snorts and grunts.

After a few minutes Virgil commented, "You ever seen the like? Why, that old sow's pure loco over that varmint."

"Yeah." Gabe kept a wary eye on Alfonse, in case the hog decided to protest Gabe's presence.

Virgil stepped out in front of Gabe, shaking his head. He watched the two hogs rooting on the ground in front of the dilapidated barn and sighed heavily. "Pure wears me out just watchin' 'em."

Gabe's lips quirked as he shot a quick look at the old man's back. Virgil's overalls looked as though they hadn't seen wash water in over a year. And he had so much junk crammed into every pocket, his wiry body appeared to be covered in huge, misshapen lumps.

A bright, clean spot of white caught Gabe's attention, and he narrowed his gaze to study it. A corner of what looked like an envelope hung half out of Virgil's back pocket. Now, what would he be doing with a letter? Not only could he not read, but Gabe seriously doubted that Virgil knew *anyone* willing or capable of writing to him.

"What's that in your pocket, Virgil?"

"Huh?" He looked at Gabe, then followed the man's line of vision. His brow wrinkled in confusion, Virgil dutifully dug into the pocket. He pulled out tobacco, string, a length of rawhide, a bear claw, and finally the envelope. The old man stared at it blankly for a long minute, then his face cleared and he looked at Gabe with a smile.

"Sure! I recollect now. That banker from town?"

Gabe nodded uneasily.

"Well, he brung this letter for Miss Loralie. She weren't here, so he give it to me."

"When was this?"

"Oh . . ." Virgil tilted his head back and stared up at the cloudless blue sky. Tapping the edge of the envelope against his gray stubbled chin, he said slowly, "Must be . . . three weeks now, I reckon."

"What?" Gabe snatched at the envelope. "Why the hell didn't you give it to her?"

"No need to shout, Gabe. I ain't deaf." Virgil sniffed imperiously. "I stuck the dang thing in my overalls here, and I ain't worn 'em but once or twice since." He shrugged. " 'Sides, letters from bankers is always bad news." Nodding, he added, "I thought to spare her some."

Gabe gritted his teeth. There was no reasoning with Virgil. Besides, the damage was done. He glanced back at his house and told himself he should run the letter right over to her. And yet . . . his fingers ran over the flap of the envelope. She was hurtin' right now. Wouldn't it be better, he asked himself, if he looked at the letter first? If it wasn't important, then he wouldn't waste her time with it. And if it was . . . well, he'd deal with that when the time came.

"You gonta read it?" Virgil leaned toward the other man as if he could somehow understand the fancy writing on the mysterious paper.

Gabe looked up, guilt wavering in his eyes. "No," he lied. "It's Loralie's mail. I'll take it to her. You feed Alfonse and Henrietta."

"Now, Gabe—" Virgil's hand swept around to hold his spine.

"Don't start, Virgil. Just feed the damn hogs!"

"You're sure everything's all right now?"

Loralie looked up at Tessie and smiled. "Yes, Tessie, thanks."

The housekeeper eyed her speculatively, and Loralie fought down a blush. Rationally, Loralie knew that Tessie had no way of knowing what had gone on between Gabe and her during the night. But somehow, she couldn't help feeling that the other woman had guessed more than she should have.

"Then I'll be back in the kitchen." Tessie smiled and winked. "You give a holler if you need anything."

Loralie nodded and tried to ignore the wink. When she was alone again, she covered her face with her palms and wasn't the least surprised to find her cheeks flaming hot.

It had been like that all morning. Every time she let herself think about Gabe and . . . She fanned herself ineffectually with an open book. Oh, Lord, what *had* she done?

Suddenly she grinned. Memories of the night before washed over her, bringing a flood of sensation and remembered warmth. She could still feel Gabe's arms around her when she woke up this morning.

Loralie closed her eyes and let the clear images form. Sunlight slanting through the open curtains, a soft breeze drifting into the room and brushing over their entwined bodies. Her embarrassment and Gabe's determination that she feel no shame . . . no stabs of prudish modesty in front of him.

And she remembered thinking that she'd like to wake up lying next to him every morning for the rest of her life.

Slowly Loralie opened her eyes again and looked over toward the mantel. The daguerreotypes she now knew were of Gabe's brother and sisters. She frowned for a moment and wondered why he hadn't wanted to talk about them when she'd asked this morning. All he'd been willing to say was that James, Anna, and Jenny were all due home soon.

From Tessie, she'd managed to learn that Anna was in some school back East, Jenny had been in Europe for the last six months, and James was traveling somewhere in New York. Funny that no one seemed to want to tell her much about them.

Loralie shook her head and opened her book to the first page. She'd simply ask him again when he came home for supper.

Home. Good heavens. Was she already thinking about this place as *home*?

Yes. Yes, she was. And she told herself that everything would be all right. That Gabe had proved himself a kind, gentle, considerate man. Why, he'd even taken over the care and feeding of Alfonse!

Loralie smiled and reached for her glass of lemonade. She wasn't too proud to admit that she'd been wrong. He wasn't trying to *control* her. He only wanted to love her. She sipped at her drink and smiled thoughtfully. And heaven knew, he was *very* good at that!

Chapter Nine

"You did *WHAT*?" Loralie knew she was shrieking but made no effort to calm herself. The warm, loving feelings she'd experienced hours earlier had evaporated like a river mist on a hot summer day. She glared at the man across from her and silently *dared* him to speak.

"Now, Loralie—"

"I can't believe you would deceive me like this!" She picked up a pillow and heaved it at him. It fell disappointingly short.

"I didn't *deceive* you!"

"Fine." Her arms crossed over her chest, her fingers tapping on her upper arms, she countered, "What do you prefer? Tricked? Connived? *Stole*?"

"Now, you just hang on a damn minute, Loralie Davis!" Gabe tossed his hat onto the desk behind him and stood facing her stiffly. "I ain't no damn thief! And I don't *trick* women!"

"Why not?" Her gaze swept him up and down and left no doubt to her disdain. "You obviously have very little regard for a woman's intelligence . . . to think I would believe a story like that! Surely then, a woman would make the perfect criminal victim!"

"Dammit, Loralie." He took a step closer but saw that her fingers had curled around a slim volume of poetry. He stepped back out of range.

This wasn't going at all how he'd planned. Right now she was supposed to be huggin' his neck and kissin' his face. For corn's sake. Hadn't he saved her farm for her?

That letter Virgil'd squirreled away had been a foreclosure notice from the bank. Since there were only a few days left on the note, and he knew *she* didn't have any money . . . well, hell. Who'd a thought she'd be so dang mad! He'd come ridin' up to the house, the deed to her place in his pocket, full of the joy of livin' and havin' her to come home to, and she acts like *this*!

"Ain't you gonna let me explain any of this?" he finally asked.

"No." She pushed herself to her feet and awkwardly tried to keep most of her weight on her good foot. Blowing at the lock of hair that hung over her eyes, Loralie pointed one finger at him and said much too quietly, "I'm sure your story would be most convincing. God knows, your 'acting' last night more than fooled me."

"*Acting*?" He took a step, risking the book in her hand. "You think I was *acting*?" Gabe laughed and shook his head. "You got the wrong Curran, lady. I don't act. And I don't steal from women. And I don't spend hours makin' love to a woman just to get my hands on a rattail piece of land that ain't worth the effort to blow it to Kansas!"

She sniffed. "I don't believe you. I believe that I was right all along. That you're no better than any other man. Unless you have complete control over a woman, you're just not happy!"

"What?"

"You heard me." She took a step toward him, faltered, then caught herself.

"Yeah, I heard ya." Gabe frowned, disgusted. Slowly he reached into his coat and pulled out a folded paper from his breast pocket.

"In fact, I know just the kind of man you are." She waved one hand toward the framed photographs on the mantel. "Your brother and sisters are off doing your bidding somewhere, aren't they? *That's* why you won't talk about them. It even embarrasses *you* to be so high-handed!" Loralie limped a little closer. "Anna's in school, you said. A fine finishing school no doubt, so that she can be the proper little wife for some fat, uncaring man who'll direct her every move."

He opened his mouth, then snapped it shut.

"And Jenny! Did you send her to Europe in disgrace? Had she displeased you somehow? Did she try to make a decision without your approval?"

Gabe pulled a deep breath into his body and forced himself to be quiet.

"Poor James." She shook her head. "I believe he has most of my sympathy. To be sent away from his home simply to *wander* through New York, *his* crime must have been great, indeed!" Loralie finally reached his side. She thrust the book of poetry at him fiercely, shoving it against his chest.

Tears welled in her eyes for the destruction of all her dreams. She gave herself a mental shake and told herself it was her own fault. She let down her defenses. She let a man in, and naturally, he ran right over her, crushing her heart into the dust.

"Are you quite finished now, ma'am?"

She sniffed again, lifted her chin, and stared him square in the eye. He would not see that he'd beaten her. Slowly she nodded.

"Good." Gabe crumpled the paper in his hand and tossed the poetry book down onto his desk. His hands at her waist, he lifted her into the air and marched across the room. When he dropped her on the settee, Loralie's mouth dropped open. Before she could speak, though, Gabe said quietly, "It's *my* turn."

She glared at him.

"Yes, I paid off your note at the bank." She flinched, but he went on. "Virgil had a foreclosure notice he forgot to give you three weeks ago! You were out of time. I wasn't tryin' to keep it from you." He tossed his hands high in the air. "Didn't I walk right in here and tell you all about it?" She didn't answer. *"Well?"*

"Yes, you did," Loralie agreed. "But you probably—"

"Enough!" He silenced her with a shout. "It's still my turn.

"As for actin' last night, well, you'll just have to take my word on it that no man can 'act' that kind of feelin'."

Loralie blushed and sniffed again, then turned her eyes away from him.

"Tessie!" Gabe's shout rattled the crystal drops hanging from the desk lamp shade, and Loralie jumped right along with them. "Tessie! Come here, Tess!"

"What in hell is goin' on in here?" the woman demanded from the safety of the doorway.

"I want you to tell Miss Loralie Davis here a few things about the family, Tess." Gabe's eyes never left Loralie's.

"Sure, Gabe. What?"

"First. What kind of school is Anna in?"

"Hmmph!" Tessie wiped her floury hands on her apron. "Don't know why you'd want to brag about that. Downright disgraceful is what *I* call it!"

"Tessie . . ."

"All right, all right." She looked at Loralie and frowned. "She's off to some fancy school studyin' to be a *doctor*!"

Loralie's mouth hung open.

"It ain't right, I know." Tessie nodded. "I argued and argued with Gabe here. But he kept sayin', 'If it makes her happy, that's good enough for me.' By thunder, it ain' decent!"

"And Jenny, Tess. Where's Jenny?"

Tessie's hands went to her broad hips. "That there's another one for you! Sweet little thing like that, and al she can do is talk about cattle!"

"What's she doin', Tess?" Gabe watched Loralie steadily.

"Hell, she's roamin' all over England and such lookin' for the perfect bull to make bigger, meatier calves with our cows." Tessie shook her head. "Praise God, her mother didn't live to see it."

"Never mind that," Gabe said, softer now. "Tell her about James."

"Shoot, why'm I tellin' her everything? Cat got your tongue?"

"Tessie, just do it. James?"

"Oh, Lordy. My sweet Jamie." Tessie's red head shook sadly. "Off runnin' around with who knows what . . .

dressin' up in them tights and wearin' face paint like a saloon girl."

Loralie's face registered her confusion.

"Tessie!"

"All right, all right." She took a deep breath. "He's a *actor*!"

Loralie's eyes opened wide, and a slight smile curved her lips. Now she understood what he'd meant when he said she had the wrong Curran.

"You about through depressin' me now?" Tessie complained. "I got bread to bake."

"Yeah. That's it." Then Gabe shouted out, "One more thing, Tess. What'd I tell you I was fixin' to buy today?"

"Lord have mercy, you want me to do *that* for you, too?" She looked at Loralie and shrugged her massive shoulders. "He went to town to buy you a weddin' ring." Tessie gave Gabe a good glare. "You want I should get down on one knee, too?"

He chuckled softly. "No, I don't think so, but thanks."

When they were alone again, Gabe straightened out the crushed slip of paper in his hand, then gave it to Loralie. "This is for you, too." Slowly he turned from her and walked to the side window. "I only bought it so's the bank wouldn't take it—and so's you wouldn't leave. You do whatever the hell you want with it."

Loralie looked down at the deed to the little farm and felt tears spring to her eyes again. Right on the front, on the space marked "Owner" was her name, Loralie Davis.

She glanced up at his broad back as he stared out at the yard. Lord, she'd made a mess of things. She should have trusted her instincts.

Imagine! One sister a doctor . . . another a cattle breeder . . . and his brother, an actor of all things! Loralie smiled gently. Oh, Gabe Curran might be many things, mostly infuriating, but he wasn't looking to control anyone. What he'd done for his family proved that. She looked down at the paper in her hand. What he'd done for *her* proved that.

"Gabe . . ."

"What?"

"Gabe, would you come over here, please?"

He sighed, turned, and walked back to her. "What is it, Loralie?"

She patted the seat beside her. Warily he sat down. Loralie snuggled in close and didn't breathe easily until she felt his arm slip around her shoulders.

"You said your family would be coming home soon?"

"That's right," he said.

She nodded and laid her head down on his chest. "Shall we get married right away, or would you like to wait for them to come home?"

He went completely still, and Loralie held her breath. Then his fingers lifted her chin, and he kissed her gently and smiled.

"Where you're concerned, lady, I don't want to wait for a damn thing."

And outside, in the shade under the Curran back porch, Alfonse and Henrietta settled down for a short summer nap.

WHITE HEATHER

Karen Lockwood

Scotland, August 1850

The shower spattering the castle windows was nothing compared to the storm gathering inside Annie Shaw's heart. Finally she had found someone upon whom to vent her frustrations, and she was not about to be put off.

"I repeat, Jamie Gordon, is the heather in Edinburgh the same color as in our Highlands?"

"Purple, aye."

"And does it not bloom in the summer the same as in our Highlands?"

"The heather, I warrant, behaves exactly the same in Edinburgh," came Jamie's reply as he continued to concentrate on the castle books. With his unruly red curls, Jamie at first glance looked like a man given to impulse. Instead, as long as Annie had known him, he'd epitomized the loyal worker, dutiful son, and earnest beau, in that order. If his passions seemed to be held in check, Annie supposed their wedding would bring them out. Marriage to Jamie, however, was a month away, and the fire in Annie's heart demanded some kind of response—now.

Impatience getting the better of her, she snatched the quill from his fingers. "Then why do those ladies have to stay here and look at *our* heather day after day?" Drops of ink scattered all over the desk.

Calmly Jamie blotted the desk before looking up, amused. "And since when has there been a law against Lowlanders admiring Highland heather?"

"There's not!" Frustrated, Annie moved to the window chair and slumped down, chin in hand, staring out at the

211

glen. Purple swathed the misty hills of Glencannon like a mantle, familiar and glorious. The time when the heather bloomed was usually her favorite season of the year.

But *this* summer, for the first time ever, Anne yearned to rip out the heath and toss it, bees and all, into the loch, ever since . . . since the village of Gillycairn had become a holiday destination for the Lowlanders. Only a pair, the Stuart ladies, had arrived at the inn, but they were a nuisance and their chaperone too retiring. Jamie simply didn't seem to care.

Leaning forward, she swiped at the window. "Until it rained, those ladies followed me about like sheep, acting all fine and rich while the villagers have more important things to worry about . . . surely *you* must understand, Jamie." She turned and pleaded with her betrothed for sympathy. "You're the one who found the castle accounts all in disarray, and now the villagers wonder if they'll be thrown out and sheep replaced in their stead."

"Evictions are possible. It all depends on Duncan, on what kind of man he is when he comes home."

"Well, I say those Edinburgh ladies are the ones who ought to be evicted, taffeta skirts and ringlets and watercolor boxes and all."

At that, Jamie finally blotted a ledger page, and he moved to take her in his arms.

"Annie Macaulay Shaw," he said with amusement in his voice. "You can't evict ladies bent on their purpose."

"What purpose?" she repeated, pushing out of his arms and putting distance between them.

Jamie sighed. "I see I must spell it out. Annie, it's not the heather they're here for. Lord Glencannon is the reason our wee village is suddenly a popular Highland destination."

"Duncan? What's he got to do with the heather?"

Jamie grinned. "Simple and bluntly, the ladies didn't catch themselves a husband in the Edinburgh Season, so they've come to holiday here and catch Duncan's eye."

Annie floundered for words. "But . . . even if that were true, how do we know when he's arriving?"

"Lass, it was to have been a surprise, but the Stuart ladies, it appears, got wind of it in Edinburgh. Rumor has it Duncan's returned to London and will be making his way to Scotland any day."

Annie wanted to jump for joy. Duncan. Almost home. "He'll want to rest, not entertain ladies," she said.

Jamie shook his head. "Don't you think as Lord Glencannon, he'll have to have a Lady Glencannon and create heirs? Besides which, he needs to make a *rich* marriage to save this poor village."

"Pooh, who'd want to wed a bankrupt man?"

"Rich ladies in search of a title care less, I think, for a man's bank account than for his pedigree."

Whirling, Annie stared at Jamie. "Are you saying, James Gordon, that Duncan's new title makes him fair game . . . for marriage?"

"Aye, he'll be pursued like the finest prize trout in all of Scotland."

Annie stood there, momentarily stunned. To picture Duncan as a man grown was one thing, but to imagine him taking some ambitious lady to his bed . . . well! A slow blush crept up her cheeks, and she busied herself putting away the books Jamie had pulled from the shelves.

Oh, suddenly she felt foolish for asking the Stuart ladies— Winifred and Gillian—why their sudden interest in the Highland heather. Such smug smiles they'd given her when she'd naively asked why they'd thought to come to Gillycairn *this* of all summers.

This month. The month Duncan was expected to return.

She stuffed a last book into the bookcase. "Fine ladies thinking to snare Duncan are as daft as bees humming the heath in winter. All Duncan likes to do is hunt and fish. And if the ladies think Duncan's grown any more refined stalking the wilds of America, they're wrong again! Sick and tired of refinement, he used to say."

"A lot can change in five years, Annie," Jamie said quietly. "Even you have to admit the village has changed. Why else are the villagers worried about how to put porridge on the table? Every one of us may have to emigrate."

Annie whirled. "But I don't *want* to leave the village. I don't want things to change any more."

"Even people change. Duncan, too—"

"No!" It was unthinkable. "You're wrong," she said and without another sound, save the slamming of every door behind her, took her leave. Outside the castle the clouds were parting, and she waded through the dampish heath to the stream where she and Duncan used to fish. There, alone, she sat beneath a tree, watching a rainbow come and go and finally the shadows of gloaming settle over the hills.

Annie tried but couldn't picture Duncan any way than how he'd left, a laughing youth, with golden tousled hair, fishing rod, and a promise to come back someday. And now, selfish as it sounded, she didn't want to share her girlhood friend, certainly not with fine ambitious ladies. She wanted Duncan—the Duncan of five years ago—for herself.

Drumarlie Castle stood as Duncan had left it, white turrets glittering in the sun, its baronial splendor standing guard over the banks of Loch Claymore and the village of Gillycairn, all of it awaiting the return of the laird.

Sixth Earl of Glencannon. The title still sat as unexpectedly on Duncan Munro as the next rut in the Highland road sat on the coach springs. He was glad to be home in Scotland, however, amazingly glad, and as the coach rolled into the village, he looked out the window in anticipation.

Except for a few sheep where once crofters had tilled potatoes, nothing had changed—yet. He hoped everything in it had stayed that way, that the trout still swam as ever, the red stag still bounded through the woods, and Annie was still here. . . .

Annie. Mercurial Annie. Across five years and two continents he'd never forgotten her temper. How, he mused, would she like having him for a guardian instead of a fellow ghillie? Would the tomboy in her rebel? As the coach slowed to a stop in front of the castle, the question seemed in imminent peril of being answered. The entire household—gentry, servants, and dogs—was outside to engulf him in heartfelt embraces, handshakes, or wet-tongued, tail-wagging expressions of happiness. Annie, he realized at once, fell into none of these categories, but he did not wonder yet at her absence.

Duncan's mother shed enough tears to dampen five violet-scented hankies. "One for each year you've been gone, Duncan," she wept, adding, "and you're not even the lad I bade farewell to. Left a boy and returned a man, that you did."

"While you, Mother, remained as young as I remembered." Gazing down with fondness at the new lines in her face, he chose to mention what was familiar about her. "Your spirits are good, Mother, and for that I'm a grateful son."

"So you've learned the art of flattery as well as tall tale telling in that wild land." His mother's eyes sparkled with fondness. "Every wrinkle and gray hair I own is over worrying about you."

"My late brother has to share some of the burden for that newly silvered hair, Mother."

His hasty words drew out another tear. "And so it took losing him to gain you back. Oh, Duncan, the price life extracts . . . Forgive me," she said, leading him inside the castle, "but you've changed so much."

Changed? Him? Not at all. True, he'd stopped at a London tailor to change his buckskins for more suitable gentleman's clothing, and undoubtedly five years in North America matured a man's look. But inside, no matter how long he'd roamed across the water, inside still beat the heart and soul of a Scotsman, a stubborn, sentimental Scot. "Nothing's changed, Mother, except the news. Now join me in the library. I want, without further delay, to hear what everyone's been up to, especially Annie."

Inside, he looked about for the familiar, frowned at the changes. The stag heads still stared down over the rows of books; the crack in the door still allowed servants to eavesdrop. But all the walls, once plain, were now covered in tartan. The sofas sported tartan, as did the floor. The decor was enough to make a man used to log huts rather dizzy.

"What the deuce happened to this place?"

"Your brother's idea. Tartan's all the fashion since the Queen came to visit the Highlands."

"And costly . . . Small wonder the estate's bankrupt . . . the villagers worrying about clearances . . ." His brother had been a wastrel, no doubt about it, but that wasn't all that bothered him. Annie was still nowhere in sight.

As the door opened, he looked up expectantly, but it was a manservant who came running in, arms piled high with account books, another following with a tray containing whisky and glasses perched on top of more account books stacked on his valise. Annie, he noted, was not among the new arrivals. Sulking somewhere, no doubt, or else fishing and forgot the time.

He flipped through an account book, searching for the ways, besides excessive purchase of tartan, in which his dear departed brother had squandered the estate.

"I know you never expected to have all this responsibility thrust upon you, son."

He glanced over his shoulder, touched at the motherly words. Lady Glencannon twisted her handkerchief in her hands.

"It was a shock, a sad shock. But I've had a long journey home to get used to the idea. Andrew did his best as laird, Mother, now I shall do my best, and my first concern is for you and the villagers."

"Some villagers say our Highland Games should be canceled this year, that people should not play at a time like this."

"Why not?" He'd just settled down by the fireplace with an account book and looked up, surprised.

"Because, with our villagers fearing for their very crofts, Gillycairn's people are too sad. As Lord Glencannon, you've the last word now. It's for you to say."

He didn't even stop turning the pages of the account book. "Despite . . . no, *because* of the hard times in this village, the Games will go on." His voice was determined. "I'll provide all the prizes. Pass the word to the villagers to mend their kilts, tune up their fiddles and bagpipes, practice their dancing and their wrestling, and ready their throwing arms . . . for Duncan Munro is returned, and just because I'm laird does not mean I intend to relinquish my records in the events." Nor his title as best fisherman in the glen, a title Annie had bestowed upon him.

But Annie still had not welcomed him. He was on his feet now, impatient, pacing the room, remembering.

He'd doted on Annie since childhood, when her family worked for the castle. In a show of compassion Duncan's father, fourth Earl of Glencannon, had taken guardianship of the motherless child after the castle ghillie—her father—had dropped dead while guiding Duncan's father and his sons in a deer hunt.

Nostalgic, Duncan sought out and found the family portraits still on the fireplace wall. In the place of honor over the fireplace hung the commissioned work, a formal portrait of the Glencannon heirs—Duncan and his older brother as young lads, boyish faces somber above their kilted attire. His eyes went to the companion portrait of Annie. There she was as he'd left her—a laughing black-haired lass dressed in dark tartan, ribbons in her hair, a sheepdog at her side. On a whim the artist had asked if he could paint the lovely little gypsy lass.

It wasn't usually done, his father had huffed proudly, for a grand family to commission portraits of their wards, but his mother had won the day. After all, the artist had wanted to paint it so badly he had not charged a farthing. Captured the lilt of her smile, the painter had, as well as her mischievous spirit.

"Where *is* she?" The longing in his voice would not be contained.

"My, but for a man gone five years you've grown impatient."

"Everyone greeted me but her," he pointed out.

"I've sent for her," his mother replied. "Told her the laird requests her."

"Tell me," he said while drinking in the sight of her portrait, "does Annie still bring in a trout every day to Cook?"

"Of course. She always favored her father."

"Annie's not changed, then. . . . Good."

"Never fear, she's most anxious to see you. She's got unexpected news."

He glanced at his mother in amusement. "Dare I hazard a guess? She's broken all my fishing equipment? Washed Murdock's coat in whisky?"

"Duncan, don't tease. She's nearly eighteen years old."

"Mother, I don't care if she's decorated the stables in tartan . . ." He was emptying the valise, setting out gifts for Annie, mementos of a life in the wilderness. Suddenly he looked up. "She hasn't, has she?"

"Duncan, your imagination has gone wild in America."

"Then, what's she done that's such a secret?"

"She'll want to tell you herself, I expect."

Smiling, he prepared himself for the worst. Which would be . . . that she'd fished all the trout from his own stream, his own private pool?

And impatiently he drew out his pocket watch and snapped it open, looking at Annie's parting memento of five years ago—now just a scrap of faded blue ribbon in the watch case.

"Find her."

His mother peered out into the hallway and gestured a maid to go and hurry Annie along. "I'm sure she's readying herself to greet you properly," his mother said and added on a sigh, "I've tried so hard to make a lady of her, you know."

Duncan laughed out loud and pocketed the watch. "Annie, a lady?" Unthinkable. Why, he'd wager she was up to mischief this very instant.

"Do you think he'll be surprised at how tall I've grown?" Annie stood barefoot, black hair to her waist, and leaned closer to the mirror to dab at a speck of mud on her cheek. The fishing this morning, because of a misty rain, had been disappointing.

"Aye, miss," the maid said with a blush, "but will you be surprised at him! Oh, miss, what a braw gentleman he's become. The ladies are going to swoon over their teacups. . . ."

Annie twisted around. The servants had wasted no time in passing the word.

"Now, stand still, Miss Annie," the maid said. "Her ladyship's sent up word for you to hurry, and she wants your hair done up, not looking like you just tangled with the kelpies."

Annie tilted her head at the mirror, mentally comparing herself to those Edinburgh ladies. Oh, the Stuart ladies might have ringlets and taffeta and be waiting to pounce on Duncan like trappers to the fox, but Annie had learned a thing or two herself in five years.

"Find me the plaid gown, the blue and green one with the low-cut neck, the one Lady Glencannon favors so . . . and borrow Lady Glencannon's perfume . . . and bring me some water so I can wash off the mud. Hurry, please, oh, hurry!"

From both ends they worked, scrubbing, polishing, and perfuming, until at last a ladylike version of Annie ran out into the hall.

"Walk, Miss Annie," the maid admonished, and Annie screeched to a halt, then started up again slowly—like the Edinburgh ladies—smoothing her skirt as she went.

Halfway down the stairs she paused at the sound of a male voice. Her heart went double time as she tiptoed down to the main floor. But remembering the maid's blush, she hesitated outside the library door. Duncan's return felt like a surprise birthday gift; she'd no idea what to expect. And she'd always been one to secretly unwrap and peek inside her gifts because she was simply unable to bear the suspense of wondering.

Which is why she peered through the crack in the open library door, looking to see if Duncan still resembled the eighteen-year-old lad she'd tagged after.

All she could find was a man. Duncan would be twenty-three now. But this man looked nearer to thirty. She squinted.

On closer inspection, perhaps the face did resemble Duncan. It was certainly his voice. But his roaming had done marvelous things to him, weathered his skin, forged a hard glint into those blue eyes. His tawny hair waved where it touched his cheeks, and his mouth and jaw were as craggy as the rocks about the lochs.

As for the wrappings about him, well, what fine clothes—an elegant London frock coat of black, buff-colored trousers, a plaid waistcoat.

"It's as Jamie said," she whispered, truly awed. The lad to whom she'd given a sentimental farewell token was gone.

Her palms went slick; her heart raced. Nor did she understand the strange flutter in her stomach. Why, she felt as if an arrow had just whizzed by her heart—a reaction she never had around Jamie. "Blast it, Duncan, you changed on me."

The words were no sooner out of her mouth than Duncan looked up and, worse, headed for the door. It was too late to come out and greet him like a proper lady. She was going to get caught peeking like a child.

Annie flattened herself against the wall, face buried in her arms, praying that she'd shrink and a mouse hole would open up and swallow her. Jamie had tried to tell her Duncan would be changed, but no, she'd had to see for herself. When, oh, when was she going to start taking Jamie at his word?

The instant Duncan heard Annie coming, he looked over at the door in anticipation. Expecting Annie to bang it open and assault him, he braced himself for a welcome-home hug. She'd probably smell of newly cleaned trout, he mused. He waited . . . and waited. She never appeared.

And unable to wait a moment longer, he stalked out of the library and looked behind the door. She was up to her old tricks—this time playing hide-and-seek with the door. Silently he moved toward her, arms outstretched, ready to pounce on her.

At the last second she whirled, and he froze in place, arms dropping to his sides.

"Annie?" His voice cracked so that he had to say it again. "Annie?" This was no child, and for a minute he decided he must have mistaken Annie for a fancy lady, or a comely maid.

Yet . . . here was Annie's rich black hair, Annie's eyes—dark as midnight—and Annie's smile.

But the rest of her was all different, all curves, parts of her swelling and flowing in places meant to tempt a man.

One by one the parts added up to something unexpected.

"I scarcely know you, lass." Torn between the boy of five years past and the man of today, he could only say the obvious. "You've grown up."

"Welcome home, Duncan," she said, and then the sweet wonder of Annie was in his arms. He managed a self-conscious peck to her cheek, noticing as he did so that she smelled of lavender now instead of fish fins. His head spun; his heart stood still.

Somehow he backed out of her arms, untangled himself, and, turning away, ran a shaky hand through his hair.

"I thought you'd still be the tomboy, chasing about the place, in need of taming by your guardian." No, instead it was his body that needed taming; his blood ran hot.

As if that weren't enough, his mother, he realized, stood there watching them.

"Duncan, you can stop looking as if you've seen a ghost. If you can come home a mountain man, why can't Annie be here waiting as a lovely young woman?"

Annie backed around him, moving toward the library. "You look positively white, Duncan," she said, "and we've five years to catch up on. Come along, and we'll fortify you with tea."

When he took the cup and saucer of tea from her a few minutes later, the porcelain rattled, and then he made the mistake of looking up into her eyes.

He stared like that, numb, the scone he'd accepted from his mother crumbling while butter melted over his fingers.

What he said he'd never remember. He mouthed platitudes. Andrew's death. The voyage home. The village. The new title.

"Have I changed?" she asked at last, as if trying to figure out why he stared at her so white-faced, why he wouldn't smile.

"A bit," he said in stoic understatement while he strove to control his breathing. "Your hair is different."

"I—I put it up."

And put down the bodice of her gowns to a tempting view. Indeed, in five years her cleavage had taken on a grandeur appropriate for a Highland lass.

"My gown's the latest fashion."

"So I see."

Bloomed she had, like the heather in its season . . . and he'd been lucky enough to get back to Annie in time to claim her before another man did. For that, he supposed Andrew's death had been a blessing.

Annie. First, his friend. Then his ward.

And now his desire. In five seconds it hit him. This new Annie wasn't a puzzle, but an answer. Annie, his childhood friend, could now become his wife. She would still be a part of his life, only in a new way.

He supposed he'd have to wait a few days to initiate a courtship. To get down on bended knee the first five minutes of his return might make him appear out of his head.

His mother cleared her throat. "Duncan's brought gifts for us all . . . and Duncan, Annie has special news for you. Which shall we do first?" And before either of them could get a word out, his mother decided for them. "Oh, Duncan, you go first."

A maiden in her first Season couldn't have blushed more deeply than did he. This was a woman who needed perfume and pearls. Not animal pelts and arrowheads. "I fear I misjudged how you'd grown up when I selected these souvenirs."

"Nonsense," Annie said, setting down her teacup and standing wide-eyed as a child again. "What have you brought me?"

"They're foolish things, mementos of the wild American territories. As I said, Annie—Anne—I was thinking of you as my ward, as thirteen—"

"Duncan," his mother prompted, impatient. Guileless as always, his mother couldn't see an undercurrent unless it was pulling her under water. "Give her your souvenirs," she said, clearly puzzled, and so there was nothing for it but to present the gifts.

He handed Annie a muff of fine buffalo hide.

She rubbed the fur to the alabaster skin of her cheek.

He handed her an Indian feather.

Ever so slowly she teased her throat with it and laughed.

He placed an arrowhead into the palm of her hand, and she held it up, admiring it as if it were a jewel, then turned laughing eyes on him.

"They're wonderful." She smiled at him in utter happiness. "I knew you wouldn't forget me, that nothing would change."

On the contrary. "How is my pony?" he asked, desperate for a common ground. Five years ago Annie had promised to care for his Shetland pony. "You've not grown up so much that you'd forget your promise to me?"

Standing there, clutching all Duncan's mementos, Annie's heart soared. She'd been so afraid that she'd lost the lad in him forever, but if Duncan had brought her tomboy gifts and was asking about Murdock, then he must want to continue their relationship where they left off as youngsters.

"Jamie helped me have a burr removed from one of his hooves, but otherwise Murdock's fine."

In truth, caring for Duncan's pony had eased her through the years, helped her endure the endless gown fittings, tea parties, French lessons, and piano lessons that Lady Glencannon, in her determination to make a lady of Annie, had foisted on her. Annie hated all of it, nothing more than this formal reunion.

"Murdock's in the stables this very minute," she went on excitedly and took a step toward him, impulsive. "Shall we ride ponies like we used to?"

They used to ride double. Duncan backed up a step, still wary of his reaction to her. "If the estate's in difficulties, the villagers doing poorly, then that would be frivolous of me."

Her face showed her disappointment. "The duties of a laird come first, of course."

He nodded and held his distance, tried to forget the aching need to take her in his arms. "Perhaps later, after the heather bloom is over. Will you wait till then?" Until he could find a second pony perhaps.

"Yes," Annie agreed, "that would be best." Poor Duncan, she couldn't help thinking, he looked so miserable to be home. Perhaps, she thought with a pang, he never wanted to return, hated having to give up his grand roaming because he'd inherited the lordship and a ward to boot.

"Duncan," his mother reminded him, calling his attention back. "We simply must decide about the ladies from Edinburgh."

As Annie flitted out of the room on some sudden errand, Duncan stared after her. For the first time he knew what it must feel like to have a herd of buffalo stampede over one's body.

"You wasted no time in turning her into a lady," he said of Annie.

Lady Glencannon planted a patient look on her son. "I've only succeeded in part. I keep fearing she'll shock the fine ladies here on holiday." Skillfully she brought the subject back to the visitors. "You know, now that you're home, I really can't put off inviting them—"

"What ladies?" he asked, his attention finally caught.

"The Edinburgh ladies. Annie's been most attentive to them."

"This is an inconvenient summer for guests, Mother."

Annie, he noticed, had come back and stood in the doorway, listening.

"Such elegant ladies," Annie said tartly, "can only paint so many scenes of heather before wanting more *refined* activity. They've been here well over a week," she added.

Unattached ladies, Duncan knew, did not traipse up into the Highlands to see nothing but heather. "Have they, then? And you've not taken them fishing yet?"

Annie looked up shyly from under her lashes and shook her head in that mischievous way. So she'd not been tamed completely. A little fire remained beneath all the refinement his mother had forced on her.

"Don't you want to know the ladies' names?" his mother asked in some excitement.

No. But she'd keep wanting to tell him till the English invaded Gillycairn. "Who are they?" he asked dutifully as he eyed Annie from head to toe.

"Ladies Winifred and . . . oh, mercy, I forget her sister."

"Why would you invite them here?" he said, still looking at Annie.

"Courtesy, of course," his mother said with maddening good cheer. "Their second cousin, I believe it was, married your father's cousin, and once when I visited Edinburgh, I'm sure I stayed at their town house. Back of Charlotte Square it was. Very fine, and they dressed so elegant— still do—that I felt quite the country cousin come to town. But they were already at the inn when I received their note informing me they were here, and I thought with your arrival imminent, perhaps I should wait till you got home . . ." She clenched her fist in triumph. "Gillian, that's the name of the other, and their father is in finance. A banker."

A banker! "A financier?" He turned from Annie to his mother, his full attention on the subject of holiday visitors. He'd been about to banish the Edinburgh ladies, but the daughters of a banker deserved more attention.

"Should we invite them to stay here?" his mother pressed.

Annie, he noted out of the corner of his eye, sighed and went to stare out the window.

"Mother, we'll entertain them, but within bounds. They are not staying at the castle." He calmed the rising note in his voice. "But I should like to make their acquaintance," he added more gently. When a man with an estate in financial difficulty received the daughters of an Edinburgh banker, all sorts of problems could be smoothed out. Annie, who'd always liked people, would understand and help out.

"You may invite them to tea," he decided swiftly. "I'll do my part to entertain and escort them about." He was already bored thinking of walks around the loch and down the village lane, all the while making edifying chitchat about the history of Drumarlie Castle. Still, it was good to see his mother smile, and a small sacrifice to make for the good of his village.

"Now it's time to give Annie your best wishes." His mother clasped her hands together in glee. "Annie, tell him."

Annie whirled at the window, her expression startled, settling into reluctance. He knew that look. He'd seen it when she'd plucked the feathers off his first grouse before he could show the bird off to his brother.

"Best wishes on what, Annie?" he asked with suspicion. "On my becoming your guardian?" Oh, but he'd guard the lass well. And after a suitable interval, court her.

"Best wishes on what?" he pressed.

"On my wedding." It was a whispered announcement.

He felt as if he'd been poleaxed. "Your what?"

"I'm to be wed," she stammered, looking up at him with those dark blue eyes. "The last day of August—so you see," she rushed on, "you've timed your return well, Duncan."

He slumped into the nearest chair, stunned by betrayal. "Wed? But you're still my ward."

"Duncan, surely you can look and sound more pleasant," his mother scolded. "You know James. Your own estate manager."

"Jamie Gordon?"

"Is there any other Jamie in the village?"

As a child, Jamie had been a fat, freckled redhead who always won the caber toss at the Games. They'd been childhood friends, but now he hated Jamie, instinctive, primeval hatred.

"He's grown up to be a handsome man—and most capable—as you well know."

While Duncan, desperate to hide his shock, strolled to the opposite window from Annie, his mother chattered on.

"With all the worry over poor crops, the villagers feel a wedding in the wee kirk will be all the more special this year. It's likely the last year for so many villagers here . . . so you mustn't fuss now. . . . You said everything would go on as usual . . . and the banns have already been read."

He shot a dark look at Annie, across the room from him. "Eloping wasn't good enough?"

"Of course not!" his mother replied. "For the ward of Drumarlie Castle, we're having a regular church wedding, Duncan. What is the trouble?"

"Mother, someone should have asked me!"

"You were hundreds of miles away across an ocean."

He couldn't hide his anger—no, his dismay. The news

was too much, too fast. He hadn't accustomed himself to Annie growing up or to his own desire for her. And now this.

"What do you want me to say?" he said at length.

"Say you're glad. Our own Annie. Duncan, it was your father's last wish that Anne—his little ward—wed well. Your late brother gave his blessing, and I expect you will, too. Jamie's a fine lad for Anne. If not a titled man, he's a steady man and with a fine position. He'll keep her well. You'll give the bride away, of course. Oh, do say you're glad."

He wasn't glad. As it was, he had to bite his tongue to keep from blurting out his refusal to give consent.

"Now, don't be a grump of a guardian," his mother warned.

Duncan looked at Annie. Did she really love another man?

Annie looked back at him, eyes dark, lips tremulous. How could he refuse her happiness simply because he'd returned too late to claim her for his own?

On the other hand, she wasn't yet wed.

"How long until the wedding?"

"Less than four weeks, Duncan," his mother said. "Why?"

Three and a half weeks at best. To convince her she was wedding the wrong man.

"Duncan?"

The room was silent for the longest time.

"The Annie I remember," he said at last, "is a lass of changeable moods. If she still wishes to wed Jamie Gordon on the day before her wedding, then I'll grant my consent. Not a minute before."

He stalked from the room, satisfied. A lot could happen to change Annie's mind in less than four weeks.

Annie, returning from a long walk in the hills with the Stuart ladies, was ready to scream in frustration. Every day since Duncan's return had been exactly alike. Boring. Boring. Boring. She wanted something to change, preferably for the Stuart ladies to leave. But, no. Stuck like thistles they did—to her all day and to Duncan all evening.

And now, stumbling along through the heath, Winifred and Gillian, arms laden with sketchbooks and watercolor boxes, could chatter of nothing but his lordship's charm and good looks. At the merest mention of his name, Annie's body flooded with warmth; her face, she knew, went crimson. If she hadn't been pledged to Jamie, if Duncan weren't her guardian, she'd swear she was smitten. That was impossible, of course, but something more than their looks had changed in the five years Duncan had been gone.

Since their reunion in the castle, however, Duncan had virtually ignored her, giving her little more than a polite nod. He gave all his time to Jamie talking about the estate. The estate. Always the estate. Taking second place in his attentions were the Stuart ladies, though for the life of her, Annie had no idea what he saw in them.

Lady Winifred, tall and straight as a caber post, was prissy and straitlaced from her rather sharp nose to her toes. Her younger sister Gillian's chief virtues were a giggly voice and a tendency to stare at every Highlander who bared his knees.

Both forced their hair into sausage ringlets and wore impossibly fussy gowns, better suited to the drawing room than to the Highlands. Their lacy black shawls were gathered at the bodice by identical silver brooches. The epitome of fine breeding, these ladies never failed to make Annie, in homespun and bare feet, feel the awkward schoolgirl.

Well, she'd had enough. She was going to get them to admit the true purpose behind this holiday in the heather. Shame them into leaving.

"Why did you come to Gillycairn?" she asked slyly. "Everyone knows there's heather to be seen down in Edinburgh."

After a brief pause, Winifred waved a hand airily. "Of course there's the patch here and there, but it can't grow in the streets and lanes of Edinburgh like it does here, and certainly we'd never find any *white* heather there."

"For luck," Gillian put in.

Annie had avoided mentioning white heather till now.

"Do you know where it grows white?" Gillian asked.

The whereabouts of lucky white heather was a secret she was not willing to share.

"Have you ever found any?" Gillian asked.

"Of course I've found some."

"Well, where was it?"

"I gave it away."

"Well," Winifred said in her practical tone, "naturally, we'd rather wait and search for white heather with Lord Glencannon."

"Naturally." Annie could barely contain the jealousy in her voice and warned, "But of course, after five years gone, Duncan might have forgotten where it grows."

"We'll let him decide that," Winifred decreed.

With that settled, and a decision made to leave the heath for a walk along the stream, there followed an endless barrage of questions about Lord Glencannon, whose mother had *finally* invited them to tea at Drumarlie Castle. It was more than Annie could bear. But if she could fib about white heather, she could fib about anything. If Annie made Duncan sound formidable, perhaps, just perhaps, the ladies would have their ardor cooled.

"Why did Duncan stay so long in America?" Gillian asked.

"He was the second son—banished because of his vile temper." It was a sin to lie, but Annie was desperate to send these ladies out of Duncan's life.

"Was he ever wed in America?"

"Now, why would Duncan wed when he was busy chasing buffalo and bears and . . . and Indians? Naked Indians," she added. Oh, but her answers were wicked.

Winifred raised her eyebrows, as if she weren't taken in for a minute. "Is Duncan very wealthy?" she asked, cutting to the heart of her quest.

"Wealthy? Oh, Winifred, ladies don't ask—"

"Hush, Gillian." Winifred tapped her sister's wrist with her parasol point. "Don't be a ninny. We're not dealing with a lady here."

Annie didn't have to keep a straight face anymore, for the answer to this question was close to the truth. "The estate is bankrupt, of course. Even I, poor orphaned daughter of a ghillie, know *that*. The blight, you know. That's why many of the villagers are so sad. They fear Duncan will evict them and bring in sheep in their stead."

To her immense satisfaction, Gillian and Winifred stopped in their tracks right in the middle of the lane near the stream. "Aye"—she sighed with as much pity in her tone as she could muster—"whoever weds Duncan can look forward to a long life of sheep at her castle door, and nothing but mutton to eat. Duncan is thrifty with a shilling, you know. To a fault."

Winifred and Gillian exchanged a knowing look, as if refined ladies like themselves were not about to have the wool pulled over their eyes by a country chit like Annie.

She paused. "It's the truth. Duncan has much to do putting the estate in order."

"Of course, but our father is a banker. Now that we know the circumstances, perhaps in some way we can offer help. . . ."

Annie, mouth open in chagrin, looked at first one lady, then the other. A banker father. Of course, that was the appeal of the Stuart ladies. Jamie had said Duncan would need to wed for heirs, and perhaps for money as well. Quickly she walked on, in case the heartache welling up inside her showed on her face.

It was a blessing when they turned a bend and Gillycairn Stream came fully into view. Unable to bear the chatter, Annie led them to the banks just below the village crossing.

"Tell me, Annie," Winifred asked, coming up beside her, "how does Lord Glencannon amuse himself in the daytime?"

Winifred's shadow scared away the fish Annie had been watching rise up. She stood and gave an honest answer. "Before he left, it was Duncan of all the lads in the village who held the record for throwing the hammer. But best of all, he likes to fish." Oh, how she longed to go fishing alone with Duncan, at their secret place.

The three women were looking down at the stream, which glistened in the summer sun and rippled over mossy rocks. Winifred looked at Gillian, and Gillian looked at Winifred. And so came the inevitable question.

"Can you teach us how to fish, Annie?"

Secretly Annie sighed, half at the nuisance, half at the unwillingness to share with these ladies a sport that had belonged to her and Duncan.

On the other hand, if she could not shame or scare these women away, she could change tactics. A fishing lesson would be an excellent way to make the Stuart ladies look foolish and perhaps make Duncan think twice about marrying for money.

"You realize fishing is best at dawn when the fish are hungry?" she asked carefully.

"Dawn? We're asleep then."

As Annie knew only too well. The ladies stayed up till the wee hours gossiping and playing at cards with their indulgent chaperone, so the innkeeper said on the sly.

"Winifred, is she teasing us again?"

Winifred tossed her dark ringlets. "How should I know when fish like to eat?" Ever haughty, she spoke as if Annie were a brick wall. "Besides, it doesn't matter if Lord Glencannon sees us actually catch a fish. We're simply going to impress his lordship with our knowledge of the sport and amuse him with our anecdotes. Ladies like us have our own wiles for attracting gentlemen, genteel things like conversation and flirtation."

"That may be so," Annie admitted, "but you'll need fishing tackle, too."

An hour later Annie had gathered up a pair of fishing rods and met the ladies, now in sunbonnets, at the nearest fishing spot downstream from the village crossing. The heather bloomed there, but so did wild grass and brambles.

"Duncan likes to say fishing is like life, that if a man understands how to cast a line, he'll understand what women are about," Annie said while separating the equipment into two piles. She added in a casual tone, "How many beaux have you got in Edinburgh?"

Gillian colored but recovered quickly. "We've many beaux. So many we had to escape the press of their proposals and come here to think it all over."

"Hush, Gillian," Winifred hissed. "We are each of us going to wed a Scottish peer, and nothing less, so keep your mind on your manners lest Lord Glencannon hear your brazen talk."

Annie stared. Their single-minded purpose quite startled her. Poor Duncan, busy minding the estate, quite unaware of false lures being cast in his way . . . the ladies flattering him . . . impressing him . . . Would he nibble? Allow himself to get caught? With an effort she turned back to her task.

"Now watch. Here's how you cast." Taking one of the fishing rods, she demonstrated what she meant. "You bring back the line like this. Don't jerk it like a whip, or it'll only come back and land at your feet."

"That looks easy enough," Gillian said eagerly.

Actually it was much harder than it looked. "Just sweep it around gently so it lands in the water like this."

With a deft flick of her wrist, Annie cast the line into the stream. The fly bobbed and floated with the current.

After a few moments she reeled in the line and handed one rod to Winifred, the other to Gillian. "Now you two try it." She ought, she thought, to warn them that, if not handled correctly, the line could backlash, but mischief got the better of her. If Duncan came along, as he was apt to at this time of day, she'd *want* him to see the ladies at their most inept.

Both made a ludicrous effort to imitate Annie as they first whipped at the water with their lines and then snagged an underwater branch. Painstakingly Annie helped them tie on new flies, and then they began again.

When Gillian's very next cast hit the water, the line kept right on unreeling, first in snakelike ripples and finally in a big tangle. When Annie succeeded in pulling the mess from the water, it looked as yarn might after a pair of tomcats had fought their way out of it.

"You must sit there and untangle the line yourself," Annie said. "This is Duncan's equipment, and he'll be very angry at you if anything happens to it."

"But there's a hook hiding in this." Gillian sat on the bank, whining, a tangle of fishing line in her lap, gingerly plucking at it with two fingers as if the mess might bite. "At home I don't even have to unravel my own embroidery thread."

As for Winifred, her next cast was so tentative, the fly scarcely reached the water.

"You've got to use more force," Annie directed.

Winifred reeled in her line, then gave a mighty swing of her arm, but instead of the backlash Annie expected, the line stayed behind Winifred.

"You've snagged a bush, I fear," Annie said, foreseeing a short fishing lesson and a long afternoon spent unsnagging and retying hooks. Still, this was better than tramping through the heather for endless hours—*and* the Stuart ladies were delightfully inept. Which was doubtless a source of celebration for any fish observing this fiasco from underwater.

Again and again Winifred cast her line with the same result; she either fell short or snagged a bush. If Annie had one wish, it would have been for Duncan to come along, and surely, the angels were with her, for just then she spied him off in the distance, striding toward them.

In a flash, she turned into the enthusiastic teacher, helping poor Winifred free her hook from yet another bush. After straightening her bonnet and smoothing down her skirt, Winifred, unaware of Duncan's amused eyes, was ready to cast again.

Annie guided Winifred's hand to the reel. "Let some line out before you cast." Winifred flicked her wrist and the rod whipped back.

A bellow rent the air. It was masculine and sounded as if a stag had walked into the direct aim of a gun.

Annie whirled. Duncan, brow thunderous, was standing up on the lane, and the fishing line led somewhere in the vicinity of his coat sleeve. Duncan was hooked!

Her first reaction was a smile of satisfaction.

"Duncan," she said calmly, "stop bellowing so." She tried to sound in command. "Nothing has happened to your equipment that we can't fix."

"Equipment be damned!" His teeth were clenched. Blood trickled from his hand, spotting his trousers and boots.

Her smile faded. The expression she'd mistook for anger was a look of pain.

"You've hooked Lord Glencannon!" Gillian shrieked, as clasping her hands to her heart, she grasped the severity of the situation. She tried to rise but collapsed again in a heap of tangled line.

"His lordship's hooked?" The normally condescending Winifred actually sounded close to hysteria. "Annie— Annie, what shall I do now? What shall I *do*?" With each word she attempted to reel in the line, as if thinking to save Duncan from her error.

"Don't jerk the line!" Duncan shouted and, even as he spoke, pulled from his coat a pocketknife and sliced the line that bound him to Winifred Stuart. Standing there, holding a knife up in one hand, bleeding, he very much resembled a forbidding mountain man.

Despite all the confusion, Annie remained calm. "Don't get mad," she called up to Duncan. "All it takes is a quick trip to the blacksmith's to have the barb snipped off and the hook pulled." She moved toward him, for with Winifred in hysterics and Gillian tangled in her own line, this was Annie's chance to get close to Duncan, to touch him, to offer some tender concern to his wound.

"This is your fault, Annie. I've no doubts on that score." Annie stopped, frozen by his tone. He was glaring at her. At *her*, not at the inept ladies. He held out a hand-kerchief.

"Tie this about my hand," he ordered, brusquely holding out his injured hand for all to see. The fly had impaled him right between his thumb and index finger.

"Oh, but his lordship's dripping with blood!" Winifred shrieked. Annie looked back in time to see her fall backward into the stream with a giant splash.

"Tie it on," Duncan commanded, and the instant she did he brushed her aside and headed off to rescue Winifred.

Nearby in the stream, Winifred sat in a shallow pool, a bare six inches of water lapping up about her taffeta skirt while she beat her fists at her side and splashed more water all over her bodice. By the way she screamed for help, one would think she might actually drown, and she certainly scared away all the fish within five miles. Annie looked on in abject misery as Winifred Stuart stretched out her arms toward Lord Glencannon.

"I want to go back to the inn," Winifred said through chattering teeth. "I b-believe, L-lord Glencannon, that we'd be interested in more r-refined activities than what your w-ward has shown us." As she spoke she stood wringing the water out of her skirt and ringlets.

Duncan couldn't have been more solicitous. He gave the shivering Winifred the coat off his back to wrap about her shoulders, and then he pulled Gillian up and inquired gently if she was quite all right, doing his best to keep his own bandaged hand out of sight from the squeamish ladies.

With Lord Glencannon's arm to cling to, Winifred's courage became daunting. "It was Annie who insisted we learn how to fish," she said in an accusing tone, looking very much the drowned rat. "She's been so cross and spoken so sharply when we're doing our best, and poor Gillian . . . she . . . she's been ordered to untangle the line as if she's a common servant."

Oh, but the lies were too much, and Duncan was obviously taken in.

"We'd best get you both back to the inn," he said solicitously, plucking a bit of purple heather and handing a sprig each to Winifred and Gillian. "With deepest apologies for the inhospitality of Gillycairn's streams."

Annie took a step toward them.

"But, Duncan, your hand . . . You have to take the hook out."

He looked back at her then, his blue eyes as cold as the loch.

"And so I shall . . . after I walk the Stuart ladies back to the inn. *You* stay here and untangle the fishing line," he said.

"But—"

"If you hadn't taken the ladies fishing in my stream without my permission, this probably would never have happened."

"But—"

"Gather up all *my* equipment, return it to the castle in good order—just like you found it, is that clear?"

"I hope you forget to have the hook pulled out and get gangrene!" she muttered, fighting tears. She knelt and viciously jerked at the snarled line. "Go on, then. Or next you'll be holding me responsible for the ladies catching pneumonia, I suppose?"

Duncan knew if he looked back he'd laugh out loud at Annie's outrageous charge. In truth, the Stuart ladies had a better chance of catching pneumonia than they did any fish, but he wasn't going to give Annie the satisfaction of letting her know he knew that. The little minx. Her game was as old as Eve, and despite the throbbing of the hook in his hand, he smiled to himself and offered each of the Stuart ladies an arm for the short walk to the inn.

Annie was jealous! Beautifully, charmingly jealous. And she didn't even know it. Oh, but this was a delightful turn of events. To play Annie's jealousy, he was willing to flirt outrageously with the Stuart ladies, starting at tea tomorrow and continuing until Annie came to her senses and realized Jamie was not the man for her.

"Your poor mother, trying to raise such a heathen," Winifred said when Duncan walked her away. "A saint to take on such a wild little ward."

Over his shoulder he saw Annie dangle the fishing rod over the stream. "Don't lose any equipment in the stream, either!" he shouted back.

Oh, aye, flirting with the Stuart ladies was his best lure for drawing out Annie's true feelings, and with true relish he arranged his time schedule with the Stuart ladies so he could join them for tea with his mother the very next afternoon. After all, two could play at this game of making someone jealous, and Annie was about to learn that Duncan, who'd held his own against the dangers of both the Rocky Mountains and the Sierra Nevadas, intended to tame Annie Shaw of Gillycairn before he gave the little hoyden permission to wed anyone.

It was his right as her guardian.

Duncan felt like a fool. After a half hour in the drawing room with his mother and the Stuart ladies at tea, the conversation had grown stultifying.

Did heather bloom first in the Highlands or in the Lowlands?

Was it a brighter shade of purple here?

And did Lord Glencannon know where the heather grew white?

"If I find some, I'll be sure and pluck it," he said.

Inside he seethed with frustration. Where the devil was Annie?

He'd attended this tea party to make her jealous, and she'd had the nerve to stay away. Probably sulking in her room while he endured the chatter of the Stuart ladies. Moreover, his hand throbbed still. Oh, it was properly bandaged and salved, the hook having been removed by an amused blacksmith, but it hurt. Duncan now stood long suffering, smile frozen on his face, while the Stuart ladies recounted the wonders of Highland fishing to his mother.

"Isn't Annie joining us for tea today?" his mother asked.

Duncan shrugged, but just thinking of Annie sent the blood coursing through his body, and, restless, desperate to escape the flirtatious looks of Gillian, Duncan paced. Oh, but it was no good without Annie here.

"Annie didn't send her regrets, did she?" Duncan had no sooner spoken when from outside came the distinct sound of his pony's hooves and Annie's war whoop, followed by a blur racing by outside the windows of the drawing room. His teacup clattering in the saucer from the haste with which he deposited it, Duncan strode over and pushed aside the draperies.

If this had been five years ago, he'd have sworn it was Annie racing around the castle grounds on Murdock. Such behavior was forbidden, and Annie knew it. So it must have been a will-o'-the-wisp he saw. Still, just to be certain, he had to look more closely. His breath deepened, and he had to remember ladies were present to save himself from swearing out loud.

In a thunder of hooves a lass flew by on a pony. Annie, barefoot, black hair flying loose, rode Murdock.

And Jamie rode with her.

"Oh, dear," Lady Glencannon said, coming up beside him and wringing her hands, "Annie knows Murdock's not allowed in the castle lane. I've told her over and over."

"She's riding with Jamie," Duncan said, trying hard to keep the resentment out of his voice. Jamie wasn't good enough for her. "She's gone out riding alone with Jamie Gordon," he muttered, overcome by jealousy.

"Well, that's perfectly acceptable," his mother said artlessly. "After all, they are to be wed."

Duncan's heart clenched; anger consumed him. She used to ride with him, Duncan, not with Jamie.

Duncan remained at the window, secretly enjoying the sight of Annie's long bare legs and her hair flying in the wind. "My own fault, I fear," he said absently. "I taught Annie how to ride astride."

Gillian and Winifred exchanged shocked gasps and moved up behind Duncan. "One would think she was a twelve-year-old school lass rather than a betrothed woman," Winifred said, and Gillian clucked in agreement.

For their opinion they were rewarded by a frosty stare from Lady Glencannon, who lifted her chin defensively. "Well, now, heaven knows but Annie's a good girl. She's learned housekeeping and piano playing and comportment among company. . . . She'll make Jamie a fine wife." And that was that. No one criticized her Annie.

Duncan's feelings ran deeper. Resentment still poured through him at being trapped here at tea when Annie was right outside. Ignoring everybody, he strode toward the door.

"Duncan," his mother said, "perhaps you can speak with Annie later, though she's so close to her wedding day, I'm inclined to overlook this breech of behavior. . . . Come back to tea."

Annie couldn't marry Jamie, and so he slowed down only long enough to look over his shoulder.

"Actually, I've been looking everywhere for my estate manager. It's a matter of some urgency. Will you excuse me briefly?"

"But, Duncan, what about our guests?"

Duncan turned a polite smile on the Stuart ladies. If there was one thing ambitious young ladies liked better than tea with the lord of the castle, it was touring the castle itself.

"Mother, give the ladies a look about. As many rooms as they'd like."

His mother stood there looking nonplussed. Behind her, the Stuart ladies smiled in satisfaction.

"But it's perfectly all right, your ladyship. We'd so enjoy seeing the castle . . . especially upstairs." Gillian's voice trembled with suppressed excitement.

"Where exactly is this painting of your little ward as a child?" Winifred asked as if she were an appraiser. "May we see it? Naturally, we'd like to see his lordship's portrait, too."

"I'm flattered." Duncan didn't care if they bounced on his bed, just so they were gone when he returned. Already they were heading for the circular staircase, staring up in curiosity while, across the hallway, his mother opened up the library.

With a sigh of relief he shut the castle door behind him, and at once slid out of his frock coat, leaving it in the hands of a startled gardener, and, rolling up his sleeves, headed in the direction of the stables.

Wait till he got his hands on Annie. Oh, she'd known what she was about, deliberately riding by the drawing room windows when she knew he had ladies there for tea. Perhaps she wasn't as grown-up as she looked after all, and his strides lengthened.

At the doorway to the stable, he froze. There she was, barefoot and long-legged, in a simple Highland shift. Her hair hung black and straight as one of the tree trunks in Gillycairn burn. About her shoulders, fastened by a round silver brooch, was a square of tartan, brilliant red Munro tartan.

In that instant before she looked up, he realized there was no use pretending he could turn back time, no matter how many pranks she played. She was a beautiful woman. And also his ward. Reconciling the two was hard. And maybe that's why it had taken him so many days to face her again, to trust himself to make coherent conversation.

She was not alone, of course. There next to her on a stack of hay sat Jamie Gordon, his own employee. A knife twist to Duncan's heart could not have hurt more. Jamie Gordon was a bright young man with red curls falling over his forehead and nothing to commend him save an earnest appeal in his eyes. He'd known him since a boy. A freckle-faced lad overly fond of pot pies and bannock. Chubby then. Stocky now, thick as a barrel, but with sharp gray eyes and a quick smile. Good-humored, steady, loyal Jamie.

It wasn't possible Annie could have fallen in love with Jamie, that she could want to marry this . . . this freckle-faced commoner? And in less than three weeks' time?

Standing unnoticed in the doorway, Duncan shamelessly eavesdropped on the conversation inside the dim stable.

Annie, with furious energy, was brushing Murdock's coat while Jamie Gordon chattered like a female.

"I heard Duncan brought you gifts—mountain-man type things." There was a touch too much eagerness in his voice, in Duncan's opinion.

"They're nothing I can use for a dowry," Annie replied carelessly, "but they're different."

"Don't you like them?"

Duncan, waiting for her reply, inwardly cringed.

"Of course I like them. They're from Duncan, aren't they? Do you want to see them?" Without waiting for an answer she reached away and, a moment later, handed her Jamie a tartan-wrapped bundle, which Jamie eagerly unwrapped.

One by one he held up Duncan's souvenirs.

"Oh, but Annie, these are wonderful gifts. They'll be playthings for our children."

"And for you?"

"Well . . . surely I'll never see the land and wonders that spawned these things." There was envy in his voice—no, longing. Why, Jamie, practical Jamie, sounded positively passionate.

Annie scoffed. "I knew you were smart, Jamie—guessing how Duncan would have changed and all—but I never knew you were so sentimental. Presents are all good and well, but it's Duncan the village is lucky to have back. . . ."

"Didn't I tell you he'd come back a man? Perhaps he's smitten with one of the Edinburgh ladies already."

Annie threw the brush at Jamie, who ducked, and the thing landed in the doorway, at Duncan's feet.

When Annie turned to retrieve it, she stopped still in her tracks and stared at the doorway as if she'd seen a ghost.

"Duncan! How long have you been standing there?"

Duncan's face remained impassive as he bent to scoop up the brush. He held it out to her, his eyes on her the whole time.

"You weren't at tea."

She met his gaze with a mutinous one of her own and tossed back her hair, proud. "I wasn't invited."

"It was assumed you'd be there. If it was my angry words—"

"No, it's not that. I wouldn't come without Jamie. My place is with my betrothed." She gestured to Jamie.

Inside Duncan seethed. And came up with a quick but plausible fabrication. "Actually, I came for Jamie," he said. "Inside the castle on the library desk you'll find an account book for last year. One page is marked, a page where I can't read some of the numbers. Would you decipher them for me? If you're through admiring Annie's mementos, that is."

The estate manager dropped the buffalo muff and, red-faced, stammered. "B-but of course. Is it my arithmetic?"

"I'd like you to double-check the accounts for the Widow MacLeod. Just a detail, but it is important."

"Oh, but the Widow MacLeod can't be evicted." It was Annie.

Duncan turned to her. "We'll see." Duncan, an excellent bluffer in matters of business, kept his voice casual. Worrying Jamie over the estate accounts would buy him more time with Annie if necessary. "Off with you now . . . but not Annie." A touch to her arm restrained her. "Actually, it's time I discussed my guardianship with you, Annie, and other family matters."

Briefly he met her curious gaze, then moved away inside the stable and made a great show of stroking Murdock's mane. Without even looking he felt Annie staring up at him, wide-eyed. He slanted a secret look at the lush fullness of the figure that had bloomed in his absence. Aye, she was ready to wed.

The second Jamie was out of earshot, he ceased his grooming of Murdock's shaggy mane and turned on Annie, who had moved to the other side of Murdock and was staring over at her guardian.

"I've been meaning to talk to you since the fishing accident," he began.

"What about? Isn't the fishing equipment all in order?"

Duncan jammed his hands down his trouser pockets.

"Aye, it's all in order."

"Then what is it?"

He'd traded with Indians but now had doubts about how to deal with his own ward, a sheltered, yet spirited, Highland lass. He felt stiff with her, as if he couldn't find his equilibrium with this new Annie. So he began with casual comments.

"Jamie was most impressed, it appears, with my mementos."

Her voice was quiet. "You know Jamie. He admires anything from foreign lands. He says touching an Indian arrowhead is much better than reading about it."

"Does he?"

"No one listened more avidly to your letters from America than Jamie. Though we could never get him to come right out and admit it, I believe he quite envied you, living with the mountain men."

Indeed. Duncan took careful note of this comment, but his words to Annie were deliberately casual. "A ruthless lot, all of them. One can't take anything for granted as a mountain man, you know. To explore uncharted territory, one doesn't just willy-nilly set out without a plan or provisions. I had to know which Indians were friendly and how to map uncharted territory. Only the hardy and the clever survive."

Annie smiled. "You can do anything, Duncan . . . discover places no man's ever touched . . . and then return and try to save our poor village. You will, won't you?"

Her words were sweet, but it was her smile that held him. He hadn't known how much he'd missed her smile . . . and her faith in him. He, Duncan, who had shot down buffalo and bears, melted somewhere between his heart and his head.

"Duncan? Will the village be all right?"

"As laird, I'll do what I can."

Grateful, she added softly, "I'm sorry if I teased the Stuart ladies."

He panicked at the thought of returning to tea with them. Instead, he moved around his Shetland pony and took Annie's hand.

"I'm sorry, too . . . that my gifts were so childish."

"Oh, no, I'd like any gift you brought me because it means you did not forget me."

Her skirt was just short enough to reveal shapely ankles. He had the strongest need to touch her, pull her to him by the waist and chart the unknown territory of Annie.

It took all his willpower to resist, to let go of Annie's hand. Giving Murdock a last pat on the rump, he stalked outside.

"How did you and Jamie . . . end up engaged?" he asked when she followed.

"Silly. He asked me. Does this mean you'll grant formal permission?"

"Not yet." His glance at her was stern, then he looked off at the castle in the distance. "Why did you say yes?"

Annie didn't know what to say at first.

"It was natural. He came to do the accounts, not so much while Andrew was alive, but after he . . . well, Jamie practically ran the estate after your brother died. Someone had to do it, and we'd no idea what mountain you were on, or how long it would take to find you . . . and there I was, and there he was . . ." She pushed her blowing hair back. "Why do you ask?"

He shrugged. "Isn't that a guardian's duty, to find out if the man who wants to marry his ward is honorable before he gives permission?"

Nodding, Annie looked off at the castle, where Jamie was even now working over the accounts. She was ashamed to admit her happiness, her sublime joy in simply being alone with Duncan, hearing his voice, looking at him. With a guilty pang she realized Jamie never made her feel like this.

"Actually, Annie," Duncan confessed, "questioning you about this betrothal can wait. It's the village I'm concerned over first. Will you walk with me?"

Her face lit up; she couldn't hide the adoration she felt for him. If Duncan, her childhood hero, could figure out a way to lock his tutor in the buttery and run off to meet Annie at the stream, then surely he could help the villagers. Eagerly she fell into step beside him, and they walked as in the old days through the back of the estate near Gillycairn Stream.

"I came to ask a favor. It's about our esteemed visitors, the Stuart ladies." He allowed a significant pause to fall, then continued. "As we both know, you've been . . . well . . . entertaining them." It was more of a question than a statement, and to emphasize his point, he made a great show of adjusting the bandage on his injured hand, the hand that just a day before had been impaled by a fishing hook.

Annie looked ready to cry. He steered her toward the heather-covered hillside above the stream.

"Now I find myself in a rare predicament, Annie. I want to entertain them but have not the least idea what pleases fine ladies. I'd ask Mother, of course, but you're the one who's shown them about and knows them more intimately. Could you tell me, Anne, what pleases them and what bores them—besides fishing?"

She was silent a few moments, the atmosphere heavy with a longing.

He fought to keep his voice casual. "You don't know?"

"They came to see the heather."

"But I imagine you've shown them that." In their childhood they'd raced sheepdogs across the heath, staged pirate duels with willow swords. Despite himself his voice became softer, deeper. He was aware of the scent of her, the way her dark hair blew out against his shoulder, every brush of her arm against his.

"Every day till we went fishing. They've sniffed the heather, plucked it, painted it, and even watched the Widow MacLeod make honey of it."

"They've seen ample heather, then?"

"Not white heather, of course."

"I think some other activity than heather gazing."

Annie smiled, secretly pleased. "They've not been to examine the priory ruins," she suggested quickly.

He detested picking his way through rubble and stone but forced a smile. "Ah, an excellent idea. And I suppose they don't know the medieval history of the priory? And about the ghost who pipes on the anniversary of Culloden?"

"I'd beware of frightening them away. Gillian is the squeamish sort."

He smiled to himself. "So I noticed. Annie, how the deuce the Stuart ladies stayed alive with you guiding them about is beyond me. . . . You won't play any more mischief?"

Annie looked into his eyes, and her heart raced. Shaking her head, she fought for breath, for coherent words.

"Jamie says the Stuart ladies are here because of you."

He bit back another smile. "Does that bother you?"

"Not . . ." she said carefully, "if their father is a banker who can save our village. Then it's worth all the days I've spent tramping through the heather."

Oh, so that's what she thought.

"What else? You've been the good ghillie to them—even if your efforts went awry yesterday, and I'm sorely tired of thinking of what to show them."

"Will there be the Highland Games this month? That would interest them."

"But of course. Why does everyone question what's been a tradition?"

"Because of the hard times, the famine, possible evictions."

He touched her hand again. "Annie, things will improve." Aware of the spark that touch ignited, he moved away, put at least three feet distance between them. "Trust me."

"So you can help the villagers?"

"I already promised I'd do everything I could."

"But you and I—"

Equilibrium threatened as he swung around to face her. "What about us?" A raw challenge edged his voice, as if daring her to guess how he felt.

"We were friends," she said on a shaky note.

"Now you're my ward. You shall not miss me, I imagine, once you're wed."

Of course. He'd brought her childish gifts; therefore, she was still behaving like a child around him.

Duncan stared at her, at the outline of her figure against her dress. Her thighs were outlined against the afternoon sun, her breasts shapely, her unbound hair blowing in the breeze, black and inky. This was no child.

"Do you remember riding Murdock, Duncan? Do you remember teaching me to ride?"

"Aye, lass."

"Do you remember racing me to the yew tree over there?"

"Aye—"

She was gone then, running for it.

Duncan nearly ran after her, but as common sense prevailed, he pulled up short. Five years had passed, and now, as Lord Glencannon, he should not be chasing around after his own ward. Instead, he strode over to the tree where she danced up and down with excitement. As quick as the wind, she was off again to yet another tree. The temptress.

Duncan was torn. Would a simple game of hide-and-seek really hurt? It would make her happy, make up for his harsh words of yesterday.

Temptation won out, and Duncan gave chase, catching his ward in the birch trees that grew beside the River Gillycairn, at the very tree where once he'd carved their initials. On a whim he captured her in his arms and pinned her fast, teasing.

Unexpectedly she threw her arms about him. "Oh, Duncan, I knew you weren't completely stuffy, that you hadn't forgotten our games. I'm so glad you're home."

But she was no child, nor he. Coming to his senses, he tried to untangle her.

She clung all the tighter, the outline of her breasts, the slight swell of her abdomen threatening to flare his loins into fire. "I'm sorry we yelled. Oh, Duncan, I wish time had stood still and we could just go fishing like we did before you left."

Each word vibrated right to the core of him. "I told you, we can't turn back time, lass." He pushed her away.

"Duncan . . ." Her voice was a whisper, edged with a longing she didn't even realize. Innocent longing for something he wasn't about to explain. "Why isn't it like five years ago? Why have things changed between us?"

He looked away, jaw taut, unable to offer her a smile even. "Time only moves forward, Annie. Not even I can change that."

"We could try. Duncan, remember when we used to wrestle?"

His heartbeat picked up. Quickly he slipped from her grasp and slid around to the other side of the tree and on down to the stream bank to sit.

She followed and stood above him, laughing, her long black gypsy hair blowing, tempting him to touch, to think forbidden thoughts.

"No, lass." Not now.

Before he could gather his wits, she straddled his lap like a child and capturing him by the shoulders, held him immobile, her breasts, firm now, brushing his shirt. "I've got you . . . at last, I've caught you off guard."

"Anne—"

"Ha—playing the American mountain man did not help your strength. Or has Lord Glencannon become too stuffy? Will you live out your days walking about the priory ruins?"

There was nothing stuffy about the reaction to her words. Spoiling for a fight she was, but he was determined to maintain control. As a slow heat spread down his body, he pushed her off and stood up, pulling her up with him. "Anne—"

"Annie."

"Anne! Anne, you're not a child," he told her as much as himself. "You cannot wrestle with your guardian."

She swayed against him, and for a minute they knelt close, his lips close enough to kiss her. She had baited him, gotten him to take her into his arms. Annie with her long black hair and capricious blue eyes and bare feet and long bare legs had been in his dreams more often than he cared to admit. For five long years. The years fell away, just for a few seconds, until she moved against him, and he put time back in its proper place.

He could not hold her. Nor could she kiss her guardian.

Clearing his throat, he pulled back. "I need to return to the castle. Your intended will be awaiting me."

Concern etched her face. "Duncan, you look pale," she asked. "Are you all right?"

No, he was not all right. He desired Anne, his own ward. He understood the dreams that had plagued him all the years he'd been gone. Dreams that had left him homesick. Dreams of summer and heather. White heather.

"How are your wedding plans coming?" he asked.

"Oh, but you're not going to be a fussy guardian about my wedding, are you?"

"After your childish behavior I'm not sure but what I shouldn't withhold approval forever."

Anne's smile faded. A delicious little frown line worried itself between her brows. "But . . . I love Jamie."

He turned on her. "Where did you have time to learn what love is, lass? In five short years you're sure you know what true love is?" His fierce reaction surprised himself.

She blushed. "I'm old enough . . . I-I keep forgetting how much you've changed. I know I should behave like a grown-up woman, but I-I just forget when I'm around you."

"Why?"

"Because I want so much for us to be friends again."

He ached for her, resisted the temptation to touch her face, smooth away the frown. His gaze came to rest on her lips. His body came alive.

"Five years changed me." And with that he turned on his heel and walked away.

Five steps along she caught up and blocked his way.

"Duncan . . . you said we'd be friends. You said."

He couldn't help but smile at the shyness—not the naïveté—of her question. Damn, this was Annie, his ward. She was his responsibility, and therefore he had a duty to suppress these less than paternal feelings.

"As long as I'm your guardian, that changes things."

"Duncan, can't we go fishing just once for old time's sake? The trout are running swift and biting well."

His shoulders were so broad . . . and tense. Slowly he exhaled, then turned, his expression fierce, forbidding.

"That's not childish," she said softly, anticipating his refusal. "The Widow MacLeod could use her dinner caught."

"If you want to fish, then take Jamie."

Jamie fished with a book in one hand. "Why not you?"

"Annie, you're about to wed. You must admit it's time you behaved with the decorum befitting a woman grown. Don't you see, lass, it's not proper to be off alone unchaperoned with your guardian."

"Fishing isn't the same. Besides, *you're* my chaperon."

Her logic was irrefutable and dangerous. "So I am . . . but I have an estate to run. You must ask Jamie, your intended."

"Fiddle," she said in disgust. "All he's done when he's not at your books is practice for the caber toss."

Grateful for a change of subject, Duncan asked, "You shall come to the Games?"

"I always do." Her voice held as much zeal as if he'd announced the castle was rationed to porridge three meals a day.

"Good. I have an announcement to make there that I think you and Jamie will both want to hear."

Her eyes went wide. An announcement? Could it be his betrothal? She dare not ask. So she changed the subject.

"Jamie may beat you. He's been practicing, and he's stronger and more agile than ever."

"Then I shall be pleased to hand out all the prizes to him."

"Fine then, and if you won't fish with me, then I'll go help Jamie practice wrestling."

Deep down in the soul of him, he ached to pull her back, to mold her close to him. She didn't belong in Jamie's arms, but in his. This could not go on. He couldn't stand being close to her, and he couldn't stand being away from her. Clearly something had to be done about Jamie, and it wasn't enough to merely send her betrothed off on errands. That would do little good once she married Jamie. No, something more drastic was called for. Something more permanent.

"Tell Jamie to practice well and to be sharp. I'll see him there." And with no more explanation than that, he strode off, whistling as he went.

Because now Duncan had a plan. Ruthless to be sure, but in all competitions, Duncan was a keen competitor who played to win, and the Games could not come soon enough.

The day of the Gillycairn Games dawned misty, but the sun broke through the sky just as the coach pulled away from the castle. Duncan and his mother, snapping open a parasol, settled opposite Annie in the carriage, and Annie was in a glorious mood. This was just like the old times. Almost.

Duncan, more and more frequently, made her feel ways Jamie never did. Especially today. Oh, but he looked the handsome Highlander, dressed in his kilt and hose and velvet jacket. The breeze ruffled his tawny hair; his eyes danced with excitement. At the same time he sat there like the proper laird of the manor, and she yearned to shake some of the stuffiness out of him. To wrestle with him . . . to run her hands through his hair . . . to slip her hands inside that velvet jacket, to embrace him while her cheek rested close to his heartbeat—

"You're uncommonly quiet, Annie." Lady Glencannon startled her out of her reverie. "What are you thinking?"

Her thoughts surprised herself. It was, she told herself, pure amazement at how Duncan had matured, nothing more.

Lady Glencannon repeated her question. "Annie, answer me, what are you smiling about?"

Nonplussed, quickly Annie sat up straight and made up a fib. "About the last fish I caught at the heather pool."

Duncan focused his gaze on her for the first time. "A brown trout?" he asked, a rare longing in his voice.

She nodded, heart warming beneath his steady blue gaze. "I gave it to Widow MacLeod, and I've not been back there since. I'd so like to fish once before my wedding." The wistful tone in her voice was real.

Duncan kept on staring at her but held his silence.

"Oh, Annie," Lady Glencannon said, "there's so much to do yet without fishing as well. Your wedding gown still isn't hemmed. Your dowry, your legacy from your parents has to be arranged. . . . Surely your wedding plans are much more exciting than another jaunt to some muddy fishing hole?"

It wasn't just *any* fishing hole. With a sigh Annie nodded. "I do need to work on the wedding so it'll be grand."

That settled, Lady Glencannon turned to her son. "Are you planning to make your announcement today?" his mother asked.

"Aye, but it's a surprise."

Annie's heartbeat quickened; her gaze rested on his face, on the lips she yearned to kiss, the brow she longed to caress. She supposed he was going to use the occasion of the Games to announce clearances. Oh, but that put a gray cloud over the day.

And then Lady Glencannon turned to her son. "Duncan, did you write to Mr. Stuart in Edinburgh?"

"He's already responded with a favorable reply."

The father of the Stuart ladies! Annie slouched in a corner of the carriage and with a fingernail traced a stripe of her tartan dress. Her mood turned stark black. This was worse than she'd thought. Covertly she studied Duncan from under her lashes. Had he really asked for one of their hands? Already?

Annie could only speculate what had gone on during all the late evenings he'd kept with the good ladies. Judging from the laughter drifting up through the floor of her bedchamber, they'd not been searching for white heather, unless Duncan had found some growing under a chair in the castle!

He'd been courting one of them, of course. Jamie himself had said Duncan would have to wed a rich wife. And now Annie was going to lose Duncan—to one of those insipid Lowland ladies. Yet, these were meager times, she reminded herself. Villagers like the Widow MacLeod had endured a terrible few years of famine, and relief from England didn't reach enough people. For the villagers' sake, she should be overjoyed.

Unable to resist a glance at Duncan, she caught him looking at her. Immediately he looked off the other way.

"I hope the injury from the fish hook will not make it hard for Duncan to compete today?" she asked stiffly.

Duncan turned back to look at Annie, savoring the sweet things about her. The lush black hair and blue eyes. The demure gown. Yet, at the same time, she was frugal with her smiles, and woe to him if she angered her. What was going on in her pretty head? Was she deliberately flirting or just innocently sensual? With this new Annie he wasn't certain what she was about from one minute to the next, and it was driving him crazy.

"I'm not competing in the caber toss or the hammer throw," he announced abruptly.

"But you always did before," she said, disappointed.

"I know I did, but I've decided to retire and judge events instead." With a rueful smile Duncan held up his bandaged hand. "The title of best fisherman will suffice."

She tilted her chin pertly. "Since you won't go fishing, how do I even know you're still worthy of that honor?"

Her eyes were wide and dark, and her mouth slightly parted. Kissable. He cleared his throat. "Nevertheless, I'm retiring. Perhaps Jamie will win all the prizes after all, do you think?"

"I wager," she taunted, "that you forgot how to compete in all the Highland sports while you were roaming America."

"On the contrary, the skills needed to survive in the wilds of America make the Games look tame. I practiced all my skills—sometimes to stay alive." He waited, gauging her reaction to the mention of America. It was, perhaps, time to put his plan into action. Either that or grab her and kiss her breathless in front of his mother.

"Was your life in danger in America?"

He nodded, satisfied. Annie had not only nibbled but taken the bait. Perfect. Settling back, he made America sound as different as anything her dear little heart could ever desire.

"It's a strange place, Annie. The mountains don't at all resemble those of our Highlands. A place for a man to visit, but not easy to settle into. In short, lass, a wild dangerous place. I would not dream of sending you there for even a look."

"But there's fishing . . ."

"Nothing like the fish of Scotland. Not as tasty."

"And hunting."

"Buffalo are surly beasts. And they're so easy to kill, there's no sport in it."

"There must be something I'd like. People surely?"

"The people come from all over. You've got to know ten languages to communicate. And that doesn't count the savages."

"What else?" She looked up at him with such utter trust.

"Lots of different things. Tepees and sod houses, but no Highland reels. No bagpipes. Lots of sagebrush, but not a speck of heather. There's still nowhere like Scotland, Annie, and a lass like you belongs in the Highlands, not in that barbaric land."

"Why'd you stay so long, then?"

After an uneasy look at his mother, he turned back. "Do you think, lass, I had a choice? I packed and set out on the return journey the same day I received Jamie's letter about Andrew. A joy it was to return to Scotland and my home. I'd not realized, in truth, how much I missed Scotland." His gaze rested on her, and it took a moment to realize the coach had stopped till the coachman turned.

"It's the lasses that keep *me* in Scotland, m'lord," said the driver, who'd been listening, over his shoulder. "If you'll pardon my boldness, but as Burns himself said, it's the sweet, sonsie lasses what can't be beat."

"Indeed," Duncan agreed, while handing the two women down from the carriage. "Scots lasses are the bonniest of all—even Lowland lasses," he added for good measure. "Trust me, Annie," he said softly as she brushed against him, "the hard times here won't last."

A piper played a welcoming tune as a cheer went up from the crowd at the arrival of Lord Glencannon with his mother and ward, and at once, Duncan plunged into the crowd, greeting old friends.

All those villagers who lived too far to walk had come by pony cart. From the farthest parts of the glen, they came to the meadow in Gillycairn. The Stuart ladies were already here and had spied Duncan, and this very instant were strolling toward him.

"Will you behave today, Annie?" he teased.

"Haven't I behaved while you were gone roaming?"

"You've allowed Jamie Gordon to grow sweet on you. Go find him now, think about how lucky you are to have found a good man like him. And tell him later I shall talk with him as your guardian, question his suitability as a future husband to my ward." Duncan smiled, touched by Annie's bleak look.

"Lord Glencannon," she sniffed, "can do as he pleases. Will I need to show the Stuart ladies about? Or will you?"

"The Edinburgh ladies are our honored guests. *I'll* need to show them about, introduce our local athletes and dancers."

"A diversion from tramping through the heather."

"And from fishing lessons."

"To be sure." Then, unable to hold back her curiosity, asked, "Which of the ladies is your favorite?"

Her question startled him. Then, as he saw Jamie Gordon approach Annie, Duncan relaxed and smiled. "Ah, but a gentleman doesn't reveal favorites, does he, not unless he's ready to commit his heart like Jamie—eh, Jamie?"

"Annie has always been my favorite lass," Jamie replied, slipping an arm about her.

"There, that's settled. I'm to have no favorite ladies— not yet, at least."

She tilted her chin in mutiny, a fire in her eyes.

Was that passion, banked? Or a childish tantrum, held in check? If he'd not been laird and had to set an example, he'd have yanked Jamie Gordon from her this second.

Patience, he told himself, for the day was young, and Jamie Gordon would be very thirsty later. And turning on his heel, Duncan hurried off.

Annie watched him bend over to kiss the Stuart ladies' hands, raw jealousy coursing through her.

Oh, how she hated them.

Dressed in Edinburgh finery—taffeta gowns with enormous skirts and flounces, they stuck out here like French corsets amidst humble Highland shifts. Her heart ached in dread. Before the day was out, by the closing ceremonies, Duncan would doubtless announce himself betrothed to one

of those fine and fancy daughters of a banker father, while
she, Annie, poor orphaned daughter of a ghillie, was to wed
Jamie.

She tried to tell herself it was right and fitting. As Lord
Glencannon, Duncan could never wed a mere ghillie's
daughter anyway. With a brave smile up at Jamie, she
took his arm and walked away to enjoy the festivities.

There was comfort in the tradition of everything. As
always, the field was ringed by spectators, all holding pic-
nic baskets, while pots of ale cooled under shade trees.
In the background came the familiar homely wail of pipes
practicing for their contest.

She managed for most of the morning to avoid Duncan,
until it was Jamie's turn to compete in the hammer throw.
And then, of course, Duncan was there right beside her,
watching.

She ignored him. "Jamie! Jamie! Show them you're the
best Highlander!"

Winifred and Gillian, standing on the other side of
Duncan, waved their fans and gave her bemused looks.

When Jamie won, Gillian giggled. "What shall Lord
Glencannon award Jamie for a prize?"

"Shall it be his blessings in marriage?"

"No," Winifred whispered in an aside. "It shall be his
condolences because his estate manager is marrying a
hoyden."

Gillian's giggle was the final straw for Annie.

"I believe all the castle can afford this year are sacks
of oats," Annie said and turned away, tears pricking at
her eyes. It was true. Duncan's brother had given away
fancy prizes, even after the blight started. Silver cups when
the villagers could have used food. This year Duncan,
with practical good sense, was giving food, so the rumor
had it.

Finally, at long last, Duncan, Lord Glencannon, stood up
in front of the fiddlers, braw in his kilt of red tartan, his
thighs strong, hair tousled, looking very much like the lion
home from the fray. As the Master of Ceremonies called
out the winners' names, Lord Glencannon handed out the

prizes for the best at the hammer throw, the caber toss, the Highland fling and the Saber Dance, and the piping and fiddling . . .

"He's so handsome, sister." Gillian, twirling her parasol, sighed audibly.

Was it Gillian, then, whom Duncan favored? Annie watched her while Duncan spoke.

"Handsome doesn't matter," Winifred said. "What matters is that Lord Glencannon is a Scottish peer."

There was no denying Winifred's single-minded purpose, even though it made Annie cringe. No, as the prettier, softer one, Duncan would probably favor *the other* sister. And then an alarming thought occurred . . . what if he had kissed one of them?

"Before I close the award ceremonies," Duncan was now saying, "I've an announcement."

This was it. The black cloud in her heart threatened to spill over into tears, even before Duncan spoke.

"Despite rumors to the contrary," Duncan said, "there are to be no evictions in this village."

Annie looked up, surprised.

"If the help from the English is not enough, then I as laird will contribute the rest of the relief. . . ."

A gasp of surprise went through the crowd, except from the Stuart ladies, who stood there twirling their parasols and looking smug.

"And moreover, I will donate a prize to everyone today attending the Games . . . a prize of grain to plant. If potatoes won't grow in Gillycairn, we'll not let that send us away. We'll try barley and hay, and then another crop and another, if need be. But no one will be evicted. . . . Everyone here today who so desires shall return next year to the Gillycairn Games. . . ."

After a split second of silence the villagers applauded wildly, and as the words registered, Annie turned openmouthed to stare in wonder. Oh, Duncan . . . Then it *was* true. If he could do all this, he had to have money . . . and that meant he must be marrying one of the rich ladies from Edinburgh.

Again, raw jealousy coursed through her. She wished the ladies had both fallen into the stream and had drowned. But then she stopped herself. If Annie had succeeded in driving them away, then the village would well and truly be lost. Evicted for the wealth of sheep. As a loyal resident of Gillycairn, she was honorbound to feel *happy*.

Someone snuck up beside her. "Isn't it grand news?"

"What?" She turned and saw through the haze of her tears only red curly hair. Jamie. "What's so grand?"

"Duncan's news, of course. Weren't you listening? He's promised to save the estate without evicting crofters, without making people emigrate."

"Do you know his secret?"

"Sudden wealth, of course!" Jamie tugged her off to watch the dancing of a reel. "Duncan is going to be a rich man. Didn't I tell you he'd figure something out?"

Annie should have been happy. Why, then, did she feel as if the bottom had dropped out of her world?

Duncan looked across the crowd, searching for one person and one person only: Annie, who'd looked so bonnie today in the carriage. He'd watched her mood fade to glumness, and he longed to see now how she was taking this news. He found her in Jamie's arms, and longing slashed through him, heating his blood. Whistling to feign casualness, he walked up to the engaged couple.

Annie drew away at once and held out her hand to Duncan. "Thank you, Duncan," she said properly.

After looking at her outstretched hand, he slipped his hand in hers and watched numbly as she shook it. "You're a wonder saving the village. Now my wedding day will be one of joy."

Her glum expression might have vanished, but it had found a new home in Duncan's heart. For if there was one thing he didn't want to spend the rest of his life doing, it was shaking hands with Annie as if they were mere acquaintances. Oh, but it was past time to dispose of Jamie Gordon.

"I shall have to treat Jamie to an ale," he said easily. "A toast to the man who wants to wed my ward." And without even a by-your-leave to Annie, he gathered up an ale jug and led Jamie off to a secluded grove near the piper's hollow, where they sat leaning against a pair of trees.

Within a half hour Duncan had plied Jamie with two cups of ale. "Jamie, I need a financier, and the ladies seem eager to recommend their father. What is your advice?"

"Oh, Mr. Stuart of Edinburgh is well recommended."

"And then I shall need a man in America to tend to the investments I left behind. What is your advice there?"

"As estate manager for the castle during these years of the blight, I've no advice on America, only surprise at its riches."

"Aye, trapping and land are profitable. And that doesn't count this California gold rush now in force."

Jamie's eyes glowed with suppressed longing. "America, it seems, is a land of many surprises. A wonderful place."

"Wonderful?" Duncan questioned. "But I thought everyone dreaded emigration?"

"Oh, that was the fear of being evicted and destitute."

"Indeed, Jamie, it's one thing to be cast out, another to choose one's fate, would you not agree?"

In the background fiddles played reels while the villagers danced and engaged in general revelry. Duncan poured more ale. Like a fisherman letting out the line, Duncan cast out a few more choice words.

"Have you ever, Jamie, wondered yourself what lies across the ocean far beyond these hills?"

"Oh, I yearn to hear about the far places." It was said in a tone of hushed reverence. "These hills are all I've known."

"I thought so." Duncan sipped his ale, while watching Jamie over his cup. "Of course," he said, pausing, "to tell tales of the American West is a dangerous temptation to lay on a man . . . especially a man about to wed and settle down."

Jamie frowned, as if the thought perplexed him. "I'd not be tempted. Merely curious. For me, the lure of America will forever remain a dream, a regret."

"Pity. A man shouldn't have to live with regrets all his life," Duncan suggested. "In truth, America, especially the

West, is beyond words. A man has to see it to believe it."

"Tell me a bit," Jamie urged, eagerness shining through his voice. "A wee bit. I've a good imagination."

Smiling to himself, Duncan secretly exulted. The hook had taken. And so Duncan began. Whatever he'd told Annie, Duncan was now about to tell the exact opposite to Jamie, because as any good fisherman knew, different fish snapped at different lures.

By the time Duncan was finished telling about the gold rush at Sutter's Mill in California, Jamie was thoroughly enraptured and stretched out on the grass, arms behind his back, looking up with a dreamy gaze at the clouds.

"Or if a man prefers the Great Plains, he can find buffalo. So many, the land there stretches out in one brown pelt." Then, for good measure, Duncan added, "In truth, a man could write a book about all the tales to be told after roaming in America."

"Yes." Jamie leaned forward, eagerness on his young face.

Duncan felt sorry for the Gordon lad. Oh, but what a streak of wanderlust he'd suppressed. Time to pull him back to reality and see how hard he fought against the hook.

"But I am being cruel, for with your wedding so close, you cannot now have grand adventures. Once a man weds and fathers bairns, it's too late to travel, to have a grand adventure. . . ."

"But so many Scots have emigrated lately. It doesn't have to be too late."

"You'd not jilt Annie, my own ward?" Duncan asked quickly.

"No, no, of course not . . ." The struggle between two desires flitted across his face, first longing, then guilt.

He thought a moment. "Do some take their lasses?"

Nodding, Duncan poured more ale into Jamie's cup. "But as her guardian, I have a say in this. The West is rough, especially in the mining camps. Full of danger, too. Annie should not have to live in shantytown tents, or have to face the loose women and thieves and vigilantes who—"

"Of course not, Duncan. I'd leave her somewhere safe."

Duncan affected a look of utmost relief. "With Annie's best interests agreed upon, then would you consider serving as my agent in America?"

Jamie's yearning was palpable. "I want to, but—"

"I could pay for passage for a man to serve as my agent in America. Passage for one."

"For one?" Jamie took in the implications of that.

"Times are lean, as you well know."

"That means I would have to go ahead of Annie."

"Aye, I'm afraid you would. Would she follow you out there to such a different place from our Highlands?"

"Oh, she would—any woman would. It—it's her place to follow me." He rose. "I-I have to find Annie."

Duncan called after him. "When word gets out, I'll have ten adventure-seeking men at the castle doorstep, so let me know as soon as possible."

"I'll tell Annie at once how it's to be."

"And you'll let me know how my dear little ward reacts?"

"James Gordon! Are you daft? You cannot mean it!" Annie's voice rose higher than when she'd caught the biggest trout in the Gillycairn Stream. The pony started in its stable, and outside the kitchen of Drumarlie Castle chickens scattered.

"We'd have a new life, a better life, lass."

"*Duncan* told you that?"

"Who else but Duncan could know how wonderful America is?"

"That's not what he told *me*."

"Aw, but as your guardian, Duncan is protective of you."

"He lied!" Annie kicked out at a heather shrub and sent purple bells flying into the Highland dust. "He lied—" Her voice broke.

"Nay, lass, the tales about gold are real. Duncan says gold was discovered in California, but that the West is no place for a fine-bred lass like yourself."

"My guardian said that?"

"Annie, don't look at me so."

"Why do you want to go? There's no need, now that Duncan's saved the village."

"Because I've lived my entire life in this one glen." His voice shook with passion, a passion Annie had never heard before. "Annie, this is a chance to see the world for myself."

"You're right about that, James Gordon, because if you go, you'll go by yourself. Yourself!"

"I'd come back for you, or send for you."

"No, I'm Highland born, and I've no desire to roam."

Oh, but Duncan was playing at mischief. Telling Jamie the wonders of America for a man and at the same time making it sound as if no woman could handle it. She'd half a mind to go and show Duncan up . . . except . . . except . . . a tear spilled over, and she couldn't think.

"Anne, it's not as if we're being evicted," Jamie said. "Not at all the same. I want to go." A fervor that Annie had never heard shook his voice. "I've never admitted it before, but I'd be less than a man if I stayed here all my life wondering what might have been."

"A grand adventure means more to you than me?"

His face set in stubborn lines. "This place and a fancy wedding celebration for the village mean more to you than me?" And without waiting for a reply, he added, "A proper wife's supposed to follow her husband. Anywhere."

"I don't want to be a proper wife if it means I have to leave my home."

"You're a stubborn lass, Annie. I'm sorry for that."

"There's nothing to be sorry for," she said. "Except for the villagers because we'll ruin their summer—take away from them the wedding celebration they've looked forward to."

"Can't we postpone the wedding, then, until I send for you?"

"We'll cancel it!" she yelled. "And if you go, don't bother sending for me or coming back, ever!"

"You're jilting me?"

"Go on to America—and good riddance!"

Jamie's face set in stubborn lines. "Good riddance yourself, Annie Shaw, and Lord Glencannon's going to have his hands full ever finding you another man who'd risk his manhood in wedding such a willful lass!"

"I don't care! Do you hear me, Jamie Gordon, I don't care!"

When she looked up from her tears, Jamie was gone, and her fury had a new focus.

Duncan. Picking up her skirts, hair flying, she rushed away to find Duncan, her deceitful guardian. It might be all good and well for Duncan to marry some rich Edinburgh lady because the village depended on him. But that didn't mean he had to ruin Annie's wedding, too.

She found Duncan exactly where she expected. Roaming about in the heather with the Stuart ladies, who followed him like taffeta-clad sheep.

"Annie Shaw," Winifred called, spotting her first, "Lord Glencannon finally consented to help us find some white heather. What do you think of that?"

Winded as she was, Anne rounded on them only long enough to give them an earful. "He's a lying blackguard who'll never show you any white heather because none grows here, and if I were you ladies, I'd not be wanting to catch him. I'd pack and go back to Edinburgh where the lads are honest."

Ignoring their shocked expressions, she continued running toward Duncan, who, at her outburst, had turned. Good. The better to beat her fists against his chest.

"I hate you! I hope all the kelpies in the loch kidnap and drown you." The words just burst out, and at the same time she fell against him, pounding. "You've ruined my wedding, and if you're my friend at all, you'll tell me why!"

With quicker reflexes than she anticipated, Duncan grabbed her wrists and pulled her hard against him. She gasped, shocked into silence.

Looking over his shoulder, he nodded to Winifred and Gillian, who stood, sketchbooks and opera glasses in hand, looking at Annie as if she were temporarily possessed.

"Will you ladies excuse us while my ward and I discuss her wedding?"

And taking Annie by the arm, he dragged her back down the hill through the heather to the empty stable. Immediately he pulled her inside, where she jerked away and threw herself down upon a stack of hay.

Duncan was sorely tempted to pull Annie against him again and comfort her, stroke away her tears. Oh, but the lass needed taming, the sort of taming that a gentle tumble with her in that haystack would take care of. But that was a momentary weakness. First, he had to know what had happened between her and Jamie.

"Annie." He affected an expression of deep concern. "Tell me what the trouble is."

She sat up, tears coursing down her cheeks, her expression furious and heartbroken. "J-Jamie's going to go to America. To that heathen place."

"Ah, then he's going to take my offer."

"You've ruined my life!"

"Annie, Annie, what kind of man do you think I am? I left America in a hurry, with unfinished business."

"What sort of business can there possibly be in that heathenish place?" she sniffled.

"Trapping, for one. I had to leave as soon as I learned Andrew had died. Why, I left my meager belongings in a little log cabin. I left my horse with a friend. My bank account still sits untended. I need a trusted agent to go back and finish packing or selling my things. And Jamie was anxious to go in exchange for passage so he could see the place for himself. It's as simple as that. Does that sound as if I'm an evil laird?"

"Jamie thinks he's going to strike it rich in some place called California."

"The gold rush lures a lot of men."

"Well, you could have waited to tell him about it until we were wed! That's why you withheld consent for my wedding, isn't it? Hoping you could hire him away."

Tears flowed all the harder, and his heart melted. Closing the space between them, he cradled her head against his chest, where she sobbed uncontrollably. When the tears subsided, he listened to the thudding of her heart. Still he held her, delaying his next question as long as possible.

Finally, she hiccupped and pulled away, swiping at her damp face. She looked up at him, dark blue eyes full of agony, tears tracking twin paths down her cheeks, hair delightfully mussed. "He-he'd rather go to America than stay here in Gillycairn. Can you imagine that, Duncan? Can you?"

"No."

"And it's you who—"

"Are you going with him?" Unable to wait another second he interrupted, voice husky. He feared that perhaps he'd risked and lost, and so he had to know, had to know this instant. So help him, if she said yes, then he'd kidnap her.

She didn't even answer him. "Duncan, why would you tell Jamie how wonderful America is and offer him a position there? My own betrothed?"

"Are you going with him?" he said, grabbing her by the wrists and staring down into her eyes. The question was ground out. Oh, but the lass was tempting him to insanity.

"Are you going?" he repeated.

"No, of course I'm not going!"

So great was his relief that he nearly stopped breathing, and a second later he broke into an enormous grin.

"I don't see what's so amusing, Duncan Munro," she accused.

He wiped away a tear from her lash and looked down at her.

"Lass, don't you see, it's not a question of whether I want him here or not. I lured him with tales of gold and adventure, I confess, but I only did it to see which he loved more—you, my gentle ward, bonnie Annie, or his secret dreams of roaming."

"That was very clever of you, but you had no right!"

"Annie, I'm your guardian," he reminded her. Now all he had to do was get her to admit the truth—that he was the one she loved. "Annie," he said softly, "why do you shed tears? Is it because the man you love has hurt you? Because he has humiliated you?"

Surprised by his question, Annie sniffled and looked up at him. He was looking at her so funny. Half tender, the way a guardian was supposed to look. And half . . . well, furious . . . as if he were angry at her for once again making a fool of him in front of the fine rich ladies.

"Annie, why this temper?"

"B-because you ruined my wedding. There's a wedding gown that may as well be packed away in lavender for all the use it'll get. There's heather ale stored up that may as well be drunk, and the new kertch will never grace the crown of my head."

"Did I ruin all that?"

Oh, he didn't look a wee bit sorry. Gently he took her chin between his fingers so that she was forced to look deep into his eyes.

"Anne Macaulay Shaw," he asked carefully, "what's so awful about the idea of joining Jamie later? It's not as if you've no dowry. And you know he'd make a better life for you. He might even strike it rich and come back for you."

"Rot. How many Highlanders ever come back?"

"I did," he reminded her, and leaning down, he kissed her gently on the cheek. "Now, what's so awful about joining Jamie in America later?"

His voice vibrated deep within her; shivers ran through her so that she could scarce recall the question. The tears in her eyes made the gold of his hair glitter, and she turned away in case Duncan read the truth trembling on her face.

"I can't join him. The idea is too awful to contemplate."

"Why not? What's so awful?"

Leaving Duncan. That's what was so awful. And that was the first moment she'd realized it. It was the possibility of leaving Duncan she couldn't face. He was her family. She'd just gotten him back, and now she couldn't bear to leave him and all the fun they could have. . . .

"Are you angry because he wants to roam more than to wed?" he asked with a fine edge to the words.

She shook her head. "Duncan, I can't explain it, but I only know *I* don't want to roam any farther than our old fishing stream."

"Why?"

"I want it to be like it was in the old days."

"Why?"

"B-because I want to stay here with you."

"Me? I'm only your guardian. I thought lasses tried to escape their guardians." His voice was soft, and a sly smile lit up his eyes. His questions wouldn't stop. What did he want her to say? Duncan's face held part mischief, part tenderness.

"Why are you asking all this?"

Perhaps, Duncan considered, he ought to get down on bended knee and propose and put himself out of his agony. After all, there was still the possibility she might get over her anger and impulsively run after Jamie. Not until he'd claimed her for his own could he relax. But he had his stubborn streak, too, and he was determined to get her to admit her feelings, to say she loved him. Not Jamie, but him, Duncan.

"Why do you want to stay with me?" he asked once more.

"Because tradition is what this village is all about," she said. "Or did you forget that while you've been wooing the Stuart ladies and chasing buffalo around America?"

"I'd not forgotten. Women do like their fancy weddings."

"Yes." Suddenly the spitfire again, she pulled away. "Why should you care when you won't even tell me which one of those prissy ladies you're to wed, and all for their money and—"

"Anne Shaw, stop talking, and I'll try to explain."

Oh, but the little hoyden needed a lesson taught.

"Annie, there will be a wedding in the wee kirk while the heather blooms. I promise you that."

She looked at him. "Your wedding?"

"Aye, it's time I created some heirs for the estate."

"In that case I shall retire to a little croft and write guidebooks for Lowland ladies who visit the Highlands."

"Indeed?"

"Well, whether it's Winifred or Gillian you wed, she'll not want me about the castle as a hoydenish spinster."

He caught her hand and stayed her. "Ah, now, lass, it won't be that bad."

"Yes, it will."

"But you'd not miss the wedding of your oldest friend Duncan, would you? It wouldn't be the same without you there, you know?"

"There's been no announcement," she said simply.

"Well, as laird, I can obtain a waver on the rules for regular weddings, don't you suppose?"

She nodded.

He looked her up and down. "Whatever kind of wedding it is, you're the good luck to me, Annie. I need you there."

Biting her lip, she shook her head.

"Annie, promise?"

"On one condition . . ."

He was afraid to ask, afraid she'd ask him to name the lady, and held his breath. "What condition?"

"That we go fishing," she decreed. "That for one last week before your wedding in the wee kirk, you could be Duncan of five years ago, and I could be Annie Shaw, not your ward, but just Annie. . . ."

He was silent, then drew in a deep breath and looked her up and down, gaze narrowed. "You drive a hard bargain, lass."

"It's only a week."

"A week can be long."

"The white heather still grows there," she countered.

"Ah, then you told a fib to the Stuart ladies," he said.

She nodded. "If you can lie about America, then I can lie about our Highlands," she countered. "But a sprig of it will bring the bride good luck. It will be a bonnie wedding. I'll see it's every bit as beautiful as any bride could wish."

"Good." A pause, then, "And in the week before, we'll do what you asked. We'll make things as they once were. We'll turn back time and go fishing. Is that worth a truce?"

At her nod he took a deep breath. But it wasn't over yet.

He was determined—before this week was up, he'd catch more than fish. He'd get his own Annie to admit she loved him, body and soul. He only prayed that no one in the castle, if they guessed what was up, would give him away.

The very next morning, Duncan's mother, handkerchief in hand, awaited him at the foot of the staircase and followed him through the castle rooms to the library, where he'd left his pocketwatch.

"Annie's so sad, Duncan, and has been ever since you lured her betrothed away. . . ." She followed his gaze up to the painting. "Andrew wanted her likeness moved to the servants' hall . . ."

"Move Annie out of Drumarlie?"

" . . . but I convinced him that some things couldn't be replaced."

"If Andrew ever put Annie in the servants' quarters, I'd go to the grave to have his hide."

"Then do something nice for her," his mother urged.

"Nice for Annie?" He stared up at her likeness in the painting. "Annie and I are going fishing, Mother. Is that enough?" He suspected a request to spend time with Annie was but a preliminary to the main concern.

"As a matter of fact, ever since Annie's wedding was called off, some rumors have it that it's Lord Glencannon himself who'll wed in the wee kirk."

"Oh. Who says?"

"Everybody is talking, Duncan. Even the Widow MacLeod knows more than me. I shouldn't be the last in the village to know what's going on."

"I don't know myself what's going on."

"Duncan, don't talk in circles. Is there or isn't there going to be a wedding?"

"Isn't a late August wedding at the wee kirk one of Gillycairn's traditions?"

His mother nodded, then asked carefully, "My own son wouldn't think of wedding—say, one of the Edinburgh ladies—without informing his mother?"

"Trust me, Mother. If I were to wed one of the Edinburgh ladies, you'd be the first to know."

"Well, to tell the truth, I was hoping I'd not end up with either of those ladies as a daughter-in-law."

"Oh?" Turning from his perusal of Annie's portrait, he looked at his mother. "Who would you like as a daughter-in-law, then?"

His mother's gaze swept up over him to the portrait of the gypsy gamine. "Actually, I always wished Annie could stay here—not just her portrait, but Annie herself."

He grinned at his mother. "Then, Mother, I suggest you not be late to the wee kirk on the last day of August."

Lady Glencannon gave him a startled look, then an answering smile.

"You mean—"

"I want her."

"There've been no banns called," she cautioned.

"Don't worry," he vowed, heading for the door. "If I have to, I'll wed the lass on the steps of the wee kirk with the entire village as witness."

Four days later Duncan and Annie were fishing at the heather pool, a quiet widening in the Gillycairn Stream, the one place in all of Gillycairn where a smattering of heather grew white. The bush nestled near a large rock upon which they used to sit as children, dangling wet feet over the edge, giggling over silly stories.

Like the purple heather, this bush bloomed lush, and Annie moved to kneel at it, touch it, marvel at its bristly beauty. Only one day remained till the mysterious wedding in the wee kirk, and today she would pick white heather for the bride. Which one of the Stuart ladies would it be?

"Are you ready for my wedding, Annie?" Duncan asked, as if he, too, were thinking of the Stuart ladies.

"Aye, except for making a bouquet of the white heather."

Duncan made no comment on the little bush of white heather, as if it had no sentimental value to him. Instead, he went about fussing with his fishing equipment.

"Come here, Annie, and get your rod ready. The heather can wait, but not the fish. They're ready to bite."

As on the earlier days in the week, conversation waxed prosaic. He asked her advice on how to make the next year's Highland Games bigger and better. They talked of the Queen, of the salmon, of the heather. Ordinary childish things.

The time together should have passed like in the old days, when there'd been perfect contentment in each other's company.

But it wasn't enough, and she wasn't content. What drove her crazy was wondering which of the Stuart ladies he was going to make his bride—Winifred suited the role of Lady Glencannon . . . but Gillian was the prettier. . . .

"You're quiet, Annie," he said at last while tying a fly onto his line. "Is there anything wrong with the fishing?"

Annie, standing a few yards from him at the stream edge, stared straight out at the water and shook her head. "I'm not getting any nibbles."

"Try another lure, then."

Truth be told, she could try every imitation fly in Duncan's collection, and she'd still be miserable.

For she'd been wrong.

Oh, so wrong. She didn't want to fish like in the old days. Each day, within five minutes, a restlessness came over her, a restlessness inside her heart, her body.

"You've got your way, Annie," Duncan said carefully while casting his line again. "Aren't we doing things exactly as we did five summers ago? Haven't I tried to turn back time for you? Am I holding up my end of the bargain?"

"Of course you are." He was treating her exactly as if she were thirteen. Only, she no longer wanted him to think of her as a thirteen-year-old tomboy. Or as his ward, for that matter.

She longed for him to see her as a woman grown. She wanted him to touch her as he would a desirable woman. But no matter how many times she stole a look at him, he never looked at her as if she were anything but a child.

And of course it was too late to confess her true feelings for her guardian. For he was to wed a rich lady from Edinburgh, and in any case, she was just a poor orphaned ghillie's daughter. Oh, but the days had dragged, and she thought today would never end.

A cold mist had lain over the water when they'd arrived at dawn, and though the sun had chased away the beastly weather, the ground was still muddy. Mud splattered Duncan's buckskins in the most intriguing places—on his right calf, his left knee, his thighs, both of them. On his white shirt his cuffs were damp where he'd dipped a net into the water.

He ignored her slow inspection. "Annie, hand me the green fly, will you?" Still oblivious to her, he reeled in the line and knelt by his tackle to tie on a new hook and fly.

She'd been staring at his profile, wanting to kiss his eyelashes, his brow, his mouth. Whenever he moved, she lost her breath. When he turned to look at her, she forgot words, breath came tight. The only sound was the ripple of the water.

"What's wrong?" he asked when he caught her staring at him. "You haven't misplaced the green fly, have you?" When she handed it over, he bent to the task of attaching it to his line. "Do you want a different fly on your line, Annie?"

His voice had gotten so deep in the years he'd been gone. "I perhaps should quit and gather the heather—"

"Nonsense, the fish have been taking the fly well off my line. I've a feeling I'm going to catch the fish of my life today."

Calmly he stood there and trolled the line out into the water. Instantly a fish jumped out, hook in mouth, but as soon as the fish lashed the surface, the line broke.

"Lost him," he said, looking intently at the water.

His mouth, she noticed by the sunlight, had a slight scar at one corner—a new scar, and it was located in just the right place to be kissed.

When he turned, he was frowning, as if annoyed at her. "Annie, isn't there a blue fly mixed in with the tackle?"

Automatically she handed him a feathery blue imitation insect, and he tied it to her line, then handed her the rod. "You try," he said with maddening good cheer.

And then he rolled up first one sleeve and then the other and took up his rod again. Stubborn Scotsman.

Annie stared at the dark hair that showed beneath Duncan's sleeves.

"Watch out," he said. "You're going to troll right into that branch." He came up behind and placed a hand over hers to guide her line elsewhere. "You're not concentrating, Annie. What are you daydreaming about?"

She turned to look at him. The breeze was tousling his golden locks. "I think . . ." She wanted to press her lips to the hollow of his throat, right where the buttons on his shirt left off to reveal fine tanned skin. "I think the stream is too muddy today. Duncan, I really want to stop fishing," and she began to reel in.

"Nonsense," he scoffed. "After all the days you begged me to fish. Have a wee bit more faith. Now, we're not going to quit today. They're biting, Annie."

"They're rising short."

"No, try again. They'll like that bait. It'll do. Aye, more than do."

At his yawn she smiled and cast again. Entertaining the Stuart ladies till the wee hours of the morning, then rising before dawn for these fishing jaunts was catching up to him like a candle burning at both ends. Oh, but Annie wasn't the least bit sorry for him. She hoped he fell asleep on his wedding night and disappointed his bride.

Out of the corner of her eye she watched the movement of his hands, the way his forearms flexed with each jerk on the fishing line. "How can you stay calm so close to your wedding?"

"You keep me calm, Annie," he answered easily and leaning back, rested his head against his buckskin jacket. "That's why fishing every day is so ideal. Just like it used to be, right?"

"Right down to you falling asleep in the heather while I catch the last fish?"

"Even so."

In a few minutes he was asleep, his catch of fish beside him near the white heather bush.

She was unable to tear her eyes off him, so when her line drifted into shore, she moved a couple of steps nearer Duncan and cast again. While her line bobbed, now she was able to stare in unabashed longing. She stared at his lips, yearned to lean over and wake him up with a kiss right on that tiny scar.

Shivers ran down her body, and, with fishing rod in one hand, she knelt over him, her own lips hovering near his. Her own yearnings ran as fierce as a Highland stream, and she touched her lips to his. Tasting, touching him, she forgot all about the trout. "All week you've tried so hard to be the lad you used to be," she whispered. "But I was wrong, Duncan, about wishing for the past."

She inhaled the scent of male skin, touched the bristly growth of his unshaven jaw, and then leaned her cheek sideways against his mouth, so that she could feel the exhale of his breath against her face. This was her last chance, ever. "Oh, Duncan," she said on a sigh, "which lady are you going to wed tomorrow?"

As Duncan lay there, using all his willpower to feign sleep while her hair teased at his eyelids, he forced himself not to grab her. The little minx. What he wanted was to pull her into his arms, seduce her there on the ground. But any good fisherman knew a mere nibble was no guarantee of a catch. If he were to tug the line too soon, she'd wriggle away. But the week was nearly up, and his patience sorely tried.

He had one hope left—that she'd kiss him again, and then he'd grab her, net her, and she'd be his.

As she moved beside him, he lay there, anticipating a sweet, warm kiss from Annie. He could almost taste the honey of her lips, smell the lavender of her hair. Bend down again, Annie, he pleaded to himself. One wee soft kiss . . .

Splat. The next thing he knew a trout slapped against his face, and the closest thing he got to a kiss was a cold, wet mouthful of scales. His eyes flew open just as Annie made a leap for her catch and fell against him. For a few confusing seconds, Duncan, Annie, and the flopping fish were all tangled together.

Duncan broke free first. He tossed the trout into a net and was on his feet as quickly as if an Indian had gotten the drop on him. "It's a good-size catch, Annie," he commented, eyeing the fish in appreciation.

When he looked back at Annie, she was staring up at him, eyes wide, as she shoved hair off her face.

"Do you always wake up that easily?"

He nodded. "A habit I picked up as a mountain man." Duncan reached into the net and unhooked Annie's trout from the line.

"Then you were awake when I kissed you." It was an accusation. Kneeling down, she angrily plucked the white heather, an entire bouquet of it.

"Annie . . ." Duncan came up behind her, but she refused to turn. "I confess I was awake the second I felt your lips brush mine. No man could nap through a bonnie lass whispering against his face."

"I'm sorry." Still, she wouldn't turn.

"I'm not, except that you won't tell me why you kissed me."

"I don't know." Snatching up the heather, she stood.

"You do."

He stood and stared down at her, surprised at the sudden lump in his own throat. Standing there so solemn, dark hair flying in the wind, white heather in her arms, she made a prettier picture than the painting back in Drumarlie Castle, and he knew he couldn't bear to be parted from her ever again.

"Annie . . ."

She began to tremble.

"What's wrong?"

"I've changed my mind."

"Have you?"

"I don't want things to be like they used to."

"What, then, would you like now?" Calmly he began to put away his fishing tackle. "Tell your friend Duncan."

Annie had been about to blurt out that she didn't love Jamie, but that would only lead to secrets.

Including the biggest secret of all. She loved Duncan.

With all her heart. Oh, he was beautiful, and she yearned to press her lips to the place beneath his ear where one lock of golden hair waved in the breeze. . . .

"Annie," he said, and she pulled her gaze back to his face. He was smiling at her, as if she were a little sister. "Tomorrow at dawn, when the mist is still low over the glen, we'll have our last fishing excursion."

"I'm afraid not. Actually, Duncan, I'm tired of pretending that I'm thirteen again. Besides, there's the shortbread to rebake because I broke the last batch in a rage. And there's the kertch for the bride's head to iron since I wadded the last one and threw it into the fire." Turning her back to him, she buried her face in the bouquet of heather.

He came up behind her and put his hands on her shoulders. "Annie."

She pulled away, aching, yearning. Oh, how she envied Duncan's bride. The woman he would make Lady Glencannon. And she decided she couldn't bear knowing which of the Stuart ladies he'd chosen.

"Duncan, don't be touching me when after tomorrow you'll be a married man. Go fishing with your bride-to-be. Don't touch me anymore."

There was a long pause.

"What happens when I touch you, Annie?"

She couldn't breathe. She couldn't think. Nothing worked. Not her lungs. Not her mind. "Nothing. That's what's wrong. I'm sorry. I don't want to go fishing anymore. It was a foolish idea. I can't stand it anymore."

"But what happens, Annie?" His breath was warm against her hair.

No, this was wrong. He was to wed another. Despairing, she dropped the heather at her feet and watched it pile up like so much summer snow. "Don't you know, Duncan?"

Yes, he did, but before Duncan had a chance to gather his wits and pull her to him, she ran away from him.

There was no use chasing after her. After all, she knew a hundred hiding places about this glen, and he'd forgotten half of them in the years he'd been gone. Oh, if he'd known her less well, he'd have searched high and low in some of the more likely places . . . in the priory . . . in the caves by the loch . . . in the cellar of the inn . . . in the old hollow tree in the birch forest.

But he wagered she'd not hide for long. Soon enough she'd end up where she belonged.

He picked up the scattered heather and with his knife cut all that remained; there wasn't a sprig of white heather left at the stream when he was done, but it did overflow from his tackle bag, tiny white bells of it tangling with all the hooks and flies.

Back at the castle Annie was nowhere to be found, and his spirits sank. By now she should have turned up. Ignoring the staring servants, he jerked aside one set of tartan draperies after another in case Annie was hiding behind them. Finally he sent word to the Stuart ladies at the inn, regrets that due to an emergency with his ward, he could not meet them this evening for cards. He closed with a reminder to join him at the wee kirk tomorrow, then pulled out his pocket watch. Where was Annie?

There was nothing more to do but make his way to his bed-chamber, where he slammed the door, stripped off his shirt and splashed himself with water. He was toweling his face dry in front of the mirror when the crash sounded in the adjoining sitting room, and he went to investigate. A squall had come up, and the rain was blowing in his open window, waving the draperies wildly. He'd not taken more than two steps toward the window when he froze in his tracks.

A dark-haired, long-limbed gypsy, hair wet from the rain, appeared from around the curtains and perched on the open window to his bedchamber. Annie. And she didn't see him.

"Where have you been?" he asked.

Startled, she grabbed at the window, looking as if she'd been caught with her hands in the shortbread tin. "On the roof," she said, swinging her legs over the ledge and dangling them there nonchalantly while her gaze ran up and down his buckskin breeches to his naked chest.

He kicked the door shut. The instant it slammed, he leaned against it, arms crossed. He possessed the ability to ask two, at most three questions of Annie before he wrapped his arms about her beautiful shoulders.

"What were you doing up on the castle turrets?" Still in need of taming she was, answering with a mere shrug.

Oh, but it had been a long week of trying to pretend she was thirteen years old, of trying not to touch her every time he saw her in breeches.

"You took the white heather, didn't you?" she asked, sliding off the ledge and moving along the wall.

"Aye."

She followed his gaze to the armoire, where, in his concern over Annie, he'd dropped the fishing tackle in a heap.

"Did you want it?" he asked in a taut voice, reaching for the white blossoms. He held a bouquet out at arm's length, tempting her. Assorted blue and green lures clung to it, dotting it with color. "Is this what you want?"

She held out her hand. "I need it for your wedding."

"Come and get it, Annie." Like bait for a trout, he held it out, daring her to come near.

She moved toward him, as if an invisible line had been stretched taut between them. Closer and closer and closer she came.

Grabbing the heather bouquet, she tried to back away, but he was quicker and seized her by the arms.

"Duncan, we need to talk."

"Not in my bedchamber," he managed, his voice husky. Then his mouth came down on hers.

Stubborn, willful Annie gasped and pulled back.

"Duncan!"

He pulled her to him and kissed her again, so long and hard her head tipped back. When he was done, she stood pressed against a wall, head still back, trying to recover her breath.

"Duncan," she said at last, "don't you see, fishing together turned out to be a mistake, a bad idea?"

"On the contrary. This is a very good idea." With an arm on either side he pinioned her against the wall. "Why did you run away? What happens when I touch you?"

"I can't think," she cried. "I can't fish when all I can think about is kissing you . . . and when I'm kissing you, I can't think about anything else. . . ."

Pushing the heather out of his way, he leaned down, his mouth closed on hers again, passionate, hot, out of control. With a groan he crushed her to him and kissed her yet again and again, more tenderly, as if he were making up for five long years.

Duncan! The world spun, went taut, tauter, then snapped; she wanted to protest, but the only sound she managed was a moan, and then he was gathering her in his arms, and she was clinging to him, giving in. Desire had been biding its time all week, perhaps all their lives.

Her knees weak, she sank to the floor, and Duncan sank with her, never breaking the kiss as he rolled her onto a silken buffalo robe. His hands began to roam. Oh, the places Duncan could roam with his hands and with his mouth, too, awakening sensations she'd never known existed. They clung. They kissed until they were breathless. There'd never been modesty between them, and now in the heat of need, pure physical need, there was no maidenly pause, no ability to wait.

"It's my fault I can't stop, Annie. I'll stop if you want, but I need you—"

"Don't stop." No one invented the fire between them. It simply sprang into being, as if it had been waiting to be discovered, then blazed out of control. So it was for Annie with Duncan. The fire ignited, and not all the rivers in Scotland could have quenched it.

She pulled him closer, jealous of the moments, of the years they'd lost, craving this new closeness with Duncan. And then he filled her, taught her all she could know of perfect companions.

Oh, but loving Duncan was better than anything in her beloved Highlands—gentle, wild, soft, furious—and tender, as at last, irrevocably, Duncan came home to Annie. Well and truly home. Afterward, they lay there sated upon the robe, while rational thought slowly returned.

He seemed to have trouble catching his breath, and she

spoke first, as she trailed a hand up the contours of his chest, stopping over his heart.

"I think," she said, "that this is rather more fun than fishing."

He dipped his head to kiss her throat. "You *think*? Annie, lass," he murmured between kisses, "we'll have to end these doubts," and he gathered her close again.

"I'm not sorry we did this, you know," she said at length. "I'd rather die a spinster than never know all of you, Duncan." After a pause, she whispered, aching, "I wish you much happiness."

"I plan to be very happy," he said and levered himself up. There was a smile on his face, not tender, but triumphant. He wrapped a tartan shawl about her, slung his shirt on, then donned his buckskin trousers, all the while grinning.

"You needn't be smug about this," Annie said, pushing her tousled hair out of her face. "I'm still leaving. And . . . and I'll be happy without fishing because it's clear we can't be friends, and your wife is not going to approve of me as a mistress . . . and . . . I'm a fallen woman." She sank back.

"I understand how it is, you see," she babbled on. "Wedding one of the rich ladies is a noble sacrifice for the village."

"Annie, stop talking." He placed a finger against her lips, then kissed the crown of her head over and over. Softer and softer came his kisses, ending with a brush of his lips on her forehead. The last kiss, the gentlest one, stole her breath.

"Annie," he said close to her ear, his voice a low rumble. "I'm a rogue indeed for stringing the ladies along, teasing them, but not so much a rogue I'd tumble one lass when I was to wed another lady tomorrow."

"You're making no sense, Duncan."

Dropping to his knees, he caught her to him. Passion burned in his eyes, making them all the bluer. She'd never seen him look at her this way. "Annie," he explained gently, "men who are smitten and a day away from wedding don't bed any woman but the one they love."

She hadn't thought of it that way.

"Then who are you wedding?" Was there another rich

lady in this village? From the look on his face, he was clearly teasing.

"The lass I wed tomorrow has found white heather and given me a sprig."

"She has?" Her heart sank. "You took the Stuart ladies to look for white heather, didn't you?"

"But the only place it grows in Gillycairn is at our fishing hole."

Which led to only one conclusion.

"The only person who's given me white heather is you."

"Me?"

"Annie, Annie, there's something I want to show you."

He pulled out a gold watch, flipped open the lid, and held it close to her. "See here, Annie? Remember the day I left Scotland . . . you gave me this?"

Nestled inside the lid of the watch was a tiny blue ribbon, a ribbon she'd tied as a child. The white heather had crumbled, but the stem was still there. A little sprig, dried and yellowed. Five years old.

"It was good luck," he said in a husky voice. "Always pulling me back to Scotland and to the memory of my hoydenish little ghillie, or maybe some sixth sense telling me one day she would grow up . . . and I would know how much I loved her . . . how much I love you." With one hand he snapped the watch shut, and with his other he pulled her close to him again.

Happiness radiated throughout her heart. He loved her! Still she was afraid to think it true. "But—but you let me think you were going to wed one of the Stuart ladies."

"You assumed that, Annie," he said softly, amused. "Why would I wed one of those supercilious ladies?"

"For money to save the estate, of course. Because their father is a banker."

"Aye, and a fine banker who shall keep good care of the fortune I made in America."

"Your fortune?" She planted her hands on her hips. "You said all you left behind was a log cabin and a horse!"

"The cabin sits on a gold mine, Annie, a mine I had no time to stay and work, so you see, I don't need the Stuarts' money. I need their father's expert advice as a financier so he can invest my fortune."

Was it possible the ladies meant no more to him? Standing there, she looked into his face, searching for the truth.

"Do you really think," he pleaded, "that Duncan Munro, the lad you knew, could wed one of those prissy misses?"

"Well, perhaps the giggly one."

He shook his head and reached over to cup her face in his hands. "I've loved you from the moment I laid eyes on you outside the library door. Now, tell me why you stayed here with me, your guardian, instead of following Jamie to America . . . tell me."

"You're a braw man, Duncan, not a lad anymore, and so . . . I just couldn't go away with Jamie."

"But tell me why, Annie. Why?" He whispered the word against her lips. "Why . . . why?"

"Because . . . I love you, Duncan." The words trembled on her lips.

The fight was over, and she was his. Briefly he shut his eyes, then clasped her close to his heart. "Ah, Annie, lass, for those sweet words, I tricked Jamie into going away for a grand adventure. But I proved my point, even if it was a long torturous week, sitting beside you casting for fish when all I wanted was to take you in my arms."

"You've behaved in a wicked fashion, Duncan," she murmured happily. And he'd done it all for her. Only one worry remained. "And what if Jamie had not been so taken with your fancy tales of riches and adventure to be had in America? What would you have done then?" She pulled back to look into his eyes.

"I imagine I'd have kidnapped you, lass, and run off with you. Blame me for being devious, Annie, but not for loving you, not for wanting to make you mine, my desire, my bride. Say yes."

Audacious Duncan. Oh, he was ruthless indeed. She drew a deep breath and nodded. "Oh, Duncan, yes. If you only knew how much I love you."

Suddenly she thought of the one thing that could spoil

all her happiness. "But, Duncan—you can't wed me. You're a laird, and I'm but a common ghillie's daughter. You're expected to wed a fine lady and have heirs of pure-bred—"

He was kissing her again, claiming one inch of her after another. "There was one thing I especially liked about America, Annie," he murmured, "and that you would like, too."

"What's that?"

"In America a man weds who he loves, not who fits his social class. I liked that best about the place. . . . Now, do you want to wait and call the banns so you have your fancy wedding—in September?"

Shaking her head, she bit back a smile. "Tomorrow. The last day of August. The villagers expect it."

"Then we can't let them down, can we?"

"But, Duncan," she asked, "if you really had chosen one of the Stuart ladies, which one—?"

Shaking his head, he put a finger to her lips. "Truth be told, if they were fish, I'd toss them both back. But it's been an uncommonly long August, Annie, and I'm weary. Now, stop talking and bide a wee." As she moved close, he gathered her in his arms again.

Oh, and a grand wedding it was. The most beautiful ever, the villagers declared when it was over, and the bell in the wee kirk was tolling for the day Lord Glencannon of Gillycairn took Annie Shaw, daughter of a castle ghillie, for his bride. Afterward, they stood in the sunshine, he in his kilt, she in her fine gown, white kertch on her head, prayer book in hand. A sight for sore eyes they made standing there surrounded by purple heather.

A radiant wedding, villagers told Annie afterward, adding that the happiness of that day would warm many a long winter night for years to come.

The last time Annie saw Winifred and Gillian was outside the church when they came up and wished her well and curtsied to Lord Glencannon, frosty smiles fixed on their pale faces, especially when they saw the sprig of white heather on the prayer book.

"So you found some after all," Winifred said.

"While fishing," Annie replied happily.

"You're a lucky ward, then, to snare Lord Glencannon himself, your own guardian," Winifred sniffed and pulled Gillian away to their waiting carriage.

As the residents of Drumarlie Castle stood watching their visitors depart, the dowager Lady Glencannon came up to her new daughter-in-law. "Well, Annie, I think they're off to search elsewhere for white heather."

"Poor lasses," she lamented for the Stuart ladies, tucking her arm into the crook of Duncan's and nestling close.

"Oh, they'll fare well enough. They're determined," Duncan observed.

Duncan's mother nodded. "Aye, I've sent them to another castle where the heather's still blooming lush. A castle where two eligible lords abide."

"Have you?" she said and, for her smile at Duncan, was rewarded with a kiss. "I hope they took a souvenir of the village," she murmured for Duncan only to hear.

"What's that, love?"

"Fishing nets," she supplied. "They'll need them yet, I'm sure," she said as her husband handed her into the carriage.

Oh, but it had turned into a perfect summer, Annie wrote to Jamie, and, after wishing him many grand adventures, reassured him that all had turned out for the best.

" . . . for within a day of Lord Glencannon taking me as his bride," Annie put in her letter to Jamie, "the village miraculously cleared of the fine ladies come on holiday to tramp through the heather.

"Other ladies straggled in later, of course, but alas, as soon as they heard about Lord Glencannon's marriage, they all decided that another village with another castle would have a prettier show of heather after all. Just as you predicted, Jamie, aye."

And inside the letter to the wild gold country of California,

Anne Macaulay Shaw Munro, the new Lady Glencannon, enclosed for Jamie a wee sprig of Highland heather.

White.

Because, in matters of love, no matter where friends roamed, everyone needed a bit of luck.

Turn the page for a special advance
preview of the new novel by
Pamela Morsi, author of
"Making Hay" . . .

WILD OATS

A charming story of love and laughter
that will warm your heart
and fill your dreams!

COMING FROM JOVE
IN SEPTEMBER 1993

If someone had told Jedwin Sparrow a month ago that he'd be sitting, hat in hand, in the parlor of the infamous Cora Briggs, he'd have not believed it.

She sat primly in the rocker, her hands genteelly folded in her lap. Her eyes were wide with curiosity. The neatly tucked pleats of her bodice could not disguise the generous curves of her bosom. But the voluminous skirting of steel-gray poplin completely obscured any suggestion of the nature of her lower body. Jedwin caught sight of one scuffed brown leather toe peeking out beneath her skirt. The sight entranced him like a mesmerist's pocket watch. His mind raced ahead from the supple smoothness of sleek brown leather, to the thin warmth of cotton stockings, whose length would be topped by lacey garters leading enticingly to wicked ladies' underdrawers.

Jedwin's mouth dried like cotton as he stared at the decently covered woman before him and imagined . . . imagined . . . sin.

"Your purpose, Mr. Sparrow?"

His speech was planned, rehearsed, revised, committed to memory, discarded, reworded, and reformated. He opened his mouth and waited for it to pour out. It didn't.

He cleared his throat and tried again.

"I'm James Edwin Sparrow, Jr.," he began.

"Yes, I know," she said.

Jedwin cleared his throat again.

"I'm the sole owner of Sparrow Mortuary, one of the most prosperous and growing businesses in Dead Dog."

Mrs. Briggs nodded. "Says something about the town, doesn't it."

Jedwin missed her meaning and her amused expression as he concentrated on the grosgrains on his hatband. "It seems obvious to even the most casual observer, as myself, that in the eight years since your divorce from Luther Briggs, your situation here has become increasingly untenable."

Mrs. Briggs's eyebrows furrowed in concern. "If some civic group has asked you to suggest I leave town, Mr. Sparrow," she said with a quiet firmness, "I will have to tell you that you are not the first to make such a request. I, however, have no intentions of leaving."

Jedwin raised his head abruptly. "Oh, no, ma'am," he said, hastily discarding his speech. "I don't want you to leave at all!"

Mrs. Briggs tilted her head with a puzzled expression. Her lips were slightly parted, and Jedwin could see her straight white teeth, so bright that the contrast made her lips appear unusually flush.

Jedwin took a deep breath and barreled in before he lost his nerve.

"The recent panic and depressed farm prices have hurt all of us, Mrs. Briggs," he said. "One can't help but notice that your house is in need of some repair, and the paint is peeling so badly that whitewash can no longer suffice."

Jedwin watched her blush with embarrassment. Being poor was not immoral or uncommon, but it was humiliating. Especially to have those facts pointed out by a visitor.

Jedwin attempted to soften the criticism. "I, of course, can have no knowledge of your arrangement with Luther Briggs."

He paused, giving her opportunity to speak if she would. She did not.

"It appears, however, that he has not been overly generous and that you could benefit from some financial assistance."

"Financial assistance?" The question was rigid with coldness.

"I am willing to provide you with a modest stipend for your discretionary use."

Cora Briggs was sitting stiffly in her chair, staring at Jedwin Sparrow as if he'd suddenly grown two heads.

"Why would you be willing to provide this 'modest stipend,' Mr. Sparrow?"

Jedwin's hands were sweating profusely, but he resisted wiping them on his trousers. This is what he'd come to say, and say it he would.

"I would like you—" he began.

Her brown eyes were narrowed on him.

"I would like you to—to become my—if we could—perhaps we—I was thinking that—"

Jedwin froze up, unable to get the words out of his mouth.

"Mr. Sparrow." Her words were soft and cool as she looked him straight in the eye. "Are you offering me an indecent proposal?"

"Yes, ma'am, I am."

If you enjoyed this book, take advantage of this special offer. Subscribe now and get a

FREE Historical Romance

No Obligation (a $4.50 value)

Each month the editors of True Value select the four *very best* novels from America's leading publishers of romantic fiction. Preview them in your home *Free* for 10 days. With the first four books you receive, we'll send you a FREE book as our introductory gift. No Obligation!

If for any reason you decide not to keep them, just return them and owe nothing. If you like them as much as we think you will, you'll pay just $4.00 each and save at *least* $.50 each off the cover price. (Your savings are *guaranteed* to be at least $2.00 each month.) There is NO postage and handling – or other hidden charges. There are no minimum number of books to buy and you may cancel at any time.

Send in the Coupon Below

To get your FREE historical romance fill out the coupon below and mail it today. As soon as we receive it we'll send you your FREE Book along with your first month's selections.
